AWP
MARCH 8–11, 2006
Hilton, Austin & The Austin Convention Center
RITZ
Visit www.awpwriter.org for more information
AUSTIN

StoryQuarterly 41

STORYQUARTERLY, founded in 1975, is an independent magazine of the short story published by an Illinois nonprofit corporation. Reading hiatus will be observed for 2005-6 only, while Stegner Fellows guest-edit *StoryQuarterly 42*. Editors will welcome short story submissions beginning October 1, 2006, thru March 31, 2007. Upon resumption of our reading, please send submissions online only, through our *Submissions* link, reachable through: http://www.storyquarterly.com. Member of COSMEP, CLMP, indexed in American Humanities Index. Opinions expressed herein are not necessarily those of the editors. For subscriptions, see our website; for advertising rates, or business only, contact us at: storyquarterly@yahoo.com. Single copy: $9; 2 years: $15; 5 years: $40; Student/Group rate: 5/$30; Life Subscriptions: $250; Sample copy: $7. Further information at http://www.storyquarterly.com

Distributed by:

Ingram Periodicals	B. DeBoer	BookMaster Distributors	Ubiquity Dist. Inc.
117 Heil Quaker Blvd.	113 Centre St.	30 Amberwood Parkway	607 DeGraw St
P. O. Box 7000	Nutley, NJ 07110	P. O. Box 388	Brooklyn, N.Y
LaVergne, TN 37086	201-665-9300	Ashland, Ohio 44805	11217-3120
615-793-5000		419-281-1802/800-247-6553	718-875-5491

ISBN: 0-9722444-3-3 ISSN: 0361-0144

Cover design by Marylee MacDonald

StoryQuarterly 41

Fifth Annual Robie Macauley Award
to Sharon May for
"Through the Water of the Clouds"
Judged by
Alice McDermott

FIFTH ANNUAL
ROBIE MACAULEY AWARD FOR FICTION
$500 to
"Through the Water of the Clouds"
by SHARON MAY
Judged by
ALICE MCDERMOTT

"'Through the Water of the Clouds' casts a spell. With its simple lyricism, it offers the reader a love story that is neither inflated by false sentiment nor weighed by fashionable irony. It is a story rich in sensual detail, in detail of place and detail of time, but one that nevertheless manages to give primacy to emotion, to longing and loneliness, to sorrow and hope, and to do so unabashedly, without structural contortions or preening displays of authorial cleverness. It is a quiet, straightforward story that nevertheless lingers in the mind. Fiction's ability to remind us of what it is to be human is apparent here. A lovely piece of work."

– *Alice McDermott*

Manuscripts were submitted blind (no author's names) to Alice McDermott.
The winning story can be found on Page 75, Sharon May on Page 545

Editor's Note: SQ Thirty Years Later

1975: Back in the mists of the Twentieth Century, the intentions of our SQ founders' fit the setting: a war had ended, feminism had found its voice, and peripheralized people had begun to elbow their way into a place at our table. SQ founders wanted the unheeded voices heard in that era of change, and responding to the call came glorious new writers—not all women to be sure but the list does include first publications for Lorrie Moore, Jhumpa Lahiri, and early work by Anne Beattie, Rosellen Brown, Janet Burroway, Gail Godwin, plus so many others; there is real satisfaction in assisting such births, plucked from a voluminous slush pile. Still, SQ determines not to become complacent. We fully intend to continue to challenge ourselves. In this issue, for example, we energetically join the global narrative with two translations of Spanish work—presented in both languages, appropriately for our bilingual country. We welcome technology too, and the way it is opening new doors. With the success of our online submissions site, we will move forward into online publishing, three quarters a year, while we continue our large anthology annually. We may not ever go to bed with a good computer instead of a book, but short stories do seem well-suited to online publication, and we'll be doing a lot more of that next year. Bilingually too.

Best of all—*announcing a special 2006 issue*—a group of Stegner Fellows will be special editors next year, choosing the fiction and composing our next issue, *StoryQuarterly42*. During this year only, 2005-2006, *StoryQuarterly* will take a reading sabbatical—no submissions will be accepted—while awaiting the choices of our editors in California, spearheaded by editors Kaui Hart Hemmings and Edward Schwarzschild. From what we've heard, the results promise to be fresh and exciting. We think you'll be as curious as we are to see how their choices lead us into the future.

M. M. M. Hayes

CONGRATULATIONS TO OUR ILLINOIS

Gina Frangello's SQ40 story "Atilla the There" was awarded an Illinois Arts Council Award for 2005. Her first novel, *My Sister's Continent*, is forthcoming from Chiasmus Press. She is the Executive Editor of *Other Voices* magazine and its new fiction press, OV Books, and her short fiction has been published in many literary magazines, most recently *Swink, Prairie Schooner, Blithe House Quarterly* and an anthology, *Homewrecker*, forthcoming from Soft Skull Press. She guest-edited the anthology *Falling Backwards: Stories of Fathers and Daughters* for Hourglass Books (2004), has taught literature and fiction writing at several Chicago universities, and has freelanced for the *Chicago Reader* and the *Chicago Tribune*. In 2002, she was also the recipient of an Individual Fellowship for Prose from the Illinois Arts Council.

About "Atilla the There": "I lived in Amsterdam for my husband's work on and off for two years, and like other times I've lived overseas, found that the comparative solitude inspired–or forced–me to rethink my identity at home, as an American but also in more individual ways. I came home and gleefully dropped out of my Ph.D program, wrote more, and began the process of adopting my twin daughters from China. A few of the characters in this story were shamelessly based on members of my writing group in Amsterdam and on other friends I made there–Amsterdam is also such a beautiful, complicated city that I wanted to write about it from the moment I arrived. My character's core issues, though–facing his past and confronting stereotypes about gender and sexuality–are probably common strains in much of my fiction and transcend my experience of place."

Arts Council Winners!

Gina Frangello for "Atilla the There"

CONGRATULATIONS TO OUR ILLNOIS

Stephanie Soileau's *SQ40* story "*La Boucherie*" won an Illinois Arts Council Award in 2005 and was chosen for inclusion in *New Stories from the South 2005*. Stephanie's fiction has also appeared in *Gulf Coast*. She is a graduate of the Iowa Writers' Workshop and now lives in Chicago, where she teaches at City Colleges and School of the Art Institute. "Several years ago, a livestock trailer did tumble off the interstate into downtown Baton Rouge, and there was speculation that the missing members of the herd ended up in stewpots and freezers. There seemed an obvious link between this and the *boucheries* my grandmother described to me, communal slaughtering parties that used to happen in rural Louisiana through fall and winter; each week or so, one family of sharecroppers would donate livestock and everyone would take a chunk of meat home with them. It seemed that my grandparents and their neighborhood friends had carried a form of these communal rituals with them to the city. There were no cows killed in the garage (chickens, maybe, and squirrels, absolutely), but there was the same devotion to good neighboring. Fatima is based on several Sudanese women I knew in Iowa City, one of whom was the daughter of a leftist Muslim political leader who had been hanged for sedition. When I knew her, she was herding 3-year-olds in a preschool for a little above minimum wage."

Arts Council Winners!

Stephanie Soileau for "*La Boucherie*"

Congratulations to our

ROBERT OLEN BUTLER for "Christmas, 1910"

Butler's *SQ40* story was chosen for incluson in the *Pushcart Prizes* 2006 and is from a recent collection, *Had A Good Time*. An early book of stories, *A Good Scent from a Strange Mountain*, won the 1993 Pulitzer for Fiction. Ten novels, three collections and a book on the creative process later, he has won a 2005 National Magazine Award (his second), a Guggenheim, NEA and a Rosenthal Fellowship from the American Academy of Arts and Letters. A collection of very-short stories, *Severance*, will appear in America after a 2005 debut in France (as *Mots de Tête*), where a ballet based upon it was performed in Lyon. His fiction has appeared in *Best American Short Stories, New Stories from the South* (8 times), as well as *The New Yorker, Esquire, The Atlantic Monthly, Harper's, Zoetrope*, GQ, *The Paris Review, Ploughshares*, McSweeney's and many others. He teaches Creative Writing at Florida State U.

2005 Pushcart Prize Winners

GREGORY BLAKE SMITH for "Presently in Ruins"

Gregory Blake Smith's *SQ40* story "Presently In Ruins" won a Pushcart Prize and will be included in *Pushcart Prizes 2006*. In addition to short fiction, Smith has published three novels, the most recent of which–*The Madonna of Las Vegas*–just appeared from Crown/Three Rivers Press. Of "Presently In Ruins" he says, "Unlike most of my writing this story has a firm foot in autobiography. Faced with a debilitating disease, my own father several times tried to kill himself, and the moral and emotional questions that chase their tails in that story were ones I lived with for a time. On the other hand, I never got up the courage to kiss Elizabeth Skibisky, so realism evidently has its limits." (Note to Indiana State Police: the author's father is still alive.)

SAM SHAW for "Reconstruction"
Chosen for *Best American Mystery Stories of 2005.*

A recent graduate of the Iowa Writers' Workshop, Shaw is working on a novel involving aviation, hard rock mining, and tropical birds. Another of his stories appears in the current issue of *Open City*.

"The first draft of 'Reconstruction' took shape just after Thanksgiving, 2002, in a tryptophan haze. Certain details—the stuffed bobcat, the cockatoo—were borrowed from life. Otherwise, its origins are largely mysterious. Many thanks to Marylee Macdonald for improving this story, M.M.M. Hayes for publishing it, and Otto Penzler and Joyce Carol Oates for affording it a second life in print."

D. Ellis Dickerson for "Post Cretaceous Era"
Chosen for *Year's Best Fantasy and Speculative Fiction*

Dickerson is a Ph.D. student at Florida State, and has had cartoons in *The Atlantic* and fiction in *Gettysburg Review*. "This story began from an assignment in a class I took while writing greeting cards for Hallmark, several years ago. The teacher told us to list our obsessions, things we'll never stop loving. The first two things on my list were 'dinosaurs' and 'cities,' and the story practically self-generated from there.

"As I write this, I'm about to hop in my car and begin a month-long, 1800-mile journey from one end of I-10 to the other, starting in Jacksonville and ending in Los Angeles. With any luck, I hope to have an I-10 travel book, *Travels With Ritalin,* or *How I Spent My Summer Stipend*. If my luck continues, I'll finish my first novel by the end of December: *By Dick! A Novel About the Well-Meaning Voyages of St. Brendan*."

STEVE ALMOND's *SQ39* story, "Rumors of Myself," was chosen for inclusion in *Flash Fiction Forward*

Steve Almond's nonfiction *Candy Freak: A Journey Through the Underbelly of America* has become a cult classic. He recently published *The Evil BB Chow and Other Stories* and has been anthologized in *Pushcart Prize 2002*, *New Stories from the South 2002* and *Best of Zoetrope*. The update of the popular *Flash Fiction*, an anthology of short-shorts containing no more than 1000 words, from W. W. Norton and edited by Robert Shapard & James Thomas, will appear August 2006.

EMILY RABOTEAU's "The Eye of Horus,"
SQ40 Robie Macauley Award, chosen by André Dubus,
was cited in *Best American Stories of 2005.*

Emily Raboteau holds a BA from Yale and was a *New York Times* Fellow at NYU. Recipients of the *Chicago Tribune*'s Nelson Algren Award, a Jacob Javits Fellowship, a fiction fellowship from the New York Foundation for the Arts, and a Pushcart Prize, Raboteau's stories have appeared in *Tin House, Callaloo, Missouri Review, Hartford Courant, African Voices, Transition* and *Best American Short Stories, 2003.* She lives in Brooklyn, teaches in Harlem at City College, and in 2005 published her first novel, *The Professor's Daughter*, of which this story was a part. She says, "I wrote this story both to expose my own brattiness and to honor my mother's strength."

REBECCA CURTIS for "Wolf at the Door"
Speculative Fiction Fountain Award: Honorable Mention

Rebecca Curtis teaches writing at the University of Kansas. Her fiction has appeared in *The New Yorker, Harper's, McSweeney's*, and elsewhere, and is forthcoming in the Australian edition of *Harper's Bazaar*.

"I grew up in central New Hampshire, which might not qualify as rural but has big rural pockets. My parents' house was rather isolated, up on a mountain and set in a small field surrounded by forests. As a kid I had the idea, or maybe just dreams, that there were wolves in the forest. They were always the 'Little Red Riding Hood' type of wolf—walking, talking, and very tricky."

SYLVIA SELLERS-GARCIA's "The Correspondence," winner of *SQ*'s 3rd Robie Macauley Award, judged by Richard Ford, was cited in *Best American Stories of 2004*

Sellers-Garcia was a fact-checker at *The New Yorker* when she won the Third Robie Macauley Award in 2003. That year she began Ph.D. studies at Berkeley. She now lives in New Hampshire, where she is working on a thesis and polishing her first novel, focused on Guatemala and it's violent history, a subject personal to her as her mother and relatives still live there. In 2003, she said, "The course of the fighting made deep impressions. Thinking of similar conflicts elsewhere in Latin America and the world, I wanted to see what people do, collectively and individually, with such memories... how memories are shaped so they might be compatible with a social agenda, adaptable to a self-image, or simply bearable."

Karen Russell

SQ intern publishes first fiction in *The New Yorker*

KAREN RUSSELL, a Northwestern intern here at *StoryQuarterly* in 2002–2003, was a highlight of the SQ office. She graduated from NU in 2003 and went on to grad school at Columbia U, and we first glimpsed her wonderful work with "Haunting Olivia," June 6, 2005, in *The New Yorker*'s special issue featuring debut fiction. Its excellence was no surprise. Karen kept us all in tears of laughter that year, and did an incredibly good job on subscriptions too. She would come to work relating one bizarre real-life scrape after another: There was Karen's high-calorie diet, in sympathy with an unmarried sister who was researching their genetic fertility prospects; another day we heard, "Yesterday the pizza man stole my cell phone! I tried calling myself and he answered, in Spanish, so I told him, I'm so glad you found it! I was just going to call the police." (Karen's Spanish is fluent, wouldn't you know). She met the pizza man in the cafeteria and over coffee got her phone back. *This woman is never going to run out of material!* About her debut, Karen reports, "*Caramba*! I'm happy and shocked and terrified . . . *The New Yorker* thing is great, but I still have so much growing to do, and now I'll pubesce in public."

Measures of Sorrow

Jacob M. Appel

I'd taken an apartment on the wrong side of the park. This was pre-gentrification, before community empowerment, when the neighborhood's leading commercial enterprise was No-Eyed Jack, a blind barber who cut hair for tourists. My acquaintances were quick to note other local resources: "a wide array of pawn shops," "check cashing on every corner," "national leadership in tire irons per capita." Their warnings didn't faze me. I was a born-and-bred New Yorker, after all, city-savvy as a street urchin, and I looked forward to the cachet that my address—on an avenue named for an obscure president and then renamed for an obscure civil rights leader—might carry with left-wing coeds at Greenwich Village parties. Besides, it was all I could afford.

What I call "an apartment" was, properly speaking, a semi-finished basement in a once-luxurious prewar brownstone. My door opened onto a narrow, pipe-lined corridor; the windows afforded a knee-level view of the sidewalk. Men sent to read the water meter frequently mistook me for the building superintendent. This responsibility actually fell to Hector Acosta, an adult son of the Dominican landlady, who also raised gamecocks on the rear fire escapes. Two dozen roosters crowed me awake every dawn.

Otherwise, I had no complaints. My new neighbors saw me as a novelty, rather than a pioneer, so they welcomed me warmly.

Crossing the park proved another matter. That no-man's-land between police precincts offered the only practicable route to the university—no cabbie wanted a cross-park fare—but its deserted trails concealed machete-wielding opium fiends and sociopaths set to garrote me with piano wire. Or so I imagined. My parents had raised me on the hazards of urban parkland; the revival of *I'm Not Rappaport* rekindled my suspicions. Although I walked briskly—with my right fist in my jacket pocket, where a would-be attacker might mistake it for a handgun—these trips to and from campus framed my days with terror. When other students asked about safety, I feigned nonchalance. Why admit that in mid-September, I was already alarmed over the shortening days, panicked that my schedule might converge with the twilight? Months of intense anxiety had left me ready to embrace the most ludicrous of alternatives. Which is, more or less, what I did.

*

It was a Saturday afternoon—a final huff of torrid Indian summer. I'd just returned from a sidewalk sale, where I'd purchased two small bookcases and a stepladder to use in changing light bulbs. The bookcases were light, but bulky, exhausting to carry three long blocks. I ditched them in the passage, propped open the door and retreated into the kitchenette for a root beer. Holding an icy aluminum can to my forehead was cheaper than air-conditioning. So was soaking my t-shirt in cold tap water and drawing it over my head. Sensing a shadow, I looked up and found myself face to face with a sharp-featured, cocoa-skinned stranger—a presence as unlikely as the Cheshire cat. The man might have been twenty-five. Or forty. He wore an aloha shirt, sunglasses tucked into the collar. His arrival dazed me so thoroughly that I forgot to shout for help.

"The day is very hot," said the intruder. "Not a day for the transporting of furniture."

Even by Manhattan standards, this development was unprecedented: a stranger had followed me into my apartment to report the weather. He'd also carried my bookshelves inside and deposited them behind the sofa.

"You are wondering from where I come," said the intruder, who did speak with an accent—though his origins hadn't crossed my mind. "I once told people that I come from a nation of which they have never heard," he explained. "But that is not of interest to most people. There are many nations of which nobody has ever heard. So now I say that I come from a nation no longer in existence, an island under lava, which is as much the truth. This is of interest to them far more."

I caught sight of a screwdriver on the countertop, and considered lunging for it, but my intruder no longer seemed threatening. Merely inept. Muggers didn't wear open-toed sandals. Nor could I imagine one so self-possessed. You'd have thought that in the man's Caribbean birthplace—which he named and which I hadn't ever heard of—the custom was to follow strangers home.

A bit awkwardly, as though handshakes were not among his island's traditions, the intruder extended a hand nearly as large as a baseball glove. "Ollie," he introduced himself. "I am residing on the second floor."

I kept my arms at my sides. "Do you want something?"

Ollie answered with a mesmeric smile—one that announced: if I want something, I'll find a way to get it. He had teeth as white as Meerschaum, but jagged, and canines like alabaster stalactites.

"May I sit down?"

I said nothing. My visitor removed a cardboard box from a nearby folding chair and seated himself in reverse, his elbows resting on the squared-off back. He'd brought with him a small stack of books, which he'd placed on the carpet and which he adjusted periodically, maybe to emphasize his ownership.

"I think more clearly when I am sitting down," he said.

"I'm rather busy," I answered.

"The blood has less gravity against which to fight, sitting down."

I walked to the kitchen table, no longer feeling endangered, merely annoyed, and in an effort to appear busy, sorted through the previous day's mail. "I have a dissertation to write."

"It is for that reason I have come to see you."

Our interaction had advanced from the implausible to the impossible. My dissertation in the Department of Judaic Studies examined two ancient Hebraic commentaries on sorrow. According to *Beit Hillel*, the precise number of tears to be shed before the Messiah's arrival was fixed. Those not wept in one generation would inevitably pour forth in another. A second school, *Beit Shammai*, rejected this. These rabbis maintained it was the volume of tears, not their number, that was predetermined. No lay person in their right mind could have cared less.

"You're interested in my dissertation?"

"I am interested," said Ollie, "in your knowledge."

"Meaning?"

"I want you to teach me. To tutor me."

Tutor him? A marriage proposal seemed as reasonable. "In what?"

Ollie paused–to collect his thoughts or for dramatic effect. "Everything," he said. "Everything that they teach at the university."

I expected Ollie to grin, to reveal a joke at my expense, but he didn't. He couldn't have been more serious had he sought religious instruction from a monk. "I have been attempting on my own," he added, passing me his collection of books. "I have learned that you cannot learn everything on your own. You need a teacher to place your knowledge in order."

His three books were Heidegger's *Being and Time*, Packenham's *History of the Boer War* and *The Complete Short Novels of D. H. Lawrence, Volume II.*

"Order is important," I conceded.

"So you will teach me?"

I thumbed through Heidegger. The dog-eared paperback had lost its cover and the pages flaked easily. Some sentences were highlighted in red. Others in yellow. Question marks cluttered the margins. Although I hoped to avoid bad blood, particularly with a fellow tenant, I refused to yield under pressure.

"I don't know you." I drifted toward the door, hoping he'd follow. "I'm sure if you phone the university, there are always graduate students looking for money. . . ."

Ollie shook his head. "I do not have that amount of money," he answered. "I am driving a taxicab."

"So you want me to teach you for free?"

"For trade." He stood and rested one of his feet on the chair, his elbow braced against his elevated knee. "I have seen you crossing the park," he explained. "You move like a fox in a dog pound."

I snapped shut his book. "So?"

"So I will be your chauffeur. I will drive you to the university and I will drive you from the university." Now, he grinned. "No more fox-trotting."

"In return for . . . ?"

Ollie didn't answer directly. "They say this is the land of opportunity," he said. "You are my opportunity."

He extended his oversized hand again. "Let us shake upon it."

"I'll think it over," I said.

"No, no. Let us shake upon it and I will drive you now."

I had no reason to visit the campus on a Saturday afternoon, nor was I clear about my attitude toward this man's odd proposition, but I am non-confrontational by nature, and a ride in his taxi seemed preferable to further argument. So I shook his hand. He held mine a bit too long, the sort of clasping, fleshy handshake that Bible-thumpers attribute to homosexuals. But there was no hint of the romantic in his smile. If anything, his expression was too familiar for romance. Too confident. I wasn't at all surprised when he stepped backwards and sized me up—the sort of "second look" one might give to auction-bought livestock. He nodded. He appeared to believe that he'd struck a winning bargain.

Outside the skies had turned dark. Thunder rumbled in the distance. We found Ollie's cab blocking a bus stop, a bright orange summons under one wiper blade.

"Do not be alarmed," said Ollie, as though his parking ticket should trouble me. He tucked the summons into his shirt pocket. "It is a trick. An empty envelope that I obtained last year from an abandoned automobile."

"Clever," I said—although this was an ancient ploy.

"Only when used properly." He removed a flyer from the windshield. *THIS VEHICLE HAS BEEN TOWED TO THIS LOCATION BY THE NEW YORK CITY POLICE DEPARTMENT. DO NOT SUMMONS.* The date and a *NYPD* insignia followed. "I print these in the public library."

When I settled into the passenger seat, I spotted another of my new acquaintance's deceptions. Ollie's taxi was a large yellow Crown Victoria with a service light on the roof—but it was not a "yellow cab." The hood lacked the necessary medallion. In New York City, I warned him, that's a prison offense.

"Which is the true crime?" answered Ollie. "To drive without a medallion? Or to limit the number of taxicabs by artificial measures? They say this is the land of capitalism. I am capitalizing."

Ollie rolled down his window and lit a cigarillo. Not the moment, I decided, for a crash-course on market regulation. "Can I ask something?" I asked. "What's this all about? Why this urge to know everything? Most people hardly know anything."

"I will tell you," answered Ollie. "It is not so remarkable. I am wishing to make an impression upon a woman."

That I could relate to. I had memorized all of Shakespeare's sonnets to win the heart of a folksinger. It didn't work.

"Who is she?" I asked.

"She is a graduate student at your university. Her name I do not know."

I responded with matching syntax. "Her name you do not know?"

"Her name I do not know."

I waited for Ollie to say more, but he didn't. Instead, he honked his horn at pedestrians edging into a crosswalk. "What do you know about her?" I asked.

"I picked her up two weeks ago. I remember the precise date. It is the same date upon which I picked her up last year."

"Let me get this straight. You want to impress a girl, whose name you don't even know, because you've given her two rides on the same date."

"Not at all," answered Ollie. "I am wishing to make an impression upon her because she is the most beautiful woman I have ever seen. That I have picked her up two times on the same date is a sign that I may succeed. You have read the play *Romeo and Juliet*? I believe that Romeo falls in love with Juliet before learning of her name."

"Jesus Christ. You've got it all figured out, don't you?"

"I have never picked up another passenger twice. On any days." His expression turned grave, almost wistful. "A beautiful woman is not easy to obtain. One must seize one's opportunities."

Ollie tossed his cigarillo out the window and eased the cab to the curb. Broadway and 116th Street. "As you say in this country, door to the door service."

Rain was falling in heavy, piercing drops. Ollie let me off and pulled back into traffic. I realized, too late, that I hadn't arranged for a ride home—that I had no choice but to "fox-trot" across the park.

*

Our first "lesson" took place the following evening in Ollie's apartment. He occupied a cozy studio overlooking a neglected yard. School kids had appropriated this lot for a battlefield, raising a fort from discarded cinderblocks. There were also two abandoned bathtubs in which an elderly woman cultivated marigolds. What had once been a stockade fence lay rotting in the crabgrass. Inside, Ollie's quarters were sparsely furnished and immaculately clean, but the room lacked personal landmarks. No photographs. No souvenirs. Its most distinguishing feature was a well-manicured spider plant. The sterility reminded me of the model units that resorts use to market timeshares.

Crafting a curriculum that encompassed "everything" posed a challenge, particularly because of Ollie's haphazard knowledge-base. He could name the popes dating back to Boniface VIII—and their dates of service—but he'd never heard of Annie Oakley or Charles Lindbergh. I joked that he should read all the books in the library alphabetically, like the Self-Taught Man in Sartre's *Nausea*, but he took my suggestion quite seriously, and rejected it. If I did that, he said, you would be unnecessary. So we started at the beginning: Homer. Thales. Anaximander. Initially, I had envisioned myself a present day Henry Higgins. In reality, Ollie learned far better than I taught. He read with an intensity that most college freshmen reserve for alcohol—transforming our "lessons" into fast-paced discussions that often left me feeling undereducated. In the course of our first week, we ploughed through Thucydides, Xenophon, Aristotle.

The enterprise proved more pleasant than I'd anticipated. Graduate students have few social outlets, and even fewer opportunities to produce anything tangible, so I took pride in Ollie's expanding knowledge, much as a stonemason might in a rising cathedral. Also, grudgingly, I grew to enjoy his company. It was impossible not to. My student's homespun theories of justice, as entertaining as they were ass-backwards, rivaled the best of Mark Twain or Shalom Aleichem.

One autumn evening, when we were about six weeks into our survey of all previous thought, a photograph appeared on Ollie's desolate bureau: a candid shot of a brunette smoking in a café. To say she was "beautiful," you might as easily describe Mozart as "musical" or Caligula as "unpleasant." I have never seen hair so black or skin so white. The girl was laughing, eyes closed, mouth open, like the women in beer advertisements. I tried my best to ignore her, to focus on Seneca's tragedies. I was Ollie's tutor, after all, not his confidante, nor did I wish to give him the satisfaction of showing my curiosity. But even from a photograph, the girl's looks were head-turning.

"Okay, you win," I finally said. "Who's that?"

"Laurah Townsend," Ollie replied—as though the picture had been collecting dust on his dresser for decades.

I'd grown accustomed to these oblique answers, to the cat-and-mouse routine that usually followed. "Who is Laurah Townsend?"

"The woman I am wishing to marry," he said. "She spells it with an 'h.' Laurah. Do you believe one pronounces it differently?"

Somehow the stakes had risen to matrimony. "How'd you get the picture?"

"I followed her from her place of residence," he said. "I was very careful to record the address when I dropped her off."

"That's stalking," I objected. "You can't do that."

"Scouting, my friend. Not stalking. If I had been a Shakespearean hero, I would have sent forward a messenger to make inquiries."

"If you'd have been Cro-Magnon man," I snapped, "you'd have clubbed her and dragged her back to your cave. In this country, it's goddam stalking."

Ollie kneaded his forehead with his fingertips. Then he crossed to the window and began watering the spider plant from a green plastic pitcher.

I found myself fearing that he might take my outburst for xenophobia. Or worse.

"This is very healthy," he finally said. "As in the Dialogues of Plato. We are sharing a difference of opinion."

I shook my raised fist à la Jackie Gleason—but smiled in spite of myself. "Did anybody ever tell you that you're infuriating?"

"The watering of plants I find relaxing," Ollie answered. "It is like urinating on an empty bladder."

"Seneca," I prompted. "*Hercules Oetaeus.*"

"You have now seen Laurah Townsend. Do you think you will be able to help me to date a woman like that?"

"I don't know if I could date a woman like that."

Ollie looked up from the plant. "You do not have to do so," he answered. "That is not of importance."

*

While my student/chauffeur knew no shame in flouting automobile regulations—it eventually came out that he even lacked liability insurance—Ollie kept his bargain with me to the letter. ("We have an agreement," he explained. "With the State of New York, I do not have an agreement.") Every weekday morning, at precisely eight-thirty, Ollie's cab pulled up to our stoop. His arrivals were as punctual as Mussolini's trains, as consistent as Immanuel Kant's afternoon strolls, by which, we read in November, the housewives of Koenigsberg once set their clocks. The regularity of our departures contrasted with the timing of my return trips. These grew earlier by the day. I spent increasingly more energy brushing up my Shakespeare (and Milton and Dryden and Swift), and concomitantly less quantifying unhappiness. Even in the world of Talmudic studies, my dissertation seemed iconically trivial: who cared about the relationship between liquid cubits and fluid ounces? Or precisely how much Rachel wept for her children? Exposure to the classics had torn off my blinders. I degenerated into one of those ghostly graduate students who publish nothing, yet are passionately engaged in maintaining the illusion of scholarship.

My commercial activity also shifted away from the campus. I washed my clothing at the corner laundromat that doubled as a bingo parlor. I bought groceries from a tiny Korean woman who made change through bulletproof glass. I even registered to vote at the local firehouse, although our precinct hadn't had a contested election since the days of Father Divine. In a matter of months, freed from the daily terror of crossing the park, I felt more comfortable in my new haunts than I ever had in my old ones. When the animal warden commandeered Hector's roosters—the same police force that couldn't keep crack out of our playgrounds—my indignation matched that of the most belligerent community activists. If I'd once been the only graduate student in the Department of

Judaic Studies who apologized for Al Sharpton, now I admired him. However, my true baptism didn't occur until after the New Year—sometime between Mill and Darwin—when I braved a trim at No-Eyed Jack's.

This tourist landmark was located on the far side of the boulevard, sandwiched between a Western Union office and a storefront church. It had only one barber chair. The "hot seat" faced several rows of cushion-lined benches from which, every weekday afternoon, and all day Saturdays, tourists paid to watch the maestro at his craft. (Jack had an arrangement with a sightseeing company that also organized gospel brunches. They provided the audience; he supplied the show.) The walls displayed photographs of the barber in the company of a wide assortment of celebrities, including an enormous portrait of him with his arms draped over the shoulders of Stevie Wonder and Ray Charles. Taped to a support beam, between two sections of mirror, a sign announced: *If I Were White, I'd Be a Surgeon.* During performances, Jack sported garish monochrome suits in chartreuse, mauve and vermillion. On weekday mornings, serving a local clientele, he didn't bother to tuck his T-shirt into his dungarees.

I settled into the barber chair and asked for a trim, hoping the man was a fraud. My stomach quivered when he removed his glasses to reveal two porcelain eyes.

"We was wondering when you'd come in here, Teach," he said.

I wasn't sure whether to answer. I did not want to distract him. "You know me?"

"Everybody knows ya, Teach. You're the guy is teaching Ollie."

Where was this leading? I wondered. Would I end up instructing the barber's children in Sanskrit? "Ollie comes in here?" I asked.

"Everybody come in here," said the barber.

He ran his calloused fingers over my scalp, my brow, my neck. I'd heard he shaved men with a straight razor, but I wasn't that daring.

"My boy Ollie swears up down and sideways you the most excellent thing since Lena Horne. Says ya gonna be best man at his wedding."

"He said that?"

"Uh-huh. Now lean forward." Jack adjusted my head and lowered his open scissors in front of my eyes. Then he drew back swiftly. "Before we start," he said. "You wanna see my collection of ears?"

I told myself I'd survive, because others had survived—no different than air travel or tattooing. My fingernails dug into the leather armrests.

"Don't let me be scaring ya, Teach. You can always trust a blind barber. He's got a lot more at stake."

He snipped the line of hair across my forehead. Straight as a railroad tie.

"Nobody will give you a difficult time in this neighborhood," Jack said—switching abruptly from Newyorkese to the King's English. "You tell them where you live and they will assume that you're much worse off than they are."

*

Several months later, Ollie announced that he was "ready to practice." After a lengthy discussion of the Boxer Rebellion, (I couldn't imagine Laurah Townsend bringing up John Hay's "Open Door" policy on a first date, but as Ollie insisted, everything was everything), we were relaxing in my apartment—his ceiling had started to leak. "You will be Laurah," he explained. "I will be me." He lit a votive candle in a teacup and set it on the Formica tabletop.

"How can I be Laurah?" I asked. "I don't know the first thing about her."

"That does not matter. I do not either."

"So you want me to pretend to be a girl I've never met and to act as if we're out on a first date."

"Precisely," said Ollie.

"What sort of restaurant is it? What am I wearing?"

These questions were intended facetiously, aimed at exposing the absurdity of such role-playing, but instead they egged Ollie on. He drew me a floor plan of the Italian bistro and described everything from the frescos of Florentine street-life to the specials listed on the chalkboard. When he informed me I was wearing a leopard-print skirt, form-fitting and three inches above the knee, I gave in. "Okay, Okay. I get it," I said. "Whenever you're ready."

Ollie straightened his back, folded his hands. "Laurah," he asked—as though conducting a job interview, "in what course of study are you at the university?"

"I'm a graduate student in the Department of Judaic Studies."

"Intriguing," answered Ollie. "I too am interested in the study of Judaism."

"Are you now?"

He ignored me. "In which area of Judaism are you studying? Possibly the *Mishnah*? Or the *Gemara*? Or Prime Minister Eshkol and the Six-Day War?"

"I'm studying tears. It's not very interesting."

"I am certain it is much more interesting than you believe."

"No," I snapped. "It's not."

Ollie paused and tapped his fingertips together. "If it is not interesting, why have you chosen it as your course of study?"

I pounded my fist on the table. "Jesus-fucking-Christ. You're on a date, not running the McCarthy hearings. Don't ask questions with difficult answers."

Ollie frowned. "I did not understand that inquiry to demand a difficult answer."

"Well it did," I said.

"How so?"

I exhaled deeply and thought backwards from ten. "Try to make her feel comfortable," I advised. "Ask open-ended questions. Let the girl steer the conversation."

"Let the girl steer the conversation," echoed Ollie—surprised, as though I'd pitched styrofoam as snack-food. "Very well. Why do you not ask me some questions? I will practice through observational learning."

"Okay," I agreed. "That I can manage." But formulating questions turned out to be far more taxing than I'd anticipated. I hadn't been dating much myself that winter—okay, not at all—and my skills were somewhat rusty. I could think only of questions which called for factual answers: Who invented the combustion engine? Where did Stanley find Livingstone? If the goal had been to stump Laurah, rather than to woo her, I'd have hit pay-dirt.

"Tell me about your family," I finally said. "Do you have brothers or sisters?"

This was the first I'd ever asked Ollie of his past, sensing it was a subject he preferred to avoid, but I wasn't taking advantage of our role-playing. It was the only question I could think of not suited for a game show.

Ollie's smile never wavered, but the muscles stiffened in his shoulders. "I have no brothers and no sisters," he said.

"And your parents?"

"It is important to be always forward looking," answered Ollie. "That is why I have come to America. A past is not necessary in this country. You can reinvent yourself like Mr. Gatsby."

"But Gatsby failed."

"That is not here, nor is it there. What is important is to look always toward the future. I am also thinking of the Biblical story of Lot. Does not the wife of Lot look backward? And for this transgression is she not turned to salt?"

I cupped my fist in my palm. "Maybe you need Henry Higgins."

"Excuse me?"

"You can't use the word transgression on a date. You sound like Reinhold Niebuhr. What kind of cockeyed school did you go to anyway?"

"I did not go to school at all," answered Ollie. "I am an autodidact. Like President Lincoln. I taught myself English from a foreign service manual."

What awed me most about Ollie's admission was that, to him, this method of education didn't seem the slightest bit limiting. Far from it. I imagine he believed it preferable to learn the language from a government drill-book.

"Other than my use of the word transgression," asked Ollie. "How did I fare?"

"You don't want to know."

"But I do," he said. "And I have one more question. What is this you mean by these McCarthy hearings?"

*

That's when my real teaching started. Ollie's greatest hurdle wasn't a shortage of information, but too much of it. Or maybe it's more accurate to say that he lacked a framework with which to distinguish common knowledge from the $64,000 question. All facts had equal value, to his thinking, until proven otherwise. He did not understand, for instance, that if you quoted Churchill, you were most likely referring to the British prime minister. You might as easily be referring to Arabella Churchill, the mistress of James II, or Canadian actor Berton Churchill. Nor was Ollie bashful about asking: Do you mean the Augustan courtesan? Or the colleague of John Wayne? Or might you be referencing the eighteenth century general? With some effort, I trained him to assume Winston without inquiry—a principle that he learned to generalize. Darwin was Charles, not Erasmus. Marx, unmodified, meant Karl—never Groucho. So far, so good. But why didn't the Marx Brothers include Karl, Eduard and Hermann? And was it permissible to ask whether Chamberlain was Neville or Wilt?

All summer I taught Ollie to forget things. "Neville, okay," I said. "Maybe Wilt. But never Owen. As far as you're concerned, there is no Owen Chamberlain."

"Are you certain?" asked Ollie. "He was a winner of the Nobel Prize. To him we owe our entire understanding of anti-protons."

"I'm sure we do," I said. "And for that I'm truly grateful. But he is not important."

Ollie massaged the bridge of his nose. "If you say he is not of importance," he agreed without conviction, "then I will speak no more of him."

Later, of course, he would second-guess my judgment and deliver an impassioned defense of Owen Chamberlain's research on fundamental particles. How could I not think proton-proton scattering important? Ollie valued knowledge too much to yield it without a struggle. My task was like spring cleaning with a packrat.

And then—one morning in September—Ollie fired me. He expressed his intentions as we passed behind the cathedral, under the shedding maples, where two priests had recently been stabbed. They'd had no chauffeur. No "door to the door" service. Police barricades still cordoned off the sidewalk.

"This evening," Ollie announced, "I will dine with Laurah Townsend."

"Tonight?"

"One full year has passed since she last rode in my taxicab. Two full years have passed since she first rode in my taxicab."

"But you can't. Not yet." My initial objection had been on Ollie's account–to prevent him from acting prematurely. Hadn't Branch Rickey held back Jackie Robinson? Then I realized that I stood to lose more than he did: my employer, my chauffeur, my closest friend. Ollie had placed all of his eggs in Laurah's basket. Most of mine had ended up in his. "Trust me," I said. "Let's give it another few months."

"This evening," answered Ollie. "I have already made arrangements. I picked up Laurah Townsend yesterday afternoon and invited her to dine."

"And she said yes?"

"She did not say 'no'," said Ollie. "She laughed. This evening I will pay a visit to her café."

"Uninvited?"

"Not invited," answered Ollie. "Not uninvited either."

I sensed the futility of objecting further; it would have been easier to postpone a solar eclipse. Moreover, I'd lost track of my loyalties. Didn't Ollie's success mean an end to our lessons? And what would his failure mean? My next thought highlighted the absurdity of my predicament. I'd wanted to ask: Can I come along? Or, in the least, Can I watch?

"Maybe I'll drop by that café," I said. "To check up on you." Meaning what? To play duenna? To play voyeur?

Ollie nodded thoughtfully. "I would like that very much," he said. "Like the tourists at the shop of the barber. You will be my audience."

*

The café, Just Desserts, was located on the "right" side of the park. It had replaced Lenin's & Trotsky's, a smoke-hazy Kerouac hangout, but had retained the former establishment's Soviet décor. Warsaw Pact flags hung from the exposed rafters. Behind the cheesecake display, placards advocated for Sacco and Vanzetti. In the men's room, a flint-faced Stalin glowered over the urinals. But the clientele had evolved: where denim-clad anarchists had once played darts, junior faculty now rehearsed lectures. Prices had also doubled. On weekends, stroller-fettered couples bought six dollar *lattes* for takeout. The old and new patrons shared one characteristic: they were almost uniformly white. Not a stamping ground for Caribbean cabbies.

I arrived two hours early, hoping to snag a good seat. Laurah Townsend, as I'd anticipated, had already claimed a chair by the window. The woman was as stunning as she'd appeared in the photograph, but considerably older. Maybe thirty. Even thirty-five. She wore an angora sweater and a gray linen skirt—a far cry from the low-cut blouse and skintight pants that I'd imagined. She was writing in pencil, gnawing the stub of her eraser. Crumpled balls of yellow paper littered her workspace, and every few minutes she increased the chaos with a page torn from a legal pad. The table's perimeter was hemmed with books. I installed myself nearby and pretended to read the newspaper. I was doing nothing wrong, I assured myself. Nothing illegal. I was no different from any other graduate student enjoying an espresso in a public coffee shop.

But I knew otherwise. I was, in Ollie's language, scouting. At one point, I peered over the newspaper and our eyes met. Laurah smiled: a tender, teasing smile that lingered until I looked away. Scouting might be sketchy; but flirting crossed the line—the sort of transgression that bordered on evil. Fortunately, the rightful suitor showed up before I had a chance to do damage.

I hardly recognized Ollie. My student had shaved his beard, traded in his sandals and beach attire for khakis and a stylish pink shirt. He winked at me, but crossed directly to Laurah—either over enthusiastic or afraid of losing his nerve. When he spoke—deliberatively, as though measuring each word—his voice held the same confidence it had that first afternoon in my apartment.

"Excuse me," said Ollie. "I believe that yesterday I had the privilege of driving you in my taxicab."

"Oh, you," said Laurah. Her surprise reminded me of my own shock at Ollie's first appearance. She flipped over her pad.

"I know what you are thinking," continued Ollie. "You are thinking that many taxicab drivers do not dine in this café."

"No," said Laurah. "I guess not."

"I drive a taxicab only to earn my livelihood. To give me leisure time to focus on my studies." Ollie leaned forward to see the titles of her books. "Secrets of the Atom," he read. "Oppenheimer vs. *HUAC*. You are studying physics?"

"The history of physics," said Laurah. "You've heard of Schrodinger."

"I assume that you mean Erwin Schrodinger who won the Nobel Prize for his work in quantum mechanics. It is not likely that you mean W. A. Schrodinger, the Bavarian horticulturist."

Laurah tucked her pad into her backpack—as though preparing to leave. Ollie frowned and then his expression turned unexpectedly gleeful. "Are you, by any chance, familiar with the research of Owen Chamberlain?"

"You know about Owen Chamberlain?" I could sense the girl's discomfort ebbing slightly, her appetite genuinely whetted. "You're studying physics?"

"Not at all," answered Ollie. "My interest is entirely avocational. I believe the research of Chamberlain is underappreciated." I did not see the man move–but somehow he ended up seated. "What I am studying," he said, "are Talmudic commentaries on tears. My hope is to quantify the sorrow in the universe."

"Tears?" asked Laurah.

"Tears."

Ollie served up a cogent, lucid summary of my thesis. He reduced seven years of research into a series of provocative anecdotes, exploring a broad swath of emotion from the humorous to the heart-rending. In his voice, the project actually sounded interesting, a topic worthy of investigation. What stung me most was his self-assurance–that he never once looked in my direction.

"I am deeply interested in misfortune," Ollie concluded. "That is what happens when one is of a nation which is no longer in existence."

"Your family. . . ?" asked Laurah.

"All of them. All of my brothers and sisters," he said. And then he spoke of the cascading lava, of the horrors he had never shared with me, until the girl was dabbing away tears of her own. When I left the café, they were still locked in conversation.

The sun had already set. I drifted toward the park–bracing myself for the passage through the darkness. I carried inside me this story, of Ollie's education, and my own, but I knew nobody with whom to share it. You can measure a man's sorrow, and the world's, in the number of stories that perish unheard.

Girl Talk

Laura van den Berg

"He could be a cad," my mother says, examining the wallet-sized photo of my lover. The diner is empty; the blinds are partially closed; pale beams of sunlight hold particles of dust. I am facing the back door. The light inside the exit sign over the door has burned out; its letters are dark and colorless. My mother cocks her head, and the red vinyl booth squeaks underneath her thighs. It is the middle of the day, and we are both drinking iced tea spiked with the rum she brought in a tin flask. She holds the photo in a stream of daylight and dust, as though the right lighting will uncover all the dark things behind his eyes. "Yes," she concludes. "He's bad all right. Run. That's my advice."

"I don't know that," I say, plucking the photo from her stubby fingertips and pressing it face down against the table. I wrap my lips around the straw and suck in a mouthful of tea and rum.

"Take my word for it." She fishes an ice cube out of the glass and rubs it all over her face and neck, polishes the gray pockets underneath her eyes. The diner is hot.

"But I'm young," I say. "It's my job to be optimistic."

She digs out another ice cube and slips it between her lips. "That's all fine," she says, sounding at once hollow and angry, crunching the ice with her teeth. "But you should know what to do in the event of an emergency."

The Last Girl on Earth

Mary Michael Wagner

Judd and I are pulled off the road in a rutted spot watching the dirty cord of the river. It's the first hot day of spring and a grassy-hay smell drifts into the open window. Behind us on the road cars sometimes swoosh by. We won't know until tomorrow morning when we walk into school whether we were spotted cutting last class; it could mean a month of detentions, maybe suspension. Right now, we don't care.

"Look at that. The moon's out." Up in the sky a piece of moon shows like a pale scab against the blue.

Judd glances through the dirty windshield. "Means the Devil's beating his wife."

"Nuh-uh. That's when it's raining when the sun's out."

"Oh, yeah." Judd's trying to light a thick kitchen match against the bottom of his shoe, something his friend Robby thinks is cool. The match splinters and he fishes another from the box on the dash.

"Why don't you just use this?" I hand him the box with the wide-ridged lighting strip facing him. I notice the bottom of his shoe's smoking a little bit. "You're gonna melt your shoe."

"Ever notice how Robby's girlfriend never says naggy shit like that to him? She's … supportive."

"She's not smart enough to be anything else." I slide across the seat towards him. I'm thinking about kissing his neck.

He raises his shaggy eyebrows, "She's got other qualities."

"That's really original, Judd." He's talking about her *D* cups.

"What? What did I say?" He laughs. His match finally lights and he holds it to the end of his Camel filterless. He inhales deeply. I move back over to my door, stick my bare feet out the window, letting the breeze move up my legs. I glance down at the small swells on my chest.

"Oh, now you're not talking to me?" he says. Out of the corner of his eye, I see him trying to blow smoke rings that look more like blobs.

"I'm ready to go," I tell him.

"You'll have to walk then."

"Fine." I slide out of the car, slamming the door. I walk to the edge of the road. When I see a car coming, I awkwardly hold out my thumb. I can see Judd watching me through the side mirror, his face clouded by smoke. I can tell by his slouch that he's smirking. The car roars by—a mom driving a station wagon full of little kids. Then there's a Cadillac. And then there's the quiet of the road with a cloud of gnats. I think, What if my mom drives by? I'm about to go and climb back into the car when Judd hangs an arm out the window, calls back to me. He's laughing hard. "Hey, Jess, you're supposed to point your thumb up, not down."

"Shut up," I say, letting my hand drop to my side.

Then I hear a rattling sound, spot a car coming over the rise.

"We both know you're getting back in the car," he says.

It's a truck. I stick my arm out, thumb up. A blue pickup with its taillights smashed out and a muffler full of holes swerves off the road and skids onto the gravel ahead of me. I start running towards it.

Judd yells after me, "Jessica, come on. Let's go." I look back and see that he's opened his car door, is halfway out. But I'm running towards that blue truck.

"Jessica, you idiot, get back in the goddamned car." His voice goes sort of high. "Whatever," he yells after me.

I can hear my breath I'm running so hard. The passenger door of the truck swings open; I lift myself up onto the seat and the truck shimmies back onto the road, rubbing a cloud of dust from the ground.

"Where can I drop you?" The guy smiles, showing tiny straight teeth, so small you'd think they were baby teeth.

"Town's fine," I say.

The guy keeps his eyes on the road. He has this enormous, pointy Adam's apple like he's swallowed a deck of cards. When he swallows it looks painful. His ears come out of his head at right angles—the sort of ears that you know were flicked on a school bus when he was a kid. But he has the bland, kind face of somebody who would just shrug off being called "dumbo," who would be a better person because of it.

"My boyfriend's a jerk. Why do boys have to ruin everything?" The guy doesn't look at me, but smiles in an understanding kind of sheepish way, because he was a boy once, too. I don't give Judd the satisfaction of turning around, but imagine him, the front seat covered in matchsticks, speeding along behind us.

I reach over and turn the radio on. No music comes out of the speakers, just a scratchy sound like the end of a record playing. I twist the knobs, but nothing else happens. There's a box of dog biscuits spilling out onto the floor of the cab, and my skirt's covered in fine white hairs, but there's no dog anywhere. I'm thinking about turning around and waving at Judd, motioning him to pull up alongside the truck. But I don't. Not yet. I want to make him suffer a little. I think I can even hear the rattling sound of his engine behind us.

I'm used to grownups wanting to ask questions. What grade are you in? What do you want to be? But this guy just watches the road. There are two creases in his forehead like he's thinking about what he's got to pick up in town. I roll down the window, but it only opens a few inches. Still, through the crack, I can decipher the cold smell of the river and see it glitter in the spaces between the trees.

I think about what a waste it will be to be suspended for this. I'd imagined Judd and me making out in the patch of sun in the backseat then going out for greasy onion rings and ice-cream sodas.

"You know," I say to the guy, "I think maybe I should just get out. My boyfriend's gonna kill me. He's following right along behind us." The guy looks up in his rearview mirror.

"You want a little inside advice on guys?" he says. "A secret?" He looks at me for the first time. When he turns a little I can see the crisp, white triangle of his T-shirt showing beneath his button shirt. My dad never wears a shirt without a T-shirt underneath. That's the way I think of guys, all buttons and layers.

"I know a lot," I tell him.

"I'm sure you do. Like I bet you could tell me secret things about being a woman that I wouldn't know anything about." A little current of feeling goes down my back, like something being unzipped, at being called a woman.

"Guys like a girl who does whatever she wants," he says, "girls who barely give him a second thought. They eat it up."

I think about how I always wait in the same spot outside of school for Judd to drift down the stairs after talking to his goony friends. Did he like that or didn't he? Laura Petit, not that pretty with hard, green eyes, broke up with a guy every month, but there was always another waiting.

The truck rumbled past the water tower, and for the first time I notice that the tower lists ever so slightly to one side. I wonder if it could fall.

"Come on," he says. "Scoot over here. Let's make him jealous."

"I really like him."

"Of course, you do. Come on over."

I scootch over and the guy slips his arm around me. I can smell the clean, spicy, fatherly smell of his deodorant or after-shave or whatever it is.

"What's he doing?" I say, laughing.

"Practically peeing his pants," he says. Then the guy slows down and turns off the main road, away from the river and away from town.

"Hey, Hey, Hey, Hey." I don't know—that's what flies out of my mouth.

He starts grinding uphill away from everything. "Relax," he says.

I scoot out from under his arm and back over to the passenger door. "Look, I really have to get home. It's late."

He keeps driving.

"You know," I tell him, "Judd's probably written down your license plate number and everything."

The guy flicks a look up into the rearview mirror. Then smiles. I turn around. Through the grimy window, no cars. Just a view.

Maybe the rattling sound had been the guy's truck all along and not Judd's. Suddenly I feel my heart beating in its tiny little compartment. Has it been hammering away like that all along and I hadn't noticed? My voice pools down in my shoes. Finally, I say, "I thought you said we were going to town."

"Relax," he says, "I've just gotta drop something off first."

"I should just get out and walk."

"You're out in the middle of nowhere."

The vibration of the muffler goes into my bones.

"What are you going to do?" I ask him.

He shrugs. "You'll be in town before you know it."

The guy's focused on the road, both hands gripping the wheel. He never lists onto the shoulder the way Judd does. He slows down to go over the single, homemade, lopsided blacktop speed bump stuck way out here by some family with little kids. I study the dropping speedometer, wondering what would happen if I jump now. I'd roll like people who jump off trains in the movies. When he sees me looking at the gauge he speeds up so we thump hard over the bump, rattling the gas cans in the truck bed.

This woman came to our school once. She talked to all the girls in the school gym, just the girls; the boys watched some filmstrip on tornadoes. This woman was like seven feet tall with a braid as thick as a man's arm and I don't know what she had to worry about, but she told us if someone was trying to assault us, that's what she called it, that we should try to talk to the guy like he was a human being, and get him to see us like a human being, too. "Humanize, humanize, humanize," she kept saying. I thought she was going to make us stand in a circle and sing.

I give it a try. "Where's your dog?" I ask. He doesn't say anything, but I imagine a mutty dog all slobbery and nuzzly and instantly I feel better. I ask the guy if he has any kids. I ask him if he gets good mileage, what his name is, if he's ever taken a vacation to anyplace nice; finally he tells me to be quiet. I start telling him about my eight brothers and sisters and this seems to be okay. As long as I don't ask him anything, he lets me talk. I tell him how my sister's frizzy hair is always getting matted in my hairbrush even though I try hiding it in my sock drawer or how my older brothers will finish the last of the cereal and put the empty box back on the shelf and you won't know until you reach for it and it's all light in your hand. I start trying to humanize myself, talking on and on about my family and the house we live in. Nobody listens to anybody. The sun's behind us somewhere.

A pickup truck drives towards us. I place my hand on the door handle, but the guy shoots me a look. I put my hand back in my lap. The men wave at each other as we pass. Pieces of hay float off the bed of the passing truck and sift through the air. We roll over a flattened skunk and the smell rises up in the cab, then disappears. I see something working in the guy's jaw and I try to remember if that means he's mad or scared.

"You know," I tell him, "my family's going to the fair tonight. I told my mom there was no way I was going. 'I don't care how snotty you act,' she says, 'I know you love that Ferris wheel.' I just rolled my eyes. But you know, now that I think about it, I really would kind of like to be home in time."

He nods.

When I was a kid that's all I cared about. The fair. One time after the hour drive to the fairgrounds my dad realized he'd switched his pants and didn't have enough money, and said that two of us would have to stay in the car. Marjory, who actually believed she was Nancy Drew, with her Nancy Drew flip-up curl haircut said, "Mommy, I'll stay behind. I don't mind." Mom beamed at her, dabbed her eyes.

All the rest of us went mute. We hunkered down, trying not to stand out. It was my dad who said my name. He reminded me that I'd gotten to ride a Shetland pony at my friend's birthday party the Saturday before. I threw myself down, wrapping my arms around my father's shins, burying my face in his weekend pants. I couldn't stop my voice–its awful whining. It was my mom's disappointed face that got me up off the ground.

I yelled at her, "It wasn't even a horse. A Shetland pony with stupid hairy ankles."

For hours I stared at the back of Marjory's head, which made small bobbing movements as she followed the words of her Nancy Drew book. The dust bellowed into the open windows and coated my tongue. The sun had fallen slightly behind the spokes of the Ferris wheel. I stared straight into it, even though it was supposed to make you blind, then I wet my pants. I remember the hot, wet feel of it at first, and then how it cooled as it ran down my thighs. It soaked the seat, some of it spilling over onto the floor. Marjory heard it hit the plastic floor mats, then peered over the back of the seat. She just slid out her door and hopped up onto the hood of the car, opened her book and kept reading. I rested my head back against the seat. When my parents came back and they found out what happened, my dad grabbed my arm. I was ready to be punished. I tipped my face up to receive his hand. But he only shushed me. "Shh, shh now." He wasn't the kind of man who even hugged us, but he picked me up like I was a little baby, and sat with me in the front seat. I made a wet spot on his pants. I don't remember what he said. Something nice.

The truck's shaking and rattling. The asphalt is pocked with enormous potholes and sprouting grass. I try to wet my pants. I sit there and try. I don't know what else to do. I squeeze muscles. I press. Nothing. I feel like if I squatted only sand might pour out of me like a punctured sandbag.

"I've gotta go," I tell him. "I mean I really've gotta to go. I think I might have an accident." He reaches his big hand in the murk under the seat, pulls out a sticky glass mason jar and hands it to me. It feels like its been rolled in honey. There's fuzz and lint caught in the stickiness.

"Don't make a mess," he says.

"Couldn't you just pull over? I could go behind a tree." I was a fast runner.

"We'll be at my house soon."

I watch out the window. The cracked asphalt turns to gravel. "These rocks are probably terrible for your tires," I say, but he drives on. I think about the speed bump and how the truck had slowed down. I start to turn around to see if Judd is behind us yet. But I don't. I can't. I know he's home by now lying on his bed listening to the stereo with his headphones. He's probably on the flipside of "Dark Side of the Moon." Was he thinking about me?

The truck rumbles over a cattle grate, making my teeth chatter. Even after we've crossed over it, my teeth keep chattering. Out in the fields the cows are leaning against each other. I look out the window at the cows. Nice cows, I think. Nice cows.

"Cows always make me . . . I like them," I say. I like hearing the sound of my voice. "This one time," I tell him, "at the fair, I went with my dad to the livestock pavilion. There were rows and rows and rows of pens—all cows and steers. The smell was nice, like rolling in soil. It made me feel, I don't know, like dandelions could grow out of my ears. I was standing so close to him . . . my dad . . . and he wasn't saying anything and there was this woman in shorts leaning over a fence petting the nose of a cow. Its nostrils grew larger then smaller as it breathed. My dad and I watched until she walked away. It was a soft place . . . sawdust under our feet. As we were leaving, before we went to find the others, my dad turned to me and said, 'You'll never get the things you really want.'"

The guy turns off onto another gravel road; a wake of dust rises up behind us. I want to ask him about how the humanizing is going. Except we get farther and farther away from town, deeper into the hills. The road has more cow grates and turns from gravel to dirt. I don't even look at the guy anymore. I just look off at the cows. Out in a field one is off by itself lying down, spread on the thick green grass like a cape. I think about how much room they have out there in the big open field.

"They seem so happy out there, you know what I mean, Mister?" I've never called anybody Mister in my whole life.

"When I was a kid," he says, and I can feel the truck slow the tiniest bit. "When I was a kid," he says again, "I wanted a dog." He takes one hand off the steering wheel and lets it drape out his window.

"I guess every boy wants a dog," he says. "But my dad says, 'who's gonna take care of it?' even though I was the one that took care of the cow, fed her, milked her and all of that. So my dad tells me if I can teach the cow to fetch, he'll get me a dog. So, I try. I spend hours and hours tossing a tennis ball, sometimes just beaning it in the head with the ball, I'm so frustrated. I even made a ball out of grass. Nothing. But that dumb cow started following me around the pasture, nibbling my belt loops. I guess he was ... kind of like a dog. When he died ...." The guy trails off, but his face looks different, and I notice that his jaw isn't working anymore. His face has the soft, kind profile of somebody I know, like maybe my math teacher.

"Did your dad get you the dog?" I ask him. He turns to look at me. The truck has slowed now, I'm sure of it. I smile. "Did he?" I say again. I really am curious.

"That's not the fucking point," he says. I see the pulse start up in his jaw.

I don't say anything, because I know it will be wrong. But then out of nowhere this squirrel goes streaking across the road and the guy hits the brakes hard, throwing me against the dashboard. Suddenly, I'm burning. My throat fills with this tremendous heat, like I've swallowed a bottle of rubbing alcohol, and I'm yelling at the top of my lungs, "Jesus Christ. Why don't you watch what you're doing?" I've never yelled at anybody, much less a grownup. Then I'm laughing–this hiccupping laughter, almost like sobbing.

"What's so fucking funny?" the guy asks.

He tells me to quit, but I can't. I think to myself, now maybe I will wet my pants, which makes me laugh even harder.

Then the guy swerves off the road and starts tearing across this rutted field toward a grove of trees. We're bouncing so hard I keep thinking pieces of the truck are going to shake themselves loose and fly off into the air. Branches slap the windshield, leaves blow into the truck, big thick roots the size of a man's thigh, crisscross all over the ground. Each time we bump over one of them, the truck tips up into the air. Then suddenly, he slams on the brakes. There's one brief moment, almost like happiness, I'm floating, then, slam, I hit the dash. My teeth go into my lip. I taste blood in my mouth.

Run, run, a voice says inside my head. I reach out and touch my hand on the door handle. He reaches over and gently rests his hand on my other wrist. The weird thing is, his hand doesn't feel awful. Not really. I'm surprised, it's so warm, almost comforting.

"I'm gonna let you go," the guy says, but he holds my wrist harder now.

"Okay," I say.

"Don't worry. You'll be home before you know it." His voice has gone soft and tender. He's telling me the truth. He's going to let me go. He's said so. There's a feeling flooding my body. Is it relief? He slides across the seat, saying, "I'm gonna let you go." He slides his arm around me. I lift a shoulder toward my face, smelling my skin. This is me, I think, this particular smell, no matter what, this will always be my smell.

"I thought you were going to let me go."

"You need to rest," he says. "Lie down and rest."

A voice inside me is saying, don't do it, don't lie down. But my body is like those auditorium chairs, folding. His hands. He has hangnails, lots of them. It looks like he has bangs along his cuticles. His body is over me somehow but not yet against me. There is only the slow dull heat of being close—a feathery feeling on my skin.

"I'm gonna let you," he says. "It's what you've wanted all along, isn't it?"

"Yes," I say, "Yes."

In places the seat springs poke through. Everything has gone soft in me suddenly, like laces being undone. There is loud breathing and I'm not sure if it's his or mine. Only moments have passed, but I'm getting used to him, the weight of him, the press of things I can recognize—belt buckle and shirt buttons. Then, like in fog when you move one step closer to an object and it suddenly materializes, a thought sharpens inside me. "My dad wouldn't let us have a dog either," I say into his shirt.

For a moment he is very still. Then he heaves himself off of me. Pushing his body upright, he pins my hair to the seat and it burns at the roots. "Why can't you ever shut the fuck up?" he says.

I realize from its sudden absence that I have been smelling his shirt, a clean but mothball kind of scent and underneath that the cutting, warm smell of his skin. A small breeze whistles through the window crack. I open my eyes and he is sitting with his hands resting on the steering wheel. His face is still. I sit up in the seat beside him. He wears the deep, unknowable look of my father and the fathers of all the girls I know. Never any clues such as tears, just a stillness, a holding that always fills me with an unbearable curiosity. I stop myself from saying, What's the matter? What did I do?

We sit looking at the clearing—a place thick with tall grass and blackberry brambles. A feeling of loneliness so intense rises in me, the kind of loneliness that you can feel only on a winter day at dusk. "You know," I tell him, "I don't know why, but I keep thinking about the fish tank in our living room. I try to tell my mom, 'There's too many fish in there.' They're always bumping into each other and into the glass. If I had money I'd buy twenty tanks. I wouldn't fill any of them with colored gravel or underwater statues or floating plants, just clear, beautiful water. I'd drop just one fish in each of the new tanks so they could roll and float all alone in the silky water."

He doesn't say anything. My face burns, like I've just done something unseemly or gross. I must have because he tells me to get out.

I sit there looking ahead, my eyes filling with tears. I want to tell him I'm sorry.

"Go on," he says.

"How am I gonna get back?" I ask.

"It's not that far."

He reaches across me, pulls the handle and the door opens. I'm surprised to see it swing open so easily. I sit there a moment staring at the open frame of the door.

"Christ, what the fuck am I doing?" he says softly. I think maybe he's changed his mind, and that he'll pull the door shut. But he motions me out.

I step out into the gnatty, bright air. My legs feel wobbly, the way you do after you've been on a boat for a long time and you step off onto solid ground.

"It's gonna be dark soon," I tell him.

"There's nothing out here that's gonna hurt you."

He yanks the door shut, not looking at me. Then he starts the engine and tears out, churning up tufts of grass. The back-end of the truck skids around in the field. I gingerly feel all over my body, like a doctor feeling for broken bones. I am dizzy with what I think must be gratitude, relief. After all, I have been saved from something.

When the truck reaches the edge of the clearing, brake lights show. I can hear my heart in my ears for a moment, but then the gravel of the road crunches under the truck tires as he swings left back down the hill. I listen until the sound of the truck is gone and there is only the hum of katydids and grasshoppers and toads, and over it all the rustley sound of leaves.

I begin the long walk downhill towards the river. Way out a country road you think everything's gonna be wild and clean, but there is garbage strewn all along the way in the weedy grass—a mattress with orange rust stains, a one-armed doll, old cans lacy with rust, pantyhose, smashed animals including a decaying cat—all of it just lying around at the edge of the cracked pavement.

As I'm walking, sometimes the lights from houses puncture the darkness. Down gravelly roads I glimpse dilapidated barns, but mostly there are only the road and pastures and cows for a long way. When I see headlights angling up the road, I hunker down beside trees or bushes. Once when there is no cover I just lie down in a ditch beside the road. When I stand up my hair is coated with burrs.

I already know I will never tell anyone. What would they say? What did you think would happen, getting in a car with some man you didn't know? My mother might say, "You're just lucky something a lot worse didn't happen." Already there is a sort of tenderness forming in my throat, the beginning of a secret.

In the overgrown expanses between houses, I hear the deep rumble first. An old engine working hard. I duck behind an oak that would look majestic and beautiful in somebody's yard but is lost in a tangle of leaning trees out here. The headlights come over the rise. It's a truck. Between the darkness and my squinting against the blast of headlights, I can't tell what color. My father could tell you the make and model just by glancing at its dark silhouette.

After it passes by me though, there is a sudden flash of brake lights. My heart hammers. And before I realize that the truck has only slowed to take the bend in the road, I have run out of my hiding place and am racing towards it through the open field. Even after I am standing stock still, inside me the impulse to run still throbs. A slow, sinking feeling settles in my chest. And now I know–this, this is what I can never tell. The secret beneath the secret. The moment in the close air of the truck cab, with the dark shape of a man falling towards me, when I'd felt like the last girl left on earth. Instead, walking down this rutted dirt road towards the river, rubbing a blister on my heel, I feel like there are hundreds of girls just like me. We are fanning down the dark hillside each of us holding our breath, watching for headlights in the road.

An Inside Story

Mark Strand

On the fifth of January of this year I received a small package from my aunt in Montreal. It contained a black clothbound notebook of unlined paper in which my mother had kept a journal. The first entry was dated November 27, 1930, which was my mother's twenty-fourth birthday. In all, there were forty-seven entries, some barely half a page long, others several pages. The note my aunt appended said only that the journal was clearly intended for me. She had glanced at it and there were parts that had to do with painting and poetry. It didn't matter that I was not alive at the time it was written, what mattered was that I was the one who would understand it. It had been found, she said, buried under a few moth-eaten sweaters, some dresses, and a pair of shoes in a small suitcase she found while cleaning her attic. (My aunt at ninety-four was finally preparing to take up residence in a retirement home.) Apparently my mother, who was to spend the next few years in New York City, had decided not to take the suitcase with her.

In the few photographs I possess, dating roughly from the time of the journal, my mother appears composed, even elegant, but in her eyes there is a dreaminess, a distant look, as if distraction might have been a habit. She smiles but does not look particularly happy. Whenever my mother talked about her early years, the years before she was married, it was always with a wistful disparagement. She had been, she said, tall and awkward. She was good at school, but not as good as her sister. She was considered artistic and standoffish. Since she felt uncomfortable with her peers, she spent much of her time alone, reading or drawing. She went to teacher's college for two years, then, against her parents' wishes, dropped out and began taking art classes. The next few years were spent painting, and moving from one part-time job to another. She spoke of herself as one would a close relative. Her tone was offhand, almost disinterested. She never mentioned having kept a journal. Nor did she ever go into detail about her painting, what it was like or why she stopped. And what is most surprising, given the contents of the journal, she never mentioned the importance for her of poetry.

In selecting from the journal, I have, in the interests of continuity, kept only the entries having to do with painting or poetry. I wish that my mother had included some of her poems, but she did not, nor did she give much indication of the kind of paintings she made.

NOVEMBER 27, 1931 *(my birthday)*
I have reached a cross roads, or perhaps it is an impasse. I have begun to think that I will never be the painter I want to be, even though I have no idea who that painter might be or what she might paint. I know only that she would be more pleased by her work than I am by mine. Every day I wake up and can't wait to paint over what I had painted the day before. All I see is ineptitude and uncertainty. Because I have no image of what I'd like my paintings to be, I use the paintings

of others to give me direction, which turns out to be no more than a "look" or a way of putting down paint. And because my handling of paint lacks the sureness of my models, my failure is all the more visible. This need to find solutions to my own pictorial predicaments in the work of others is as troubling as my clumsiness and only doubles my dissatisfaction.

NOVEMBER 28

Connected to my reliance on the paintings of others is the feeling that I leave too much of myself out of my own paintings. I don't feel that who I am can be reduced to what can be seen on canvas. But when I write, this is not true. More of me, I believe, makes it to the page. This may be because the way we know ourselves and explain who we are to ourselves and allow ourselves to be known by others is with words. I am not saying that painting does not convey feelings and ideas. It does. But what is made explicit through language can only be suggested in painting. It is probably this suggestiveness that drew me to painting in the first place, that offered some relief from the specificity that writing demands. And now, it seems that I need some relief from the vagueness I see at the heart of my paintings. Why, I wonder? Why is it so necessary that I be seen through the works that I create? Why can't I use painting or poetry as a way of making myself into someone other than who I am?

NOVEMBER 29

Reading over what I wrote here yesterday and the day before, I have come to think that what I find lacking in my painting is my ability to paint. Diminished by my work, I blame the art and not myself. Maybe my greater satisfaction with poetry has to do with how I see myself reflected in it. I say things that have never occurred to me before, but which nevertheless seem, if not true, at least inevitable. I seem to take in more of the world. When I paint, I experience only limitation—a predilection for the same solutions to formal problems, the same dependence on line instead of color, a marked preference for certain shapes. Now having just said that, I wonder what is the difference between what I call "limitation" and others call "style?" Maybe what I object to in my paintings is that they are simply what I am able to do, not what I have chosen to do.

DECEMBER 19

A painter will need a particular light in which to work. She is light sensitive. A poet needs a particular dark, a dark without which the discovery of light would be meaningless. For her, words are the couriers of light, which is to say meaning. A painter must invest her paintings with some variant of dark, a shadowy element that mysteriously suggests the non-pictorial and whose presence calls the obvious into question. But why would one paint if she wished to present or give evidence of the non-pictorial? To do so seems a way of undermining the primacy of what is pictures. Maybe what a painting represents is twofold—its subject matter on the one hand and its content on the other—subject matter being the thing painted, content being what changes the character of what is painted. Subject matter is the bowl in the still life; content is what the bowl tells us about the artist who painted it.

January 3, 1932

I have no idea why I write. I sometimes think it is to rid myself of what I would say. And yet, it is not as if I knew what I would say. Often, when I begin a poem, my mind is a blank and what follows is a calling forth of something out of nothing. Why I select one word over another is a mystery, especially since I have no clear idea of what I want to say. Nor am I sure about the next word or the one after that. I follow vague formal imperatives that suggest the direction of the poem. Its meaning is held in suspension and is changeable and entirely subservient to notions of what sounds or seems right. It remains purposely unfinished so that any judgment of its worth would seem premature, and finally unfair. Eventually, I catch the drift of what I am writing. When that happens I begin to fear that I may have created too smooth a path towards too obvious a solution. My uncertainty may be necessary, for when a poem becomes too easy to write, its downfall is imminent. Well, maybe not its downfall, but its resemblance to other poems already written by myself or by others. I tend to remember combinations of words especially as they resonate in the poems that I read. And there is always the possibility that they will resurface in my own poems, not by design of course, but quite unconsciously. The result is something that sounds secondhand. I am not sure what makes my poems sound like my poems (if they actually do?), but I know when they start to sound like somebody else's.

JANUARY 26
When I write I confirm an impossibility—that of shaping nothing. And yet, that nothing becomes a something—words of a poem that suggest not the nothing of their origin, but the something that is their destiny. I am constantly surprised that I am able to cover a blank sheet of paper not with just words but with words that cohere and make sense. Although I mistrust poems that arrive too quickly on the page, I often have the feeling that I am not entirely in control of what is written, that my poems write themselves, and I am merely a middleman or enabler.

JANUARY 27
Clearly I was exaggerating when I spoke about the nothing that is the poem's origin. Where does a poem begin if not in the language that I supply? Who could say that a poem exists outside of language? And yet it seems to me that the more a poem eludes language the more it is convincing. It will create a pause, a space in which we are in touch with something distinct in our experience of the world. Suddenly, in that break with the run of ordinary events we celebrate the very objects and experiences that had resisted our attempts at describing them. And they become ours in a new way.

FEBRUARY 3
I sometimes feel that in a poem the world is sacrificed to that dark, elusive universe of the poet's intentions. In the end—when the poem is finished—the actual world will have become the ghost of the verbal one.

Their positions are reversed. What had been buried is visible and what had been visible is not buried. In this sense, the act of writing is a form of subversion. The writer appropriates according to her desire. She writes not for others but for herself. Her consciousness is fixed on the writing of herself into language. Then a further subversion ensures; the poet turns away from the poem in which the features of the world have given way to the existence of a self and begins another poem. Is this an admission of the inadequacy of individual poems or is it a sign of the self's continued quest for its own image?

FEBRUARY 15

What I wish for my poems is a latent futurity so that they might be read in a different social, political, and literary climate from the one into which they were born. I do not want them to be the victims of a period style. I wish them a long life of pointed irrelevance. If a poem speaks for no period, then maybe it speaks for all periods. I wonder. I wonder if it is possible to will oneself out of the times one lives in. Probably not. But one should not feel imprisoned by one's own time. Perhaps I am making too much of this. Of all art forms, the lyric poem may be the one least susceptible to change. It relies on the continuity of human subjectivity and assumes, therefore, a connection between privacy and universality. Otherwise it would not be possible for us to read and understand the poems of the past.

MARCH 4

I am beginning to think there is another life that exists inside of this one, a life without particulars except to make this one seem artificial and pointless. The other life is the hallucinated blank, the self's lost town from which, I would like to believe, poems come. Unfortunately, the more it is explored, the more ordinary it looks. And yet, it is always there, beckoning, offering, without ever being specific, something else. What is that something else? Surely it is not poetry. And how can its vagueness be thought ordinary? Unless of course it manages to be always the same, undermining whatever satisfaction I may experience in doing my work. Why do I feel that something so destructive is necessary? Why, I wonder, must I struggle with my own self-generated skepticism? Why should I make things so hard for myself?

MARCH 5

It is beginning to seem like my engagement with poetry is an attempt to establish the record of an inner life. Maybe what I write is a sort of autobiography in which the texture of feelings, of stray thoughts and moods are central and give the ghostly recollections of place a tone and a weight they never had in my paintings. For me, "rightness" in painting had to do with actual visualization. In poetry, or I should say in my poetry, there is no actual visualization. One senses a presence instead of being shown it. One knows what a scene contains without actually seeing it. It is the suggestiveness of poetry that I find beguiling. Poems, even the most finished, or perhaps especially the most finished, harbor something impenetrable, a core of mystery that a reader can sense, but not, finally, penetrate.

MARCH 6

It occurs to me that maybe I meant something else when I said "inner life" or "another life." Maybe I didn't mean life at all. I am not sure what life means when used to describe what a poem signified. I begin to think that what I hope to create is "no life" or, better yet, something beyond life, even beyondness itself, the properties of which are not strictly speaking those of the poem—that is, those elements of the poem that make it an artifact. "Beyondness" seems to exist apart from prose elements or, even despite them. But what it is I cannot say. I can sense its presence in the way it colors a poem, shedding a particular light on what would otherwise be a plain object, say, or an unremarkable scene. It is—I can see now—a form of illumination, mysterious and revealing. I can recognize it but I cannot will it, although sometimes when I am writing I can feel something like its formation. I can think so hard about a thing that is surface not only changes, but ceases to be. It ceases to be a thing and becomes meaning. I know that this need to make meaning as it is enacted by my poems and perhaps satisfied by them is finally insufficient. There is something too rarified about the meaning that I make. How do I change, assuming that I really want to? Would it matter if I used colloquial language, so that my poems were more like talk, creating the illusion of directness and simplicity, and even sincerity? Would that make my poems any less rarified? Probably not.

March 10
I had a dream in which I was reading my poems to friends, the words slipping effortlessly into place, enunciated with precision, moving outward, each tied to each in a magical progression, always manifesting the urge, the seminal, basic, unpredictable urge to be part of a rhythm, a fusion of sounds, a body of meaning, so that belief, however short lived, would be inescapable. I woke up happy, but convinced my poems would never be what I want them to be.

March 31
I know nothing. I am nothing at those moments when it must appear to others that I know something. But how can I now speak for what I am or am not at those moments when I am selected by circumstances I don't understand to bend my ear to the world's intimate breathing and listen for what it wishes to tell me.

April 2
Today I destroyed all of my paintings. My relief is immense. What made me think that my small talent could make pictures that would stand alongside the paintings of others? Simple vanity. I thought that because they were mine they had value. I was wrong. What I wanted when I painted was the very thing that paint hid, that is, its materiality got in the way of mystery. With each brushstroke I covered what for me was most important—an energy, an intangible at the core of experience. The surface I created was one of strokes

that clumsily added up to barely identifiable, poorly oriented objects, and no more.

MAY *1*
I continue to write but my enthusiasm, even my interest, is waning. I labor over small issues like whether I should use a definite or indefinite article here or add a subordinate clause there. I will spend a week turning a single sentence around, then end up throwing it out or going back to what it was originally. I suppose this is what people call writing. The changes I make will never mean as much to anyone else as they mean to me—no one else will be able to gauge their importance. I wonder, then, if my constant rewriting is a ritual that I must endure to prove to myself that my writing is good or even just passable. And at the same time, I know that my constant rewriting takes some of the life out of the poem. Those rough first drafts have an energy that the later drafts lack—that is, unless I am able to recapture some of the enthusiasm I had early on. Increasingly, however, I find I am not able to. Increasingly, I find myself looking for other things to do.

MAY *10*
I have not written anything in over a week. I just don't have the desire to sit down and start grinding out words. Nor can I bear to look over the poems I have managed to complete. Actually, I am afraid that I'll find them to be no more than evidence of habitual self-delusion.

> *JUNE 1*
> I am beginning to think that my poems will follow my paintings into non-existence. Why not? What would be the loss, and to whom?

And that ends my mother's journal.

I am astonished by how much her experience of painting and writing poetry corresponds to my own. I, too, gave up painting to concentrate on poetry, but I never bothered to articulate the reasons why, nor do I think I could have, given my general inability to articulate my motives for making less important decisions. It dawned on my mother that she could never be a Matisse or a Picasso whereas it dawned on me that I could never be as good as some of the students with whom I was in art school. Even now, I find it difficult to be articulate about many of the things my mother discussed with apparent ease. And that may be why I continue to write. My mother got bored writing, hating the tedium of rewriting, whereas I tend to like it. She found it exhausting, I find it necessary. For her, it measured the distance from the promise of the initial prompting to write, for me it is what the initial prompting urges me toward.

In three years I would be born. In her forties my mother, then living in Lima, Peru, where my father was a Pepsi Cola executive, became an archeologist, writing her Master's thesis in Spanish on the kinds of tools the Chibcha, a Pre-Incaic civilization, used in the carving of stone figures. This is as close as my mother ever came to a resumption of her career as an artist. As far as poetry goes—I cannot recall my mother, who read a great deal, ever sitting down with a book of poetry. When I began to write poetry, she was encouraging, but offered no advice. She died just before my first book was published.

When the Toasts Stopped Being Funny

Steve Almond

This was in an airport bar, the four of them squared off and late to somewhere else, on holiday from offices, files, throwing toasts like punches: to leather jackets and chardonnay and potato skins and snow delays and new friends and old flames and every sin rearranged to seem romantic, less mistaken.

Their stems swung forward and their glasses clanked, and when the drunkest of them, a loud blond, belted out her appreciations to valium and vibrators, all four howled and clanked again and tried to remember the last time their naked bodies felt a part of God.

It was nothing like grace, this sorrow.

Then they drifted off to be swallowed by gates and planes that were dreams they would never see from the ground.

FIFTH MACAULEY AWARD WINNER

Through the Water of the Clouds

by

Sharon May

You ask me if I have ever been in love, and I see worry gather in your eyes. It tenses your eyebrows and pulls at the edges of your mouth. Your face is always like this, open as the sky above the rice fields. Like now. You're afraid I may have a wife somewhere in the camps, or in Cambodia, but instead you ask, Have I ever been in love?

I don't want to talk this morning; I'd rather just listen to the clatter of traffic outside, the murmur of the fan set at the foot of our mattress on the floor. The weak current of air pushes in waves, making watery patterns in the mosquito net, which we have not bothered to tie up yet. The breeze slowly dries my skin, except where our bodies still touch. In these moments I feel oddly at peace. For the briefest time, no past exists, no future, no one but the two of us, here. The dead who normally crowd my mind have retreated beyond the single screened window, beyond the rice fields whose scent fills this room.

It is our one day off from working in the refugee camps, the one full morning we have together before we must prepare for the week—you writing lesson plans, I finishing paperwork to convince the Thais to let me bring supplies into the Cambodian camp, to the people I survived the war with. Only I got out. I came back. No one really understands this, why a refugee would come back. And I don't want to think about it. I don't want to remember. I would rather make love again, not caring about the heat or the way the sweat sticks to our skin like sugar water, not caring that it is almost 10 AM or what our Thai neighbors will say because we have not yet emerged from the house. They will talk about us anyway, the Cambodian man and American woman, not even married; they will make rude comments as we pass by in the market later this afternoon, while I feel secretly grateful you do not know Thai.

So I say nothing. But then you ask again, more softly this time, as if you're afraid someone in the next room might hear, "Have you ever been in love?"

You look at me so directly I'd consider it rude if you were a Khmer woman. Your blue eyes seem almost transparent, with pale needles of gray, and as you watch me I see the color deepen, the way monsoon clouds rush to darken the sky just before the afternoon rain. I know what you really want to ask lies underneath the words.

"You have been here too long," I say. "You are almost Khmer."

You look at me, half-angry, half-puzzled. It's true. You ask this question like a Cambodian, but still your face is too open. You can't hide anything—anger, doubt, happiness. It always surprises me and makes me afraid for you too. You reveal too much. Maybe this is what I like in you.

I noticed it that first night I saw you at the Aran Army Base, at the Fourth of July party the Thais hold every year for the Americans. You stepped from the main hall, your face flushed from dancing. You didn't see me because I am a Khmer man. I was leaning against the wall, a little drunk. I remember the smell of citronella smoke rising from the mosquito coils set under the tables. The heavy bass of the Western music inside the hall shook the walls, making them shudder as if from mortar fire.

Laughing, you ran your hand through your hair and admired the pineapples stuffed with fried rice and the grilled ginger fish. You looked so much younger than the other volunteers and journalists who usually come here, maybe twenty, hardly older than I was when the Khmer Rouge took over. I wondered what you were doing here, in this place of refugees and soldiers.

Pointing at a plate of spiky red rambutans, you asked the red-haired nurse who works in Khao-I-Dang, "What's that?" in your American accent. You seemed like close friends, but with Americans I can never be sure. You act like you've known each other ten years, but maybe it's only ten minutes.

The nurse named the fruit in English, going down the table, like a list of diseases: rambutan, mango, mangosteen, papaya. You tasted everything, until you reached the durian, the fruit I like best, set at the far end, away from the rest of the food.

"I wouldn't touch that," the nurse warned.

You wrinkled your face at the smell, like most Westerners do at first. Then you picked up a piece of the golden flesh. This surprised me. "Tastes weird," you said. You tried one more piece, but I could see you didn't like it nearly as much as the mangoes. You kept returning to them, even though their season was past and they were no good, the pale yellow mangoes the Thais usually eat with sticky rice. In Cambodia, these mangoes are deeper in color, almost orange, like the robes of the monks, and the taste is stronger–sour mixed with the sweetness.

I almost wanted to say something to you then. But of course I couldn't. Even now, I want to say something, as you watch me so intently, propped up on one elbow, sweat beading on your upper lip, waiting for me to answer your question. You have let the sheet fall away, so that you lie completely uncovered in the bright heat of late morning, and while earlier I felt desire, now I want to shield you.

I pull the sheet up over your hips, but you tug it away. "It's too hot," you say, pushing it down with your feet to the bottom of the mattress where the mosquito net has started to come undone. "Should we get up?"

"Do you remember the party at the Aran army base?" I ask. "The Fourth of July party?"

"Yes." You sit up and hug your knees to your chest. "Seems like a long time ago."

I want to say, it doesn't seem so long ago for me. This is my curse: I cannot forget. Your excitement that night seemed strange to me, because I don't like that place. I don't even know why I go to the party each year. Maybe because everyone else on the border does, and it's easier for me to go than to explain why I don't. Maybe, too, it's because there is a small, secret pleasure in walking freely where once I was imprisoned.

You see, my first night on the border was also spent on that army base. The cell where I was held wasn't far from the hall where you danced, where the feast was laid out for the foreigners. You wouldn't know this. I've never told any foreigner I was imprisoned here. I don't want them to feel pity. We were all so skinny then, right after the fall of the Khmer Rouge. You couldn't tell men from women; we had all been made the same by hunger. It was almost a relief to be put in prison. I felt I had arrived. No more minefields to cross, a little food. Still, part of me could not believe that after escaping to freedom, I was put in a cell as dark and damp as the holes the bullfrogs make in the rice fields.

And there you were, not far from this place, enjoying the party—eating, drinking, laughing. I couldn't touch the banquet spread out on the tables. The food had no taste to me. Inside the hall, the deejay was playing "Black Magic Woman," which I used to listen to before the Khmer Rouge took over. I followed you inside and watched you dance. You wore large red earrings and a black dress with no sleeves, only thin straps, so your neck and shoulders were bare and pale. I wondered how someone could wear black and red, the colors of the Khmer Rouge. You had to be new here not to know, and new not to know to stay away from that Australian doctor you were dancing with—a man known for his bad reputation when it came to women.

"Pitchai," I said to the deejay, my Thai friend, "I want to hear Khmer music." I had given him cassettes smuggled out of Cambodia, songs from before the war.

"No problem." When he switched the music, most of the foreigners, including the doctor, left to go outside and smoke cigarettes and eat water buffalo hamburgers. But you remained, looking confused as Thais and Khmers gradually moved in from the edges of the room to *ramvoung*. When the ring of dancers crossed where you stood, you joined them, only your feet didn't quite match the rhythm and your hands twirled awkwardly in the air; you seemed a part of the dancing circle and yet separate.

"Pitchai, you see that woman?" I said in Thai. "The new American?"

He looked up from the mixing board. "The one who can't dance?"

"Yes, her."

"What about her?"

I paused, then without realizing, said out loud what I was thinking. "I'm going to marry her."

"Sure, brother." Pitchai laughed, showing the space between his front teeth. "She won't last here a week."

It was then that you finally sensed I was watching you, or maybe you just heard our voices. You turned your head and looked straight at me—not at Pitchai, who was still laughing, snorting like a horse—right at me and smiled a beautiful, open smile. And I remembered Apsara, and the day she loosened her *krama* and let it fall briefly to her shoulders. And I thought of a Khmer love song from before the war, "Who Smiled at Me Last Night," which I like to sing to you now sometimes when I have drunk too much. I thought of so many things in that single moment. Then you turned away and continued dancing.

I can still see that smile. You don't remember, I know. I saw later how you smiled at everyone, even the Thai soldiers, without thinking, without even realizing what you were doing. And I thought, you do not know the meaning of a smile.

And so I'm afraid you will not understand this story. But still I will try to tell it, because I have not forgotten your question and because you are waiting, chin on your knees, so quiet now, so still except for your eyes, which have changed color again, lightening from blue to gray.

*

I wasn't looking for her, any more than I was looking for you. It was the first year of the Pol Pot time, and I was thinking of how to survive, how to free the country, not about finding a wife. No—don't look at me that way, so worried. We never married. I never even said a word to her, not one. I was not the kind to spend my time dreaming of women. But still, that night of the Moon Festival, I noticed her.

Before the war, this used to be the traditional courting time, when unmarried men and women could talk to each other.

Even during that first harvest under the Khmer Rouge, men and women were allowed to make *ombok* together. As a child I always loved this festival, because it was when we made *ombok*, toasted new rice, which looks round and flat, like the Western oatmeal I cook for you in the morning when I can see you are tired of rice and fish.

But the truth is, that night of the festival, I didn't want to go anywhere. I just wanted to sleep. I'd already worked all day, and I felt weak from malaria. But of course I couldn't refuse, because the Khmer Rouge would accuse me of being lazy and not wanting to serve the revolution.

We worked in a field under the full moon. One group heated the rice in a pan. When the kernels started to pop, the rice was poured into a mortar and pounded flat before it cooled. Then it was winnowed, tossed from baskets, so that the light chaff hung briefly in the air, then disappeared on the wind. Finally, a last group cooked.

I was assigned to pounding the rice, across from a woman. We had to lift and pound alternately, using two pestles and the same mortar, careful not to break the rhythm. I hadn't been so close to a woman in a long time, but I didn't look at her at all, just worked, watching the warm kernels of rice being pounded flat, the skin starting to separate. I was thinking of the harvests when I was a boy, how the *ombok* was cooked with coconut milk and sweetened with small, delicious egg bananas—I could almost taste it on my tongue—and how we'd mash it into sticky balls and toss them into each other's mouths, laughing. At night, my older brothers would put us to bed early, but we could still hear the young men and women running under the houses, throwing balls of *ombok* and giggling in the dark.

As I worked, I didn't look up. I wasn't thinking of the woman across from me. I didn't watch her like I watched you the night you danced at the army base. No. I was thinking of the past, remembering the taste of *ombok* and the laughter under the houses. The pestle grew heavier in my hands and my chest began to ache. But the woman across from me kept working, and there was an ease and gentleness in her movements, in the effortless way she pounded the rice, that finally made me look up. She wore loose clothing and a *krama* wrapped around her face so that all I could see were her eyes, which were turned down to her work. As I watched her, she glanced up at me. Quickly I looked away.

I tried to hold the pounding stick so that she couldn't see my blistered palms and know that I was a city person with soft skin. Then, I couldn't help looking up. Each time, her glance met mine, her eyes clear as water, I kept working until my hands stung and my chest burned. Finally, I asked someone to switch while I went to wash blood from my hands. When I returned, she was gone.

After that night, whenever I saw a group of women working, I looked for her. Sometimes I found her, but her face was always hidden by the *krama*. She never talked much to anyone, and when she walked she kept her eyes turned to the ground like a monk. This made me pay more attention to her.

In the traditional way, you don't talk to each other. You observe the person, how they work, how they speak to the old people. You listen to what the old people say about them. I learned that her father lived in my village, not far from the hut where I stayed with the old couple who had adopted me, whom I called Grandfather and Grandmother. They told me her father was a rice farmer, who knew traditional medicine. Before the war, people used to go to him for help. Even during the Khmer Rouge time, people still went to him secretly for medicine.

Her younger brother worked in my group of ten. He was quieter than the other boys, hardworking, with very skinny arms. You could see the ribs in his slim chest. Sometimes he joked but in a polite way. Even though I was from the city, he respected me and called me older brother, never comrade, except in the nightly indoctrination meetings, when he had to.

"Older Brother, my sister's name is Apsara," he told me. Apsara, like the dancers carved into the walls of Angkor Wat. We were digging dirt to build a dam, but it would dissolve in the first rains. One cubic meter per person, man or child. Her brother was only thirteen, not strong enough, so I often did his share. Sometimes I told the boys stories to distract them from hunger, to keep them from crying or sitting down. If they didn't work, the food ration was even less or nothing at all.

"Apsara?" I said. "That's an unusual name." I'd never heard of any Cambodian woman, much less the daughter of a rice farmer, having this name.

He seemed proud of his sister's name. "The night before she was born, my father had a dream of an *apsara* rising from the sea." He told how the dancers were born in the *Churning of the Sea of Milk*, flung from the foam up through the clouds and into the sky, just like in his father's dream. He knew a lot, this country boy. When he stopped to rest his hoe on the ground, I didn't remind him to keep digging. "My father says in the old stories the *apsara* is the one who passes through the water of the clouds, who can live in both earth and sky."

Of course his sister Apsara was not a dancer or a sky creature. She was a rice farmer. She didn't wear jewelry or show her skin like the dancing women. She always hid her face behind an old *krama*—made of cotton, not silk, checkered green like the rice fields and blue like the sky just after the sun has set. No matter how hot it was, she wrapped the scarf around her face and pulled her wide-brimmed, palm-leaf hat down over her eyes. She wore a loose long-sleeved shirt over a sarong, and even though she was skinny, I could tell her shape was elegant. Under her sleeve cuffs, I caught glimpses of the pale insides of her wrists, and the brown skin of her ankles beneath the hem of her sarong.

It used to be that when someone from the countryside fell in love with a city person, they couldn't marry because the farmer was considered too low. Under the Khmer Rouge, things were reversed, but the result was the same. I knew I couldn't hope to marry her because I was a "new person" from the city, and she was an "old person" from the countryside. She was also a group-of-100 leader, promoted because of her family's clean class background as rice farmers.

I don't know if anyone else thought she was beautiful. It seemed no one else noticed her or talked about her that way. I heard of no soldiers wanting to marry her, as with the prettiest girls. I thought, maybe she was smart enough to hide her beauty and avoid a forced marriage. But to me it was obvious, even while she was carrying rice seedlings on her shoulder pole; there was a grace to the way she moved, as if she were gliding on air, not walking at all. It was the first time in my life I had felt this way.

Wherever I worked, I looked for her, and when I found her, often, at the same moment her eyes found me too. It happened this way many times as we worked in the fields or passed each other on the road or along the earthen ridges between the rice paddies. But always she hid her face in the folds of the *krama*.

When I became sick with malaria and couldn't work, she came by frequently to pay her respects to grandfather and grandmother.

Sometimes she left a bit of food, a packet of rice, or some dried fish. Whenever she walked past the hut she would slow down to glance in. If she saw me there, she would continue on, because she wouldn't talk to the old people in front of a young man. But if she didn't see me, she would stop to talk with the grandparents and from the back room, I listened to her voice through the thatched walls.

While I was still sick, one day I recognized her footsteps as she slowed down. It was a bright, hot day, so quiet the buzzing of the flies seemed unbearable. The grandparents were in the back, out of sight. When she glanced into the hut and saw I was alone, she loosened the *krama* and let it fall to her shoulders, revealing her full face. It was a gesture so subtle that anyone watching might have thought it an accident. Then she shocked me—she smiled, an open smile, meant only for me. I remember that smile even now, the clarity of her eyes, her face no longer hidden. I forgot everything—malaria, hunger, even the Khmer Rouge. I said to myself, *I have someone*. In that moment, I knew she felt the same way, that she too had been watching me quietly. She knew exactly how I felt. When she smiled, that was her answer.

Then she calmly rewrapped the *krama* around her face, showing only her eyes, and continued on her way. She never said a word to me and I never spoke to her.

The next day I heard she had been sent away to work in a youth mobile team. I stayed in the hut, still sick, dreaming of her. I hadn't forgotten my city background and that we couldn't marry, but I could wait. I knew the Khmer Rouge couldn't last forever.

I don't remember how long she was gone. Some weeks. The rainy season ended, and we began to run out of food. The village grew quiet, the wind stronger and colder. The heads of the rice plants, once flat and green, began to swell and turn golden—pregnant, we say in Khmer. This used to be a time of joyful anticipation, but now it was the season when the most people died of hunger, waiting for the harvest.

Finally, I heard she had returned to see her father. I waited for her to stop by and talk to the grandparents, as usual. When she didn't, I told myself she must still be out working. The next day, I heard people talking next door. The huts were so close and the walls so thin, you could hear everything, especially the shrill voice of the village cook. Usually I didn't pay any attention to her gossip, but this time, I had to ask, "What happened? Who died?"

"Comrade Apsara."

"Who?"

"Comrade Apsara, the daughter of the healer."

I didn't believe it.

"Her body's at home," she said. "You can go see for yourself."

I walked slowly toward her father's hut, telling myself, it's not her, not this woman who smiled at me. From a distance I saw the front wall of the hut open, and I stopped. Inside, on a raised bamboo platform, lay her body, dressed all in white.

Her father sat cross-legged beside her, smoking a hand-rolled cigarette. He wore black trousers and a faded green-and-blue scarf draped over his shoulders, partially covering his skinny chest. I recognized it as her *krama*, the one she always used to hide her face. My legs were shaking, but I tried to keep my face smooth. I told myself the Buddha's advice: *life is always changing: we are born, we are sick, we die*—sooner or later. Maybe soon it will be me.

Then I saw three Khmer Rouge women headed toward the house to pay their respects. They pushed shiny black bicycles that couldn't be ridden over the rough ground, and they wore clean black uniforms with new red-and-white checkered *kramas*. I recognized one as a district leader and the other two as subdistrict leaders.

Her father saw them coming too, but he didn't greet them. Instead, he turned to the body of his daughter and took a slow drag from his cigarette. As he exhaled, the smoke spread out and disappeared into the thatched roof above him. Then he began to speak, loud enough so that the Khmer Rouge could hear.

"Wake up, daughter. Wake up! Don't you know it's time to go to work?" His voice was hoarse, as if coming from a deep, dry place. "Come on, don't sleep. What's wrong, are you lazy? It's time to serve the revolution. Look, your comrades are coming for you."

The three women stopped as if they had been hit by bullets. I was stunned. I looked at her father, his face broken with grief, and saw no tears in his eyes.

"Don't pretend to be sick," he continued, loud enough for everyone to hear, even though his voice was cracking. I couldn't believe he dared to say this right in front of them. "It's time to go now. Why do you sleep? Your comrades are waiting for you."

Without a word the three Khmer Rouge women lowered their heads and turned their bicycles around. Even as they walked away, her father kept talking. "Look, your comrades are going to work now. Daughter, why don't you wake up!"

When I got back home, the neighbors began to gather wood, precious wood usually used only for cooking fires, but in this case, to honor her with a cremation. I didn't want to go. I stood at the back of the hut where I once hid to listen to her voice. From there, I watched the column of smoke rise from the fire.

Her brother told me later that if she'd been allowed to come home just one day earlier her father could have saved her, but the Khmer Rouge wouldn't allow it. They said she wasn't really sick.

By the time they finally let her come home, it was too late. She died of a disease that poisoned her body, and afterward her skin turned black and purple; that's what people said. But I didn't see. All I could see, from a distance, was her body dressed in white on the platform. I couldn't go close, just like I couldn't go near the cremation but could only watch it from far away until I saw no more traces of smoke.

As evening grew dark, I went to the burning place, just outside the village, on a piece of ground so hard not even grass or thatch could survive. A few banana trees clung to the edge of a muddy pond, but the soil was poor and even these trees, which are easy to grow, looked stunted.

The charred ground held traces of fire. Already her family had collected the burnt bits of bone. I looked up from the gray earth to the dying banana trees, to the sky turning red. This was the place where the person I loved disappeared from the earth.

I could still find this place. The ground will still be gray, even though years have passed. No one can change the color. Even if grass grows over it, underneath you will see the earth is gray, in the shape of the burning place.

*

Sometimes I wonder, why do I talk to you like this, spilling all these words?

Now you are the one who is quiet, sitting there so still in the corner of the mattress, waiting, perhaps thinking. You are no longer even looking at me. Nothing moves in the room except for the mosquito net undulating in the weak gusts of the fan. Your eyes are cast down, studying the creases in the pillow.

Maybe I have become too open, careless, almost like an American. Maybe this too is the fault of the army base, where I was imprisoned after I said good-bye to Apsara and to Cambodia, and where that night you smiled at me as you danced. I know you don't remember, even if you try to pretend for my sake that you do. I don't blame you for not remembering, or for not being able to lie. I think this is something you've never needed to do.

For me it is different. I've learned how to feel one thing and show another. In this way, I survived. What I have not learned is to forget. Not her smile. Not yours. Nor the morning when you missed your ride—panicked, talking in such a rush, something about the alarm that I couldn't quite understand—and so I drove you into the camp. That morning we passed the whitewashed walls surrounding the army base, and the women bent over in the ditch outside the walls, waist-deep in water, harvesting lotus seeds. Palm-leaf hats shielded their faces, and in my chest I felt the words rise up, pressing against my throat. I told you a small story about Cambodia, and you listened, your body suddenly still, your eyes fastened on me—just like they are now as you look up at me—and I wanted to tell you then, as I do now, what was lost. I still see the dead in front of me—talking, laughing, smiling.

When I talk to you, I think you see them too.

I want you to know this is why I can no longer taste, thinking of those who died of hunger. This is why I could not touch the food laid out on the tables that night I first saw you, but only watch you eat. But instead of telling you this now, all I can manage to say is, "I am a dead man."

You frown at me, a deep wrinkle between your eyes. "Don't say that."

"I am a man who lives with the dead."

"Please don't say that."

"It's true. I give you my memories, and now you have to live with them too."

You look away, tucking your hair behind your ears, as you often do when you're uncomfortable. I worry I have said too much, afraid you will not understand. But then you reach for my hand, entwining my fingers in yours. In the pattern of light and dark, the crisscrossing of our skin, I allow myself for a moment to imagine a shade in-between. A child.

"We should get up," you say.

The mangoes I sliced last night are waiting in the fridge. I searched the market yesterday, testing the fruit, smelling the base of each stem, but all I could find were poor Thai varieties that have been picked too green. They will be stringy and tasteless. I feel sorry I can give you nothing better than this. When I see the pleasure you will take in this fruit that has no flavor or scent, I will recall the taste of Khmer mangoes and I wish I could bring this taste to you instead.

There are many ways to love. I never said a word to Apsara, not one. And to you, I say so many. But no, I do not say, I love you. Even now I can't say it, as I feel the warmth of your hand resting in mine, as I see you waiting, still hoping, perhaps, to hear these words before we must rise and tie up the mosquito net and leave the sanctuary of this room. I don't like to say this word, love, so short in English, such a small word, insignificant. It disappears as soon as it is spoken. Maybe that's why you think you must say it all the time, because it is so light, scattering like ash. Even in my language I don't say this. I don't say this word that rolls down my tongue and lingers—*srolanh*, long and drawn out, curling at the end, as if it would not end at all but rather continue, beginning all over again.

Don't Listen to This

Steve Almond

This lousy park, pretty and stupid with trees, doesn't deserve our beauty, what we did together with our bodies. We never touched each other here (as I recall) though we did most everywhere else.

When I was a boy, a couple used to make love in a park like this, droopy with eucalyptus, while I watched them through a trellis. And those noisy enjoyments which I barely understood then are all I can think of now, as we call an end to our affair, which was—in the language of current politics—*fueled by ecstasies of sexual congress*, and built to explode.

My mother always warned me that passion fades, but the lesson never took. I should know by now, old as I am, a ridiculous bachelor flashing my scalp to the world. So, in this dark, puddled park with its muddy vagrants, we are trying to make right, setting out along the path of *no longer*, a pair of nervous pilgrims swallowing back the ache.

We tried it rough so many times (remember?) but could never undo the tenderness of slipping into each other. We tried to be sensible, but grew bored of lying.

I can see now, by the set of your mouth and your final tone that you will not succumb to the body. Perhaps you've been cured of this disease of over-involvement. I haven't. I feel diminished for yielding to my need, rather than completed, and still I want the tip of you in my mouth. And all those clenched moments, rhapsodic with sweat—don't listen to them no matter how I beg, don't listen to them, don't.

Slave Quarters

Stephanie Dickinson

We passed a Royal Street nightclub. A jukebox was playing 'Red Roses for a Blue Lady,' and you could still hear glasses of tinkling ice and tourist men in white shirts toasting women who smeared lipstick on their cuffs. It was our anniversary, the night that Bluejay and I celebrated the fluke of us.

"Go for it," Bluejay said, starting into the crosswalk. "You have thirteen seconds before the light changes." I didn't believe in him as a self, he was a protein synthesis.

The "Don't Walk" light was flashing. I hesitated. In front of me was urine that glistened like a handful of dragonflies. I thought of the old fisherman's saw: the secret to fishing is pissing. It makes even the sunfish run. The curb was the place you could go missing, where you could become one of those latticed buildings broken into a million good times, one party on top of the other. My hair felt like silky rain. I'd brushed glitter through it. I wore a jean mini with silver buckles, a matching jacket, and silver epaulettes on its shoulders. The label, Jean Gaborit.

"You blew it. Better wait, Memory," he shouted from the opposite curb.

There really wasn't anyone behind my eyes, just eyes doing what evolution had made of them. Eyes were a success story and that's why fish and reptiles and birds and mammals all had them in one style or another. Otherwise I was a jumble of microbes and chemical reactions and when I died my cells would begin powering down from lack of oxygen until two days later even my skin would expire.

I saw the headlights of an oncoming Imperial taxi. I calculated how many seconds would get me into its path. I waited. Then I took three steps and wedged my heel into a crack, almost toppling headfirst. "Yes," I said, bracing myself for the instant of collision. The smash of egg cells into nerve cells, the connective tissue separating.

"Mama," a tall man in a dress cried as he ran into the street. He threw his shoulders from side to side as he came toward me, one huge hand on one hip, the other extended in front of him like a stop sign. His legs were birds wading. He was even taller than Bluejay, maybe six-foot-three. I caught his stare, his mouth-like eyes. I thought of the Ragin' Cajun at Lake Pontchartrain, the roller coaster with two vertical twisters. He reached down and snatched my heel free of the crack, whisking me out of the way just as the taxi careened past. "Sometimes it happens to me. Don't give it away, baby," he winked, twisting past me. "Sell it."

I felt let down. I had dressed up for nothing. At the curb Bluejay waited in his white suit. His eyes glinted in his Cajun-Jamaican face; eyes that could turn on a dime—get hard or fill with light, eyes as prehistoric as those that had shone from tyrannosaurus skulls. He was handsome: wide nose, big head, high cheekbones, a long neck, and nutmeg skin. At a glance you couldn't see the cuts that zigzagged over his arms and chest, the ones made with tin can lids and bicycle chains, souvenirs of the battles he'd fought growing up. The juvenile detention centers.

You might not notice that he was deaf in his left ear until you talked to him and he answered you too loud.

"The taxi almost clipped you. I don't like you playing chicken," he said. "You must be losing your snap."

"Swagman," I said, calling him the Australian word for hobo. "I can't run on a full stomach." We'd eaten on Esplanade at The Siam Café. Thai food and wine on pillows on the floor. "I want to go home and hold you." I said, thinking how sweet I would love him in the shadow of two bottles of blue Valium stockpiled in the medicine cabinet. I might have missed one exit opportunity but there was always another.

He grinned. "First we've got an errand to take care of for Valentino. We've got to go by a house and pick something up. I've got the key."

"Where at?" I asked, tired of doing favors for Valentino, a Maf seafood restaurateur. "This is our night."

Seven years ago today we met. I was fourteen and Bluejay, an old man of sixteen the first time I saw him crossing Grandma Nonny's front lawn carrying a two-gallon gasoline tank and pushing a lawn mower. July 10th. His lips were red and moist, like a heart in the middle of his face—his mouth the one thing lawn mower grease hadn't touched. Nonny said passion bloomed only at night and that daylight made it shrivel, but there was bare-chested Bluejay pushing the mower into the brightest sun. He asked me out for a Sunday school date, the only kind Nonny allowed, saying, *No way was I going to end up like her daughter, my mother, pregnant at fourteen.*

When Bluejay picked me up he gave off sparks in a white church shirt. I had on a linen coat. As soon as we got a block from the house I took off the coat and showed him the dress that I'd made of real magnolia leaves and petals, picked dry from our tree and sewed on Nonny's machine. I loved thread and needle and stitching things together. "You're the chick with the rich grandmother," he had said, "and you're wearing leaves." I curled up my nose. "Who says she's rich. Why would we live in a boarding house if she was?" He came right back. "To save money. Keeping a tight fist around pennies is how you get rich."

A boy with dimples didn't have to be rich. I liked how he looked at me like I was an apricot, a fruit that would ripen on his palm, and a fruit he could hold or tease with his teeth. I liked how he looked at me as if he knew about the water and ions inside me. The unequal number of electrons and protons. I liked how he listened to my lips so he could hear better when I talked. We both felt it. It was his hair, how our hands fit together, how we'd break into a foot race at the exact same second, how he could break a window in a vacant apartment and slide me inside against the jagged glass. When he kissed me he warned that his loving was so good I would need it. Like the Chinese girls in Gold Rush California fed opium until they craved it. Then they lived in lean-tos, giving their bodies to the miners who bathed once a summer. I rolled my eyes, told him it was my loving that would make him crawl. In honor of those midnights when we spoke secretly, when we wanted each other's breath like water hyacinth, I rubbed myself with dogwood lotion.

"Didn't you hear me?" I said. "Where's the house he wants us to see about?"

"Ferret Street. Valentino's bought some slave quarters over there. He's remodeling them into rentals for college kids. In one of them there's a stray dog that the sheet rockers have been feeding. Valentino wants us to pick the dog up and bring it to his place."

I let out a long breath, "That's the weirdest errand he's ever asked us to run. Why didn't Valentino send his lazy son?" A nerve in my eyebrow twitched. He was a *grande beede*, a big clumsy man who controlled the She-Crab Palace and time share show rooms where they sold cocaine and invisible real estate.

Bluejay swatted my butt. "Mem, didn't you like The Siam? Who do you think paid for that?"

Case closed. Taxis honked. The dark much darker and dirtier on Bourbon Street than Esplanade. Buildings with short balconies on their second and third stories. You could feel all the lies that had been told here, generations of untruth. The street wove and dipped, full of potholes, the high curbs smelled of vomited hotdogs. We had come to another "Don't Walk."

"See those wheels," Bluejay said, swinging my hand at the Thunderbird accelerating off the green light. "Pretty soon I'm going to buy one of those for you."

I didn't want one. Instead I imagined us running together like old times right into the path of the Thunderbird, knowing that a stumble would bring my life and any that someday might take root in me to an end.

I fantasized the Thunderbird's headlights throwing themselves at us like the turreting eyes of a seahorse. Bluejay and I springing through those lights. Matadors, our bodies the red capes flung down before the stampeding steel bull. I could feel the car's breath as it passed by, *skinny asses you almost got kilt.*

"Mem, come on. It says 'Walk.'"

I craned my head. The sky was the color of a rusty hinge.

*

Ferret Street ran parallel to Saint Charles Avenue, a street with tree roots that could twist inside you if you had to walk over the sidewalks. Long ago the planter mansions had been built on the avenue with the slave quarters hidden behind them. Spanish oaks shared space with low-roofed dwellings that had been rented for generations by Tulane students. From one end of the block to the other only an occasional TV lit up windows.

Bluejay eased up on the gas of the Mustang. "It's 807 Ferret. Read the numbers for me, Mem. I can't see them." On the seat between us sat a bag of Kennel Rations and Gaines Burgers.

"They still make these things, huh?" I asked picking up an individually wrapped Gaines Burger. "They're like Dingdongs. Why does Valentino want the dog? Why didn't he tell the sheet rockers to take it to the Humane Society?"

"Do I look like the answer man? I don't get into his business."

"Maybe you should."

Bluejay reached under the seat for our flashlight. "You're a regular detective tonight except when it comes to finding number 807."

"793. We're close. There it is, Bluejay."

Bluejay parked. We sat in the car listening to the engine tick and looking at the saddlebag-style dwelling built for two families and painted the color of yellow mud. Here in the slave days the only illumination would come from a grease lamp, an iron bowl filled with grease and a rag floating in it for flame. I grabbed the Gaines Burgers. We got out of the car. There was a magnolia tree in the yard and the blossoms had opened. The scent was so strong. A white room you could walk into and be gone. Bluejay took the key out of his pocket. Then he pretended to toss it in the bushes. Standing still the mosquitoes began to bite, I slapped at the thin green quivers in the stagnant air. Finally, he fit the key in the door and led the way inside where it was stifling.

I touched the wall feeling for the light switch. "Nobody's remodeling this place," I said. "It smells old."

He swept the flashlight over the hearth that took up the lion's share of the room. The light rose like flood water, up to the hooks that once held iron kettles, then it washed over the bake oven, over a footprint imbedded in the chimney–everything here remembered, every blackened brick having a secret. Hands that knew only scald and stir, lug and scrub. Hands that spent entire lives deciphering the marks of fire on flour. Someone had stuck feathers into spaces between the chimney stones. Vodoun gifts to please the sweet *loua* spirits. Some of these slave quarters had pits where hunters found animal skulls filled with clay marbles and Spanish coins–white magic offerings.

"Looks like someone's living in the fireplace," Bluejay said.

A sleeping bag was spread out in the fireplace and a smell emanated from it. Styrofoam takeout containers littered the floor. When Bluejay moved the flashlight over the door that must lead to the bathroom, noises seeped through from the other side. One long whine and two short ones, and then another long and two shorts like the dog was talking to himself.

Bluejay closed his hand over the knob and turned. "Maybe it's a pit bull. I can handle that. A German Shepherd might be harder. Could be Valentino didn't send his lazy ass son over here because Junior can't handle a feisty dog." The door was now open far enough to shine the flashlight inside. The beam caught the sink and a cocker spaniel peering up. His eyes were bloodshot. Loops of salvia hung from his muzzle. He strained at the leash that had been tied to the bathtub's nozzle, the leash too short for the dog to turn his head. Bluejay tried the bathroom light switch. No juice. Bluejay set the flashlight on the sink.

I untied the leash. "Don't be scared. Poor dog, poor dog. We're not going to hurt you." No one could look into the eyes of that animal and be afraid of what he might do. When I flipped up the toilet lid the cocker spaniel stuck his snout in the bowl and noisily lapped. "Poor baby, what have they done to you?" I got down on my knees. His fur unraveled over his paws, and when he lifted his head from the toilet he looked like a sad eyed seventeenth century cavalier in a ringleted wig. I held out the Gaines Burgers that smelled like beef stew and the dog swallowed it. I fed him another. He sniffed at my fingers. Instead of being silky his ears were gritty and coarse.

"Can you give me your paw?" I asked. He lifted one and when I shook it he whimpered. I could feel the cracks in his pads. They would need to be cleaned and antibiotic ointment put on. What did Valentino want with this dog? The only animals he seemed to love were the ones he ate, shrimp and boudin, oysters and she-crab. "What's going on here, Bluejay? This feels totally strange. He's covered in piss, we have to wash him." I turned on the water in the tub.

Bluejay reached over and twisted the faucet off. The dog flinched when Bluejay lifted him. "Mem, let's just get him out to Valentino's. You sweep the flashlight around in front of me but keep it down."

Being in a forbidden place made my senses come to life. I could see into the shadows, smell an old floral Airwick, I could hear Bluejay's boots click on the tiles.

Bluejay laughed. "Don't do that. This dog just licked my face with a tongue he had in the toilet." He carried the dog out to the car and gently lifted him into the back seat. I got in the back seat too. The cocker spaniel looked up at me as Bluejay backed the Mustang out of the driveway, speeding us along I-10 highway. I broke out another Gaines Burger. This one smelled like liver and onions. The dog licked it from my hand, and then buried his snout against my leg. I stroked his fur of frayed rope. I scratched his belly, and he sniveled. He wasn't a he after all. I could feel rough nipples like the dog recently had a litter. "It's a girl, Bluejay." She was a mother. What had happened to her children? Most likely some human had taken them from her. Animals didn't leave their offspring in the dirt beneath a sweet corn tree unless they intended to return. My mother gave birth by herself, in the neighbor's backyard of overgrown okra, and left me in a hole she'd scooped. But she didn't have the heart to cover me over with dirt. Beauty, the neighbor's mutt found me, cleaned me with her tongue, and barked until the two-legged ones came. In the backseat, I felt the stitches, a line of them crisscrossing the dog's stomach, and there was something under them. "There's a big hard growth on this dog's stomach. Maybe a cyst."

"Couldn't be cysts," he said. "They're soft and small."

"Not necessarily. Why would you open a dog and sew her back up with the stitches and leave the cyst inside her?"

"They're not cysts, Memory, I already told you. Maybe it's like an afterbirth. A piece of puppy that didn't come out."

"She likes me. We could keep her."

"No way. Valentino told me he wants the dog delivered."

We were about to cross the Huey P. Long Bridge; the girders were throwing their reflection in the moonlit water like the stilts of the river god, but a rusted one. Lafitte lay about five miles on the other side. Bluejay tapped his fingers on the steering wheel as Tin Pan Alley played on the radio. I thought of Nonny who loved the Mississippi, the longest and best word in the world to spell. She adored Huey P. Long who built the bridge when he was governor, and she remembered being a girl in braids the day the Kingfish was assassinated. The wind coming in the

Mustang's windows smelled of river, a rawness that reminded me of oysters. I pictured Nonny shucking her oysters with a putty knife, slurping that weird jelly. Then Nonny at the stove frying those she didn't eat—cornmeal and grease spattering the wall. Oysters were screaming in the skillet. I heard them. "Eat, Memory, oysters make you smart." I shook my head. "No, Nonny, I hear them crying." She tried milk and red pepper flakes over oysters. I stirred the mixture, but wouldn't eat. "No, Nonny." She wiped her hands on a dishrag and gave me an ice cream sandwich. On her sixtieth birthday, Nonny sealed up our kitchen and left the oven gas on. The police came and got me out of school. I never went back. After the funeral expenses, there wasn't enough left to pay back taxes on the boarding house. Bluejay had been wrong about her being rich.

Seeing the bridge I had a premonition that something would happen to this animal if Valentino got his hands on her. "Bluejay, pull over. I don't want to go to Lafitte. Call Valentino. Tell him the dog wasn't there. Tell him there wasn't any dog."

He turned the volume on the radio down, checked his side mirror. He didn't lie to the old man. Valentino trusted him like a son.

"Then tell him I asked for the dog as an anniversary present. Bluejay let me keep her."

"I thought we were going to make love and you're talking dog," he complained.

"And you're talking Valentino. Make love to him."

What if he did see Valentino as a father? Weren't we both short on parents? Maybe Bluejay thought he was being honorable, an obedient son, but he didn't understand how he'd been dirtying himself: running all the errands for Valentino, debt-collecting, breaking into houses, slashing tires, jamming horns to blow for hours, spreading Valentino's restaurant's stinking fish carcass garbage in a competitor's parking lot. But bending someone to your will was like trying to move the refrigerator with your thoughts.

Then the back of the Mustang wobbled and the right tire started to drag. Bluejay eased his foot slowly down on the brake and gripped the steering wheel. "Oh, fuck." The car started to shimmy, the tire scraping. The spaniel lifted her head and whimpered. "You've got to be kidding. We've got a blow out. Not tonight."

I'd gotten my way. After the blowout we'd had to be towed home to the sublet on Magazine Street; the spare tire had a hole in it too. Bluejay called Valentino and told him we'd buy a new tire in the morning and deliver the dog to Lafitte first thing.

Bluejay poured a cognac, and then put his arm around my waist and walked me backwards into the bedroom. My nose pressed against his shirt. I inhaled leaves, earthy brown, how he always smelled because he didn't sweat. That was the Choctaw in him, the reason alcohol hit him more because he couldn't excrete it through his pores.

He smacked on the liquor. "Here." He lifted the glass to my lips, the syrup trickling over my chin. "Take a nice sip, babe." His barbells and dumbbells stared up from the floor.

I took the sip in. I loved how cognac melted the outer layers away, how it seeped into my gums like swallowing the hum of wasps.

"Give me your lower lip. I want to eat it," he teased. He pushed me onto our bed, the push he used to make it better. My hands were moving inside his shirt, bringing him out of it, tracing the scar shaped like a fishhook under his left nipple, the healed cuts that nicked his ribs, touching the sweet hairs that dusted his belly from his naval down to where the gingerbread man lived.

"Mem, lie flat," he whispered. "Bring your beautiful ass down to the edge of the bed." He gripped my ankles and yanked. My hair swam over the sheet. His tongue started at my toes giving me a long leg lick. He squeezed my upper arms and shook me. This was where we met to become voodoo dust, turn orange in the blue fire. The cocker spaniel yipped from the backroom closet. "Bluejay, did you hear her? I better see if something's wrong." "Nothing's wrong." Bluejay knelt before me and I set my feet on his thighs. "Don't move." I laughed at the giddiness that comes from skin. Then the dog began to bark. "She must be hungry," I said. He covered my mouth with his hand. "Hush."

Was the dog hurting? What had been done to her? Usually, we were one by now, one flat boat drifting into the overcast. Then I let go.

It was still in the center of the bayou, except for the mullets that blurted from the water like they were being shocked.

Afterwards I stared at the walls painted an eon ago the discolored orange of loose face powder. The parquet floor in the foyer dipped and slanted like the street. We were apartment sitting for the mother of Valentino's latest girlfriend who was in California for six months. The girlfriend didn't like Magazine Street, or the outside steps that led to the apartment. Rent was free. But then it really wasn't free, was it? At the far end of the room sat a table in an alcove of windows on all sides. A tasseled olive-green tablecloth hung crookedly.

"I'm jealous," Bluejay said when I got up. "I mean you gave her my sleeping bag."

"We should call her Thelma after my mother."

"You didn't have a mother."

"Not much of one, but I did. Her name was Thelma. That's what I want to call the dog."

"Wrong. We're not naming her. We can't keep her, and believe me if we could we wouldn't name her Thelma."

I threw on cutoffs and a tube top and padded into the kitchen, switched on the light, and saw two cockroaches dart into a wall crack. They were invincible. I thumped the defrosting hamburger into the skillet. Bluejay hardly ate anything else. I loved vegetables, but he hated them. Not zucchini, not peas, not broccoli or pickles. Not lettuce or onions or cherry tomatoes. He told me his Jamaican mother used to keep vegetables in Tupperware containers, pickles especially, and they'd get warm and stink. When they took bus trips she would make him eat the bad smelling pickles. His mother was a dark woman he wanted to run from, the palms of her hands like eggplants.

"Thelma, are you hungry?" I cut on the light in the spare bedroom. Everything was pink, the walls, the bedspread, the lampshade, and the floor boards. The bedroom of Valentino's mistress when she was an innocent. I knelt in the closet door. "Hey, Thelma, are you hungry?" I'd made her a bed in the crawlspace that went back under the eaves. When I put the hamburger bowl down, the cocker spaniel looked at me. "Yes, Thelma, it's for you." I stroked her ears that now felt like corn silk.

"Nonny told me it was the neighbor's dog that found me in the sweet corn and started to bark. I was saved and now it's my turn to help you." Thelma rolled onto her side still trying to nip at the stitches in her belly. When I pressed the lump, she keened. I pushed against it and she snapped her jaws, but not drawing away from me.

"Thelma, did someone put something inside you? Would you let me look?" She kept licking her stomach, trying to gnaw apart the threads that had bunched like a reef of acorn barnacles. "I'll be right back, Thelma."

I went to my sewing machine and found needles and thread before stopping in the bathroom for towels and cuticle scissors. I opened the medicine cabinet and shook out two blue 10 milligram Valiums and dropped them into my side pocket. When I passed the bedroom the lights were off and Bluejay snored. Once he fell asleep nothing short of a three-alarm fire would wake him. In the kitchen I climbed onto the counter taking down the bottle of cognac and pouring what was left in a salad bowl and adding milk. I balled a slice of wheat bread and slipped in the Valium before dipping it in hamburger grease.

"Here, Thelma, a treat." She ate it. "Take a little cognac, Thelma, so I don't hurt you." She dipped her tongue into the liquor, and then sneezed. "Good girl. Try some more." I dunked a washcloth into the mixture and touched her with it. She sniffed, her nose rummaging the towel. "Right now I have to be top dog, Thelma. Will you do what I ask?" I stroked her head and sang to her, "Waltzing Matilde, Waltzing Matilde, Who'll come a-Waltzing Matilde with me." I worked the scissors into the stitch nearest the lump and snipped.

"That didn't hurt, did it, Thelma?" I took another stitch. Stay with me, Thelma. I'm a gifted seamstress. I used to make all my clothes."

Her jaws snapped. She lunged at me. I watched her teeth sink into my hand, but I didn't feel the bite. Pain came when she let go. I cut a strip from the towel and wrapped it around the blood.

She cowered as if afraid I would hit her. "I'd never do that," I said, and sang again so I wouldn't hear the soreness in my hand.

"And he sang as he watched
and waited 'til his billy boiled,

Who'll come a-Walzing
Matilde, with me."

Then she slumped, the pills and cognac kicking in. "I'm doing this because I love you. Because I love you." Later when it hurt more I got my fingers around her muzzle and held it shut. I hummed to her,

"Along came a jumbuck
to drink at the billabong,
Up jumped the swagman."

I poured cognac for us both and talked to her about whatever came into my head. "I always operated on broken things, sewing bird wings back on even when they lay apart on the ground. I sewed my own forehead up when a neighbor boy threw a mug at me. I've put tons of stitches into Bluejay. It doesn't hurt." I was a full-fledged surgeon as the closet's moth light fluttered down. The lump felt harder the more I moved it to the opening. What would it reveal? Heroin, afterbirth, Miss Mary Sheila's face in the frosted door pane when I locked her out of the 6th grade classroom? "Thelma, you're going to feel a little pressure. A little pressure," I repeated. "Ready?"

She was drowsy. Her ears went back and she made the tiniest of sounds when I pushed it out of her. I had the glop in my hand like a goiter cut from the neck of a swamp maw maw. I still didn't know what it was, but I didn't give a crap either. Not tissue but tin. I set it aside and wrapped the towel around her middle. My hand had bled more than her belly.

"Up jumped the swagman,
leapt into the billabong,
'You'll never catch me
alive,' said he."

Later when Thelma was asleep, I rubbed the slime off the thing that had been inside her and saw an oval tin that pastels came in. I giggled. The kind of expensive pastels you bought in upscale stores in the Godiva chocolate section. I let the water run hot before I washed the hand Thelma had bitten.

"Who'll come a-Waltzing
Matilda with me?"

*

I was dreaming but not all the way asleep. I was in the Club Jolie Blon. In the middle of the bar was a blue-lit aquarium. Bluejay was waiting for me somewhere in the club but I couldn't find him. I stopped to admire the reefs of pink coral. A platinum tetra floated by. Little red fish with long tails. Then tetra blue flames. The fish were swimming, had to keep swimming to keep breathing. My hand was on fire. Flickering frantic bits of light. I stuck it in the aquarium. I flattened my lips against the glass. Then I heard a noise that wasn't in my mind. The footsteps didn't know where they were going. There was someone in the room.

I was about to reach for the bedside lamp when I heard the closet door slide on its rollers. I heard Bluejay taking his sleep breaths. I had hidden the glop I'd found inside Thelma after I stitched and bandaged her. I wasn't sure what it was but I knew it would be trouble. Dry heroin, opium paste, embalming chemicals. Not meth. It didn't have that peculiar odor of cat piss and apples. Whoever was in the room was looking for it.

"Where's the fucking light?" a male voice hissed.

"Like I live here. I dunno."

Two of them. Air drifted in the open window meaning they'd gotten in by the back stairs, hopped over the unused balcony, and jimmied the door. Again the closet door in our bedroom moved on its roller. A hand was in the air close to my face. I let my lids close almost all the way. Pretending to be asleep was a game I used to play as a kid when Grandma Nonny bent over me on Saturdays trying to wake me for Seventh Day Adventist Church, an all-day sit on folding chairs. She could never tell if I was asleep. My lashes were long like feathers and cast shadows onto my cheeks. They disguised the slits of open eye. Now I relaxed every muscle. The bedside lamp went on.

Between the closet and the bed stood a tall man in a black ski mask. He was about to search the wrong closet if Thelma was who he was looking for. She lay curled up in the spare room closet. His elbows stuck out like his bones were loose under his windbreaker. A shorter man in a red hooded sweatshirt leaned against the night table. The tall one lifted Bluejay's trousers and shook the wallet free. The hooded one had a thin face and a red mouth. His mustache drooped like shoestring licorice. The cold stink of booze wafted off them. I shivered down to my toes before going cold all over.

"Where's the dog?" the tall one said.

The red mouth said, "Maybe it's in the bed."

"I only see two lumps"

"Look at that chick's hair. I bet she can sit on it."

The tall one disappeared into the closet. I could hear him flipping through the hangers, the dry cleaning plastics hissing. The woman who lived here must have kept all the clothes that ever touched her body. Chrysanthemum evening gowns, polka dot summer dresses, shoulder padded jackets with Dentyne gum turned to putty in the pockets. I could feel a sobbing coming out of my ears, chest and shoulders, but not my mouth. Not for me but for the dog that seemed braver and better than anyone I'd ever met. Bluejay snorted twice and smacked in his sleep.

"They didn't deliver the dog, they've still got it." The short one jiggled from leg to leg at the side of the bed. His eyes seemed glued to me. I had on panties and nothing else. His lips were bright red because he kept licking them. Like ants kept crawling over them. Redness ringed his mouth. He couldn't stay still; he kept jiggling and licking. He was inching closer. I didn't want to see the ring he licked around his mouth about to turn into the sky above my face. The hood of his sweatshirt fell showing off a rooster's comb of brown hair. Did he see my eyelids flicker? No, I was safe in the darkness. I could feel his gaze where the sheet fell between my breasts, where he could see the rise and fall of my ribcage. He got down on his knees and crawled under our bed.

The tall man came out of the closet, hissing, "Paul, where the fuck are you?"

"Looking to see if pooch is under the bed, which she isn't." The red mouthed one stood up.

Were they the ones who had cut Thelma? I was proud of her for making no sound. She either sensed danger or didn't bark or the cognac had filled her with dreams of fantastic smells.

"You didn't even take care of the phone. Where's your head?" The one in the ski mask spotted the phone and yanked the jack from the wall. Now I let my lids go all the way shut, skinny lids like common moth wings.

"Maybe they ditched the dog. Maybe it shit in their car and they threw it out." The red mouth moved away from the bed and soundlessly walked toward the door. He must be wearing sneakers. I didn't hear what the tall man spewed into his ski mask as he carried the phone into the hallway. Air started to stick in my throat; pulses were opening under my chin. Bluejay snored on, his leg kicked over me like a table. Out there in the wilds of the apartment, drawers were being pulled, and books tumbled from shelves. The TV went on.

The tin wasn't inside the dog, but in the empty Irish oatmeal can under the sink in the kitchen. I would give it to them, but how could I convince them not to kill the dog or Bluejay? It was time to wake Bluejay, but how could I do it without sound? I lay on his left side next to his deaf ear. Whenever I startled him in his sleep he would jerk up from the pillow into a sitting position. Then he would shake his head and cry out, "What, what?"

"Where's the remote?" the tall one shouted.

"You're going to wake them."

"Let 'em wake. They're gonna have to pretty soon. I want some MTV."

"Shit for brains, you can change the thing manually."

"Well, do it for me."

I was following their voices.

"Bluejay," I said in my lowest strongest tone. He drew another deep breath. "It's not in the dog anymore." But he slept on as if everyone he ever loved were still alive.

"Would you look in this cupboard? There must be hundreds. I love these little booze bottles like on airplanes," the tall man said. "They're called miniatures. Shit, they've got Kailua, Amaretto, Frangelico, Green Chartreuse. I'm going to taste test a couple of them."

I could no longer tell who said what. All I knew is I did not want either of these two to take my life. More drawers were pulled. The lights went on in the mistress's room. The tall one must have figured out how to change the TV manually. MTV vomited talk not music. My mind darted around the room searching for escape. Unlock the window, shove it up. But it was two flights down to the ground, probably not fatal. Better to jump and live. Dry heroin was probably what was in the tin. You could make lots of street heroin from it. I thought of the girls at Caligula's in yellow silk teddies who did what they did for it and whatever else they could get. They didn't belong to themselves, with their full lips so red like the plush blood of calf livers had found its way to their faces, their innocent lips. Those girls looked out under their half-closed lids of mercury, faces with poked out eyes. They had famine bodies and enormous chests. Bluejay took me there when I was in high school. Once he delivered their angel dust from Valentino. I watched their eyelids do a rise like in thermometers. "Do you like their bodies?" I asked Bluejay. "Yeah, I love mammary glands that look like bicycle air pumps filled them up." I imagined those girls and their balloon breasts floating into the clouds.

Now I heard the men come closer. The red-mouthed one stood in the door. "I want to watch them sleep a little while longer."

Sweat was collecting along my hairline and on my upper lip. Relax and take deep breaths not these short jerky ones. The mattress dipped, he was sitting down. He must have finished a liquor miniature. Amaretto mixing with the beer. Once I'd flown with Nonny from New Orleans to Houston. The flight attendant served Nonny a drink from those little bottles on the airplane flight. *I'm safe in the 747 somewhere over the Texas Panhandle. When I fall asleep at cruising speed there is no land below, but when I wake lights have drifted from the blackness in an effervescent orange mist. After Beaumont the darkness doesn't come back, it opens its mouth and out come swarms of cloudless sulfur butterflies, and I wonder can there be any wilderness left. I press my face to the Plexiglas. From Beaumont west, a single teeming megapolis, bracelets of interstate, snakes of agitated car lights, satellites and monstrous blinking things. The Lone Star State.*

The red-mouth drummed on his knees. His jeans needed to be laundered. I waited for his hand to reach out, and then I felt his fingers combing through my hair. I thought of clouds that billowed above the lawn those summer afternoons when time didn't move. I'd lie in the grass and kick my leg in the air pretending to stir the clouds with my big toe. He lifted a strand of my hair and put in his mouth. He smelled it. He touched me with one finger, pulling the sheet down the center of my body. Like the line you made with the point of your knife before gutting a white trout.

"Paul, I've found her! Get in here," the tall one yelled.

Then I heard the most blood-curdling yelp.

I rolled and leapt up from the bed. "Nooooo, leave the dog alone." My feet ran. They knew what was happening. All the lights were on in the spare room. The tall one had taken off his ski mask and was wiping his face on it. I got down on my knees before the crawlspace door and when the cocker spaniel saw me she tottered to her feet. Her eyes were wide with bewilderment. "No, girl, stay there. Lie down, girl."

"Let her come. Keep letting her come," the tall one said, his face breaking into what he must have thought was a smile. He had a knife. Everything felt different when a weapon appeared, yet familiar because who wasn't used to blades and squirting metal on TV. I envisioned myself shirtless and in peach panties with an outline around me the way the police would see me. The stillness of the plum-colored canopy bed was being invaded and the stuffed rabbits and elephants awakened.

"I've already taken it out of her," I said calmly. "There's nothing inside her."

"Bullshit," he snapped.

"She's bandaged."

"I'll do it. I'll cut the dog," the red-mouthed one sneered from the doorway. He reached into his beltline for a knife. The blade was split into two like a bird's beak.

The tall one was looking into the closet crawlspace. The cocker spaniel was just beyond the reach of his hand, cowering there. "Yeah, she's wearing bandages." When he walked toward me I smelled his adrenaline, a gutting-fish odor. His lips drew away from his teeth, and one of his incisors overlapped its neighbor and jutted out. "Okay, give it to me."

"*Us*, man. Give it to *us*," said his buddy.

"How do I know you won't knife us afterwards?" I asked.

"That's a chance you have to take."

I shook my head. "You'll never find what I've hidden."

The red-mouthed one held his knife like people did guns on a shooting range—pushing the blade forward, arms straight out, shoulders at right angles, and elbows locked. Bluejay had taught me what to do when someone had the drop on you. Stay cool. Wait to erupt, become a chair flying into the china. Throw yourself into a seizure. A good seizure with foam at the mouth and blue eyelids. Take that lamp with a Chinese lantern shade with the brass base and hurl it.

"You've got my word we won't hurt you," the tall one said, "if you hand the stuff over."

The three of us crowded into the tiny kitchen between the gas stove and cabinets. The counters held pepper mills and lovely porcelain teacups with wisps of willow trees. I could hear the tall one curse under his breath.

"Look at them roaches," he said. "They can live up to a week without a head. Then they die of thirst."

The veins bulged in his neck when he watched the roaches skittering over the stove. "Where's the bug killer?"

"Stop!" his friend shouted. "Forget the roaches, you gat."

"The roach spray is under the sink," I said.

"I ate roaches in the peanut butter as a kid," the tall man said, kicking open the cupboard. He seemed to have forgotten why he was here. "I ate jelly and cockroaches. Cockroaches in

Pepsi-Cola." Maybe his life would have been different if people had gone up to him as a kid and given him kisses instead of cockroach sandwiches. He found the Hot Shot Roach Killer. "Sir Francis Drake once captured a wooden ship filled with millions of roaches. That was his booty."

"You're nutting up, yat," the red mouth snapped. "Let's just get the stuff."

The tall man turned the burners on and sprayed Hot Shot into the gas. Flames whooshed up in a torrent of green. He aimed into the flames and sprayed again, the gas made a popping sound like a balloon bursting and a second sticky black fireball rolled up. "Got you and you!" he guffawed. The smoke alarm went off. I could feel the kitchen vibrating. The red-mouthed one banged the smoke alarm with his fist. The green and indigo paints shivered. The tall one lifted a bottle of apple vinegar from the counter and whacked the alarm until the cover dangled by a wire.

I heard a roar. I saw the blue flame snorting from Bluejay's gun hand. He stood naked in the entryway. My ears were ringing. Everything slowed down: the vinegar bottle falling to the floor, the red-faced man trying to run and Bluejay going after him, the cocker spaniel barking. I was alone with the tall man. His head tilted at a weird angle and blood spurted from his chest like a drinking fountain. Then pieces of blood went flying. Red tetra bits. I'd seen men shot on TV more times than I could count.

There was no place for him to fall. He crashed onto the stove. *Oh, no.* His hair caught fire. A hundred fireflies, and then one big flame spreading to his sweatshirt. I tried to beat it out with a kitchen towel. Then I filled the skillet with water and threw it over his head. The fire sizzled out. I could see his scalp.

Bluejay stood in the doorway. He no longer had the gun. "Are you okay?"

I nodded. "The other one?"

"Got away."

"Is he dead?" I asked. My hand was swelling up but I couldn't feel it.

"Pretty sure he is."

I leaned over the sink and looked out the window. Lights went on across the alley. I twisted off the stove burners. The tall man slumped between the cabinets. The fire had blackened the skin on his forehead. His eyes stared at the broiler handle.

"We should call an ambulance," I said.

"No. He doesn't deserve one."

"Who's going to call the police?"

"I'm calling Valentino to see what he wants me to do. I heard you say you took the stuff out of the dog. Where is it?"

"So you knew about that stuff inside Thelma all along?"

"I didn't hear you. Who's Thelma?"

"The dog. You knew it was in the dog."

"Mem, where the fuck is it?"

If I closed my eyes his voice wasn't much different from theirs only louder. It had taken the smoke alarm to wake him. "It's in the Irish oatmeal can under the sink."

"Mem, you better wash up."

I filled a bowl with fresh water for Thelma. I heard him grab the can and pop the lid. I walked out of the kitchen. My feet shuffled over the parquet floor picking up grit and dust balls. Two dusty pink couches on either side of the room faced a TV on wheels, the metal kind rolled into junior high classrooms. The TV had been left on. A hippie bus was driving through a field of wheat. A girl wearing only her hair ran from the bus through the waving grain. My head pounded telling me I was in the eye of a migraine where you could see blue sky and stars.

Hanging from the louvered closet door in the hall, the jean skirt I'd worn earlier, a matching jacket, and epaulettes on its shoulders. The French tart.

"Don't be afraid, I won't let anything happen to you," I coaxed the cocker spaniel. She limped out of the closet into my arms. She licked my neck. I couldn't stop kissing the top of her head. "I'm going to get clean and then we're leaving." She was frightened of the bathroom so I carried her into the bedroom. "Wait here for me." Then I went into the bathroom.

I refused to look in the mirror. The sink leaked like a nose. I stood on the braided rug and let my knees knock. I wanted to go back to Nonny, who would soap my hands with a glycerin bar, Nonny whose water was better than water, the droplets bigger and softer. Next to her sink sat a bowl where an orchid floated. It filled the room with the aroma of sleep. I could see red veins in the white petals. The flower was always for me.

Bluejay came into the bathroom, opened the medicine cabinet and reached for the Spice Stick. "I plugged the phone back in. Some of Valentino's guys are on their way over. You okay?" He was trembling. "I'm not expecting you to bow down and call me Christ, but I saved your life."

I stepped past him into the shower. My arms were speckled with blood. I looked up and the showerhead was raining blood. I sponged the droplets. I couldn't get clean. But there wasn't really any me. I imagined how it would be pulling the deadbolt. I would carry Thelma out of the sublet with someone else's feet, someone else taking the hard steps down the street like wading into a rutted potholed road.

Kursk

Maria Elena Suarez

I am watching about submarines when you come out of the shower with your freckles and your solid shoulders. We have talked about everything possible except that our baby died in my body before it was born, and that you are worried about me. In a way though we talk about only that, and when you ask me if I want apples from the store, you are really asking when I will be alright again, what you can bring me to make me alright. You sit very close to me, still in your towel, and together we watch doomed Soviet sailors on television. The narrator tells about the failing of the nuclear submarine, about the utter ruin for the men inside. It sinks slowly and there is no hope of power resurgence just in time, there is no hope of rescue, and it is a slow, ballet drift down to death through universes of cold water. As you leave the room to get dressed, the physical ocean has overwhelmed them, and they will die soon. The water gathers over them, more and more of it all the time, and they watch it collect on top of them. They can hear its weight as it crowds in on them, and they understand completely what it is to be helpless, to be a collection of tissue and blood at the hands of an entire ocean. I apologize to the sailors in a whisper. The camera pans slowly across a picture of them all together before the accident, in clean uniforms and smiling, back when they had lives and choices, when they could drive away from the ocean or towards it. I tell them I am sorry for not getting them out. If I were strong enough, I whisper, I would have protected you. If my body were strong enough, I would have kept the violence from your bodies, I would have been a guard against everything that pushes in. Back, now, in jeans and sweater, you put your arm around me with a gust of new soap and skin scrubbed clean.

Kadongo Kamu-
One Beat

Doreen Baingana

I am ashamed to say it is an American who tells me about the performances of Kiganda music called Kadongo Kamu here in Kampala. I met Ed at the Open Mic Nite at the National Theater complex, a rowdy drunken Monday night showcase of local pop talent. I live in the United States, so when I see an American here in Uganda, I'm curious to see what kind he or she is, and it is easier for me to ask what he or she is doing here. That is what I am asked all the time in the States even after ten years, so why not take revenge? Ed says he is studying traditional Ugandan music. An ethnographer, he says, which to me is a long name just to say he wants to have fun away from home. He came over here as a volunteer music teacher a few years ago and loved it. He found other reasons to come back again and again. Who can blame him? He seems to know his stuff, though. He asks if I have heard Paulo Lutalo's music.

"No, I haven't, but why don't you talk normally?" He is attempting a Ugandan accent for my sake.

"I travel a lot, so sometimes I get an accent from the last place," he tries to spin. I don't entirely believe him, and soon he speaks like himself. He is white, tall, with big long forearms and huge hairy legs rarely seen here. Calves the size of small chickens.

Men here don't wear shorts that much, but the few legs I see are wired tight and thin. Ed's watery green-gray eyes look vacant until you get used to them. His head is sparsely covered with dirty blond hair that sticks together. A reddish tan, not the best. He wears the standard back-packer attire: a hanging T-shirt and baggy khaki-colored pants with pockets bulging out everywhere. You know the look.

I guess I should describe myself, too. Well, I have less of an American veneer than I should have after ten years in the States. I am a standard urban Ugandan female, which means I dress like any woman trying to look hip in any city around the world. Bell-bottomed jeans, a thin clingy pink blouse declaring, "I ROCK," long brown braids down to my waist flecked with gold that I flip this way and that as if it's my own hair, fat platforms. A uniform of sorts.

Ed and I talk some about his deejaying in Seattle and my community radio work in Baltimore, we vehemently agree that the war on Iraq sucks, and then he invites me to a Kadongo Kamu concert later this week. I'm not sure if he is showing off his knowledge or is genuinely interested in it. Of course I know the music, I tell him, I just don't listen to it much. Hardly ever, actually. It is Kiganda music and I am not from that tribe. I don't admit that the main reason is that Kadongo Kamu is street music, lower class, not for the educated.

See, for me, at least when I was growing up anything foreign was cool. We got cassette copies of radio tapings of Kool and the Gang, New Edition, Phil Collins and Whitney from anyone who traveled abroad, mostly the UK. Even the radio talk between records, the noisy, slurry stream of ads. London weather was fascinating. The voices that were not in our English were like arms reaching us from another world. They were not intended for us, of course, but who cared? Half the lyrics escaped me, but at least they were in English. Anyway, the Luganda used in Kadongo Kamu is that of market sellers and taxi-park lay-abouts, not the simpler, less slangy one my friends and I speak.

But you grow up, and inevitably you start going out, sometimes to outdoor joints—a few wobbly benches arranged on a dirt floor in front of wooden kiosks that sell everything: Sunlight soap, Ambi lightening cream, saucepans and handbags made in China, phone cards, water, fried *mandazi* and, most importantly, cold cold beer. As you swallow it down your dust-coated throat in the cooling twilight, wiping sweat from your brow and upper lip, wandering men or barefoot boys come up holding a one-stringed harp, *ndingidi*, or an old guitar. Your date or your uncle orders them rather rudely to sing, and waves a well-worn, one-thousand shillings note.

The musician, with a mouthful of ssebo, *sir, ssebo*, scrapes and bows and prepares himself. If he has an *ndingidi* he may squat down to play. The guitar player remains standing, placing one foot with its dusty black sandal made up on a bench from old tires. His gnarled toes tap to the beat. The young boys' voices strain high like starving birds, but the men sing it best with voices as scratchy as old records, throats corrugated by years of crude *Waragi*–war gin. Imagine Louis Armstrong as a village African. Kadongo Kamu is talk-song about events of the day, with a refrain that rises like a wail from the past. It is the original rap, far older than the Black American urban beat, with guitar twangs that reveal Blues' beginnings. Folk music about everyday drama so absurd and yet so real that it unexpectedly twists your heart.

The wandering musicians find you; a concert you have to seek out. I am back home on holiday and looking for my own drama, so why not Kadongo Kamu? On this smoky blue evening of the show, Ed and I plan to meet at Nakivubo Stadium, which is in a rather unsavory part of town next to a crushingly chaotic taxi park for *matatus* to all parts of the city, and a bus park for transport to every rural corner of Uganda. I go to the parks only when absolutely necessary, but have never been to the Stadium, and not just because I am not a football fan. I don't tell Ed this, nor does he offer to pick me up. I guess he is not trying to impress me, or he assumes I will find my way there; this is my city, after all. His invitation is American-casual-friendly, so I am not sure if this is a date, or what. And what if I don't find him there? I'll be all by myself at the Stadium at night! But he should be easy to spot; he will be the only *mzungu*, most likely. He had better show up.

I gamely venture into the last throes of downtown evening, as the night threatens like faraway thunder. The dust is swept up and flung down by the day's last rush of old Toyotas, minibuses, grumbling, quaking painted buses. Hazy yellow street lamps come on, flashing car lights glance on red night eyes, then away as the cars swerve round corners. Scraggly thin mongrels climb and search through the day's rubbish heap: black-green slimy banana skins, *Uchumi* plastic bags now dirty puffs of fallen cloud, jagged edges of broken brown glass, squashed-open rotting tomatoes, burnt oily rags, gray bones. Starving cats slither through holes in half-built, half-fallen walls. Fat bustling women with huge double-globe buttocks—wrapped in swathes, acres of cloth patterned with bright frenzy—drag worn-down blue or green *sapatu* underfoot, a screaming toddler in one hand, and enormous rice sack in the other. Slim dark boys run up and across the street like shadows, chasing mischief to the honk of impatient taxis looking for the day's last cash. Shouts, baying, squeals, a crash—it's ignored—more shouts, a wail. It's just another good night in the ragged bottom of the city.

I weave through safely, toward metal gates and high cement walls. A policeman searches me perfunctorily, playing the local war on terror. He won't find anything with such a half-hearted try. Two men next to him collect money for the show. They wear our version of gangsta hip: tent-sized sports shirts in shiny yellow and red, *Red Skins and Dallas Cowboys* stamped loudly across each chest. Matching oversize shorts, caps turned backward, sneakers like boats—all made in Dubai, from head to toe. One of them holds up his palm, fingers spread wide: five thousand shillings. I have a ten thousand shilling note. He gives me a five thousand note back. I can't really see his face.

Inside the high cement walls is a wide, flat, green field milling with people. A wooden stage has been set up on the north side and in front of it thickens the crowd of about two hundred. Close up, stadium lights shine on upturned faces, and further back the illumination throws a mix of shadow and light on scattered bodies. Beyond that, long coats of shade merge into darkness. Buses that brought the performers park behind the stage, where they are all still gathered. A number of bands will perform tonight, basking in Paulo Lutalo's light.

I wander through the crowd, rejecting persistent offers of baked plantains and roaster peanuts from sellers. I made it here, so I am less apprehensive, more excited, but where is Ed? Oh, there, talking with a man who doesn't even reach his shoulder. I come up. "Here you are!"

"Oh, hey, Milly. Meet...Moses, is it?"

"Yes. How are you?" Moses reaches out his hand to shake mine, something Ed did not do. They turn back to each other and continue talking. I stand there silent for a few minutes, then step away back toward the stage. Let the men talk. The musicians are warming up. Finally, Ed comes up.

"Did you know that guy?" I ask.

"No no, he just came up and started talking to me."

"About what?"

"He's a musician. Plays pop music—not this traditional stuff."

"What did he want?"

"Jeez, Milly! We were just chatting."

"Really?"

"He thought I might be a record producer. That I could take his records back to the States and promote him."

"See? You're a *mzungu*, after all."

"Nothing but. Thanks for the reminder." He squirms.

"It's not so bad, though, is it?" I insist. He shrugs impatiently.

"Come on, you're somebody here."

"Oh, and I wasn't before?"

"You know what I mean."

"Attention and ass-kissing isn't much fun when you know why."

"Just because I'm white. How fucked up is that?"

"You sound like I do in the States!" I can't keep my voice from rising.

"Okay, okay!"

"At least you get positive attention and are liked, at least on the face of it."

"Yeah the prostitutes just love me."

We both laugh. Then comes a pause of relief.

"Can they start playing already?" Ed says.

"I'm getting a beer. Want one?"

"Sure, thanks."

I walk away still miffed. What has he to complain about?

Along one wall are set long tables with tubs full of bottled beer and soda. I ask a woman behind the table for two Bells and hand her a five-thou note. She holds it up to the light and scrutinizes it for a long moment, then crumples it in one hand, flattens it out and examines it again. I am about to ask what's wrong when she shakes her head and silently passes the note to the man sitting next to her. He inspects it, too, but doesn't take too long. "It's fake," he says in Luganda.

"What?"

"*Nyabo*, this is not real money. We can't accept it."

"But they just gave it to me. Back there, at the gate." I point helplessly.

He shrugs. "Sorry, we can't help you."

He drops the limp dirty-blue note on the table. I pick it up and turn it over and over. I can't tell the difference, of course. I stand there feeling like a fool. "They cheated me. It's not my fault." I am more upset than angry.

"You are the one who brought big notes." He has no sympathy whatsoever. "Are you going to buy drinks or not?"

The woman points to the stage. "Look, they're starting."

I dig through my purse and find some coins. She briskly wipes off two wet, cold beers and hands them to me. "Don't mind, auntie. Take the note to the bank. They may refund you." She smiles and I am grateful.

That was a bummer. It wasn't much money, but still. Well, I was expecting something to go wrong, so better this than a knock on the head and my bag grabbed. I know my fears are exaggerated but I can't seem to completely shrug off my childhood Idi Amin days of insecurity. Nothing drastic happened to me or my family, but rumors and stories stewed in our heads and, at least for me, I am repeatedly reassured. But incidents like this jolt me back to that uneasy something-bad-is-about-to-happen feeling. Just for a moment I long for America.

I go back to Ed and tell him the sorry tale as he gulps down his beer. "You shouldn't carry so much money, you know," he says, ever the savvy traveler.

"Thanks for telling me now."

He chuckles, takes another long swig, and wipes foam from his upper lip. "God, that really hit the spot. Thanks, Milly." He doesn't offer to pay for his drink. I am too polite and peeved to ask. This is definitely not a date.

The Bukalasa All Stars finally begin and we move into the thick of the crowd. Kadongo Kamu has evolved from an *ndingidi* to a guitar to bands, though all forms are still played. It remains spare, with the emphasis on the lyrics. What I didn't know is that the singers now dress up and act out the songs. A big, fat, matronly woman comes out in a *busuti*, the traditional Kiganda dress, which drops down to her feet and has huge, puffy sleeves like pointed hills perched on each shoulder. A wide, hard belt embroidered with shiny thread is knotted below the waist and stomach. To look good in a *busuti*, you need to have a round protruding stomach and matching bulbous buttocks, which this performer has. Others must pad their behinds with pieces of cloth wrapped around and around. A busuti would hang limp on me, though that's not the only reason I have never worn one. The first singer is followed by a man in a white doctor's coat, suit pants, glasses, and a stethoscope around his neck.

"Robert Mugalula," Ed shouts in my ear. He pronounces it Muga-LUU-lah.

"It's MU-galula," I shout back. I, too, know a thing or two.

The band lowers its introductory melody, and the performer launches into how hard he works as a doctor. He operates on his wife early in the morning, then services the nurses at his clinic, and then in the evenings helps out a lady friend, who, by the way, makes him the best roast pork ever. Mugalula moves across the stage and gestures lewdly as he sings, making us laugh out loud. He has studied what the whites call gynecology, he boasts, and adds in a bit of local medicine, too. He loves his work and applies himself vigorously, so why does his wife complain?

On cue, she moves to the front and tells her side of the story. Her parents encouraged her to marry a doctor and yes, he gives her everything she and her children need. But he is too generous; he gives himself to every woman he sees. What kind of a husband is that? The couple sings a refrain together:

> Abaange, *people, let us tell you about marriage,*
> *It's not an easy thing, you see,*
> *I thought it was about sharing everything,*
> *But he/she complains about me.*
> (They each point at each other)

The woman tells us about the worst day of her life. One evening, she followed the good doctor after work and saw him enter a slummy-looking house. She soon heard moans and groans and crept to the nearest window, which was small and gritty. What kind of a *malaya*—prostitute—did her husband pick anyway? She saw them zealously at it and, furious, threw a stone through the glass, shattering it. She raced back home, sent her children to the neighbors and waited for the slimy cheat.

They both act out the next scene, vying for the audience's support. The man arrives home, and the wife pulls a knife out of the front flap of her *busuti* and runs at him. He mock fights her down and throws the knife away. She cries and sings from the floor: she is leaving, before she is killed in her own house. Who was trying to kill whom? the husband responds. Anyway, where can she go? She has nothing, her parents won't take her back, her children must stay here. Come to your senses, he reprimands. You are my wife; you're going nowhere. Ask for anything, and I will give it to you. But just leave me alone to do as I please.

The woman turns back to the audience. This is her only home, she laments, so she will stay, for now. But since he wants to keep on treating other women, she will look for her own medicine, too. The audience laughs and claps to the beat as it joins in the final repeated refrain. The couple bows deeply to loud applause, steps back and off the stage.

Some of the crowd shout crude advice to them both. "Stick with each other, you deserve each other." The women side with the wife, saying, "Mwatu, my dear, get yourself a better, stronger doctor!" "Get your own degree!" The men back the husband. "He is a doctor, what do you want him to do?" "She enjoyed the treatment, doesn't she want others to enjoy it, too? Selfish woman!"

The Luganda is so concentrated, I have missed most of the language tricks and dirty metaphors, colloquialisms and deeper political messages. For all I know, it could really have been about the president and his numerous political bedfellows. But the comic overblown acting was entertaining all on its own.

I ask Ed, "Did you follow?" He knows the basics of Luganda.

"Enough. That was awesome, wasn't it?"

"Yeah, but I'm not sure why you like it so much. It's all in the words."

"I know, but I get to actually listen to the music since I don't have to concentrate on the words."

"The music is kind of the same throughout."

"Some people would say the same about reggae. The music—I mean, didn't you just hear it?"

"You're right."

"I'm always right."

"Whatever!"

*

Another group gets on stage, but Ed wants to talk to Robert Mugalula. We walk around back to the huge buses with empty black windows. The two are sitting on a grass mat on the ground underneath the stage, between tall wooden legs that hold it up. They sit side by side quietly, comfortably, like an old couple. They appear humble almost, which is surprising after all that rowdy stage action. Mugalula drinks from a bottle of beer and passes it to the woman, his wife, or girlfriend perhaps. Ed doesn't know her name. They may be two of the best paid musicians in Uganda, but here they are sitting calmly on the ground straight after such a performance, not mobbed by anyone. The woman is still in her *busuti*, the man has taken off his white doctor's coat and is not wearing a huge cowboy hat. She gets plates and dishes out of a basket by her side but stops when she sees us approach.

I tug at Ed's shirt to stop him, but he gets closer, leans over, and reaches his hand out to Mugalula. Ed knows we shake hands a lot here, but doesn't know when not to. He greets them in English, says, "The show was great!"

I add quickly in Luganda, "Sorry for bothering you when you are about to eat. We can come back later."

The woman turns away and continues bringing out her dishes. The man ignores me, but says "Thank you" to Ed, shortly.

Ed goes on. "Where can I get good recordings of your work? The ones on the street are not clear at all."

"I am very sorry about that. Keep trying. Buy only the ones covered in green." Mugalula makes a shape of a CD case with his hands. He is distant and polite, dignified even; he does not pour himself all over the *mzungu* like the other young man did. Mugalula and his partner are the exact opposite of the gesticulating, foul-mouthed couple on stage. They must be tired. I tug at Ed's shirt again to make him leave, but he gives the musician his phone number. Ed is the one gushing now. "I would love to record you live. Could I? You know, for radio, back in the

States?" The woman murmurs something in Luganda that I don't catch. Mugalula replies, simply, "I will call you."

Finally, we leave their shadowed space. As we walk back to the light, Ed's eyes glitter as if he has just talked to Bruce Springsteen or someone. "I must have those two on my world music show."

"World music." I roll my eyes. "The term should be banned."

"That would be totally cool, you know, it would be a first." He rubs his hands together with excitement.

"First in the U.S." I correct with irritation. "Anyway, nobody would understand a word. By the way, it's not polite to talk to people when they are eating or about to."

"God, I hope he calls me."

"Also, if people are sitting on the ground, it's kind of rude to lean all over them. You should get down to their level."

"I'm gonna bug those guys on Radio-XFM to get me his tapes."

"Are you even listening?"

"What? They weren't offended, were they?"

"Would you have noticed?"

He shrugs. "Stop fussing."

We remain silent for a while and I think of leaving, but Paulo Lutalo hasn't gone on yet. Ed is still in euphoria, humming the refrain of the last song. Why am I so bothered? I say, "It was nice to see you as the groveler for once."

"I am a fan, Milly, in case you hadn't noticed. I grovel when groveling is due." We laugh, he more than I. "You know, you should try enjoying your music a little more," he says smiling. He touches my shoulder, a peace offering.

"Oh thanks, what an amazing and new idea!"

We get more drinks and wander through the crowd. Ed immerses himself back into the live music and comic acting, while I look on. He even dances to one hectic tune, his large frame jerking clumsily; he is in it completely. People standing by us stare quite openly at him, amused by the antics of this out-of-place *mzungu*, but he doesn't notice, or care, or he relishes it, perhaps. Look at him, almost albino-like here, with his pale reddishness, pale eyes, pale hair, his shabby faded clothes and rubber sandals that some of us wear only in the bathroom. How he towers over everybody as if he has been eating everyone's food. Like the doctor who sleeps in any bed he pleases. I would have to be deaf, dumb and blind to be this free. He is comfortable with the world, anywhere. I am jealous? I turn away.

The black night has now completely replaced the dusty daytime commotion. The crowd rekindles, surges forward, and breaks through my mind track. Paulo Lutalo is now on stage. He doesn't act, doesn't have to; his sonorous voice is enough. He is old school, decorous, more subtle. He sweeps away soap opera and digs deeper into our questions and regrets. There are no answers. You live with the laughable and ominous and tragic and stoke it all with sex. There is death, too. Of course.

Lutalo turns us into one lithe living thing, eating and sharing and tasting the same dish from one huge plate. He moves to a slower final song. Ed turns to me and smiles. Eyes back on stage, he takes my hand. For a moment I hold still. I feel his warmth, my palm safely cuddled in his larger one. The dark air is full of deep bass. He moves his fingers, but I slip my hand out. I prefer to enter the lips of the night and disappear. Like music.

A New Kind of Gravity

Andrew Foster Altschul

Around one in the morning I go out to the alley with Horace to bum a cigarette and trade the evening's tragedies. I'll pick him up at his cage in the basement, rap on the reinforced glass, point to the clock over his head. We check the monitors to make sure all's clear, no belligerent drunks or clever husbands waiting in ambush. Mattie would fire us both in about a minute and a half if she knew we did this. If she looked back at the night's security tapes, saw the steel door propped open with a brick, the two of us leaning against the outside wall like we were on school recess–she'd have no choice, everyone knows that.

"Play with your own life if you want to," she said when she hired me. She looked me in the eye, shook my hand, but didn't raise her voice. "Don't fuck with someone else's. That's our rule here." Mattie always says things that way–real plain, like she's just talking. But Mattie's never just talking.

I tried to laugh about it with Horace once, my first week on the job, trying to get chummy with the other guard. I did a pretty good impression of Mattie's monotone, her cold half-smile, the way she presses her palms together when she's lecturing you. Horace didn't think it was so funny. He unbuttoned his uniform and showed me the thick, brown scar where a husband had knifed him on the sidewalk at eight in the morning and taken his keys. Mattie shot the guy in the vestibule, then gave them both first aid until the ambulance came.

It's not that we can't smoke in the building—nicotine practically holds this place together. There are meeting rooms on the second and fourth floors with big, industrial ashcans that are always overflowing. There's the dingy third-floor kitchen, and there's the roof. But to get there you have to walk down those sad hallways, posters of Paris and the Grand Canyon, "One day at a time" in flowing letters across a sunrise. You can hear the women in their rooms, praying or sobbing or talking in their sleep, yelling at their children or reading bedtime stories. Some of the rooms are dead silent. The meeting room walls are cluttered with photocollages and news clippings and needlepoint, third-grade spelling tests and divorce papers and Spanish prayers. Me and Horace like it better out in the alley, where it's just the dumpsters and the weather, a few minutes of bare freedom.

The women don't come out here. They don't stand on the roof or stroll in the city park or take their kids to little league practice. Some of them can't even hold jobs anymore, haven't left the building in two, three, ten weeks. When they do leave, we usually don't see them again for a while, until they come back with their noses broken or their elbows dislocated or worse.

"Look at them," Horace says out in the alley. He doesn't have to look up to know they're there—sleepless faces in the windows above, staring out at the shabby buildings, jealously watching us smoke outside. "Pathetic," he says. "Pathetic specimens."

Horace is on a roll. Sometimes you'd think he hated the women, the way he talks. But he's been here six years. I've helped him and Mattie wrestle a bodybuilder into a four-point restraint, the guy so amped you could smell the crystal. I saw

Horace's face while we held the husband down, howling into the concrete. I don't have to ask whose side he's on.

Tonight he's worked up because he saw on the log that Lucille Johnson checked back in. "You explain it to me, Charlie," he says, blowing out the smoke like it insulted him. "You tell me why a woman like that ought to be coming and going from here, wasting her life in this place. Don't she have brothers? Don't she have a father? And nobody doing shit."

Horace gets especially enraged by black women at Skyer House. He says it's a private thing, the community ought to take care of it. "Woman in my neighborhood gets beat up like that she's not gonna need no safehouse. She's not gonna need no restraining order," he says. He flicks his cigarette across the alley, where it bursts into a small orange shower against the dumpster. "That kinda shit only gonna happen once. You know why?"

I've heard this speech a hundred times. "Because black men know how to treat their women?" I say.

Horace gives a sour laugh. "Black men know how to treat animals," he says. He crosses his arms and nods. I grind out my cigarette with the toe of my shoe.

"Get back?" I suggest, checking my watch. There's a 1:30 A.M. rerun of *The Honeymooners* that I don't want to miss.

"Talk about humane," he's growling as we head for the door. "I'll show you some fucking humanity."

I kick the doorstop away and try not to look up—even though I know I will, even though I know who I'll see when I do: a seven-year-old girl in Wonder Woman pajamas, waving at me from the fourth-floor window. I wave back, point to my watch and pantomime sleep, but Camila only stares from behind the bulletproof glass. It's the same every night: I trudge upstairs to my cage in the lobby, and in the monitors I can still see her standing there, a tiny figure looking at the place I've left, while

I triple check the doors and clean my gun and wonder if the day will come when I'll have to kill her father to keep her safe.

*

The doorbell chimes at seven in the morning and I don't even need to check the monitors to know what's out there: a husband on the front stoop, fidgeting with his clothes, trying not to eyeball the camera. He'll be freshly shaved, maybe wearing a tie. He'll definitely have flowers, red roses from the Korean shop on the corner—they do a hell of a business. Some of these husbands are big, real big; some of them aren't. Some of them look like the bottom of the barrel, some look like accountants. But when they walk past you, you get the same feeling, like a smell they give off, like something hot and rotten has been packed inside them, crammed down into a space too small to hold it in.

Soon there are footsteps clicking down the stairs and April Pittelli floats past the cage in her best dress and an hour's worth of makeup. She's wearing a big smile, despite her swollen jaw, glowing like a teenager getting picked up for the prom—she's leaving, she says, we can give her bed to someone who really needs it. It's what she always says. She stops to give me a hug before I buzz her out. In the monitors, I watch them embrace, her husband crying, smothering her in kisses. They hold hands as they walk away.

The first time I had to let one of the women go, I started arguing with her, incredulous. Mattie shook her head at me from across the lobby. "It's not your decision," she said later. "No one can take care of them but themselves."

It's true. You can't stop them. Even the fourth or fifth time—when they've come back to lay low a while, let their bones heal, their hair grow back—when that door chimes they practically fly down the stairs. The caseworkers talk about how scared the women are, how they go back because they don't know what else to do, or they can't support themselves, or for the kids. But it's the smile that gets me, the way they throw open that door and fall into their husbands' arms. You'd think they really believed this time would be different. You might as well tear up the restraining orders in their file, shower them like ticker tape out the second story window, make a big celebration out of it.

But then you'd just have to call the courthouse for new copies in a week or ten days, when she comes back in a squad car with cigarette burns on her arms or a high wheeze from broken ribs or, worse, injuries you can't see, whatever spirit she'd had left replaced by shaking hands and a self-loathing so deep she won't find the bottom for months.

When Mariana came back the first time, wearing a neck brace and gripping Camila's hand so tight the little girl was trying to pry it off, I opened the door and put an arm around her to bring her inside. She closed her eyes for a second, and I thought she might cry on my shoulder, but then she pulled away and yanked her daughter up the stairs and disappeared. Mattie called me into her office a minute later and gave me another warning. There's no such thing as positive male attention here, she said, slicing the air with clasped hands. You open the door, you close the door. You see a raised hand, you grab it. You see a knife, you shoot it. These women are not your friends, she said. They're not your girlfriends. They're sick. And let me tell you, you don't want to catch what they've got.

*

For a while it seemed every woman I dated had an ex who hit. For some it was unpredictable, a kind of reflex—the hard shove in the middle of a fight, the drink thrown against the wall; for others it would be premeditated, methodical. It started with Teresa, my old fiancée. Soon after she moved in with me, she told me about her ex, how he used to cry while he wrapped a towel around his fist so he wouldn't bruise her. She sat on the edge of the bed, her back to me, and I held a pillow over my face while she told me how sorry he'd feel afterward, how she believed it was a different person, like something taking over his body.

He put her in the emergency room once, she said, and when she came home the next morning she found him in the bathtub—he had shaved his head and was trying to slash his wrists. When I asked why she didn't let him do it, she closed her eyes and twisted her mouth into a smile, as if there were some things about love I just couldn't understand.

I heard so many of these stories they stopped surprising me. I didn't know what it was about me that attracted women who'd been with such people. I'd have dreams about running into the guy on the street, smashing his face into the pavement. This was when I still worked at the mall, I'd find myself taking it out on some stupid shoplifter, pinning him to the wall by his neck.

What got me was that they all went back. Maybe they'd go into counseling or quit drinking together, but it didn't make a difference, after the first hit it wouldn't stop. None of these assholes went to jail. No one pressed charges. Teresa's ex was the only one who even got arrested, and that was because he pulled the phone out of the wall when she tried to call 911. Apparently pulling the phone out of the wall is a federal offense.

*

The last thing Horace and I do each morning is put the kids on the bus. The counselors bring them down the back stairs and they file past Horace's cage with their bookbags and lunchboxes, when we see the bus pull up in the monitors we stand outside the steel doors and the kids pass between us. It's almost like any other bus stop, just a bunch of kids going to school—except that these kids barely make a sound, they don't tease each other or complain, and they need two men with guns to make sure they get on the bus alright.

Sometimes a father will be out in the alley, but usually he'll just call to his kid and wave. "Tell your mother I love her," is what they usually say. We have lines painted on the pavement at 100 feet and 200 feet, so they can see exactly where they'll be violating their order. Sometimes, watching a father out of the corner of my eye, I catch myself hoping he'll cross the line, give me a reason.

Horace says he's never seen a problem at the bus. The fathers know there's not much to gain here, what with the mother locked inside and armed guards and all. He says they just come to feel like fathers for a few minutes. Maybe they hope their kid will wave. Maybe they think their kid will run over to them, crying, "Daddy, daddy!" We have to stop them if they do.

I've worked out a deal with Camila's caseworker where I'm allowed to pat her on the head before she gets on the bus. She used to run over to me and hug my legs—her caseworker watching, alarmed, I stood there and tried to gently pry her away. Now I'm allowed to say, "Have a good day at school," and she's allowed to blow me a kiss.

Last week her father showed up in the alley. I knew he was there because Camila walked out the door and froze and immediately started to cry. "Camila," he shouted. "*Te quiero,* Camilita. *Tu mamá, dile que le amo.*" The caseworker had to carry her onto the bus. I turned to see a middle-aged guy in cords and a fisherman's sweater. I figured I'd get some kind of dirty look or

Spanish curses, but he wasn't even looking at me. He just stared at the bus pulling away and gnawed miserably at his thumbnail.

In the evenings things are more informal. From eight o'clock, when I come on, until ten, all the women are in meetings. The night counselors are supposed to plan activities for the kids, but mostly they have them do their homework or watch TV. I sit in my cage with the day's logs and drink coffee, read up on any new residents or watch *Wheel of Fortune* on the little black and white. Eventually, out of the corner of my eye, I'll see half of a face and a few strands of hair peek around the corner of the stairwell. I'll pretend not to notice, looking over the notes on the console, and she'll sneak down the last stairs to spring up at the door of the cage.

"Boo!" she yells, and I pretend to fall out of my chair.

"You shouldn't sneak up on a man with a gun," I said to her once, thinking that was kind of funny, but I could see from her face that it wasn't. Another time I put my hands in the air and said, "Please, don't hurt me!" like it was a stick-up. That wasn't funny either. You really have to watch yourself.

Camila brings her homework downstairs and I let her sit in my chair and swivel around and I help her with math. She has her times tables down cold, but she's completely blocked on long division. Last night I had to tell her again that it doesn't always come out even, that sometimes there's a remainder.

"This is stupid," she said, shoving the book onto the floor. She started pressing buttons on my console and I could hear the electric lock on the front door clicking in and out. I quickly checked the monitors, which thankfully were clear, but I still didn't want her fooling with the doors. I picked up the book and the pencil and put them back in front of her, but she didn't stop.

"Camila, you can't touch those," I said, and when she kept doing it I reached out and put my hands over hers—so gently I didn't even breathe—and moved her arms away. "We have to keep the doors locked," I said, rolling the chair back.

"Why?" she said.

"That's the rule. That way everyone's safe."

"But what if someone wants to come in?" she said.

I pointed to the monitors and said anyone who wants to come in can talk to me through the intercom. She knows all this. We've been through it before. She said she wanted to go outside and use the intercom. She wanted me to buzz her inside. When I said no, she said I should go outside and she would buzz me in. She wanted to make sure it wasn't broken.

"I'm not allowed to go outside," I told her.

"You'd get in trouble?"

"I'd get in trouble."

"You'd get a *castigo*?" she asked. I didn't know what that meant, so I just nodded.

We finished the last problem and I told Camila it was time to brush her teeth. The groups were letting out upstairs, the women spilling out of the meeting rooms, zooming on caffeine and affirmations.

"My daddy wants to visit me," she said, erasing and carefully rewriting her name in the exercise book, brushing eraser shavings all over my console. "He said he wants to take us home."

"You saw your father today?" I asked, trying to sound casual.

"He said he wants to see my room."

I took a deep breath. I'd have to tell her caseworker. Her father's order says he can't come to her school, but they just don't have the staff to keep a lid on these things. Last month one of our first-graders was taken right out of PE. He was missing for almost a week until they found him, in a motel with his father, two towns away. They were just watching TV and ordering pizzas, like they couldn't think of what else to do.

"He says you won't let him visit me," Camila said.

I pictured her father behind me in the alley while Camila got on the bus. I wondered how many mornings he'd been out there, watching, what it would feel like to see your daughter grab a stranger's leg when you called her. I made myself stop thinking about it—Mattie says the worst thing you can do is let yourself identify with these people.

"I can only let in the people they tell me to," I said, taking back my chair. I tried to say it the way Mattie says it, slow and reassuring. "It's so everyone can be safe."

She crossed her arms in the door and glared. "My daddy loves me."

I pretended to straighten some papers, checked the monitors again. I could see the women in the upstairs hallways, leaning against the walls, on line at the payphones—waiting to call their husbands, to cup the receiver for their allotted 15 minutes, whisper how much they miss them.

"I know," I said.

"He does."

I saw Mariana in the third floor stairwell, on her way down. She couldn't have been more than 25, but she looked much older. Her hair was pulled back tightly and she walked with a stoop, her head tilted to one side like she was listening for something. She never talks to any of the other women. Camila stood in the door of the cage and scowled.

"You're stupid," she finally said.

*

"You need to be careful with Camila Lopez," Mattie said over the phone. She usually checks in around 11. Now that I'm on nights, I only see her at our monthly supervisions, or when something is really wrong. "Young girls like her behave in very sexualized ways around men. It's how they get attention."

"Sexualized?" I said, too loud. I tried to laugh. "I'm helping her with long division, for Christ's sake."

"Don't be defensive. I'm not accusing you of anything. You're not trained to see these things. You don't know the things I know."

I knew where she was headed. Horace and I are allowed to see the court orders, so we know who can do what—but only caseworkers can read the files. We hear a lot of stuff, but there's always more. I stared at the monitors, at the washed-out olive world surrounding Skyer House, while Mattie talked about positive reinforcement, appropriate buffer zones, and nonverbal cues. I could feel that tightness creeping back, that heat on the back of my neck. At my first weekly supervision, almost a year ago, I told Mattie how angry it made me to think of what these women had been through, what the kids had been through. I twisted a paperclip until it left dark indentations in my fingertips and said if a husband tried anything while I was around he'd end up in worse shape than his wife. Mattie put down my folder and told me to take the next week off to decide whether this was the right job for me. There was nothing angry or disappointed in the way she said it, but nothing encouraging either.

"It's better if you don't care so much," she said. "We don't need another Rambo. That's why most of them are here in the first place."

*

Out in the alley, I asked Horace if he thought there was anything weird about how Camila hugs me or asks me to pick her up. He propped a foot against the wall and blew smoke up toward the windows.

"Someone gotta treat these kids like kids," he said. "Else they grow up thinking everyone's just as fucked up as their mother and father. Thinking one minute you hug someone, next minute they punch you in the gut."

"Kids are naturally affectionate. You don't want to discourage that," I said, but it came out sounding a lot like a question.

A light drizzle pattered against the dumpsters and our breath came out in orange clouds. The alley smelled of burned rubber, like someone had just peeled out around the corner. "You ask me, they should lock both of them up, the mother and the father," Horace said. "You let your kid see that kind of shit, see you putting up with it, now what kind of damn message is that?

"It's weakness," he said on the way inside, gearing up for another one of his rants. "Nothing makes someone want to victimize you more than you being a victim already. They can smell it. Like a shark smells blood a mile away. There's no blood, you can swim right next to a shark and he just leave you alone. But show him you weak...." he said and shut the door to his cage. I watched him sit on his chair and cross his arms, his mouth still moving, the raspy, hollow sound of his voice through the two-way speaker.

Upstairs, I checked all the doors and windows and put on *The Honeymooners*—Ralph steamed again, Alice shaking her fist in his face. I watched Camila in the monitor, her back to the camera as she stared out the meeting room window. Some nights she stands there for hours, wrapped in her Wonder

Woman cape. Maybe she's worried that her father will come to get her. Or maybe she's hoping he will. In the months before Teresa moved out I used to stand at our kitchen window, watching the street. Sometimes I'd see her ex, driving slowly past the building, squinting up at the windows; by the time I got down there he was always gone. Other times, waiting for her to come home, I'd sit with the light off and pray for her car to appear.

After the kids got on the bus I went home and pulled down the shade and slept through the morning. I had the dream again, the one I've been having for months: I'm up on the fourth floor and I've found a room I've never been in. The windows are open, long curtains fluttering, and I don't know if someone's gotten in or gotten out. I rush downstairs but can't make it fast enough, moving in that excruciating slow motion. That's when I usually wake up, but this time there was more. This time it was Mariana's father down on the street, and then Mattie was shouting at me from the bottom of the stairs and I couldn't find my gun. "It's the end of the week!" she kept yelling, as though this kind of thing shouldn't be happening and I fumbled at my holster, trying to make it to the bottom but there were so many stairs, my feet so heavy I knew I'd never make a difference.

*

Mariana's been talking to her husband again, hanging off the fourth-floor payphone every night this week. Her caseworker got it from the night counselor, though Mariana still denies it in their sessions.

"It's the old pattern," says the caseworker, shrugging as the schoolbus pulls away. "She doesn't really have anyone else, no skills, no experience being on her own. It's either go back to her husband or go back to El Salvador." She looks up at the brick wall and bulletproof windows, the crumpled gray sky. "Or stay here."

He's coming to Camila's school every morning, says the caseworker, giving her notes to bring to her mother. This is how it happened last time, she says. She's called the school, the police; no one acts very concerned.

"There's gotta be something you can do," I say. She looks at me like I have three heads. "She can't just go back. I mean, there's a little girl involved."

"I'm aware of that, Charlie," she says.

"Maybe I should ride the bus with them," I say. "Make sure they get in the school alright."

She looks at her hands. "The school has security guards."

"Hell of a job they're doing."

"I'm just saying."

She leans against the wall, looks at me over her glasses. She's my age, or maybe a little younger, with a face that would be pretty if she let it, if she didn't pull her hair back so tight, if she smiled once in a while. Her nose looks like it was broken once. When she talks, her eyes don't blink.

"There must be something we can do," I say.

"We're doing it," she sighs, and goes right into the spiel. "We're giving her choices. We're giving her a place she can be safe, for as long as she needs it."

"What about Camila's choices?" I say, as quietly as I can manage.

The caseworker doesn't answer. It's not really a fair question. She pats me on the arm and walks inside. I can tell by the set of her shoulders how tired she is. I try to imagine her outside of Skyer House—walking in the park or driving, or maybe out on a date, sipping a drink, hair down around her shoulders. But all I can see is that exhausted expression, the lines at the corners of her eyes deepening each day. I picture my own face, shaving in the bathroom mirror. Behind me, my silent apartment, the empty refrigerator and broken stereo, one side of the closet bare where Teresa used to hang her clothes.

*

I got my job at the shelter when Mattie fired the previous guard, a kid named Trevor. She never told me what he actually did to get fired, but she said she'd always known he wouldn't last. In supervision he'd snicker and talk about irony. It was ironic that so many of the women hung crucifixes in their rooms, he told Mattie. It was ironic that their husbands were out there, living normal lives, while these women were locked up like criminals. It wasn't that he didn't have sympathy for them, she said. Just that he saw them as unwitting, the helpless butts of a cruel joke.

But cheap ironies abound at Skyer House and Mattie won't permit you to underestimate the women. "It's mutually assured destruction–just like the bombs," she once told me. We'd just watched an ambulance pull away; one of the women had swallowed a bottle of pills and collapsed at meeting. You can't stop people from fucking up their own lives, Mattie said. You can't even really stop them from fucking up someone else's, if that's what they want to do. All you can do is give them choices, offer them some scaled-down version of freedom, then stand back and cover your ears when they still decide to push the button.

*

"Now I'm going to stand there and wave and then you press this button to let me back in," I tell her. I make her point to the button three times, until I'm convinced she knows the right one. "No playing around," I say. "I wave, you push."

But Camila wants me to talk to her on the intercom. She says I have to ask permission.

"No. You just press the button. That's it."

She crosses her arms and spins around and around in the chair. "But you have to pretend I don't know you. You have to ask if you can come in," she says. She stops spinning and puts her arms around my waist. "Please?"

I glance up at the monitors. The meeting room doors are still closed, the sidewalks and the alley all empty. Horace is in the third-floor kitchen, taking his first break. "You can't ever tell anyone," I say, showing her how to key the intercom. "I'll get in big trouble."

"Okay."

"Promise?" She nods solemnly.

As I'm opening the front door, I turn back to look at her—sitting in my chair, staring at the console, her lips pursed in concentration. Outside on the stoop, I wait for a few seconds and wave to the camera, press the doorbell, grasp the handle. After a moment, the speaker crackles, but there's no voice. It crackles again, just the tail end of whatever Camila tried to say.

"It's Charlie," I tell the speaker, smiling for the camera. That's when I realize I left my keys in the cage. "Can I come in please?"

There's another crackle of the speaker, a quick clicking in and out of the lock, too fast for me to pull it open. I look up into the camera and wait, and she does it again—in and out—not holding the button long enough to open the door.

"Camila, no messing around," I whisper into the speaker. "Open the door now." But when it crackles again I can hear her laughing, saying my name. The lock keeps clicking, too fast, she's playing with that button like a damned video game, like this whole thing is just a game. Then it stops clicking altogether.

For a moment it's quiet outside Skyer House. The front of the building is patterned with lit windows—if someone looks out and sees me standing here, if they tell Mattie about it tomorrow, I can kiss my job goodbye. "Camila open this door," I say, trying to keep my voice down, yanking on the reinforced steel. "Open the damn door, or you'll get a *castigo.*" I'm starting to sweat. There's still no response, another minute I'm standing out there like a fool, then the lock buzzes steadily and I'm back inside.

"Camila," I'm saying, throwing open the vestibule door, ready to pick her up out of my chair and send her upstairs. But Mariana is standing in front of my cage, holding her daughter tightly by the arm. Camila is bawling, hiding her face against her mother's hip, holding the hem of Mariana's sweatshirt in one hand and hitting her other fist against her mother's leg. She turns to look at me, her face red and miserable, and cries harder.

"She just wanted to see how the door worked," I say, a little out of breath, feeling like I should apologize for something. Mariana looks at the floor, still gripping Camila's shoulder. Her sweatshirt hangs nearly to her knees, over old jeans. She looks so young—she could be anyone, a college girl in a dorm, or someone's little sister. Above her head, the monitors are gray and empty.

"She is a very bad girl," Mariana says quietly. Camila hiccups and sniffles. "She doesn't listen to me, she doesn't listen to her father."

"It was my fault," I say, scanning the console, the inside of the cage. "I shouldn't have let her do it."

"*Disculpe,*" Mariana says. "I keep her in the room. She will not bother you."

"It's okay," I say. "It's no big deal." I reach out to put my hand on Camila's head, but she hides behind her mother. Mariana raises her eyes, and for just a second I can imagine her as a young girl, back in El Salvador, before all this. Then I imagine her upstairs on the fourth floor, in the small room she shares with her daughter, staring out at the alley and wondering what the hell happened.

"She's a good girl," I tell Mariana, who blinks at me from the door of my cage. "She's very nice. Just like her mother."

For a second she looks like she's going to smile. But then, just as quickly, she lowers her eyes and slides past me. She mutters another apology and guides Camila to the stairs; I sit back in my chair, watch them move through the monitors, climbing back up to the fourth floor, where they'll be safe for the rest of the night.

*

The next night the front-door chime sounds as Horace and I are heading out for our smoke. I freeze up for a second, sure that it's Camila's father. I have to grind my teeth and tell my feet to follow Horace back to his cage. I have to remind myself that I'm a professional, I'm not paid to understand.

But the guy outside is white, in his thirties, jeans and a dress shirt. He stands there with his hands in his pockets, whistling at the sky. Through the monitors he seems almost friendly, like an insurance agent; if you saw this guy in the supermarket you wouldn't think twice. He's no one we've seen before, probably the husband of a new client, just testing the waters, seeing how much we'll let him get away with.

Horace keys the intercom. "Sorry, we didn't order no pizza," he says.

"I want to see my wife," the guy says. He looks right into the camera, leans forward so his face grows large in the monitor, breaks up into green pixels. His pupils are shrunken to pinheads.

"Visiting hours are over," Horace tells him. "You got two minutes to find somewhere else to be." He keeps his voice even but firm, exactly the way we were taught. He's really good at it—I've seen him put a guy in an armlock while the wife clawed at Horace's face, drawing blood, all without raising his voice. I don't know how you do that, how you lock those feelings away. I wonder if it comes out when he gets home, if the walls of his house have big divots in the plaster where he punches them, like mine do.

"You've got two minutes to go fuck yourself," the guy snarls into the camera. "She's my fucking wife, you piece of shit."

The clock on Horace's console reads 1:08 A.M. and I take out the incident log to start a report. Horace leans back and crosses his arms, trying to wait him out. You never want to get into it with a husband—especially when he's flying on something, like this guy. You keep it friendly as long as you can, let him know the limits, and hope he'll show some good sense and let it go. That almost never happens.

The husband hits the chime again, mashing the button and shouting into the intercom. Any minute now, the women will start coming out of their rooms. We'll see them in the monitors—nightgowned ghosts drifting through the hallways. The chime only sounds in our cages, but somehow they just know. It's like a sixth sense.

"Don't make me call the police," Horace says, rolling his eyes. "Make a better decision than that."

"I'm gonna decide to bust down this door and kick your ass," says the husband. He starts pounding against the door, slamming into it with his shoulder. "You hear me, fuckhead?" he screams, pointing his finger into the camera. "When I get in there I'm gonna rip off your head and shit down your neck. I want to see my fucking wife!"

"Two points for the shit-down-the-neck comment," I say. "This one's creative."

"Yeah, he a real poet," Horace says, reaching for the phone. There are women in the halls now, whispering among themselves, shooing their children back into the rooms. This will be over in five minutes when the police arrive. The only thing to worry about is whether the husband will catch a glimpse of his wife or not. If his wife goes to the window, and her husband looks up and sees her, all bets are off. I've seen a 140-pound husband throw off three cops after seeing his wife in the window. I've seen a guy make it halfway up to the third floor by scaling the front of the building—his wife beating against the glass, trying to put her arms around him. I couldn't stop thinking it wasn't human, that normal people don't behave like this. I watched him in the monitors, clinging to the bricks until the fire department came, his wife being restrained by the counselors—they weren't human, they were more like moths hurling themselves against a light bulb, some frantic, uncontrollable instinct driving them.

This is what Teresa wouldn't say to me, why she couldn't stop going back to her ex, time after time. It's not something that can be explained. It's a force of nature. We were together for two years, and she said she loved me, but I never felt it. They were just words when she said them to me. They had no force.

*

The cops finally pull up, and after the obligatory struggle—the husband spits in one of their faces, they slam him onto the hood of the cruiser, his legs wild and rubbery as they cuff him—

things are under control. Horace and I flip a coin to see who'll go calm the women. I lose, and climb the stairs to the second floor, where they're still whispering in the hall and peering out the windows. Lucille Johnson is on the phone already, slapping her hand against the wall, her face smeared with cold cream. I tell them everything's alright, to go back to bed. I keep my hands open at my sides, like Mattie showed me. I maintain acceptable distance. These women know me, know I'd never hurt them, but it's not a question of what they know. I speak quietly, and do my best not to look at the open bathrobes, the thin nightgowns and worn sweatpants, the shy smile of a woman who leans against the wall and tries to hide the cast on her wrist.

"Who was it, Charlie?" they ask, their eyes nervous, excited. They grab my arms and ask, "Is he going to come back? Where's Mattie?" I don't know whose husband it was, but it seems like she might have slept through it. If not, if she saw her husband downstairs, it could be an even longer night than it's already been.

When I've finally gotten everyone out of the hallways I remember the cigarette in my shirt pocket. Mattie will review tonight's security tapes, so I open the door to the fourth-floor meeting room, look for a pack of matches. As soon as I walk in I can feel the cold breeze—someone left a window open again—and I'm halfway across the room before I notice Mariana standing in the dark, her nightgown camouflaging her against the curtains. She's standing in the same spot Camila always stands, holding her arms around herself, her cheek damp and reddish-silver from the streetlights.

"Are you okay?" I ask quietly. I start to reach out to touch her shoulder but think better of it. Mariana just nods. "It's over," I tell her. "There's nothing to be scared of."

I shut the window and look for a blanket or a robe to put around her, but there's nothing. There's the faintest of reflections in the glass, doubling her face, and the large darkness looming behind her is just me.

"Do you need anything?" I ask. "Is there any way I can help?" As I'm saying it I can hear Mattie's voice in my head, but I just don't believe what she says. I don't believe you can help another human being by not helping them. It makes no goddamn sense.

"You are very nice," Mariana says, her voice barely audible. Her eyes are swollen from crying, the light on her face makes her look girlish and innocent. "Camila, she likes you. She says you are very intelligent."

"She's the smart one," I tell her. "She really is a bright little girl."

Mariana still won't look at me. "It is from her father. He is very intelligent."

I know I shouldn't say anything but I can't help it. "I don't think he's very smart," I tell her.

She starts to say something but stops, and that's when I see that she's holding something, a picture frame which she's pressing to her belly, the fabric of her nightgown taut against her body. I don't have to look to know what that photo is. There's no sound in the room, only the rise and fall of her chest, a siren somewhere in the city, as she holds it out to me.

"I was only seventeen years old," she says, handing me her wedding photo. Her eyes are dark and liquid, her hair tucked behind one small, ringless ear. And as we stare at each other I realize that she hadn't been scared by the commotion outside. She wasn't frightened–she was crying because it wasn't her husband, because he wasn't the one who tried to force his way inside and take her home. She pushes the frame to me, her gaze finally meeting mine, and her need for me to look at that photo, to see in it what she sees, is a tangible force between us, a new kind of gravity, bodies which somehow repel and attract each other at the same time. I look at the security camera in the corner, the little red light blinking slowly, I take her wrists and gently push them away, her skin warm on my hands, my knuckles brushing the fabric of her nightgown.

I open my mouth and all that comes out, whispered, is "Camila." We're standing much closer than we should be, something pushing us even closer, I should take my hands away but I don't. We both take a breath, and I don't know whether in the next instant I'm going to lean down and press my lips to hers or take her small, pale neck between my hands. I don't know what comes over me, but the image is so clear, so imminent, that I snatch my hands away and take a step back, the frame falls at Mariana's feet and shatters.

"Don't move," I tell her, awake now, bending to grab the frame, collecting the shards in the palm of my hand. "Stay here. I can't see it all, dammit," I tell Mariana, whose bare toes are inches from my fingers. "Just hang on, I'll carry you out or something."

There are already faces in the doorway, drawn to the sound of violence. I'm on my hands and knees, running my fingertips over the carpet, invisible splinters burrowing into my skin. Mariana snatches the frame out of my hand and then, despite my warnings, walks right past me in her bare feet. I want to reach up and grab her arm, pull her back, ask why she would do such a thing. But I keep my eyes on the carpet, scrounging around stupidly, all I see is a flutter of cotton, the flash of her calves as she pulls the door shut behind her.

*

A few days later, Camila doesn't come down to the schoolbus with the others. Horace and I stand in the sunshine, a fragile, early-spring morning, and I watch the kids' faces file past. When the bus door closes, I raise an eyebrow to the caseworker, who shrugs and turns away, heads upstairs before I can catch her.

"Smoke?" Horace says, reaching into his pocket. He casually moves between me and the door. The bus turns out of the alley, sunlight warbling off the back windows.

"I think I'll go see what's wrong with Camila," I tell him, but he grabs my elbow as I try to move past.

"Have a cigarette first," he says. "You go in a few minutes." His hand on my arm is friendly but firm, his expression studiously neutral. I know that expression, have seen it on my own face, practiced it in mirrors.

"What's going on?" I say.

Horace looks past me. "What do you mean?"

By the time I'm halfway up the stairs I can hear Mattie's voice in the front hallway and I know something terrible has happened. I take the stairs two at a time, hands clenched, wondering how I could have missed it. At the top of the stairs I nearly barrel into the four people standing outside my cage.

"Good morning, Charlie," says Mattie, taking a half-step forward to look me in the eyes. "Can you wait in my office a moment, please?"

Before I can say anything, Camila runs to me and wraps her arms around my leg, pressing her face into my thigh. Her mother calls to her, but she holds onto me, sniffling into my leg. Her father says nothing, frowning and watching her over his mustache, holding Mariana's hand. Mariana says something in

Spanish and he nods. He's shorter than his wife, wearing freshly ironed black pants and a collared shirt. Mariana clutches the roses to her chest. Her suitcase sits by the door, Camila's small backpack slumped on top of it.

"Camila, *ven*," says Mariana, her voice steadier than I've heard it.

Mattie says my name again, but I don't look at her. My hand rests on Camila's head, stroking her hair.

"*Hija, ven*," says the husband. Camila looks up at me, wanting me to tell her what to do, but I won't take my eyes off her father. Finally, she lets go and straggles back to her parents. Her father crouches to whisper in her ear. She shakes her head, but he turns her around, urges her back to me.

"He said thank you for being my friend," she translates. Mattie has her hands on her hips, watching me intently, but no one can control what's about to happen, least of all me.

"Tell him I'm not his friend," I say.

Camila starts to giggle. "No, stupid," she says. "*My* friend. Me."

Mariana starts to say something, but I've already taken a step forward, drawn myself up—it's like I can see it happening, like I'm watching the whole thing, that fucking animal shrinking away from me, trying to get his arms up, but not in time, and the sting of his face against my open hand sends a shiver through me, the sharp smack ringing in the air as he half-twirls, slides against the wall, stumbles over his wife's suitcase and sprawls to the floor. Then I'm standing over him, just waiting for him to get up, just waiting, Camila is crying, everyone shouting, but it all seems to come from somewhere else. For that instant it's just me and him, staring at each other, one of us stronger than the other, locked in a moment of perfect communication.

"Now you done it," says a voice behind me, there are arms wrapping me into a bear hug, Horace nearly lifts me off the ground, pushes me against the far wall. He stands inches from me, containing me without anger, Mattie shaking her head and Mariana sheltering her sobbing daughter, the roses strewn across the floor.

"Stand right there," Horace says quietly, barring an arm against my chest. "Don't you move." He reaches around and undoes my belt, removes the holster, faces peering from the top of the stairs, tense voices whispering. I stand with my palms flat against the wall, my throat so tight I can't swallow, while Camila's father picks himself up and smooths out his clothes, reaches for his wife's arm. It's hard to tell who's leaning on whom.

Mattie opens the door and the lobby floods with sunshine. Mariana picks up her howling daughter, her husband's arm around both of them as they walk out of Skyer House. Over her mother's shoulder, Camila looks at me one last time, her face smeared with tears, her eyes wide open and afraid.

The door swings shut and Horace backs off, still wary, ready to tackle me if I try to go after them. "Shit, Charlie, what in hell are you thinking," he says, trying to make eye contact. His voice sounds like it's coming through a tunnel. "You know that motherfucker just gonna take it out on her."

There's noise in the stairwell, women applauding, hooting and calling down congratulations. "You're my hero, Charlie!" comes Lucille Johnson's voice. I walk back to my cage—slowly, hands in the air so Horace will know I'm not a danger anymore. I sit at the console and find them in the monitors, watch them move from camera to camera, Camila's face buried in her mother's shoulder, her father's arm across Mariana's back. The image skips from one monitor to the next, the angle changing as a new camera picks them up, so for a second it almost looks like they're coming back.

Soon they've passed beyond the cameras. I can see Mattie on the stoop, catching her breath, waiting to come inside and fire me. I can hear her doing it, that businesslike voice telling me it's for the good of the shelter. I can't blame her. I've given her no choice.

She'll say it's for my own good, too. She'll smile weakly and suggest I think about counseling. She'll say it's up to me to decide what to do now. Then she'll ask for my keys and tell me never to come back.

But first she'll bring me into her office and close the door, and from a desk drawer she'll take out the tape from the other night. She'll ask me if I know what's on that tape and I'll nod, unable to speak. She'll put the tape in the player and let herself out, leaving me alone in her tidy, windowless office. And while she's upstairs, setting everything back to normal, I'll watch that tape again and again, sit right up close to the monitor and stare at the grainy image of a man–standing outside the shelter, coming in the door. I'll keep hitting the rewind button, watching him forward and backward, and wonder if that's what I really look like in the flat gray world outside the door.

En los parques, al anochecer

Marina Mayoral

La presidenta de las señoras de Acción Católica me ha pedido que escriba mi autobiografía. Quieren publicarla en una edición corta, muy cuidada, no venal, que se regalará a los miembros de la asociación para que sirva de ejemplo a sus hijas en estos tiempos tan libres que vivimos. Cuentan con la ayuda económica del ayuntamiento, que ya ha aprobado por unanimidad la propuesta en el último pleno. No me sorprende: casi todos los concejales han pasado por mi escuela y conservan un recuerdo cariñoso de su antigua maestra. Se trata—así lo he entendido—de un homenaje a tantos años de dedicación a los niños y de un reconocimiento a mi labor y mis méritos.

Yo he agradecido a la presidenta la iniciativa de las señoras de Acción Católica y la generosa colaboración del ayuntamiento, pero les he hecho ver las dificultades del proyecto, los gastos y el esfuerzo que supone y los escasos beneficios que pueden derivarse de ello. ¿A quién va a interesarle hoy la vida de una oscura maestra de escuela? Y, sobre todo, ¿a quién le será útil?

In the Parks, At Nightfall

Marina Mayoral
Translated by: Edward T. Gurski

The president of the ladies of the Catholic Action organization has asked me to write my autobiography. They want to publish it in a very fine edition—professional, not commercial—that they will give to the members of the association to serve as an example for young girls in these loose times in which we live. They are counting on the economic support of the local government which unanimously approved the proposal during their last session. It does not surprise me: almost all of the members of the town council have attended my school and maintain an affectionate memory of their old teacher. The project, as I have understood it, is an homage or tribute for so many years of dedication to the children, and in recognition of my work and merits.

I have thanked the president for the initiative of the ladies of Catholic Action and for the generous collaboration of the town hall, but I am obliged to see the difficulties for them in the project, the expenses and the effort required, and the scant benefits that can be derived. Who is going to be interested today in the life of an obscure school teacher and, above all, for whom will it be useful?

De mis primeros años poco puedo contar. Fui una niña buena y una joven seria. Mis hermanos se casaron y se fueron con sus mujeres. Sin que nadie lo formulara de manera explícita, se dio por hecho que yo cuidaría de papá y mamá y de la tía Sabina, que no tenía un duro. Nosotros no éramos tampoco ricos, pero mi padre tenía un retiro decente y la casa era nuestra, herencia de mi madre. Con eso y con mi sueldo de maestra vivíamos sin estrecheces aunque modestamente.

A los treinta años me di cuenta de que era una solterona. No es que fuera más fea o más antipática que otras chicas del pueblo que se casaron. Creo que, sencillamente, tuve mala suerte. La guerra me cogió con diecisiete años y cuando acabó había pocos hombres y muchas mujeres donde escoger. Yo era tímida y algo sosa; nunca he tenido picardía y pienso que ésa fue la causa de que ningún hombre del pueblo me echase cuentas.

Como el trabajo de maestra me dejaba muchas horas libres y mis padres todavía podían valerse por sí mismos me puse a estudiar idiomas; primero francés y después inglés, italiano, alemán.... El conocimiento de lenguas extranjeras fue fundamental en mi vida y me ayudó a realizarme plenamente como mujer y como ser humano.

A los treinta y tres años—una edad en la que tantos grandes hombres acabaron su vida—decidí hacer un viaje a Francia, a París. Ya leía con bastante soltura y me ilusionaba practicar la lengua hablada y conocer una ciudad que entonces me parecía el centro del mundo.

En París un hombre me besó por primera vez. Fue para mí una experiencia extraña y turbadora—*bouleversante* pensaba yo en mi incipiente francés—pero que no consigo evocar con nitidez a pesar de la honda huella que dejó en mi espíritu.

I remember little of my early years. I was a good girl and a serious teenager. My brothers got married and they lived with their wives. Without anyone posing it explicitly, it was given that I would be the one to take care of our parents and our aunt, Sabina, who did not have a dime. We were not rich either, but my father had a decent pension and the house was ours, inherited by my mother. With that, and my income as a teacher, we lived modestly but without financial difficulties.

At thirty years old, I was already an old maid. It is not as if I was uglier or less pleasant than the other girls in the town who married. I believe that I simply had bad luck. I was seventeen in 1936 when the Spanish Civil War caught me, and when it was over in 1939 there were few men left and many women from which to choose. I was shy and somewhat boring. I had never shown any naughtiness and I think that was why no man from town paid attention to me.

Since my work as a teacher left me a lot of free time, and my parents were still able to take care of themselves, I began to study foreign languages: first French, then English, Italian, German, *et cetera*. The knowledge of foreign languages was fundamental in my life and helped me to fulfill myself completely as a woman and a human being.

At thirty-three years old—an age by which so many great men had already died—I decided to travel to France, to Paris. I already read the language fairly fluently and I dreamed of practicing the spoken language and knowing a city that seemed to me to be the center of the world.

In Paris, a man kissed me for the first time. For me it was a strange and disturbing experience—*boulervesante*, I thought in my incipient French—but could not express with precision, in spite of the deep impression it left on my spirit.

Vi a aquel hombre en un café, en el barrio latino. Me di cuenta de que me observaba y me puse colorada hasta las orejas, cosa habitual en mí. Fingí abstraerme en el estudio del plano de la ciudad, pero él vino a mi mesa y se ofreció para servirme de guía. No había tenido muchas ocasiones de hablar, dada mi timidez, y acepté. Salimos juntos del café y paseamos por la orilla del Sena hasta el Vert-Galant. Allí, él me pasó el brazo por los hombros mientras me contaba no sé qué historia sobre un templario quemado vivo. Yo no atendía a lo que decía, sólo oía los latidos desbocados de mi corazón. Cuando me empujó contra un macizo de plantas y me hizo caer al suelo me asusté. Quise gritar, pero él me metió su lengua en la boca y me apretó con su cuerpo contra el suelo. Todo sucedió como en un sueño. No sé si eran mis lágrimas o si, en efecto, había niebla, pero todo lo recuerdo envuelto en una bruma gris y espesa, todo solitario y en silencio; sólo se oía su jadeo y después el sonido de mis pasos al correr. Volví al hotel, disimulando lo mejor possible mis medias destrozadas, el desorden del pelo y las manchas de sangre en la ropa. Recogí el equipaje y regresé inmediatamente al pueblo.

Cuando me tranquilicé, me di cuenta de que me había gustado. Recordaba con un estremecimiento de placer el sabor de su boca, su aliento, la violencia de su abrazo y, sobre todo, su entrega. Sí, su entrega: la presión de sus brazos y de su cuerpo aprisionando el mío y después su laxitud, su dulce languidez. Era una sensación compleja, excitante y sobrecogedora, que trastornó mi tranquila existencia de maestra de escuela de un pueblo de menos de diez mil habitantes. Supe que tenía que volver a sentir aquello, que la vida era insípida y gris si no podía sazonarla,

I saw that man in a café, in the Latin Quarter. I realized that he was staring at me and I blushed up to my ears, a normal thing for me. I pretended to absorb myself in studying the map of the city, but he came over to my table and offered to serve as my guide. I had not had many chances to speak in such situations, given my shyness, so I accepted. We left the café together and walked along the bank of the Seine to Vert-Galant. There he put his arm around my shoulders while he told me some story about an ancient knight who was burned alive. I was not paying attention to what he was saying, only listening to the runaway beating of my heart. When he pushed me against a bed of plants, knocking me to the ground, I was frightened. I wanted to scream, but he stuck his tongue in my mouth and pressed me down against the ground with his body. Everything happened as if it were a dream. I do not know if it was my tears or if, in fact, it was misty out, but I remember everything wrapped in a gray and dense fog, completely solitary and silent; I only heard his gasping and then the sound of my steps as I ran away. I returned to the hotel, hiding as best I could my ruined stockings, my disheveled hair and the blood stains on my clothes. I gathered up my bags and returned immediately to my town in Spain.

When I calmed down, I realized that I had liked it. I remembered, with a shiver of pleasure, the taste of his mouth, his breath, the violence of his hug, and above all, his strength. Yes, his taking me: the pressure of his arms and his body imprisoning mine, and afterwards his sweet listlessness. It was a complex sensation, exciting and overwhelming at the same time, that disturbed my calm existence as a school teacher in a town of less than ten thousand people. I knew that I had to feel that again, that my life was insipid and gray if I was not able to season

iluminarla con aquel placer que me arrebataba y me transportaba a un mundo al que sólo me había asomado, pero al que ya no podía renunciar.

No fue un paso fácil. Tardé algún tiempo en decidirme a hacer otro viaje. Al comienzo me satisfacía con la simple evocación de lo ocurrido, pero al cabo de unos meses sentí la imperiosa necesidad de vivir de nuevo aquella experiencia.

Volví a París, porque con el pretexto de practicar el idioma podía dejar unos días a mis padres y a mi tía sin más explicaciones.

Empecé ya a disfrutar y a excitarme con los preparativos del viaje, aunque me asaltaba el temor de no poder llevarlo a buen término. ¿Y si la primera vez había sido todo obra de la casualidad? Quizá nunca más un hombre volvería a mirarme con ojos de deseo ni se lanzaría sobre mí como una fiera hambrienta. Pero mis temores resultaron vanos. Tuve suerte o quizá lo que sucedía era que, lejos del pueblo, se desarrollaba en mí un oscuro instinto, un atractivo sutil que la rutina de mi trabajo y mi timidez coartaban allí.

He de decir, sin falsas modestias, que nunca en mis viajes me costó gran esfuerzo atraer a un hombre y que, incluso, me permití escoger. Muy pronto me percaté de que para llegar al culmen del placer, a una satisfacción completa y total tenía que hacerlo con un hombre de características especiales, que respondiese al tipo que se considera más viril: fornido, bien musculado, de barba cerrada y abundante vello corporal, olor fuerte y, sobre todo, de impulsos violentos. Me producía un placer indescriptible sentirme oprimida, estrujada, aplastada por un cuerpo poderoso, sabiendo que, al final, se entregaría, se plegaría a mi cuerpo y yo bebería su aliento mientras él languidecía entre mis brazos, sobre la hierba húmeda . . . Porque me gustaba hacerlo en los parques y al anochecer. Creo que esto fue un pequeño vicio, una manía que se me quedó de aquella

it, to illuminate it with that pleasure that shook and transported me to a world I had just looked into, but already could not renounce.

It was not an easy step, no. I delayed some time in deciding to take another trip. At first the simple evocation of what had happened satisfied me, but after some months I felt an urgent need to repeat that experience.

I returned to Paris with the pretext of practicing the language, so I was able to leave my parents and aunt for a few days without further explanation.

Now, I began to enjoy and get excited about the preparations for the trip, although the fear of not being able to accomplish it, to carry it to a good ending, assaulted me. And what if the first time had been a complete accident? Maybe no man would look at me again with eyes of desire nor throw himself on me like a hungry animal. But my fears turned out to be imaginary. I was lucky, or maybe what was happening was that, far from my town, some dark instinct was developing in me, a subtle attraction that the routine of my work and my shyness restricted there.

I have to say, without false modesty, that in my travels it never took a great effort to attract a man and also that I permitted myself to choose. Very soon I came to understand that to arrive at the peak of pleasure, to reach complete and total satisfaction, I had to do it with a man of special characteristics, one who matched the type I considered most virile: big, muscular, with a strong chin and abundant body hair, a strong odor, and above all, with violent impulses. To feel physically overwhelmed produced in me an indescribable pleasure—pressed down, crushed by a powerful body, knowing that in the end he would submit to my body and I would drink in his breath while he lay listless between my arms on the wet grass . . . because I liked to do it in the parks at nightfall. I believe that this was a small vice, a peculiarity that I acquired

primera experiencia en el Vert-Galant. No siempre he podido darme ese gusto, pero cuando lo consigo mi placer es perfecto, absoluto, incomparable.

Despúes de la segunda vez me puse a estudiar inglés con aplicación y al cabo de seis meses me sentía capacitada para hacer un viaje a Londres. Más tarde fueron Roma, Berlín, Colonia...; siempre grandes ciudades y siempre previo estudio del idioma correspondiente.

Estos viajes no sólo me han proporcionado todo el placer de que he disfrutado en mi vida sino que me permitieron hacer bien a los demás. Los niños de mi escuela aprendieron conmigo los rudimentos de idiomas que les permitieron destacar en su trabajo de adultos o, al menos, emigrar en mejores condiciones. Su contribución a mi homenaje es buena prueba de que estiman lo que hice por ellos. Y otro tanto he de decir de la paciencia y cariño con que atendí a mis padres en su larga enfermedad y a mí tía Sabina en su vejez de inválida exidente. Eran mis propias cuñadas quienes, avergonzadas de que todo el peso de la familia cayese sobre mí, me animaban a emprender aquellos viajes de los que siempre volvía con renovados ánimos.

No digo esto por disculparme. Yo sé que lo que hacía puede parecer moralmente censurable, pero ésta es una cuestión entre Dios y yo, y con nadie más accederé a discutirlo. La única persona a quien revelé en parte aquella necesidad mía de poseer de vez en cuando a un hombre fue a mi confesor, a don Luis, un alma pura, un verdadero santo que comprendía que de alguna parte había de sacar yo fuerzas para vivir encerrada todo el año con tres viejos enfermos y una patulea de niños alborotadores. Pero no acababa de entenderlo por completo. Me decía:—Hija mía, ya

from that first experience in Vert-Galant. I have not always been able to give myself that pleasure, but when I manage it, my pleasure is perfect, absolute, incomparable.

After the second time, I began to apply myself to the study of English and after six months I felt qualified to take a trip to London. Later it was Rome, Berlin, Cologne, always big cities and always with prior study of the corresponding language.

These trips not only have provided me all of the pleasure that I have enjoyed in my life but also allowed me to help others. The children in my school learned with me the rudiments of languages that permitted them to stand out in their work as adults or, at least, to emigrate from Spain under better circumstances. Their contribution to my tribute is good proof that they esteem what I did for them. And I also have to mention the patience and affection with which I attended to my parents during their long illnesses, and to my aunt Sabina in her demanding old age as an invalid. It was my sisters-in-law who, ashamed that all the weight of the family fell on me, encouraged me to undertake those journeys from which I always returned with renewed spirits.

I do not say this to forgive myself. I know that what I did could seem morally reprehensible, but this is a matter between God and me, and I will not agree to discuss it with anybody. The only person to whom I revealed, in part, my need to possess a man from time to time was my confessor, Father Luis, a pure soul, a true saint who understood that I had to find strength somewhere in order to live shut up all year with three sick old people and a mob of boisterous children. But he did not understand it completely. He told me: "My child, since you are not able to do without that, why do you not do it with someone

que no puedes prescindir de eso, ¿por qué no lo haces con uno del pueblo? A lo mejor os arregláis y te casas, y no tienes que andar por esos mundos de Dios.

Pero a mí, precisamente, lo que me gustaba era el anonimato, el desconocimiento del otro, el encuentro rápido, animal, de dos cuerpos que se desean y luchan hasta que uno vence. Sólo eso. Y cuando no es así, cuando el otro se empeña en hablar, en contar cosas de su vida e indagar sobre la mía, entonces yo no puedo. Lo único que puedo hacer es sacrificarme, como con mis niños y mis viejos, dejar que el otro disfrute de su placer, sin ninguna satisfacción por mi parte.

Don Luis no podía entenderlo, ni yo quise nunca entrar en detalles, pero la cosa era bien clara y para mí no tenía dudas desde que pasó lo del Eusebio.

Un día, muertos ya mis padres, cuando andaba yo por los cuarenta y tantos, Eusebio, el de los ultramarinos, que había vuelto de Alemania con dinero, se me metió en casa con un pretexto tonto y me arrinconó en el pasillo de abajo, junto a la escalera. Jadeaba y farfullaba incoherencias mientras me apretaba contra su cuerpo. Olía a sudor acre y por el cuello entreabierto de la camisa le asomaba una mata de vello negro y lustroso. Me gustaba. Siempre me ha gustado enredar los dedos en el vello y sentir la piel húmeda y el latir de la sangre en el cuello, en el sexo, en el pecho. Busqué como otras veces la fuente de aquel latido violento que pasaba de su cuerpo al mío y me dejé arrebatar por él. Mi boca se pegó a su boca, mi mano buscaba ansiosa su corazón, iba ya a poseerlo cuando, inesperadamente, el Eusebio se apartó un segundo para mirarme a la cara y me dijo:

—Y por la tía Sabina no te preocupes: la juntamos con mi madre y tan contentas las dos.

from town? You make an arrangement with someone and he marries you, and then you do not have to wander all over God's world."

But for me, precisely, what pleased me was the anonymity, the lack of knowledge of the other, the quick encounter, animal-like, of two bodies that desire each other and fight until one conquers the other. Only that. And when it is not like that, when the other insists on talking, on relating things about his life and inquiring about mine, then I cannot. The only thing I can do then is sacrifice myself, as with my students or my aging parents and aunt, to let the other enjoy his pleasure, without any satisfaction on my part.

Father Luis was not able to understand it, nor did I ever want to give details, but the matter was very clear to me and I had no doubts after what happened with Eusebio.

One day, my parents already dead—I was in my forties—Eusebio, one of the Spanish emigrants who had returned from Germany with money, got into the house with a silly excuse and cornered me in the downstairs hallway, next to the stairs. He was panting and sputtering incoherently while he pressed me against his body. He smelled of bitter sweat and through the open collar of his shirt protruded a matt of black, shiny hair. I liked that. I have always liked to run my fingers through that soft hair and feel the sweaty skin and the beating of the blood in the neck, and in the chest of the man. As at other times I searched for the source of that violent beating that was passing from his body to mine and I let myself be captivated by it. My mouth pressed against his, my hand searched anxiously for his heart, I was already going to possess it when, unexpectedly, Eusebio moved back a second to look me in the face and he said to me, "And don't worry about your poor aunt, Sabina. We can put her together with my mother and the two of them will be so happy."

No pude seguir. Guardé la navaja en el bolsillo de la falda y lo rechacé. Le dije que venía gente o algo parecido y nunca le di la oportunidad de acercárseme otra vez.

No fue el temor lo que me llevó a actuar de ese modo. Yo hubiera podido tener mi satisfacción como otras veces y decir después que me había atacado y que yo me había defendido. ¿Quién dudaría de mi palabra? ¿Quién pensaría en otros motivos? Pero si no sentía placer, ¿para qué hacerlo? Así que tuve que seguir con mis viajes, que cada vez, hay que decirlo, presentan mayores dificultades, porque no es fácil a mi edad encontrar un hombre que reúna las características que yo necesito. Otras mujeres buscan compañia, ternura, amistad, entendimiento intelectual o espiritual, o, incluso, un simple placer fisiológico que puede comprarse con dinero. Yo no. Para mí, placer quiere decir deseo puro y mutuo, encuentro de dos cuerpos anónimos, lucha y posesión completa, total.

Pero me temo que esto no lo van a entender las congresistas de Acción Católica, ni los concejales del ayuntamiento, ni los ex alumnos que han colaborado en mi homenaje. Por eso le he dicho a la presidenta que será mejor que me den una comida y una de esas bandejas de plata que llevan los nombres de todos los participantes, y que, acaso más adelante, cuando yo haya muerto, publiquen estos papeles por si a alguien pudieran serle útiles.

I could not continue. I put the knife away in the pocket of my skirt and I rejected him. I told him that people were coming, or something like that, and I never again gave him the opportunity to get near me.

It was not fear that made me act that way. I would have been able to have my satisfaction like the other times and say later that he had attacked me and that I had defended myself. Who would doubt my word? Who would think of any other motive? But if I did not feel pleasure, why do it? So I had to continue my travels, and I have to say that each time presents greater difficulties, because at my age it is not easy to find a man who meets the characteristics I need. Other women seek company, kindness, friendship, intellectual or spiritual understanding, including a simple physical pleasure that one can buy with money. Not me. For me, pleasure means pure and mutual desire, the meeting of two anonymous bodies, battle and possession, complete and total.

But I am afraid that the delegates of Catholic Action are not going to understand this, nor the members of the town government, nor the former students who have collaborated on this tribute to me. So I have told the president that it will be better to give me a dinner and one of those silver platters that bears the names of all the participants, and that perhaps later on, when I have died, they can publish these papers in case someone would be able to find them useful.

How to Clean Up Any Stain

Danit Brown

If there's a simple, logical explanation for everything–or, at least, an elegant one–then somewhere in Ann Arbor another man was running around with Marvin's name. There was plenty of support for this theory: people Marvin had never spoken to kept telling him they were so glad to hear from him again; letters from the library, complaining that he'd hung on too long to books with titles like *How to Clean Up Any Stain*, and *Dinner for One?*; and, to cap it all off, the dentist, who told him she'd been expecting someone else before pointing at the spittoon. "Rinse," she ordered. "I haven't seen teeth like that since they started fluoridating water."

No wonder then that Marvin had trouble smiling. And if there was comfort in numbers, it wasn't much: his daughter and wife had cavities too.

"So we had a bad dentist in Tel-Aviv," Ayala told him. "It isn't a sign, you know."

But to Marvin, it seemed like a close call, evidence that moving back to the States had been necessary: hadn't he only narrowly managed to whisk Ayala and Osnat away before their teeth rotted out completely? He stood in front of the mirror in the men's room and bared his teeth in what looked like a snarl. They seemed more crowded than he remembered, his incisors worn down, as if he'd spent an inordinate amount of time gnawing on something: a bone? a stick? a chew toy?

Back in his office, he pulled out the university phone directory and looked himself up. There he was: Marvin Greenberg, Mathematics. And there he was again: Marvin A. Greenberg, Statistics. What were the odds? He consulted a map and discovered that the statistics department was across campus, tucked in with computer science and operations research. And somewhere over there was another Marvin Greenberg, one with a middle name that started with A, who spent his evenings learning to cook dinners for one while his library fines kept right on accumulating.

*

On the way home, Marvin stopped at the Village Corner and bought himself a can of Sprite. He loved Sprite. In Israel, it came in glass bottles that exploded if they got too hot, so he never bought any: he didn't want Osnat's possible disfigurement on his conscience. Instead, he had Sprite only in secret, when the speech therapist he went to in order to lose his American accent had him gargle to practice his *R*s. Not that it helped—he may as well have walked around with "rich and gullible" scrawled on his forehead, the way Israelis tried to take him for every lira he had. He had put in thirteen hot, difficult years drinking non-carbonated, vile grapefruit *Mitz Paz*—because, to tell the truth, he didn't trust the water—and now he was paying the price with three cavities and the ridicule of his dentist (No doubt Marvin A. Greenberg had perfect teeth, without even a hint of yellow). Still, as some sort of acknowledgement of Ayala's misery, and of the fact that everything tasted different here—even yogurt, even cheese—he continued to avoid drinking Sprite at home, even though in Michigan it came in plastic bottles. He knew it was asking a lot, moving them all here. But hadn't she asked a lot too? And even if she hadn't, technically, hadn't he done a lot anyway? Besides, it was a warm day, and how would Ayala ever find out?

When he got home, Ayala was on the phone to her sister in Israel. She called her sister every week, sometimes twice. "Uh huh," she was saying. "Uh huh . . . uh huh . . . ." There was no telling what they were talking about. Sometimes, after watching Ayala nod vigorously for up to twenty minutes, she would finally say something and Marvin would realize that all they were talking about was the weather, or a recipe for *pashtida*. It seemed like a waste. Phone calls were expensive, and Marvin thought that if all you were going to do was nod and say *uh huh*, it was more economical to write a letter.

In the living room, Osnat was watching the six o'clock news for signs of the nuclear war she was sure was upon them, and writing her weekly letter to Ronald Reagan. Marvin didn't know where she got her paranoia. He and Ayala had tried to explain to her that a nuclear holocaust was unlikely, and that, even if it wasn't, the Soviets would be satisfied taking out only New York and Washington, D.C., both of which were hundreds of miles away. It was as if Osnat didn't know what to do with all the vigilance she'd learned living in Israel, and turned it instead against the sky, constantly gauging its color and appraising the changes in the weather: were clouds really supposed to look green? Was that thunder, or a fighter jet? In Osnat's yearbook, kid after kid had written, "Have a great summer, and try not to worry about the nukes." Not that Osnat listened. Instead, she fired off missives to the White House. There was something pathetic about her diligence. Sure, there had been that girl, Samantha Smith, who got a trip to the Soviet Union out of it, but she had written only one letter, and she had sent it to Andropov, and she had been ten and not nearly fourteen, like Osnat. Still, it wasn't as if Marvin's heart were made of stone. After the third form letter, he started intercepting the replies from the White House and swapping in his own: "Thanks so much for writing. I'm doing all I can for world peace, so please don't worry so much about nuclear war. Concentrate on getting good grades instead." It was surprisingly easy to write letters as Ronald Reagan, and by the sixth or seventh he was including little details about Nancy renovating the Oval Office, trips to the National Zoo, and descriptions of state meals that included disgusting foods like snails and frog legs. He'd hand Osnat the latest letter and ask her what was new with the Commander in Chief, but if Osnat was excited to hear about reupholstering the chair Lincoln had sat in, she sure did a good job of hiding it. Instead she rolled her eyes as if there was nobody on earth more boring than Marvin, and she did it so convincingly that sometimes he found himself worrying that maybe there wasn't.

*

Okay, so Marvin had been lax about getting them all to a dentist. They'd been in Ann Arbor nearly two years, renting a house in a neighborhood near the stadium. There really was no excuse for waiting so long, except that he was busy at work. Thank God for the modem, or he'd never be home at all. Anyway, it was easy to forget your teeth when they didn't hurt, and when you had forty exams to grade, eight dissertations to go through, three lectures to prepare, and two grants to write. But now it was August, and Saturday, and summer, and—at least on the home front—he was finally catching up: dentist, oil change, lawn mower, storm windows. With all the chores done, there was no good reason not to go looking for the other Marvin Greenberg.

"I don't know," Ayala said. "Maybe you should go alone—what if I see him and like him better?"

"The man is learning to cook from a library book."

"Not a bad idea," Ayala said. "Maybe you should try it."

It was hard to tell when she was joking, so instead Marvin invited Osnat to come along and together they walked over to Marvin A. Greenberg's building, which was covered with sheets of ivy that rustled with birds getting ready for the long trip south. Inside, the hallways were tiled and neutral, like something out of a hospital. Marvin pointed at Marvin A. Greenberg's name on the building directory in the lobby. "There's another man here with my name," he told Osnat. "Only he's a statistician." When Osnat didn't look impressed, he added, "What are the odds?" Of course, she didn't get it.

They took the elevator to the third floor, and walked up and down the hallway, reading the names on the offices. No one was in, and Marvin A. Greenberg's door, when they found it, was locked. Still, there were plenty of clues: the door was covered with cartoons about dogs, of all things, and alternate lyrics to Frank Sinatra: "Bayesians in the night, assessing chances, we'll be sharing risk before the night is through. . . ." Marvin groaned.

"*Ma?*" Osnat asked.

"Speak English," Marvin told her. She needed the practice, and anyway, English was easier for Marvin—he'd almost forgotten how easy. There were thousands of words in English: all he had to do was open his mouth, and there they were.

"What?" Osnat asked again.

"Bayesians are statisticians—they figure out probabilities," Marvin explained. "Maybe three people in the world get this joke."

"So he is like you," Osnat said, then scurried out of reach so that he wouldn't swat her.

"Actually," Marvin said, "my jokes are much funnier. You'll discover that once your English gets better."

*

In the city phone book—what luck—the other Marvin Greenberg had no problem with listing his full name: Marvin Alvin Greenberg, as if Marvin and Greenberg together didn't already invoke massive amounts of nostril hair, golf pants, and game after game of shuffleboard. The other Marvin Greenberg's brazenness made Marvin, who was careful to keep his own middle name—Sheldon—under wraps, a little nervous. Over the years, he had developed a theory that in any group of people there was a finite set of naturally occurring roles. Usually, he found this oddly comforting, a kind of catchall explanation for why certain things worked, and others didn't: someone had to be the best, and someone had to be new, and someone had to be the idiot. All you had to do was figure out who had occupied your position before to see where you were going to end up. It was how he stayed focused, able to believe that all Ayala and Osnat needed was time, that eventually they'd realize he wasn't asking too much, only doing what others in his same position had done before him. Take the group of Israelis he and Ayala occasionally met for dinner: Israeli women and their American, academic husbands who kept stumbling over the gendered nouns in Hebrew and nodded when their wives talked longingly about tomatoes and cucumbers, when really, deep down, they were glad—ecstatic even—to be back in the States, throwing big, bloody slabs of meat on the backyard barbecue and eating them in front of a color TV. It wasn't anything they said, but he could see it anyway—their relief was something palpable, like sweat or body odor. And it wasn't as though he and Ayala particularly liked any of them—he certainly would have never chosen to be friends with any of the men—but being with them was a lot like checking your reflection in the mirror: if your reflection seemed fine, then you probably were too.

Of course, he was well aware that this all was abstraction, mere speculation, and nothing compared to the startling concreteness of another man who possessed your name, an occupation that was a more practical variation of your own, and the kind of self-confidence you only wished you had. And who topped it all off with cavity-free teeth.

"It only costs $50 to pull a tooth," Marvin told Ayala after they brushed their teeth that night. "It's cheaper than a filling."

"Are you crazy?" Ayala said. "I'm keeping all my teeth."

"Not you," Marvin said. "Me." He wiped his mouth with a towel. "Who would know? They're way back there."

"I'd know," Ayala said. "You're going to get fillings, like a normal person."

"Or maybe a gold tooth. Then we could cash it in when I retire, and move to Florida." Marvin could tell Ayala was getting mad by the way she screwed the cap back on the toothpaste tube without wiping off the excess toothpaste. Still, he kept going: "Then I could be the Marvin Greenberg with the gold tooth."

"Or the one without a wife," Ayala said.

"He doesn't have a wife," Marvin said. "He's cooking for one, not for two."

"Maybe she's on a diet," Ayala said. Then she sighed. "Anyway, I thought we were going back to Israel when we retire."

"We are," Marvin said. "Of course we are. Why wouldn't we?"

*

Another letter had arrived from the White House, thanking Osnat for sharing her concerns and assuring her that though a more personal reply was not possible, Ronald Reagan was doing his best for the country. After dropping Ayala off at the dentist, Marvin drove into work to borrow the secretary's typewriter. When Marvin first started writing the letters, he'd worried about not having anything that could pass as official White House stationary, but then he figured that his version of Ronald Reagan would use his own personal stash of paper anyway—it was more intimate. "Dear Osnat," he wrote. "With fall semester starting soon, Nancy and I hope you will do your part to make trickle-down economics work by going back-to-school shopping with your mother." Sometimes he really cracked himself up; he hoped Osnat was saving the letters somewhere. Sure, if Samantha Smith hadn't gotten there first and written Andropov, it could have been the three of them touring Red Square and writing best-selling books about how the Soviets are people too, but wasn't this letter exchange meaningful in its own, more private way? Wouldn't Osnat look back one day and think, "Boy, my father really must have loved me to intercept all that mail?"

Ayala was in a bad mood when he picked her up from the dentist. "Am I drooling?" she kept asking. "I feel like I'm drooling." She squeezed her bottom lip between her thumb and index finger. "Nothing," she reported.

"So it didn't hurt?" Marvin asked, hopeful.

"Are you crazy? Of course it hurt." She tugged at her lip. "I feel like a cow," she said. "Give me some hay or something."

"I wrote Osnat another letter," Marvin said.

Ayala sighed. "You know I wish you wouldn't do that."

"Come on," Marvin said. "It's fun."

Maybe he was imagining it, but Ayala rolled her eyes. "It's misleading," she said. "Dishonest, even. Besides, I thought you were going to drive by that other Marvin Greenberg's house."

"This was more important."

"Don't think I haven't noticed you staring at his name in the phone book," Ayala continued. When Marvin looked over at her, she added, "See? I pay attention. Maybe it's because I'm the only one in this family without a double." She leaned back in her chair and sighed. "No sir," she said. "No double vision for me."

Marvin concentrated on his hands on the steering wheel. They had traded the used station wagon they bought when they first arrived for a nice sedan with automatic transmission and power windows and locks. "America?" he had said to Ayala before driving it off the lot, and she had answered, "America," maybe even with an exclamation mark at the end. Now it was all Marvin could do to stop himself from saying, "I pay attention too." He was getting better at not responding. Adjustments always took time. He knew this from experience. And as humiliating as it was to deal with irate bank tellers impatient with her accent, at least no one was whisking Ayala off to basic training with a bunch of eighteen-year-olds who stole your blankets every time you went out for a piss.

"I'm sorry," Ayala said. "I hate dentists." She patted his thigh. "I don't know why you're so obsessed about this guy. It's just a name. It doesn't mean you'll have anything else in common."

*

At home, Osnat was in the living room, watching TV. "Did it hurt?" she asked Ayala.

"Not one bit," Marvin said quickly. Osnat's appointment was scheduled for Monday. He imagined her sitting in the dentist's waiting room, staring at all the Polaroids of the other, smiling kids who were in the No Cavities Club, and wringing her hands. He tried to signal to Ayala to play along, but she didn't: "Well, maybe it didn't hurt your father," she said. "But it did hurt."

"A lot?"

"Of course not," Marvin said. Osnat looked skeptical. "It only hurts for a few seconds," Ayala said. "Then you go numb."

Marvin fished into his backpack and pulled out the letter from Ronald Reagan, which he'd resealed into its original envelope. "Look," he said. "You've got mail."

Later, while they were eating a dinner comprised entirely of easy-to-chew food—scrambled eggs, cottage cheese, soft white bread—it was hard not to notice how old they all were getting. There was Osnat with arms and legs and a face that were all bony and out of proportion, and Ayala with laugh lines and wrinkles on her neck and coarse silver hairs that insisted on standing up and declaring themselves. And here he was, responsible for them, providing, for God's sake, and all they could talk about was Ayala's sister's new color TV, as if they hadn't had color television for two whole years. "I can't believe they made him pink," Osnat was saying about some cartoon character, and Ayala was agreeing: "I thought he was brown." They weren't even giving America a chance.

"All right, so he's pink," he said finally. "Anything new outside the world of television?"

Osnat mopped up what was left of her eggs with a piece of bread. "So," she said, "maybe when football starts, I could sell cookies. I bet Lizzy makes lots of money."

Lizzy was the ten-year-old who lived down the block. Rumor had it she'd been selling cookies to fans heading to the football stadium since before she could talk. You had to admire that kind of business initiative from a toddler.

"If she makes any money," Marvin said, "it's because her parents pay for the ingredients." He pulled a pen out of his shirt pocket and flattened out the napkin he'd been using. "Let's see. How much is a bag of chocolate chips?" Ayala and Osnat exchanged looks. He knew he wasn't supposed to have seen them, but he had. "What?" he said. "Anyway, I don't know if the market can bear another girl selling cookies. Lizzy has the advantage of being first, and of being younger and cuter."

"Fine," Osnat said and Ayala said, "Marvin."

"What?" Marvin said. "I'm not saying Osnat isn't cute. I'm just saying she's thirteen."

"Fine," Osnat said again. "I won't sell cookies."

She stood up and started stacking the dinner plates. Her lips were pressed into a straight, flat line, as if someone had ironed all the expression out of her face: a two-dimensional girl in a three-dimensional body.

"Hey," Marvin said. "Hey." Osnat reached for his silverware, but he moved his fork away from her. "Don't worry about the dishes. I'll do them."

*

Although he knew that any man walking by on the street could be the other Marvin Greenberg, Marvin found himself favoring tall, middle-aged white men with dark hair—no one would name a blond, blue-eyed baby Marvin, would they? He imagined the other Marvin Greenberg talking on the phone, stroking a well-kept, bushy beard. When Marvin had tried growing a beard in his twenties, it sprouted scraggly and sparse. The other Marvin Greenberg—virile, hairy, and vigorous—would have no such problems. Perhaps he even played football in high school, rather than chess.

"All right," Ayala said. "That's it. This has gone on long enough. We're going right up to his house and ringing his doorbell. Next you'll start imagining he's some kind of body builder—"

"With no back hair," Marvin said. "Maybe I'll start waxing."

"If he's virile," Ayala said, "he has back hair. And anyway, if he's such a demigod, why is he a statistician?"

Marvin played it out in his head: first he'd finish washing the dishes, and then they'd watch *Wheel of Fortune*, and then they'd all get in the car and drive over to what would no doubt be the other Marvin Greenberg's mansion, complete with a hot tub and a live-in maid. Then what? "I don't know," he said, rinsing out the dishcloth. Meeting your own double seemed as if it should be a private moment.

"Marvin," Ayala said. "Enough. Enough already. There are more important things to worry about."

"Like what?"

"Like Osnat," Ayala said. "Like me."

Even though she was smiling, her eyes were hard and wet. Marvin focused on the fine lines around her mouth. "But don't you see?" he said. "You're all I worry about. Why don't you think I worry about you?"

Suddenly Osnat was standing in front of them. "Are you fighting?" she asked. Behind her, Marvin could hear the applause of a studio audience, and the opening strains of the *Wheel of Fortune* theme.

"We're discussing—" Ayala started to say, but Marvin interrupted her: "Of course we're not fighting."

"Because it's not important about the cookies," Osnat said. "It was just a thought."

*

It was Marvin who took Osnat to the dentist on Monday after Ayala begged off, saying it was too soon and that she could still smell that burning tooth smell from the drill.

"They don't burn your teeth," Marvin said.

"You know what I mean," Ayala said. "You take her."

Of course, they would have eventually heard the news, but that morning Marvin felt unprepared for the shock of it: there she was, Samantha Smith, grinning at them from every newspaper box, as if reproaching Marvin and Osnat with her own fine fluoridated-from-birth teeth. He'd recognized her picture right away, and even started to say, "Now what?" when the headline registered and he realized that she was dead, that she and her father had been killed in a plane crash in Maine the night before. He turned away quickly, hoping Osnat wouldn't notice, but she had. "Wow," she said. Then she shrugged and made her pronouncement: "Bummer." But except for that, as far as Marvin could tell, she was fine.

In the waiting room, while Osnat was in with the dentist, he studied Samantha's picture on the front page: the freckles, the side part, the wide smile. In addition to the trip to the Soviet Union, the TV special, and the book contract, she had recently taken up acting. If you ignored her untimely death for a moment, it seemed unfair to get so much in return for one letter. Timing really was everything.

"On the bright side," he told a numbed and drooling Osnat during the drive home, "if she hadn't written that letter, she never would have been on that plane. Life in the public eye involves a certain amount of risk. It's the same with the Kennedys, you know."

"Who?" said Osnat.

"Anyway," Marvin said, "you have that nice correspondence going with the President. It's probably good that Samantha Smith got there first." At least they were both still alive, he wanted to say. And at least it would be Lizzy, and not Osnat who, two years down the line, would be run over, cookies and all, by a drunk fan driving home from the football stadium.

*

It was a hot day, and the students were already beginning to trickle back into town. Even with the air conditioning, it was hard to concentrate. Over lunch, Marvin bought a can of Sprite from the vending machine on the first floor of the other Marvin Greenberg's building and then parked himself on a bench across from the entrance: that way, he'd be sure to see him leaving for lunch. He was curious to see whether the other Marvin Greenberg would trigger some sort of signal—goose bumps, chills, a ringing in the ears—the kind long-lost siblings reported feeling right before finding each other. Man after man left the building without even glancing at him, and not one of them felt familiar. Samantha Smith leered at him from the newspaper boxes that lined the corner.

Back at the office, he called Ayala. "I'm just worried about this whole Samantha Smith thing," he said. "I mean, they're practically the same age, and she writes all those letters. I thought she'd be more upset. Why isn't she more upset?"

"Marvin, it's not like they actually knew each other."

"But it's still a connection," he insisted. "Like me and the other Marvin Greenberg."

"Enough," Ayala said. "Enough. God, how many times do I have to say it? Enough. I know you have this elaborate theory, but Marvin, it isn't fooling anybody."

"I'm not trying to fool anyone."

Ayala sighed. "You think Osnat doesn't know you're the one writing all those letters? You think she doesn't know we fight? She's thirteen. She's not stupid. And neither am I."

"I never thought you were."

"Then why do you do it?" Ayala asked. "Why do you keep pretending we might go back to Israel, when you sure as hell know you won't?"

*

On the news, they replayed clips of Samantha Smith's visit to the Soviet Union. Osnat sat on the couch, knees tucked up under her chin. She had dark hair, like Samantha's, but Osnat's was wavy, and her skin was too sallow for freckles. Whatever wholesome, all-American quality it was that Samantha Smith radiated as she toured Red Square, Osnat didn't have it. Still, as wrong as it was, Marvin couldn't shake the strange feeling of relief that he had somehow only narrowly avoided a great disaster.

"So," he said during a commercial break, "Mom told me you know about the letters." He didn't know if he should look at Osnat or at the TV screen, so instead he concentrated on picking a loose thread from the couch cushion. "Are you mad?"

Osnat shrugged. "I'm almost fourteen," she said. "I know Ronald Reagan is too busy to write back."

"So why didn't you say something?"

"I don't know," Osnat said. "I guess I figured it wasn't hurting anything."

She sounded so resigned Marvin felt frightened. Where was all that youthful optimism everyone always talked about? "I just hate it that you're so worried about nuclear war," he said. "You weren't this scared in Israel."

Osnat rolled her eyes. "Dad," she said, as if he should have known better, as if he really didn't understand her at all, "when the world ends, it won't matter where we live. It won't matter at all."

*

Every imaginary conversation Marvin had with Ayala ended with her packing her bags and leaving. Sometimes she took Osnat, and sometimes she didn't. Either way, Marvin's evenings stretched out long and empty before him, filled with stacks of canned soup and frozen dinners eaten in front of the TV. This was what happened when you strayed from careful planning and fell in love with the natives in a country you were only planning to visit for its archeological artifacts. It was easy to get swept up in the novelty of it all: the sun, the heat, the contested borders. Everywhere you looked there were Jews—buying groceries, writing out parking tickets, emptying garbage cans—and that deceptive blank-slate feeling of new neighborhoods rising in the sand and drip irrigation turning the desert green. And he loved Ayala, who picked him over hairier men with calloused hands and combat experience, and who didn't mind that he sang in the shower and was nervous around anything with an exoskeleton. He had been young and believed the Beatles that love was all you needed, and now here he was fifteen years later, and it turned out he needed more: a job worth going to, a language in which he could tell jokes, snow. He wanted to be selfless and giving, but wasn't his turn supposed to come too? Wasn't it his turn now?

Ayala was outside, filling the bird feeder in the backyard. Marvin wanted to go out and talk to her, but he didn't know what to say that wouldn't sound as if he were choosing his own happiness over hers. There was still an hour of daylight left. It was time to seek a greater wisdom.

"All right," he announced from the back porch. "I'm doing it. I'm going to see the other Marvin Greenberg."

*

Marvin walked briskly, swinging his arms and concentrating on the way each foot rolled forward from heel to toe. The other Marvin Greenberg, he had noted with little surprise, lived on the other end of his very same neighborhood, on a shady street that boasted large brick houses with two-car garages. It was exactly the kind of street Marvin would have chosen for himself if he already had tenure: America.

Now that the air was starting to cool, people were outside, sitting on front-porch swings and watching Marvin walk as if he were a parade of one. Marvin stared straight ahead, hoping it would make him seem more purposeful. He could hear children shooting baskets off garage doors. Hello, he thought, imagining himself marching right up the front walk and ringing the doorbell. Hello, I'm Marvin Greenberg. Hello there, I'm Marvin. Hi. Hello. But when he finally got to the right house, there was a man on the front lawn, large and sweaty and steaming mad, cursing a lawnmower that was lying on its side. "Damn it," he was saying. "Damn it. Damn it." Marvin kept right on walking, but when he reached the edge of the lawn, he stopped. He wanted a better look.

"Need some help?" he asked, even though it was Ayala who was normally in charge of the mowing.

"Thanks," the man answered, "but no thanks. It's a heap of junk, this machine." He looked nothing like Marvin had expected: he was shorter, for one thing, and nearly bald. There were grass stains on his pants and he was wearing a white T-shirt that was brittle and yellow under the arms. No wonder he was still hanging on to the book about stain removal. "What I need," the man announced, "is a riding mower."

"I'm Marvin," Marvin said, extending his hand. "I'm new here."

"Marvin?" the man said. "I'm Marvin too. Marvin Greenberg."

Marvin braced himself for a bone-crushing handshake, but when it came, it was nothing special. "Huh," he said. "My last name is Greenberg."

"What are the odds?" the other Marvin said. Then he laughed. "I've been saving that up for weeks. You're the one in mathematics, right? Hang on a sec. I have a bunch of your mail." He disappeared into the house, and came out holding two beers and a small stack of envelopes. "I kept meaning to stop by, but you know how it goes," he said, handing Marvin a can.

"Yeah," Marvin said. "I know exactly."

*

Later, after Osnat was asleep, Marvin lay in bed and watched Ayala give herself a manicure. She cut her nails square and close, then trimmed her cuticles. Earlier, with the other Marvin Greenberg, it had been so simple to sum up the essentials of his life: a wife, a child, a clean shot at tenure, thirteen years in Israel and now some time in America where, by all objective, quantifiable standards, life was easier. No one could argue with that. Bringing your family back to America was a no-brainer, in the same way that no one questioned families who moved from the city to the suburbs. Compared to the other Marvin Greenberg, with his estranged wife and broken lawn mower, Marvin's life seemed full, exciting even, garnished with danger and exotic locales.

Now though, with Ayala on the edge of the bed rubbing lotion into her hands, Marvin knew—he *knew*—that the last thing they needed was to talk everything over yet again. These things took time, but you got used to them: the lush, green lawns; the clean streets; the big cars; the way people smiled and asked about your day. A body could resist for only so long and then it had to adjust, the same as it did to the local water and cooler temperatures, until suddenly you were sweating when it was only 45 . What Marvin needed was patience. Ayala and Osnat would begin to see things the way they actually were: how tired everyone looks in Israel, the way everybody yells, how there's nothing natural about hennaed hair.

"So," Ayala said, "fat and balding, you say?"

Marvin nodded. He lifted up the covers so Ayala could climb in, then pressed his mouth against the warm skin between her shoulder blades. It tasted like soap. "But he knows how to do laundry."

Ayala snorted. "Anyone can do laundry." She was quiet for a moment, and then she took a breath. "Marvin—"

"Ayaloosh," Marvin interrupted her, "let's not talk about it. Let's not talk about it tonight." What he really wanted to say was, Trust me. Trust me to do what's best. But here it was, his life: his wife stopped at the beginning of a sentence, all that breath waiting to be exhaled, and him pressed against her, hoping she wouldn't continue, hoping she'd forget exactly what it was she wanted to say.

Announcement

Steve Almond

Congratulations to Hector and Consuelo Acuña on the engagement of their daughter, Felicidad, who they never thought would amount to much of anything and secretly feared would return home pregnant from one of her many sweaty summer dates with Ronny Hask, a near graduate of Weed Senior High, who would like to be a pilot for a small airline someday, if he can overcome an inner ear syndrome averse to his balance. The couple plan an October wedding at St. Sebastien's (assuming construction on the new rectory is complete) with reception to follow at Red's Marathon Lodge.

The Hask family, natives of nearby Hudspeth, will sponsor a rehearsal dinner at the Pasta Factory, where the two families will make loud innappropriate remarks about the couple and, more softly, about one other.

Consuelo is sure to cry most of the afternoon, because Felicidad is her only daughter after six Acuña boys (may they each rest in peace) and because they love one another so much they once fought with butter knives in the dinette area.

Ronny's mother, Dee, will also tear up, though more quietly, because that is how they do things in her family; sorrow appears as something illicit, something to be smoothed over by time and patience, the beatitudes of faith.

Let God watch over this young pair as they lie vibrating with desire and wake damp and foul in their mouths and later, after they have moved on to another town, mugged of their naïvete, and all their lives seem a struggle to stand under the weight of what they have done, and what has been done to them, let God still watch.

Contrails

Paul Maliszewski

November 5, 2001

Dear President Bush,

I was sitting outside on my porch the other day watching two female cardinals chase each other around. One hopped onto the fence, and the other scared it off. They were really going at it. A squirrel dangled from a thin, low-hanging branch, trying, I imagine, to calculate whether its interest would be best served by dropping to the ground or scurrying back up to someplace more secure. The squirrels here at my new place are fearless animals, I tell you, or maybe they are just plain aggressive. I was right in the middle of trying to determine whether there was any meaningful difference between being fearless and being plain aggressive when I noticed a series of crisscrossing jet contrails in the sky. The first and second ran roughly parallel from north to south, while a third cut a diagonal across the pair and then terminated. I am seeing more jet contrails than ever these days.

The sight of jet contrails never fails to remind me of my brother. My brother Frankie and I grew up in a house in Shreveport, Louisiana, located just across the Red River from Bossier City, home of Barksdale Air Force Base. Barksdale is where you landed in your airplane on September 11, made a brief public statement, and then took off again for Nebraska. Frankie is my younger brother and only living sibling.

Anyway, my brother and I were big fans of the B-52 planes. We played outside, throwing a football, for example, or climbing on a jungle gym my father constructed out of wooden ladders. We spied green anoles crawling up and down the outer walls of the house. They turned the color of the brick. We found more lizards on the fence that ran behind the three pigmy apple trees. There they turned the color of the fence. No matter where we found them—and we found them all over, Frankie and I, under the eaves, for example where they turned the color of a short vacation's tan—what we did is we caught them in our hands and held them until they puffed out their pink throat sacs for us. What was not to love about the pink throat sac of the green anole? At all times we kept a lookout for a B-52.

Shreveport in those days was a cotton town on its way to becoming something else, what exactly was not clear. In the middle of one set of fields, they constructed a branch campus of the state university, specializing in agricultural research. The subdivision where we lived was surrounded on three sides by cotton fields. The fourth side was a swamp. My brother and I had a friend who lived on the very edge of the subdivision, his backyard separated from the rows of cotton by a six-foot-tall wooden fence. His family let him and his sisters play tic-tac-toe on the walls of their rooms. They used pencils, magic markers, and crayons, it didn't matter. His parents didn't care. When I asked our friend if he was sure it was okay that we drew on the walls, he said, "Why not? We're renting."

Once, our friend dared my brother and I to peek over the backyard fence into the cotton field. I wasn't interested. I never much liked dares. I believe I feared the consequences of the unknown, though I doubtless did not express the sentiment in those words, exactly. What were the rewards of accepting a dare save one's boldness only slightly enhanced? My brother took that dare and what he saw—what he tells me he saw—may be best described as a scarecrow fashioned out of the crucified body of a coyote.

Today, as you know, sir, Shreveport isn't much like that. Today Shreveport has less cotton. Today Shreveport has riverboat casinos. Today what cotton fields there are remain largely unplanted, as the owners wait, sitting in large chairs beside telephones in large houses, to receive and entertain all serious offers for their land from commercial real estate firms representing Wal-Mart, Old Navy, or Target.

When Frankie and I saw a B-52 fly overhead we ran out to the middle of the yard and began desperately signaling it. 'We're down here' was the gist of what we were up to. I hopped up and down and waved my arms in the manner of jumping jacks. Frankie lay on his back in the grass, opening and closing his legs while fully extending his arms and then bringing them together over his head. If there were snow on the ground in Shreveport, which there was only rarely, once every eight years, say, there would have been the outline of an angel around Frankie. It occurs to me that the grass was St. Augustine grass, which is a large-bladed variety of grass and thus not a comfortable grass on which to lie or, for that matter, walk barefoot.

We ran to the pigmy apple trees and picked up all the fallen fruit we could find and started chucking apples at the B-52. One minute we signaled the plane, desperate, needing the crew's attention, rescue from something, and the next minute we armed ourselves. As I picked up the apples, I was never certain what side we were on. Our allegiance was fickle. I didn't know what the sides were. I should mention that the apples of the pigmy apple trees were deformed and grievously misshapen. They were all gnarled up like the fists of an arthritic grandfather who tells the same story over and again, to anybody who will listen, about how he used to do some amateur boxing. Remember, this was before Golden Gloves came along. The skin of the apples was pitted with black worm holes. Apples left on the ground for too long became small red sacks, translucent in places, filled with seeds and slime. Our apples did not look the way apples at a grocery store looked.

So we hurled the junk up, and the junk came back down. The apples struck the ground around us and broke into pieces. The grass was slick with the juice. We slipped on large chunks, and we got apple on our clothes and in our hair. The backyard smelled of apple. That was when, as a last-ditch effort, we aimed our cocked fingers at the plane and made terrific explosions. When we felt we put up a good enough fight, we threw ourselves on the ground and played dead. Frankie, always a bit on the theatrical side, clutched his hands to his chest and fell over where he stood. Sometimes he flopped around a little for effect, both legs quivering slightly and then only one. Often he managed in the throes of his final pain to croak out a few words that described the blatantly obvious. "They got me," he said. Or, "I'm dying." Or, "I'm dead." Or the like. We died so many times that year.

Keep up the good work, sir.

Sincerely,
Harvey Strub

If You Get There Before I Do

Honorée Fanonne Jeffers

I have sought out the meaning of life at Parson's Soul Food so many times, sitting at this tacky fake wood table or another one just like it across the room, eating biscuits smothered with the grape jelly that jiggles on the tip of a knife, the cheap jelly that comes in the little individual containers. I have waited for a sign. I have prayed at the altar of pig meat in this very room, though my therapist wanted to call it something else.

Before I dumped her at the end of an unfruitful relationship, Ms. Shrink tried talking to me about food hygiene. As if there is something clean or dirty about eating when there is only full or empty. My mama still had me on her insurance so Ms. Shrink and I would talk fifty minutes once a week about my latest dietary backsliding, and then Ms. Shrink would come at me.

"Why'd you do it, Ailey?"

This was after the unfortunate incident with a straight razor and that trip down to the mental hospital. I had scratched across my wrist with the razor—an illegal one Mama gave me when I first started dating back in high school, just in case some fresh boy tried to take advantage of me. There was a serious scene when I got the courage to call Mama a few minutes after I made the scratches. Mama screaming and asking me had I lost my mind and did I think she had gone through picking cotton as a child in Cusseta, Georgia, and working like a dog to put herself through college and wearing the same damned pair of shoes for the four years my daddy was in medical school, all of that to go through this? And had she labored thirty-seven hours to push my bigheaded self out, breastfed me for almost a whole year even when I was biting and her skin never was the same again, all of that for me to mess up? How could I try to kill myself when I was supposed to be the one standing over her grave one day and not the other way around?

The police, the ambulance. A nurse in her uniform with little bears printed all over. Mama refusing to hold my hand. The mental hospital. And I couldn't leave for a day and a half. It was the law.

That's what I remember, that and the redhead who leaned over me when I thought she had fallen asleep in the next bed. Her breath in little puffs when she enunciated each syllable. "Would you like to hear about my soul now?" The redhead certainly was polite, quite nice, really. I truly believe some biscuits would have helped her.

"Why'd you do it, Ailey?" Ms. Shrink had asked me. Why'd I try to kill myself?

Later, after I'd been watched for months and I seemed to have given up on the whole suicide thing, why had I binged again? Didn't I want to get well?

And the other question Ms. Shrink wanted to ask but didn't, which hung in the air like an unpleasant odor–why was I, the daughter of a former teacher and a dead physician, the child of so much black privilege, why was I such a complete fuck-up when there were other folk my color out there living in the projects, two-stepping with roaches, not even making do? Just what was my problem?

"Why'd you do it, Ailey?"

Ms. Shrink asking the question suddenly, as if she were ripping off a scab for my own good. Her blue eyes open, sympathetic, trying not to look down at her watch and calculate how much my different neuroses were costing me. According to Ms. Shrink, I was supposed to write down everything that went into my mouth. Keep a journal, record it all. A journal–this was what Mama's high option insurance was paying for.

Cheeseburgers, French fries, onion rings, fillets of fish, apple pies, hot fudge sundaes and Diet Coke.

Then I fasted for five days.

Then I ate a box of Ex-Lax like it was Swiss chocolate.

Then I ran nine and three-quarter miles.

And it was good. Amen.

Ms. Shrink didn't understand. I'd been looking for what you might call a watershed moment–that's what I'm still seeking, that epiphany when I know that the other moments were not the actual moments of truth, they were times when a false god came to me, trying to get me to drop my drawers.

Today I watch the door as usual, waiting for my sign, but only Professor Whitcomb walks through.

*

fair water alabama
march 18 1815

master jenkins
we is well here Praise God but bessie she com down with
the Croup in this stil cold wether an dont seem gettin up
agan no time soon forgiv your Humble servant this news
we put all things in the Lords hands
lifestock is well the Pigs comin alon nicely Pompey report
your heifers quickenin and chickens is many eggs is much

and big sum brown and sum wite butters in the cellar beeves and hams locked up to master if you forgiv me i ask to mariage with peter he bin wating for you but now with you gon so long he ast me i write i never did expect this tho God know i been prayin to do what the Good Book say
your humble slave sary jane

*

If I wasn't trying to finish this dissertation, I might try to report Whitcomb for following me, though he never flirts with me. No intense eye-gazing or even a lingering pat on the hand. Something inappropriate would at least be a bit exciting, instead of this fatherly stalking he subjects me to from time to time. This invasion of privacy in the name of advising and then those stories of his. The way he goes on about how he was in SNCC back in the day and did I know he met Harry Belafonte at the March on Washington and Harry sang snatches of that banana song just for giggles and grins? "Day-o! Day-ay-ay-o!"

How when he was in his own doctoral program he wore an Afro and a daishiki instead of the three-piece suits and the wingtips he does now? And he and the brothers showed up three times a week to the class of a white professor teaching Introduction to Black History—"A white boy! Teaching us about our history! Can you imagine, Ailey?"—just so they could heckle him.

"I bet your great-great granddaddy owned slaves."

"We had algebra in Africa when your kind were grooming their hair with rancid lard."

"Who invented peanut butter, motherfucker?"

Leaning on the walls, sitting on the floor to send the white boy subliminal I'm-gone-kick-your-ass-honky messages. And the professor tolerating Whitcomb and the brothers because, after all, black male rage is to be expected. Healthy even. Get it all out. Let's dialogue. I hear you. I do.

Whitcomb gets on this kick and makes me get on it too, when it's not even in style anymore, like platform shoes or affirmative action.

I remember when I walked into my first history seminar with Whitcomb, I looked around and I was the only colored face up in there. I sat down and stretched out my long legs and Whitcomb gave me this tender look. We were in this one together. And then he started to lecture.

Someone had caught Olaudah Equiano and his baby sister and split them up. Sent Olaudah across the Middle Passage by himself–if you don't count the other folk by themselves too, there in the hold of that ship.

"Did you know that he never saw his little sister again? Think of their terror; think of their heartache. Wrenched from their parents, their culture, the only land they'd ever known. How lonely and confused Olaudah and his sister were. Think of it, people." Whitcomb's thin, bourgie lips twitching with emotion.

"Think of him; think of her." Whitcomb clearing his throat trying to keep from crying.

In that first seminar he played old records for us, spirituals, from his own collection, and he explained the codes. A mystery we couldn't understand now in this twenty-first century, but was loud as gunshots to the slaves who sang them. "Listen to this!" and he would sing "Swing Low, Sweet Chariot" in a respectable tenor. Right along with the records:

If you get there before I do,
Coming for to carry me home
Tell all my friends I'm coming too
Coming for to carry me home

His face flushed. Completely unembarrassed. "Do you know what that song means? Anyone?"

I would be the only one to speak. "Well, Professor Whitcomb, whenever a slave was planning to run, he or she might sing that song to alert the rest of the quarters that an escape was taking place soon, so a diversionary tactic might take place. Or it might mean what was waiting for the slave in the future. In the case of this spiritual, 'friends' may refer to the Quakers, some of whom were known to be conductors in the Underground Railroad."

"Exactly, Ailey!" Whitcomb beamed. He was so proud of me. "And it's *George*, remember?"

I absorbed so quickly. I was so engaged, his best student. I didn't want to tell him that my teacher told me this stuff during Black History Month when I was in grade school. What I didn't learn from school, Mama had told me. So long ago, I couldn't even remember the exact words. I didn't say in class that according to the newest research, someone had found out that Olaudah actually had never been chained to the ribs of a ship or ridden the Middle Passage but was born right in South Carolina. A little historical intrigue, a fraud.

I'm sure Whitcomb had read the research but it was the spirit of the thing that counted to him. And I'd be willing to bet the rest of my alleged future in academia that Whitcomb's moment was about thirty-five to forty years ago, somewhere down south, in the middle of a cotton field, or in some appropriately weathered clapboard church, or dodging rocks pelted at the *café au lait* New England brow that it took his forebears generations of color-struck breeding to mold. Of course, he was terrified as he stood his ground those years ago. What song were they singing, those authentic dark-skinned southern negroes, the descendents of slaves, in that field or that broke down church or that gauntlet through white sheets? Surely something throaty, deeply felt and way down in some poor person's empty belly.

Wherever he was, you know Whitcomb was up underneath some folk, clasping a black hand in his light brown one, and thanking whoever he prayed to that he had the chance to change that red dirt corner of the world.

And now I am his red dirt corner.

*

Birdtail Plantation
North Carolina
21 November 1805

Dear Master Norell
Uncle Jeter done died. Iona come to see
about him Friday mornin and fount him. We put
him in the ground Saturday past because Sunday
is the Lords day. Uncle William recite the dust
and there was nice hymns too. The folk sing Ride On
King Jesus No Man Can Hinder Me. Mistress read
from the Scripture and tell us Uncle Jeter in a good
place now with no work and all the cornbread he can
eat. You know how he loved it so with his syrup on top.
I know Mistress is wise. Please Master dont think
that I ant grateful for everything you and Mistress
has did for me the whitewash and the brick hearth
built for me last Christmas. God knows I am
grateful. God knows I am Master.
The livestock is well and we prepare for harvest.
Forever your obedient slave
May

*

I was in medical school before this. History wasn't my first choice. I thought the first time, when I went to medical school, that I was on the right journey then. Mama had wanted me to be a doctor like my father, like my sister. A healer. A rich healer of small coughs and sick headaches. Someone with one hand holding aspirin, and the other hand holding money. I wanted to please her—I wanted to do that for her. My poor mama had been trying for so long with me, while I went in one direction and then another. As I made mediocre grades in high school, good grades in college but flitted from one major to another, slept with the wrong men and brought them home, once actually to her family reunion down in Cusseta, Georgia.

I generally wasted time while Mama reassured me and my daddy how much potential I had and how everything was going to be okay with faith and prayer and cussing me out every now and then. If it hadn't been for my MCAT scores and Daddy's contacts at Howard Medical, I never would have gotten in. Then I had the nerve to drop out in the third year.

In my defense, I truly thought I was going to be a doctor, Mama's forgone conclusion, throughout my childhood. I had Mama and Daddy telling me so and it took with my sister Carol, only she went to Harvard. She's living in the big Capitol Hill house with a finished basement and a temperature controlled wine cellar. She has good credit and drives a BMW. If those years of brainwashing had worked on me, I'd be set. Suffering from sleep deprivation because of those long hours at the hospital, but semi-rich with a happy mama. Now, I can't sleep four hours straight anyway and I'm broke and always going to be broke. History professors don't make jack.

I don't think Mama is happy with me but this is not my fault. It's my high school biology teacher's because he was the one who made me smell the frog. I know if I never had to smell the frog, I would be living right now on Capitol Hill, too, finishing up my residency.

Have you ever smelled a pickled frog? It is one funky, life-altering experience.

It isn't so traumatizing to look at. Aside from the head and the arms, it looks like a meal to me, like a fresh fish from the market with its belly cut open. My granny Rose, my mama's mama, had taught me how to clean catfish and perch every summer. Same difference. Sprinkle on some garlic powder, salt and pepper, roll it in some cornmeal and fry it up in a cast iron skillet. The smell of the frog, though–it's one thing to kill a creature to eat it, so that the memory of the killing is covered up by the joy of a full stomach, but to turn that creature into a specimen and make ungrateful teenagers sniff that funk through third period is just plain cruel.

Right then, in third period in ninth grade, I knew that I was not a healer but I didn't admit to Mama that I was not meant for holiness. I was not going to lay my rough hands on anyone, call them to rise up like Jesus did Lazarus. I went on the journey anyway. Failed, and I'm here, trying school again. I ran up these student loans and now each day is like the rest: walking across campus, climbing up those damned steps to the historical collection, looking in books.

Sometimes when I'm up and reading through my notes for my dissertation and I just start typing and I know I'm not going anywhere but I just keep typing, I'll stop for a minute and put on an old thirty-three that my mother gave me, a recording of her college choir singing the spirituals almost forty years ago when Mama was a soprano before she started her smoking. It's one of the same records Whitcomb played in class but mine isn't in as good a shape as his. I have an old player I bought from Goodwill and I have a bad habit of bumping the turntable to skip over the scratched parts.

Before music videos, singers had much better voices. There is just no comparison. In the days of records, nobody cared how homely you were if you could hit the tune. Those were the days. The voices on Mama's record were so meshed you couldn't tell whether you were listening to one girl or fifty.

I eat too much while I listen, but I'm more satisfied, too. Fried chicken under heat lamps, instant mashed potatoes, meat loaf, German chocolate cake, caramel swirl ice cream, Diet Coke. I close my eyes and think about those runaways Whitcomb loves to talk about, the ones who had sung the spirituals. In my mind, I can see a picture of someone, a woman, running away from home. Always a woman. Just running without looking behind.

Run, won't you hide me? Through the woods into the blank distance. Then the picture gets confused with one of those jogger girls in sports bra and tight little spandex shorts, the kind who likes to bounce along the campus sidewalk, and has the body I could keep if I could just pace myself, commit to a real diet. Anyway, that picture of a jogging girl is wrong because behind any runaway, a real runaway, was something that held on, even when she was safe up north—relatively safe anyway. Something that scared her, hummed a song. Home that crawled up in her and ate up everything there was inside.

I don't want to steal away like a secret. I want to be that jogging girl gaining on the horizon, not worried about anything, not my thighs or my next meal or where the sidewalk leads.

*

Blackberry Wood, Virginia
January 15, 1839

My Dearest Master Ben:
I take my pen in hand to write you about your home which I hope you have not forgotten.
The constitution of all is fair. I regret to write there have been thieveries in the smokehouse and cold cellar. I now have pinned the keys inside my skirts on my favorite petticoat, the lace one trimmed with ribbon fringe.
I hope you will not be angered but well pleased that I am expecting another of Gods gifts come spring. After the death of Baby my heart has grown tighter and tighter. Please forgive your servant for saying it has been too much to bear when walking through the garden to chance a look at the mound of daisies marking his grave. Perhaps this new little one will make a light space once more.
Your daughters the young mistresses grow in beauty. Miss Abigail is a flurry over her presentation and has me sewing until I feel my fingers must bleed but my pleasure is hers. Miss Sarah must find something to busy her own hands and after labors teaches the servants to read the Bible verses you chose.
I cannot help but remember how your beloved and dear wife gave me ciphering and my letters. I pray for her departed soul often.
All who cherish this earth await your return Master to your home.
I am your most devoted and loving servant,
Susan Bishop

*

The place they keep the original documents of the best white southern families is housed in a tall three-story building cocooned by trees. The flights of stairs you have to walk up once you get there are no joke. The hike way across campus and the trek up the stairs, the rapidly beating heart—this is what you have to pay for the secrets. The endless stairs where you think you've gotten to the next flight, but you actually are resting on a landing and then you have to coax your aching legs to start climbing again with those internal "I can do it" cheers. These rich alumni give money hand over fist, but the archivists won't let you use the elevator in historical collections unless you have a key. And this exercise doesn't count because I haven't eaten yet.

The sneezing from the dust is another payment as well. You have to get used to the smell of dust flying around the collections.

Finally, patience is the final tithe. Tolerance like sitting beside Granny Rose on Sunday, on the third pew of Red Mound Primitive Baptist Church trying to make sense of the spirits shouting up inside you.

I am an historian now, I suppose. I trek up those endless stairs. I sift through the papers. Things are computerized now, but that doesn't make them any less confusing in the archives, and after doing some double-checking, I found out that the librarians either were too lazy to enter everything into the computers or were sitting me in the fool's chair, pulling a qualitative joke at my expense. Better to do things the old-fashioned way so I have gone through a lot of the alphabet in the portfolios, and I'm still trying to find some stuff that will please Whitcomb. Runaways, suicides. Better yet, a few women who had killed their children and then killed themselves because of what might have been termed in the antebellum era "extreme melancholia."

A year ago, Whitcomb decided I should change my dissertation topic from the boll weevil plague in the Deep South to mad black women of the antebellum period. Or what he called "female slave resistance."

"But this topic is so much more exciting, don't you think, Ailey? You can do something; make a difference, instead of writing about the boll weevil plague. Who cares about how a bunch of fat cat white boys lost their money on cotton?" His ironic little laugh. Then the eyebrows pushed up earnestly. "Don't you want to do something for our people, Ailey?"

I am supposed to be outraged by these women and I think this is Professor Whitcomb's problem besides the fact that I haven't written one useful word on my dissertation. He wants me to get angry, because if he's mad and he's a northerner, then surely as someone who had grown up below the Mason-Dixon line, I should be ready to cut somebody deep. When I don't get mad enough to Whitcomb, he prods me. He finds an essential book that I need to read. Last year, right after he changed my mind for me about my dissertation, he handed out one of these books as an independent assignment. I cracked this one open and around page five, I realized that I didn't want to read it, but I had to because I was trying to get through this program.

There were pages and pages of descriptions. Black men burned at the stake, hearts cut out still steaming. Dicks sliced off and made into cuisine for the brothers who were forced to eat themselves while still alive and burning.

I got around to the middle of the book and there she was. Not a voice that I could chase away with a Valium or a Prozac, but a tactile jumping inside my skin, a moving in my womb: a woman, not a man, lynched.

Eight months pregnant and hung up from a tree. She danced up there so high. Awful and graceful. Perhaps the baby moved inside her and one of the mob saw the stomach leap, wondered what the woman's womb looked like within her. She was nothing to them but a hog stretched for slaughter. Fresh sausage. Someone, a curious sort, cut the hanging woman's round belly open and the baby fell to the ground, gave a pitiful sound and the mob took turns stomping the child, still connected by its cord to the mother's heartbeat, into silence. Boy or girl? The author couldn't say.

I felt the small pulsing of a child jump into me then, skip through my empty body. My jaws tightened when I read. Was that outrage? The dry mouth and the need for food? My eyes shifted back and forth–the hunger coming. I wanted to eat until my belly stretched and what was inside me pressed toward my throat. Maybe I could vomit out the ghost child, give birth the wrong way.

I haven't told Whitcomb, but I did get angry once for real, one night coming back from the library walking to my car. I didn't look around to see if anyone was following me. I felt that hunger in my gut. I felt that spirit child quickening in my womb when I walked toward the big bronze statue of a man who had sired little yellow and cream colored bastards that he denied to the end. Later on, his legitimate white children had killed some of those bastards.

I walked right up to that bronze man and I spit on him. His eyes looking out to nowhere. Or maybe he wasn't looking out but was looking inward at what he thought was his spotless soul. He was all right with his Maker, those half-black slaves he had made notwithstanding. The statue wasn't looking at me, that was for sure, and maybe I was as crazy as my mama said. Or I just wanted to be attacked by some Confederate fool; they were around campus and they didn't have any sense either, especially when they were drinking. It was an autumn Friday night at a football university.

I was ready for somebody to try some shit. After nine hours in the library, I was salty and looking for trouble. After spending my days constantly explaining just what I was doing on this campus when I wasn't on the women's basketball team, I wished somebody would try something. I had mace and the illegal switchblade. I hadn't slept more than forty-five minutes at a time in days. First I would spray my attacker down, then I would cut his clothes off of him—clean—then I would talk about his entire lineage using a few choice words. Oh I wished. Then I would go eat to celebrate. Or eat to calm the child that wasn't really bouncing under my heart but who I felt all the same.

Not one drunken frat boy said anything to me or paused. Those white kids walked past me like they didn't see. I was invisible kin to Ralph Ellison's boy. And my spit didn't even reach the bronze guy's foot, that's how high he towered over me.

*

Boston, Massachusetts
June 10, 1861

Dear Master Pinchard
I trust this letter finds you well and in the best of health. I write to inform you that my Husband Solomon and I have been living Free for these last five years with Mister Robert Rutledge the man who purchased us from you. Mister Rutledge and his Wife are known as good Christians in the city that we dwell. They have been our

> *benefactors since our migration. They are very kind to us. I now work as Cook in their household and my husband is training to be a Minister. Mister Rutledge has vouchsafed for my husband's communion.*
> *Ever since I left I worried on my Salvation and after much meditation I now write to you and ask Forgiveness. This is my Christian Duty.*
> *I Pray you will Forgive me the wrongdoings I committed. I truly regret the deception of my leave-taking.*
> *As for the other occasion with the red pepper juice, I blush to recall my Sin. I fervently Pray you have healed. I Forgive you as well the Evil done to me and my Husband. I hope you will not be sentenced to the depths of Hell for all eternity. I know how much heat vexes you.*
> *Please give my Love to Grandmother and all the Folk at Cusseta Place.*
> *Love to Mistress as well.*
> *God Bless you Master.*
> *Yours very truly*
> *Mrs Elizabeth Rutledge*
> *née Rabbit Pinchard*

*

Whitcomb's not hard to miss. First, the door to the café jingles when he walks in because they have a charming little bell attached to the doorknob. Then too, he's wearing a three-piece suit and his favorite shirt, the French-blue one with the gold cufflinks. His dome is bald now that he can't rock the Afro anymore.

When I spot Whitcomb, I throw him a half-smile I picked up on my travels. The go-away, smirky smile. Then a neutral wave and a diplomatic shifting of my chair to give him the signal that I just want to take my food home, and eat it quick while I rub my fingertips across my face and try not to burst into tears. And then take my laxatives or go for a run. I really don't want to be bothered with him.

I have been through the fire today and I'm really not in the mood: I have smiled extra wide to the stank-attitude waitress who rolled her eyes at me, despite my incredibly down greeting, "Hey Sister, how you doing?" No auxiliary verb. I pulled out my ghetto pass—though my mama is from the country, and I don't think her relocation to Capitol Hill counts as urban drift. Sister Waitress wasn't having it, though. Did she care that I'm trying to make it in this cruel, white supremacist, academic environment? No ma'am, not hardly. Clearly, she hasn't been reading her bell hooks. There was no solidarity, not this morning when Sister Waitress was wearing the hairnet and I handed money across the counter to her.

As hip as he is, though, Whitcomb just won't pick up the vibe when he sees me. Or maybe he wants company. I could stop to think about whether he was lonely if I gave a damn. The guilty, pinched countenance would tell me so much if I cared. He's not my daddy, either. Daddy's been dead for a while now and I am way past three times seven. I don't have time for any of this. My fucking food is going to get cold.

"Ailey! Will you have brunch with me?" No waiting for my response, but plopping down in a chair. Demanding his propers. He is, after all, my dissertation advisor. I am, of course, afraid of him. He doesn't think I am afraid, though. He thinks he is my friend, like your parents do when you are a teenager and they sniff reefer or sex on your clothes, and they want to have that talk.

Sister Waitress calls my number and I go up and pay. She glances over at Whitcomb and actually gives me a sympathetic look.

I bring my carry out containers in a big plastic bag back to the table and sit down. "Uh, Professor Whitcomb, I have to go soon. I bought these for a friend of mine and I don't want them to get cold." Whitcomb just gives me a serene smile. He has that New Englander knack of being rude and nice at the same time.

I open up my laptop and turn it on, start tapping on the keys without looking at him. Stop for a second and brush a little salt off the vinyl tablecloth.

Maybe Whitcomb will finish with me quickly and leave. Then I can go home, salvage my morning if I could get back to my own kitchen. I'm certainly not going to eat in front of him and I'm not trying to figure out what to say in the meantime either. This is why there are rules about fraternization in the military. Things are so much simpler when you keep the different levels segregated.

He goes and gets his plate and I try to breathe through my mouth so I won't smell when he comes back.

"So how is that first chapter going? Any end in sight?"

I start typing extra loud then on my laptop. Making intellectual noises. Clickety-clack. Clickety-clack. "Oh, it's going great. You know how it is. I was up at the collections this morning for three hours. I'm just, you know, taking a break for brunch. Then I have to go back, do some copying and some more reading. I just love it there." I scrunched up my mouth in what I hoped was a perky, studious manner. "It's going great," I say again.

I flick a glance over at his food. There is a lovely pool of melted margarine in the middle of his cheese grits. Whitcomb makes humming noises in between bites. I hear him tapping his foot under the table. Like a baby tasting his first solid food.

"This is so delicious; you should eat." He has his kindly voice on now and I know he wants to ask me about the letters.

The letters are mine, I found them all by myself. I am, if nothing else, resourceful. Even Whitcomb, who didn't know they were there until I told him, said, "It didn't make any sense, letters written by slaves, especially women. That was illegal back then, to teach them to read, to even let them hold open a book." Now he won't let them go, wants me to look for those trouble-making female slaves. A woman who would lead me on a chase. I keep looking through the catalog, which takes forever. That's the point. It discourages researchers who don't feel like looking for hours and hours—for what, they don't know—and sneezing every now and then, self-importantly, because of the dust.

The letters come from the few slave women who stayed alive and were allowed to read and write. Women walking softly through corridors, the pads of their feet not making a sound. Someone had taken a risk and taught each of these women—an unsuspecting mistress, a white playmate who didn't understand the implications of a slave who could read. Someone had thrown a black girl a careless gift and she tried to keep herself alive to enjoy it. Her unbroken body, her life depended on her remaining invisible. I'm not going to be the one to shine a light on her.

I glance up from the laptop at Whitcomb, pat the Styrofoam boxes on the chair beside me, and put the drawl into my voice. Code switch, settle deep into my Georgia mama's home training.

"That sure does look good, Professor Whitcomb, but I'm really not hungry, thank you so much. I'm just picking these up for a friend, but I appreciate you for thinking of me, sir, I surely do appreciate it. Besides, they're cold now." I hope he is catching my drift.

Whitcomb doesn't even know that the real folk, not the ones who are passing for black like him, but real folk usually don't eat here at Parson's because the restaurant is owned by a white man who bought it out from Mr. Parson's son a while back. Brother just sold out and left town. The white owner kept the same staff. That's the big, open secret among us coloreds here in town, that Parson's cook cuts some serious corners. Anyone used to her black mama's cooking can taste the margarine and Velveeta in Parson's cheese grits. And you could bust a hole in your forehead with their biscuits. I suspect they use lard, which is what used to go into an authentic biscuit until someone discovered what butter and flour tasted like together. If you don't have a black mama, though, or if you do but your black mama can't cook or dance, then I guess you are out of luck.

A bunch of folk eat at Sug's, a hole-in-the-wall greasy spoon out past the city limits, out of protest to the original Parson selling out. But also because Sug's is on another level. That woman can burn. She uses real butter in her grits, and biscuits too, butter on everything. Sug's husband makes his own sausage and their house specialty is fried souse meat with onions. Not for the weak of spirit or uninitiated. I don't go there on binge mornings because it's too far a drive out. On the few times I tried, I ended up pulling over to the side of road, not bothering to open the plastic silverware packet. I scooped the food up with my hands and licked the grease from my fingers. Jelly painted on my chin. It was a scandal.

So I do my praying where I can.

"Ailey, now I keep telling you: it's *George*. Call me George, please. Listen, let me pay for these." Whitcomb puts his fork down and reaches for his back pocket, lifting his hips slightly off the seat. He gives me a sorrowful look like Jesus.

"Have I told you how wonderful it is to work with you, Ailey? A privilege. You were so focused when you started the program. But I have to be honest with you, Sister. You deserve that from me. So I'm going to tell you that in order to finish a dissertation"—gesturing at me with the ten dollar bill in his hand—"first you have to begin that dissertation. Why don't you do some more work today and then come by the office early tomorrow morning? We'll talk, okay? Keep the change."

He places the ten dollars in my hand, picks up his fork again and digs back in. He's got a blob of grits on his chin and it moves up and down as he chews.

I start back making typing sounds and think about the ruined food I can't eat in the containers. I don't know if I can go back up there to the register and brave Sister Waitress again.

Salmon croquets, biscuits, jelly, hash browns, eggs, pancakes, fake maple syrup, Diet Coke.

I need to write all that down.

Baths

Michelle Mounts

I came into the world in a bathtub. I've seen the photograph. My mother is leaning forward in the tub, holding me up for the camera, and I am wriggling in the air, eyes squeezed shut, mouth open wide. This was in the early seventies. In the photograph, my mother's hair falls past her breasts in two thick braids. She has often told me, since then, that the day I was born was the happiest day of her life because she knew she would never be alone again.

Eighteen years later, on the night before I left home for good, my mother told me that she wanted to give me a bath. This actually wasn't such a strange suggestion, from my mother–she has never quite had a sense of what normal mothers and daughters do. But I didn't want a bath. I wanted to finish packing my suitcases, wake up the next morning and drive down to Athens, which is only two hours away from Deer Hollow, but that seemed far enough at the time.

"A bath," my mother said. "Just like when you were little. I'll fill the tub with bubbles, and you won't have to do a thing."

We were in the kitchen, and my mother was bent over at the waist, vigorously brushing the underside of her hair. When she stood up, she put on a straw hat with a wide, floppy brim and cinched the cord beneath her chin. We were going to the Kendricks' annual summer barbecue, and my mother thought the hat made her look "country." She was wearing a red-checked blouse and too-tight bell-bottomed slacks. When she turned toward me, she looked me up and down skeptically, lips pursed. Then she tugged on the waist of my gym shorts and tucked in the hem of my tee-shirt, pulling the fabric back up slightly around the waist. "Blousing," she called this technique.

I pulled the hem back out. "I have to finish packing tonight," I said. "Besides, I don't want a bath, Mom."

"And why not?" She tucked the hem back in.

"Because I'm eighteen," I said, pushing her hand away, gently. "Because people don't do that sort of thing." I wrapped my arms around my waist. "It's not normal."

My mother sighed. For all of her gestures toward her appearance, she never looked quite put together. Her lipstick strayed outside the lines of her lips, her mascara bled, and she was always missing a button or two. But she had thick red hair and a face that made you think she had probably been beautiful for a summer, years before, without her even knowing it. She took my chin in her hand.

"Well, we're not like most people," she said, studying me. "Are we."

I couldn't argue with her there.

She picked up her enormous purse from the counter and held it like a sack of groceries. The purse was a knobby, macramé sack with wooden beads and sequins sewn into it. She flung open the kitchen door and glanced at me over her shoulder. "Did you take your meds today, Maggsie?" she sang.

"Oh yes I did, Momsie," I lied, looking her in the eye.

I followed her through the doorway, breathing in the stifling air. It was August. "Woo-wee," said my mother, fanning herself. "It's like bathwater out here."

About a year before that night, I'd had what my mother called a complete nervous breakdown. She took me to a series of doctors, many of whom said I simply needed to sleep and eat more regularly, but my mother refused to believe them. One of the doctors told me that I was just very good at spooking myself, and my mother told him he was a quack, right to his face. She wasn't satisfied until she found a doctor who agreed to proscribe me a mild antidepressant.

I stayed home from school for a few weeks, taking the medication once a day and spending most of my time staring up at a water stain the shape of Africa on the living-room ceiling. I didn't have the patience to get dressed or even run a brush through my hair. During those few weeks, my mother never changed out of her pink terrycloth bathrobe. She would shuffle through the house sucking on butterscotch candies, a bottle of Windex in her robe pocket, occasionally spraying some piece of furniture down and wiping it clean with her sleeve. She would collapse on the couch at the opposite end from where I lay, intertwining her legs with mine. "You and me," she'd say. "We're not cut out for this world."

I didn't quite believe her, but I did worry. I worried about the spongy tissue of my brain, wondered if the chemicals inside were imbalanced, as my mother claimed. I pictured one half of my brain filled to bursting with viscous chemicals, the other shrunken and empty, caving in on itself. I worried about the inside of my body, the fragile web of veins covering my muscles, threading through my lungs, the soft organs hanging by sinews in the jostling dark cavern of me. I'd spend hours in the bathtub, lying very still, willing the water to clean this vulnerable feeling away. I had talks with myself. "You're spooking yourself," I'd say. "Fucking stop it. Get over it." I didn't want to leave the tub. I felt strong while lying alone in the water. If I switched on the fan and stuffed my ears with toilet paper, I could barely hear my mother's voice when she came knocking on the bathroom door, could barely hear the doorknob as she twisted it back and forth, calling my name.

I took the antidepressants. But I also began to eat six small meals a day and go for long runs in the afternoon so I'd be tired by bedtime. After a month or so, I returned to school. I wasn't sure if I'd recovered because I was sleeping and eating more, or because of the medication, or a little bit of both. But four months later, I stopped taking the medication. In another couple of weeks, I flushed the pills down the toilet and refilled the bottle with aspirin.

My mother didn't know that I'd stopped taking the pills she picked up for me every month. She didn't know that I seemed to be doing just fine without them. She didn't know that I was trying not to think of myself as a depressed and paranoid person, trying not to think of what had happened one year before. Some part of me was beginning to understand that thinking of myself as a sick person was indulgent. A trashy luxury. Like putting your finger on the burner, just to feel that quick bright heat.

But my mother had always been in love with the mind's frailties, the body's failures, and as we walked up the street toward the Kendricks' barbecue, she began to talk about the benign tumor that had recently been in her uterus. "Big as a grapefruit," she said, as if I had not heard all about it before. She described the way her abdomen felt now, when she touched it—"soft and wobbly, like a baby's fontanel"—and my stomach turned. If my father had been there, he would have been walking several feet ahead of us, humming in an agitated, determined way, a vein throbbing fatly at his temple. But he wasn't there. He was golfing with his business partners in Miami again. Before he had left, he had given me an expensive fan as a going-away present. "It's damn hot down in Athens," he'd said.

My mother put her arm around my shoulders and hugged me to her. "You're not talking much," she said, rubbing her palm up and down my arm. "And your skin is just a smidgen too cool. Are you feeling shaky?"

"I'm fine," I said. "Will you please stop asking me that every five minutes?"

"Well, sorry," my mother said. "You can't blame me for being worried."

Yes I can, I thought, clenching my jaw. My mother swatted my forearm, hard enough to sting. "Mosquito," she said, primly, and I looked down at the smear of blood on my skin.

We walked in silence past the brick homes on our street. My mother pulled me close to her again. I finally relaxed against her side and looped my arm around her waist. It seemed the right thing to do. I'd only be hers for one more day.

*

My mother lives alone, now. She has lived alone for ten years, ever since my father moved to Miami with a woman named Carol, a woman, he says, who has a good head on her shoulders. My father has breezily severed all ties with my mother and started a new life. As for me, no matter how distantly I travel, no matter how many months I am gone, my mother is always with me, her voice reaching me through telephone lines and radio waves across the ocean. No matter where I go, she finds me.

Of course, I'm the one who tells her where I am.

When I was twelve, I decided to run away from home, but I could not bring myself to leave the house without writing a note to my mother first. I told her that I would be living in the woods from then on and I hoped she wouldn't worry. She came out to the pond by the path behind our house, wearing her nightgown and rubbers, a flashlight in her hand. She dragged me back to the house, drew me a bath, and scrubbed my body so hard my skin flared red. Then she put me in bed and crawled under the covers. She fell asleep, curled behind me.

When I was in grade school, my mother and I would spend entire days in bed together. She would decide that I was sick and keep me home from school. I would open my eyes in the morning, and my mother would be leaning over me, pressing the back of her hand against my forehead. "Warm," she would say. "Very warm. Sick day for you." After my father left for work, she would crawl into bed with me and we'd spread the drawing pads and crayons around us. We'd turn the radio to an AM country station and sing whatever song they played. I loved Lorretta Lynn, and my mother said this was because I had coal-miner's blood, from my father's side. My mother loved Patsy Cline. She could sing just like Patsy, swaying gently from side to side, her eyes closed, her voice trembling in all the right places: *You don't love me anymore.* When my father came home from work at five, my mother would shut and lock my bedroom door, so he wouldn't disturb us.

As I grew older, I didn't want to stay home from school anymore. I didn't want my mother to be my only real friend. When I talked about my new friends at school, my mother would sniff. "You won't even remember their names when you're my age," she'd say.

Once I came home from school to find my mother sitting on the edge of my bed, staring at the wall. I sat beside her, quietly waiting for her to snap out of it, hesitantly touching her elbow, the back of her hand. "Do you ever hear voices?" she asked, gripping my knee. "In your head?" I told her I didn't, and she sighed. "Well, you probably will, someday," she said. "That's the way it's going to go with us."

After that day, I began to think that maybe she was right. Whenever I heard the trace of a voice in my head, I would pound my fists against my temples to make it stop. If I talked aloud to myself, I would shut my mouth quickly, wondering if this was the beginning of my long life of insanity. Looking back, I know that I was not going crazy, I know that my mother's words had become my own self-fulfilling prophecy, but at the time, I was morbidly afraid. I pictured the two of us in the future, lying in my bed and babbling like idiots, chewing on my crayons.

I continued to draw on my own, but the figures I drew became increasingly disturbing. I could never get the proportions right. Their heads were too big, their bodies boxy and awkward, their limbs jutting out at unnatural angles. Their eyes were large and strange. But my mother thought the drawings were brilliant, and she taped them to the wall above my bed. She refused to let me take them down. Because I was so wary of upsetting her, I kept them there. Mornings, I would open my eyes and see the figures above me, the pieces of them, the parts that didn't quite fit together. They seemed to be trying so hard to make visual sense, to add up to a whole. Sometimes I wanted to help them, to make them look right, but at other times, I hated them. I imagined the figures being stabbed or shot. I pictured them burning alive.

My own body began to transform, to grow longer and skinnier, fine dark hairs sprouting beneath my arms and between my legs. One night when I was twelve, I lay naked on my bed, running my hands over my stomach and the nubs of my breasts, looking down at my pale body in the lamplight. My skin tingled everywhere I touched. Then my mother flung open the door–she never knocked–and she drew in her breath sharply. I jerked onto my side, yanking the covers over my body.

She touched my shoulder, tugged on the covers. "Come on," she said. "Don't be ashamed. It's just your mom. Let me see this new body of yours."

"No, Mom. Stop it."

"Come on. Let me see."

She wrestled the covers from my body, pulled on my shoulder until I was on my back again. She was stronger than I was. Then she pressed her palm lightly to my neck, ran her fingers over my chest and ribs and the shallow plains of my hips. I closed my eyes. She spread her hands over my thighs and moved them down to my knees and back up again. She rubbed my legs in the same way she rubbed my arms when I was cold. She cupped her hand beneath my neck and lifted me toward her, and when I opened my eyes, her face was inches from mine. It was odd to be so close to her, to focus on only her eyes, her long hair falling past my cheeks. "Maggie," she said, as if my name made her terribly sad. Then she lowered her lips to mine. Her mouth was soft. Sticky and cool. She backed away, staring at me.

I didn't watch her leave the room. I rolled the blanket around me and buried my head inside its dark cocoon, counting my breaths so I wouldn't have to think. My body pulsed.

That was the night I left her the note and waited for her to find me by the pond. The night she scrubbed me in the bathtub until my body was raw, curled behind me in bed, crying, and I felt her sadness as if it were my own. The night I lay awake as she slept restlessly beside me, her legs shifting, as if she were trapped in a dream, and I thought I would never be able to leave her again.

*

When we arrived, the Kendricks' barbecue was in full swing. My mother slung her purse over her shoulder like a bandolier and put on her sunglasses, the cat-eyed ones with blue-tinted lenses. She treated social occasions with the mind-set of a soldier. She invaded the crowd in her uniform of strange, dated clothes, armed with her shrill laugh and non sequiturs, and forced people to deal with her. I don't think she knew any other way to be. She clutched my elbow and began to weave with purpose through the crowd, barking out hellos to our neighbors. Some of them helloed back, but most of them smiled, faintly, and turned away. My mother's purse was so large it whacked against people's arms as she moved, unsettling their drinks.

We kept walking, past the tan limbs and bright white sneakers, and I grew dizzy from the scents of my neighbors, their fruity perfume and bug repellant, their warm beery breath. We climbed onto the patio, and I looked down at the swimming pool in the side yard, where the Kendrick twins were splashing water in each other's faces, blonde hair plastered to their foreheads. "Girls," Georgie Kendrick called out softly to his daughters. He was the picture of Deer Hollow fatherhood, sitting in a lawn chair beside the pool in his tube socks and baseball cap. "Don't play too rough," he said, smiling. "Hey, now."

Amy Kendrick rushed up to me and squeezed my arm. "Maggie sweetie," she said. "I heard you're going away to college tomorrow." She clapped her hands lightly. "That's so exciting!"

Amy was an energetic, boring woman whom I secretly liked. I liked her ponytail and apricot skin, her normal-mom clothes—white blouse, neat jeans, sensible brown sandals. She was, I was sure, a woman who cut out coupons and did creative things with hamburger. The only thing my mother knew how to cook was a milky casserole with fish and peas in it. Most nights, she picked up carryout from Ding Ho's.

"Yes," I said, relaxing as I looked into Amy's blue eyes. "I'm leaving. Finally."

"That's just super."

"You look nice, Aims," my mother said. My mother gave everyone a nickname and tried to use it as much as possible in conversation. She slid her sunglasses down to the tip of her nose and lowered her voice confidentially. "As for me, I might look great, but I'm still recovering."

"Oh," Amy said, tilting her head to the side. "I didn't know you were sick."

"I had that tumor removed," my mother said. She pulled up her blouse, sucking in her stomach, and tugged down on her slacks, revealing the wiry black thread of her stitches. "He tried to get the thing out vaginally, but when I woke up, I had these–"

"Mom," I hissed, yanking on her arm. "What are you doing?" She would have unzipped her pants if I hadn't stopped her.

Amy smiled brightly, murmured some excuse, and rushed back toward the house.

My mother sighed. She took off her sunglasses and walked to the edge of the patio, as if she were contemplating stepping down into the backyard. Explosions of laughter, booming voices, and the squeals of children rose up, like a wave.

Her eyebrows peaked together. She looked afraid. "Come on, Maggie," she said. "Come with me."

But I turned away. I walked across the patio, through the sliding glass door, and into the Kendricks' house, where the *vuh-vuh-vum, vuh-vuh-vum* of dance music pulsed in the living room, like a heart murmur.

*

I remember the first time she threatened to leave me. I was fourteen. I came home from school and the house was empty, cleaner than usual, dishes drip-drying in the rack, magazines fanned on the coffee table just so. My mother rarely went anywhere without leaving a note for me on the kitchen table, notes she wrote in painstakingly perfect penmanship, underlining the important words twice. I walked slowly through the rooms, calling for her. It was springtime, and the windows were open, white curtains shifting in the breeze. The air smelled cool and clean.

I took a glass of ice water into my room and sat on the window ledge, in the sun. I closed my eyes and enjoyed the silence. "Don't come home," I whispered. "Stay away, stay away, stay away." But soon the phone rang, and I knew it would be her. I waited, but the ringing went on and on. I picked up the phone and held it to my ear. I could hear the muffled sound of conversations in the background, like the murmur of restaurant voices. Finally, I said hello.

"You're probably wondering where I am," my mother answered. She waited for me to respond. "Hello?"

"Yeah, Mom," I said. "I was wondering."

"Well, I can't tell you, I'm sorry, I just can't. I'm only calling to let you know that I'm not dead."

"I didn't think you were dead, Mom."

"Not now, you don't, but you'd probably begin to wonder later. What I mean is that you're never going to see me again. You obviously don't need me anymore, and your father won't even notice I'm gone, so I'm sure you both will be just fine without me. Don't worry. I'll find some boring little place to live, just like Deer Hollow, and I'll be happy as a crazy little clam. Goodbye. You know I love you."

This was the first time she did this. She would try it only a few more times. But because this was the first time, a real panic came over me. I thought of calling my father at work. I thought of calling the police. I thought of how I had willed her to stay away and how that couldn't possibly have been a coincidence. I pictured my mother driving down the interstate, glancing nervously at the rearview mirror, chewing on a fingernail and swerving from lane to lane, Hank Williams blaring. She had the habit of picking up reckless-operation citations once she got on the freeway. She'd lost her license long ago.

But about twenty minutes later, just as I was picking up the phone to call the police, my mother walked through the kitchen door, smiling pleasantly, a smudge of something on her cheek—dirt or grease. Her clothes and hair were soaked through with water, as if she had just emerged from a pool. She was carrying a plastic bag, Ding Ho's in red calligraphy on the front of it. "I got you number seventeen, this time." She tossed her keys onto the kitchen table, taking a deep breath. "The world is so beautiful today." She smoothed her damp palm over the back of my head. "It just makes you feel so ugly, you know?"

I knew she wanted me to ask her where she had been and why she was dripping wet, so I didn't, and this killed her. That night she left her soggy clothes in a pile at the foot of my bed as a reminder, but I refused to acknowledge the gesture. I didn't even speak to her for days. Walking home from school, I would will for her to be there when I got home. I would walk through the door, my muscles tensing, listening for the sound of her somewhere in the house. And then I would hear her voice. I would see her moving down the hallway toward the kitchen. I didn't want her to reach me. I just wanted to see her continually moving toward me, distant, but there.

*

Once it grew dark, Amy Kendrick lit citronella candles on the patio and the remaining guests gathered in lawn chairs in the grass. My mother sat with her legs crossed and her purse in her lap, eagerly following the conversation, her straw hat hanging by its string from her throat. The Wilsons, the Rhodes, Georgie and Amy were sipping from glasses of red wine. All of them were a little drunk, aside from my mother, who was drinking grape Kool-Aid from a plastic cup. When they laughed, my mother laughed, too, but a beat late, as if she weren't really listening. She sat on the edge of her chair and studied their faces, nodding. My mother never knew quite what to do with herself unless she was the one doing the talking.

A few feet away from their lawn chairs, the back yard met a shallow line of trees, and as soon as I walked toward it, my mother's radar went off. "Where are you going, Maggs?" she called out, twisting around in her chair.

"I'll be right back," I said. "Just stretching my legs."

I passed through the trees until I came to the path on the other side. I had walked the path many times before. If I followed it far enough, I would come to my own back yard. The path was made of cedar-chip mulch, and on one side of it, the land sloped down into a large pond. Bullfrogs croaked down in the murky green water. Fireflies blinked, as if in synch with the croaking. Moonlight shone down on the pond, penetrating the spaces between the algae, so that the water glowed only in patches here and there, and brightly, as if it were lit from within. The moon was a flat orange disk, so low in the sky that gray shapes swirled on its surface, like continents on a map.

I could see our back-deck light far up the path, and in a matter of minutes, I could be there, opening the back door, walking inside. I still needed to pack a few things. I wanted to put on my new hiking boots and admire the way they looked on my feet. I thought they made me look strong. Prepared. In Athens, there were rocky green hills to climb. In Athens, the air smelled of honeysuckle and river water. In Athens, I imagined, my calves would grow taut. My hair would grow long. I would live every day out in the world.

I picked up my pace, concentrating on our back-deck light, which was now glowing bluely, like a nearby star. But I didn't even make it halfway there before I thought of my mother sitting in the lawn chair in her red-checked blouse, her ridiculous hat. I stuffed my hands in my pockets. I turned around.

*

A few years after my father left her, my mother moved out of our house and into a condominium complex on Route 23. She tells me she spends a great deal of time staring at a television, sometimes when it's turned on. But every Saturday afternoon, she goes for walks in the woods behind the complex and doesn't come home until dusk. "I keep thinking about the trees," she once said to me on the phone. "We think we have it rough, but those trees have got it much, much worse. They can't even move. They have to watch their friends get diseases and slowly die, and they can't do a damn thing about it. Then one day—boom. Fred's on the ground. Goodbye, Fred. It's heartbreaking."

My mother has been talking like this more and more lately. During one phone conversation she'll be concerned about the trees, during the next she will become very emotional about the stray cats on Route 23. "Why don't you rescue one of those cats?" I once asked her. "Might do you some good to take care of something."

My mother didn't say anything for a moment. Then she sighed. "I guess we both know how good I am at doing that."

I wanted to tell her that she hadn't done such a bad job of taking care of me. But I didn't. Maybe I didn't have the energy to lie. I was getting ready to catch a flight, at the time, and I was already thinking of my window seat on the plane, the landscape opening up beneath me, the bright neat squares of green absorbing the untidy details, the blanket of clouds absorbing the squares of green.

"I have to go, Mom," I said.

"Yep," said my mother, and hung up the phone.

We don't even bother saying goodbye anymore. There will always be another call.

*

When I reached the Kendricks' house, I veered off the mulch path and stood near the edge of their yard, in the shadows of the trees. The citronella candles had been snubbed and no one was left in the circle of lawn chairs aside from my mother and Amy and Georgie Kendrick. It was time to go home.

But my mother was talking. It seemed she was in the middle of a story, and Amy and Georgie had no choice but to listen. Georgie fidgeted in his chair, looking down at the grass, and Amy shook her head, laughing nervously, ponytail bobbing. My mother's back was to me. No one could see me, so I stopped in the shadow of the trees to listen to my mother for a moment, contemplating taking the path home by myself after all. It was difficult to stop her once she was on a roll, and she seemed to be talking about her favorite subject, me.

"Oh, she's a very smart girl. Very bright. And artistic. Teachers love her, all you neighbors love her, everyone loves my daughter.

Maggie. And why shouldn't they? She's beautiful and athletic, she gets As on her papers and blah-de-blah-de-blah." She held up her hand and made it talk. "Blah."

My mother swooped toward Amy and clasped her by the arm. "But what you don't understand is how mentally unstable she is."

My throat constricted. I had the impulse to run toward her, but I didn't.

"What a weird thing to say, Gina," Amy said, trying to remain cheerful, withdrawing her arm from my mother's claw-like grip. "That can't be true."

"You know why you don't think that's true? You know why?" My mother grabbed hold of Amy's arm again. "Because you weren't there when she had a complete nervous breakdown."

Amy bit her bottom lip. "Oh," she said.

"Yeah, you think you know her, but you don't," said my mother, her words rapid and tense. "She has real problems. Anxiety, depression, paranoia, you name it. She's not well. She had the breakdown only a year ago, and she'll never fully recover."

"Maybe Maggie wouldn't want you to tell us about it," Georgie murmured, putting his empty wineglass to his lips.

"She's taking enough medication to kill a horse, but she could snap any second and have to go through that hell all over again," my mother replied, ignoring him. "I mean, when it was bad? When Maggie was at her very worst? I hate to tell you this"—she lowered her voice—"but she wet herself. I'm serious! Peed her pants, just like a little kid. I even had to hand-feed her at one point. And don't even get me started about the splinter in her finger. The splinter. My God! She had a splinter and she was convinced she was going to die if I didn't get it out. She said, 'Mom, I'm going to get an infection! It'll kill me! It'll kill me!' She was like a lunatic."

"That's terrible," Amy whispered.

"What do you know about it!"

Georgie cleared his throat. "Gina," he said, half-rising in his chair.

"You don't know anything about it," my mother said. "That's what."

"But she seems to be better now–" Amy began.

My mother let out a kind of trembling moan that made Georgie wince. "You don't know how I held her in my arms that night," my mother said. "All night long, I rocked her and rocked her, trying to convince her that she wasn't going to die. A splinter couldn't kill her. But she's so fragile on the inside. She's like a child, still. She has no one, no one in the world but me." My mother wrapped her arms around herself and rocked back and forth. She bowed her head to one side, and even from a distance I could see her profile, the brightness of her eyes, the downturn of her lips. "She can go away to college. She can leave. I don't care. She's going to go crazy and I won't be there to help her. She's already crazy." My mother was whispering now. "She is."

*

My mother recently called my apartment in Prague.

"Where are you now?" she asked. "Czechoslovakia?"

"It's the Czech Republic, Mom."

"Isn't it dangerous there? What about the communists?"

"Oh, they got tired of oppressing people and decided to leave," I said. "Now the country is run by an intellectual. A writer."

"Well, good for the Czechoslovakians."

I turned toward the window and the phone cord wrapped around my waist, pinching my skin. I could see the red clay rooftops of Michle beneath my window, the orange-vested street-sweeper standing on the corner, drinking a bottle of beer. The dogwoods were in full bloom, and when the wind picked up, white petals soared on the air, some of them landing on the cobblestones, some of them drifting between the buildings and out of sight.

"Where'd you just come from?" my mother asked.

"Poligny," I said. "Before that, Rome."

"I forgot where you were the other night, and I called the last number you gave me, and I ended up talking to this person who didn't speak English. It was kind of interesting, actually. I told her about the duck, and she kept saying, 'Wha? Wha?' But I think in some mysterious way she knew what I meant."

"The duck, Mom?"

"Found her by the pond, Maggie, way out in the woods. You think we have it bad, well, you should've seen this duck. She'd been shot. Right in the belly." My mother paused for so long I thought the line had disconnected. But then she cleared her throat. "I buried her," she said.

*

That night, after listening to my mother's version of my breakdown, after watching her fall apart in front of Amy and Georgie, I ran back toward the mulch path and slid down the loose soil of the embankment toward the pond. The bullfrogs croaked in alarm.

I hated her for humiliating me. Hated her more for her hold on me. Even as I had watched her rocking herself in the Kendricks' back yard, I knew that it was me she had pinned there against her chest. The one night I had woken up from a dream of a splinter entering my bloodstream, during those weeks when I had not been well, it was my mother who had told me that even the smallest splinter could cause an infection. "It's true, Maggie," she had said softly in my ear as she rocked me in her arms, running her fingers through my hair. "Even a little splinter can kill us. It's a dangerous world." I fell asleep and woke up to her kissing me—my cheeks, my forehead, my lips. She was stroking my side and saying my name. I let her kiss me. I told her I loved her. I curled into her. I kissed her back.

"I hate you," I announced to the pond. I sat by the water for at least an hour, saying this over and over, tasting the words on my tongue. I picked up a stone, held it in my fist, and closed my eyes until I felt like the stone—hard and hot and dry. I whizzed the stone across the surface of the pond and watched the water split open. I watched the waves ripple out and out.

I didn't know how rarely I would see my mother from then on. I didn't know that I would sometimes tell people that she was dead, then feel guilty afterward, admit that I'd lied, try to explain. I didn't realize how much time I would spend in the hills of Athens, camping in the snow, hiking through the woods, hunting for morels and wild raspberries, learning survival skills. How to make a salad from thistles and lemonbalm. How to soothe a bee sting with crushed plantain leaves. How to bury a hot stone from the fire in the earth, on a cold night, and lie with my heart over the mound of soil, so that the warmth circulated from my heart through my veins and out into my limbs.

I didn't know that I would discover the gothic asylum on the highest hill of Athens, the sprawling abandoned building that seemed to watch over the town. I would go for hikes on that hill, past the asylum's cemetery, past the unmarked gravestones jutting out of the earth like crooked teeth. After the asylum was shut down in the sixties, some of the residents were released into the streets, and as I walked through town, I would see them—the man with Tourrette's Syndrome who shouted curses as he gave sticks of bubble gum to passersby, the barefooted man who mumbled the Rosary and called himself Jesus, the wispy woman who yodeled for change in a muumuu on the courthouse steps. I didn't know that I would volunteer at a community center where these people came for food and conversation, to work on jigsaw puzzles of places they would never see—the Grand Canyon, the castles of Wales, the Charles Bridge, the Acropolis. I didn't know that I would see all of those places myself, after I left college, and that sometimes I would imagine the unfinished puzzles at the community center as I gazed up at the chalky white pillars of the Parthenon against the blue sky, or gazed down at the knobby, twisted branches of a juniper tree in the orange mouth of a canyon, awed for the moment, but not quite content, already thinking about the next place I should go.

For years, I would travel, teaching English to support myself, never staying in one place very long. For years, I would talk to my mother on the phone and attempt to describe the details of each new place I lived. The mist settling over the green fields of the French countryside in the mornings. The kerchiefed *babičkas* of Prague carrying home bloody bags of carp at Christmastime. The trill of a bouzouki. The peak of Mount Parnassus, and the tinny sound of sheep bells far below. The taste of hot wine. The scent of wet leather on the subway. Riding a bicycle through the hunting grounds of Rudolph II, past the five-hundred-year-old oak trees and squawking geese, in the rain. I would describe these things to my mother, and she would attempt to make some sort of response. Once, she said, "Maggie, I don't know what to tell you. Great. You're having an impressive life, all by yourself. Good for you." After that, I stopped trying to describe anything to her. And I began to listen.

I didn't know that even my mother would learn to step outside herself, slightly, by going for long walks in the woods until dusk, by bringing signs of the outer world into her home—or so I imagine. A bird's nest on the bookcase, shards of obsidian in a dish. Daisy fleabane leaning over the lip of a tall glass jar. A muddy footprint on the bathroom rug.

I didn't know any of this as I left the pond and walked home, that night. All I knew was that I hated her at that moment, and the hatred felt good. It felt right. She was going to be waiting up for me, sitting at the kitchen table in her disgusting pink terrycloth bathrobe. She would be upset that I had deserted her at the Kendricks' house. She would remind me that this was our last night together. She would look at me with that wounded expression and say, "Maggie, how could you? How could you just leave me like that?" And I would look back at her and answer her question directly.

But the house was oddly dark and quiet when I arrived. As I walked through the living room, all I could hear was the whir of the air conditioner. I turned down the hallway, and the first thing I saw was her straw hat on the floor. A bit further down, I came across the heap of her macramé purse. Then her blouse, her pants, her socks, forming a trail that led to the bathroom door. The door was ajar, and through the crack I could see a dim flickering light. I could hear the sound of water, slowly dripping.

I pushed open the door.

"You forgot about our bath," my mother said.

There were candles, everywhere. Red and yellow and purple, in small glass dishes along the floor and the windowsill above. Their flames cast shadows against the wall. My mother was leaning back in the claw-foot bathtub, her hair tied messily at the nape of her neck, the milky skim on the surface of the water parting around her breasts and knees. I saw a stack of fresh towels on the rug and a bottle of bubble bath on the edge of the sink. Romantic Evening, read its warped and cracked label. The bottle was coated in a light film of dust, as if it hadn't been used in years.

"I guess it was stupid idea," my mother said, glancing at me. "Giving you a bath. Stupid." She fished a washcloth out of the water and squeezed it over her arm, sighing. "Oh well. I suppose a bath is good for me, anyway. Good for my poor old stitched-up womb. You know."

"Have you been waiting for me here?"

She didn't answer, but I knew that she had been. I could picture her, preparing this bath for me, sitting patiently on the lid of the toilet, a towel in her lap, disappointment setting in. Deciding to climb into the tub herself. Lying there, waiting, her skin pruning in the water, planning precisely what she would say to me when I opened the bathroom door. She sniffed, pretending to be absorbed in the task of washing her arm. Her wet skin shone in the candlelight.

I kneeled on the rug before her. "Give me the washcloth, Mom," I said.

She rolled her eyes. I could see the dark smudges beneath her lashes where her mascara had bled. "Oh, you can't be serious. You? Wash me?"

"Just give it to me, Mom."

She smiled, her eyes brightening. "Okay," she said, holding out the dripping washcloth in her palm, like an offering.

I dipped the cloth into the soapy water and circled it over her neck and shoulders. She rounded over, and I pushed the cloth down the notches of her spine. I lifted her wrist and tucked the cloth between each of her dangling fingers. I spread the cloth over her chest and ran it down her ribs and stomach, my hands sinking into the water until I could feel the wiry, pointed tips of her stitches. My mother winced.

She slid down until her neck was submerged in the water. "Do my feet," she said, kicking her leg out and resting her ankle on the lip of the tub. "Do my toes." She slid further down until the water covered her chin. "Wonderful," she said as I ran the cloth over her foot. Her mouth sunk below the surface, and she closed her eyes.

I looked at her, for a moment, watching the bubbles escape her mouth and rise to the surface of the water. I looked at the soft blue veins of her eyelids, the fine hair at her temples, the pinkness of her cheeks. She was smiling a little, humming quietly, her arms floating limply at her sides. I placed my hands on her shoulders, lightly at first, and then I let my fingers sink into her skin. My mother stopped humming. Her eyes flashed open. I pressed down on her shoulders, and her eyes disappeared. She struggled, but I was stronger than she was. She beat at my chest, but I kept pressing down. I pressed down until her face, her hair, all of her was submerged in the water, held her there for as long as I felt was necessary, holding my own breath as I did so, feeling the strength of my arms, the solid pounding of my heartbeat.

Then I grasped her shoulders and lifted her up. I lifted her up, and the water spilled away from her face. My mother opened her mouth wide and inhaled, sharply, sucking air into her lungs as if for the first time.

Some of the Art of Fiction

Reginald Gibbons

"This was once a handsome residential hotel, not so very large, but now it's a halfway house for mentally ill persons on medication." My guide pointed to a brick building, six or perhaps it was seven stories high, with an entranceway that had been made smaller and darker by remodeling, after hotel elegance was no longer wanted. In the cold air moving as a cold breeze, of a kind that can be tasted in winter, the building faced a small park in which the leafless elms looked like a mad growth of endlessly proliferating antlers. "They tend to congregate"—he meant the persons who could not survive except by looking at everything through a pharmacological lens—"during the day in that café across the street to one side. It was here that Gordon Weaver, an excellent although little known American writer, drank his first Coca-Cola, more than half a century ago, in the rooms of his aunt, who lived here when it was a residential hotel and whom he would come to visit from Milwaukee when he was a boy. She kept Coca-Cola in her refrigerator."

I said only, "Oh," in acknowledgment of his information, as I looked where he pointed, because I was not giving my guide all my attention as we walked along the pleasant street. I was distracted by the two men who had begun following us as soon as we had left my guide's car, several blocks to the west. The men kept a constant distance of half a block behind us. With few walkers out in the winter day, there was a feeling of emptiness around us, and the small-town sidewalks gave the two men no cover.

But really I was just walking the four blocks from my studio apartment to the laundromat beyond the halfway house (the ex-hotel, which really had been turned, years ago, to its new use) to see if my clothes were dry. The people from the halfway house are alienated from themselves and from each other and from all the rest of us by their mental and emotional afflictions. Some of them may, with a certain focus and even cunning, pursue their own immediate interests effectively—such as a sweet or a cigarette or a cup of coffee or another pill or another ill person—but none of them, including the cunning ones, can pursue their own emotional interests and catch hold of the prize of steadiness—like a mental gyroscope that would make it possible for them to live on their own. The men behind us are the imaginary villains on whom we all—including the people living in the halfway house, the ex-hotel—would like to blame something, to whom we would like to ascribe the heartlessness that is partly in us, but which also does such great damage from its thrones in the minds of the powerful.

No one was following us; and there wasn't any guide, although there really is an American writer named Gordon Weaver and he really is a good one. Everything else I was inventing.

But really I was making up the story about walking to the laundromat. I wasn't walking there at all, I was sitting in my studio apartment in my old, rather worn armchair, which is upholstered in a now faded deep red, it's comfortable both because of its shape and because it's friendly in its shabby, familiar way. And I was writing all this on a legal pad with a throwaway roller-ball pen, although there really is a Gordon Weaver.

A golden reiver.

But really, I do not live in a studio apartment, I was not this person narrating his story of not doing something but rather imagining a narrative for himself. Instead, I was or am myself writing down and revising again and again these words which may give the impression—as I want them to do—of being those of someone who in the first place narrates a dramatic situation that suggests the classic story of a journey of a pilgrim, a seeker, led by a guide (as Dante was led by Virgil through Hell, where there were various sorts of persons alienated from God by sin, who were eternally punished for these sins against the Christian God and crimes against each other, although Dante the person did not undertake any such journey nor could have done so in reality, since no one can really travel through time to converse with the dead, but he described an imaginary version of himself along with the imagined figure of the ancient Roman poet Virgil traveling through imaginary realms which he, Dante the poet, peopled with figures drawn from Italian life of his time by writing an elaborate and exquisitely worded and shaped poem, so that he, Dante the imaginary poet-traveler guided by the imagined Virgil, could observe those imagined sinners and even converse with them, so that he, Dante the poet, could make use of these figures in order to articulate through narrative his ideas about religion, politics and the state, and his acute sense of the human range of experience and feeling, motives and desires), and who—now I mean the person whose "voice" I have impersonated in this little piece of writing, or ventriloquized as if the written text were a moving puppet—in the second place describes also some sinister figures such as those in classic American detective fiction (where the story of the journey is, just as much as in Dante but with an entirely different tone, a quest for truth, only in the case of classic American detective fiction the truth is of the explanation of some human crime and may seem trivial compared to the quest for the very truth of human existence such as Dante pursues in his account of the relationship of man to God, narratively symbolized and made absorbing by the many stories and details of Dante's realm of Hell), and who then—my narrator, again—in the third place confesses or at least explains that he, this person whom I have made up, has made up his narrative, as if he, a fictional creation of mine, had the same freedom of will that I think I have, and thus appeared to break free of his captivity in the confines, so to speak, of my mind, and who in the fourth place has also made up the confession that his confession is false. As if to play with the power of imagining.

But there really is a golden reiver, who from us has reived or reft the whole world that was—a thousand years ago, or when we were children, or yesterday, or in the moment before you began to read this little instance of some aspects but not all of the art of fiction. Thought may riot or may move as though in a slight breeze, like a single butterfly on a summer day of blossoms or like a single snowflake on a day of winter crystals. Feeling may flood suddenly, or may move like one raindrop blown this way and that on a long fall from cloud heights to the surface of a puddle in a street or a field. Blooms and blowing winds; streets filled with smoke and chaotic rushing as the police or soldiers advance and clear the intersections one by one with volleys of tear-gas canisters or bullets; the mind following a guide of its own intuitive invention, imagined as a person. Fragments. Feeling and thinking becoming a story of something that sparkles with meaning flashing off it in bursts of light even when the story itself is dark.

Dream then, and speak among your selves that are all one self, and raise a little flag to mark where an unexpected discovery, a place of heroic resistance or kind love or inspiring perseverance, however small or ephemeral or unknown, gives the lie to all this noise around us from machines both mechanical and electronic, from persons both maniacal and chronically false (whether housed halfway between the sane and the insane, or paid inconceivable sums to read news reports, or to decide to shut factories), from structures both political and sermonic, from cruel persons both critical and demonic.

But there really is a garden griever. There are two, in fact. That is a very old tale, indeed–the two of them who together must find a way to go on.

El zapaterito de Guanajuato

Elena Garro

IBA YO BAJANDO la avenida, llevaba a Faustino de la mano, mi nietecito no decía nada, aunque yo bien veía que los tres días de girar por la ciudad, sin alimento y sin cobijo, lo habían amedrentado. "Sin dinero, sin familia y sin amigos, ¿qué será de nosotros?", me iba yo diciendo, mientras veía las casas y las ventanas que me miraban pasar. Nunca fui pedigüeño y la vergüenza del hambre me hacía caminar sin ver por dónde pisaba. La ciudad es hosca por desconocida y todas sus calles, que son muchas, son ajenas a la tristeza de un fuereño. "¿Qué será de nosotros sin un alma que nos mire?" Iba yo oyendo los pasitos encarrerados de Faustino, sin verlo, para no mirarle el hambre .... "De seguro lleva la boca bien seca. Sufriendo se enseña el hombre ..." así iba yo diciéndome, cuando la vi por primera vez. Estaba dentro de un coche nuevo, encaramada en el asiento, bien abrazada al hombre que la tenía tomada por la cintura. De él solo vi el pelo negro asomando sobre un hombro de ella, y los brazos que la sostenían. Me dije: "¡Caray, aquí se besan en mitad de la calle y en plena luz del sol!" Me llamó la atención su cintura delgadita adentro de su vestido blanco.

The Little Shoemaker from Guanajuato

Elena Garro

Translated by Sara Dania Kippur

I continued walking down the street, holding Faustino by the hand; my little grandson said nothing, though I could see that the three days of walking around the city without food and without shelter had frightened him. *Without money, without family, or friends, what will become of us?* I kept asking myself, while I gazed at the houses and windows that watched me pass by. I've never been a nuisance, and the shame of hunger made me pay little attention to where I was headed. The city is unwelcoming for those who aren't familiar with it, and the streets, which are many, seem indifferent to the feelings of some out-of-towner. *What will become of us without a soul to watch over us?* I continued hearing Faustino's small, quick-paced steps, without looking at him, so as not to see his hunger . . . . *Surely his mouth must be very dry. Men can get used to suffering . . .* and I was repeating this to myself, when I saw her for the first time.

She was inside a new car, perched on the seat, in the tight embrace of a man, holding her around the waist. I could see only his black hair sticking out over her shoulder and his arms holding her. I thought, *Wow, here people kiss in the middle of the street, in broad daylight!* I noticed her thin waist inside her white dress.

La puerta del coche estaba abierta, y le vi las piernas tan desnudas como los brazos. Faustino también los vio. Y los dos vimos, cuando ella levantó una mano y le dio una bofetada en mitad de los besos que se daban. El, ofendido, echó la cabeza para atrás y ya no vi nada. No podía yo quedarme a mirar. "¡Viejo curioso!", me hubieran dicho y con sobrada razón. Faustino y yo seguimos bajando la avenida. "¡Qué genio tan vivo!" me dije y ahora me digo: "¡Ojalá que Dios le detenga la mano, para que no acabe mal!" De repente el coche nuevo pasó zumbando junto a nosotros. Vimos cómo adentro iban forcejeando: él para detenerla, ella con la portezuela abierta. El coche iba zig-zagueando, como si fuera borracho. "¡Sea por Dios, con tal de que no les salga al paso un poste!". . . . Faustino y yo seguimos bajando la avenida a la que no le veíamos fin. La mentada avenida era como todas las calles de la ciudad de México: cerrada por paredes y por casas, sin desembocadura al campo. La luz por allá es muy blanca y sin verdura, y a esas horas del mediodía, con los ojos sin sueño, los pies andados y el estómago limpio, cansa. En mis ochenta y dos años ya he visto mucho, pero nada tan desamparado como los mediodías de la nombrada ciudad de México. Faustino iba espantado. Así me lo dijo ella, cuando nos habló. Porque de repente la vimos venir andando de cara a nosotros. Su traje blanco relumbraba al sol. Parecía muy acalorada. Abrió tamaños ojos y se nos quedó mirando.

—No son de aquí, ¿verdad?

Nos vio fuereños por los pantalones de manta, los huaraches y los sombreros ardidos de sol.

—No, niña.

Se quedó piensa y piensa; ella todo lo piensa mucho aunque parezca que no.

—¿En dónde paran?

The car door opened, and I saw her legs, naked like her arms. Faustino also noticed them. And we both watched as she lifted her hand and slapped him right in the midst of their kissing. Offended, he threw his head back, and I could no longer see anything. I couldn't keep looking.

Nosy old man, they would have called me, and with good reason. Faustino and I continued walking down the street. *What a bad temper!* I thought then, and even now I think, *Let's pray God stops him from hitting her, so this doesn't end badly!* Suddenly the same new car whirred by us. We saw how they were struggling inside: he to stop her, and her to open the door. The car kept zigzagging, as if it were drunk. For the love of God, let's hope that post doesn't get in their way!

Faustino and I continued walking down the seemingly endless avenue, like all others in Mexico City: enclosed by walls and houses that didn't open onto the countryside. The light there is very white, without any greenery, especially at noon. With our eyes weary, legs heavy from walking, and stomachs empty, we tired quickly. I have seen a lot in my eighty-two years, but nothing as deserted as midday in Mexico City.

Faustino looked frightened, or so she said to me, when she spoke to us, because all of a sudden we saw her walking straight towards us, her white suit glistening in the sun. She seemed hot and agitated and opened her small eyes to stare at us.

—You're not from here, right?

She could tell we were from the country because of our calico pants, sandals, and hats, baked by the sun.

—No, miss.

She stood there thinking, and thinking. She always thinks about everything, though it seems like she doesn't.

—Where are you staying?

—En ninguna parte, niña.

Era feo mendigarle y los dos preferimos bajar los ojos. Nos dio vergüenza la desdicha.

—¿Ya comieron?

Preguntó de frente y sin rodeos. ¿Para qué mentirle, si se nos veía el hambre? Se me nublaron los ojos, la vejez no sirve para atajar a las lágrimas cuando quieren correr.

—No, niña. Ni mi nietecito ni yo hemos probado alimento, en los tres días que llevamos girando por estas dichosas calles.

Le dije todo por el niño. El orgullo hay que hacerlo a un lado cuando hay criaturas.

—¿Tres días?

Nos miró como si dijéramos mentiras y luego se puso a mirar los coches que en esa avenida nunca dejan de pasar.

—¡Hay mucha hambre, niña! Mucha hambre. No sólo nosotros la padecemos, en mi pueblo todos andamos en la misma desgracia. Por eso venimos del campo a buscar consuelo en la ciudad.

—¡Estos bandidos del gobierno!

Se enojó como las yeguas y dio patadas en el suelo.

—Vengan.

No me avergonzó su caridad. La hacía con enojo, como si ella tuviera la culpa de mi triste situación. La frescura de su casa nos consoló de la sequía de la calle. Sus sirvientas se pusieron a reír cuando nos vieron. Luego detuvieron la risa y se quedaron serias. Una de ellas se acercó a la señora Blanquita.

—Señora, ya van tres veces que llama, una después de la otra. Seguidito, seguidito.

La señora Blanquita se puso roja de mohina y apoyó la cara sobre la mano para no pensar. Todos nos callamos.

—Nowhere, miss.

It was embarrassing to beg from her and we both preferred to avert our gazes. Our misfortune made us feel ashamed.

—Have you already eaten?

She asked us straightforwardly, no beating around the bush. Why lie if she could see our hunger? My eyes clouded over; even old age can't protect you from tears when they want to flow.

—No, miss. Neither my grandson nor I have eaten anything in three days, since we've been walking around these damned streets.

I confessed everything because of the child. One has to throw pride to the wind when children are involved.

—Three days?

She looked at us as if we were lying, and then she started observing the cars that endlessly speed down the avenue.

—There is a lot of hunger, miss! A lot of hunger. We're not the only ones who suffer from it; in my village, all experience the same misfortune. That's why we left the country, to find comfort in the city.

—Those damn government crooks!

She got angry like a mare and stomped the ground.

—Come with me.

I wasn't ashamed of her charity. But she seemed to do it with annoyance, as if she felt responsible for my sad situation.

The airiness of her house soothed us from the dryness of the street. Her servants laughed when they saw us, then stopped and became serious. One approached Señora Blanquita.

—Señora, he's called three times now, one right after the other. All in a row.

Señora Blanquita got red with exasperation and covered her face with her hands as if to prevent herself from thinking about it. We all got quiet.

—Si llama otra vez díganle que no he llegado . . . o que me morí . . . .

Sus sirvientas y ella se quedaron muy tristes. Faustino y yo hicimos como si no hubiéramos oído nada y como si no estuviéramos allí. Las sirvientas nos llevaron a un cuarto para reposarnos, mientras nos preparaban la comida.

—¡Cuánta molestia! — decía yo.

—No se mortifique, señor, estamos impuestas, así es la señora Blanquita.

Y así es. Por la tarde me quedé en la cocina platicando con ellas. Les conté de Guanajuato y de las tristezas que pasábamos: quería pagarles la cortesía del hospedaje y de la risa. Al oscurecer entró a la cocina la señora Blanquita. Estaba bien triste. Ocupó una sillita y se fumó dos cigarros, sin decir una palabra.

—Vete a ver al Chino, para ver si nos fía algo para la cena— dijo de repente.

Nunca pensé que una casa tan bien puesta y una señora tan bien vestida, no tuviera ni un centavo para cenar. ¡Parecía tan rica!

—El dinero se va como agua. Es maldito, ¿verdad?

Muy verdad que era maldito. Y así se lo contesté a la señora Blanquita.

—¿Hay mucha hambre en su tierra?

—Sí, niña, mucha.

Preguntando, preguntando, me hizo contarle mi vida, mis pesares, y la razón de mi viaje a la mentada ciudad de México. Soy de oficio zapatero, le dije, pero a causa de la pobreza, ya nadie compra zapatos en Guanajuato. Por eso junté unos centavos, que le pedí al agiotista, y me puse a hacer algunos pares, para venir a venderlos a la ciudad de México, en donde todavía

—If he calls again tell him I'm not home yet . . . or that I've died. . . .

Both she and her servants seemed depressed. Faustino and I acted as if we hadn't heard anything, or as if we weren't even there. The servants brought us to a room where we could rest while they prepared a meal.

—What a hassle we must be! — I said.

—Don't get distressed, sir, we're used to it. That's how Señora Blanquita is.

And that's how it was. I spent the afternoon in the kitchen chatting with the servants. I told them about Guanajuato and about our difficult life there. I wanted to pay them back for the courtesy of their hospitality, and for their laughter.

Señora Blanquita entered the kitchen at dusk. She seemed incredibly sad. She sat down and smoked two cigarettes without saying a word.

—Go see El Chino to see if he can offer us something for dinner on credit— she suddenly said.

I would never have thought that with such a well-appointed house, and such a well-dressed Señora, they wouldn't have a cent to buy dinner. She seemed so rich!

—Money goes like water. It's wretched, no?

I agreed with Senora Blanquita that it's wretched.

—Is there much hunger in your village?

—Yes, miss, a lot.

Her asking and asking propelled me to tell her the story of my life, about my sorrows, and the reason for my trip to this city. I am by trade a shoemaker, I told her, but because of poverty, no one buys shoes in Guanajuato anymore. So I put together a little money that I got from the money-changer, and I made a few pairs to come and sell in Mexico City, where rich people still

la gente rica lleva zapatos. Salieron muy bonitos, con hebillas de plata y tacones altos. Por allá somos mineros, y nos gusta tanto el oro como la plata. En otros tiempos todo fue de oro: los palacios, los peines, los altares y en algunas casas hasta los barrotes de las ventanas fueron de oro. Pero, ya digo, eso fue en otros tiempos. Ahora somos pobres, por eso vine hasta aquí a traer mis zapatos. Rosa, mi hija mayor, los envolvió en papel de seda, y me prestó a su hijo Faustino, para que me acompañara en el viaje. Mi hija Gertrudis nos preparó la comida y nos hizo el itacate. Y la mañana de un jueves nos pusimos en camino. A las tres de la mañana agarramos la carretera y caminamos hasta el mediodía. A esa hora hallamos albergue en la casa de un carbonero, que nos ofreció su compasión, su agua fresca y también su fuego para calentar las tortillas. Con él también hicimos noche. Nos fuimos de madrugada. Al despedirnos nos deseó la buena compañía de Dios y nos dijo que en el viaje de regreso nos recogería otra vez. En nueve días que duró el viaje, lo hicimos a buen paso, hallamos consuelo en la gente de bien, que nos compadecía. A mí, a causa de mis ochenta y dos años. Y a Faustino, mi nietecito, por sus ocho añitos tan tiernos. Cuando entramos en la ciudad de México, nos fuimos derechos a la Villa de Guadalupe, para dar gracias. Hicimos noche en los portales de la Villa, junto con otros peregrinos, que también venían en busca de consuelo para su hambre y sus pesares. Allí platicando, platicando, un señor me informó que en cualquier mercado me comprarían los zapatos.

—¡Qué bonitos! —me dijo, cuando se los enseñé. Yo no me di bien cuenta de que los miró con codicia, sino hasta el otro día, cuando amanecí sin ellos. Faustino me dijo:

—Vamos a buscarlo, abuelo, al fin que no andará lejos.

wear shoes. They turned out really nice, with silver buckles and high heels. We're miners over in my village, and we like gold just as much as silver. In earlier times everything was gold: palaces, combs, altars, even the window bars of some houses were made out of gold. But, as I said, these were other times. Now we're all poor, and that's why I came here to try out my shoes. Rosa, my oldest daughter, wrapped them up in silk paper, and lent me her son Faustino to accompany me on this trip. My daughter Gertrudis prepared our lunch and made us traveling provisions.

On a Thursday morning we began our trip. At three in the morning we reached the highway and walked until midday. At that point we found shelter in the house of a coal merchant, who offered us warmth, fresh water, and a fire to heat up our tortillas. We spent the night with him. We left in the morning. When we said goodbye, he prayed that the Lord be with us and told us that we'd find him again on our return trip. We struck a good pace for the nine days that our journey lasted, and found solace in good people who showed us compassion – which I needed because of my eighty-two years, and Faustino, my little grandson, because of his eight tender years. When we entered Mexico City, we walked directly to the Villa de Guadalupe to offer thanks. We spent the night in the villa, next to other travelers, who were also in search of relief from their hunger and suffering. There, chatting together, a man informed me that any market would buy my shoes.

–How lovely! – he said to me when I showed them to him. I didn't realize that he was eyeing them greedily, until the next day when I woke up without them.

Faustino said, –We're going to look for them, Grandpa. They couldn't have gone far.

Y así fue: nos pusimos busca y busca y busca sin hallarlo. El señor no era muy alto, llevaba una chamarra de cuero, tenía el pelo muy negro y se reía bonito. Pero no dimos con él. Andábamos en su busca, sin un centavo, y sin poder volver a Guanajuato, cuando la hallamos a usted, señora Blanquita.

La señora Blanquita nos miró compadecida.

—¿Y cuánto valían sus zapatos?

—Algo así como unos cien o quinientos pesos. Nunca lo supe de cierto, porque como le dije, no llegué a venderlos.

—¡Uy, qué bicoca!

Y la señora Blanquita se echó a reír. Hay que decir que ella no es de medias tintas, o se ríe mucho, o está bien enojada.

—Quinientos pesos . . . yo se los doy y le pago su boleto de autobús para que regrese a Guanajuato.

Mucho se lo agradecí. Le di mi nombre junto con las gracias: Loreto Rosales, para servirla. Y mi nieto, Faustino Duque, su servidor. Regresó la sirvienta que se llama Josefina, y que es frondosa y de buen parecer.

—El Chino dijo que ya es mucho lo que nos fía, y no quiso darme ni un pedacito de queso.

—¡Se asará en los infiernos!

Y la señora Blanquita salió de la cocina, diciendo palabras gruesas, ella que es tan delgadita. Esa noche cenamos café negro y tortillas duras con sal. Pero no nos afligimos, porque como nos dijo la propia señora Blanquita, todos estábamos al amparo de la Divina Providencia. Apenas acabamos de cenar, apagaron las luces de la sala y cerraron las cortinas de las ventanas que daban a la calle. También apagaron la luz de la cocina. La señora Blanquita y sus sirvientas se tiraron en el suelo, junto a las ventanas, para espiar la calle, por la rendija de una cortina apenas entreabierta.

And that's how it was: we went searching and searching and searching without finding them. The man wasn't very tall, in a leather jacket, with black hair and a good laugh. But we didn't find him. We were searching without a cent, without being able to return to Guanajuato, when we found you, Señora Blanquita.

Señora Blanquita looked at us with sympathy.

–And how much were your shoes worth?

–Maybe a hundred or five hundred pesos. I never knew for sure, because as I told you, I was never able to sell them.

–Whoa, what a bargain! And Señora Blanquita burst into laughter. I must say that she's not a woman of half-measures: either she laughs a lot, or else she's enraged.

–Five hundred pesos . . . I'll give them to you and pay for your bus ticket back to Guanajuato.

I thanked her very much. I gave her my name along with the thanks: Loreto Rosales, at your service. And my grandson, Faustino Duque, your servant. Then came back the maid Josefina, who is quite voluptuous and handsome.

–El Chino said that he's already given us a lot on credit, and he didn't want to give me even the smallest piece of cheese.

–He will burn in hell!

And Señora Blanquita left the kitchen, uttering foul words for such a small woman! That night we dined on black coffee and hard tortillas with salt. But we didn't get upset, because as our own Señora Blanquita told us, we were all protected by Divine Providence. We had hardly finished eating when the servants turned off the living room lights and closed the window curtains that looked out onto the street. They also shut off the kitchen lights. Señora Blanquita and her staff threw themselves to the ground next to the windows, spying on the street through the hole in the curtain that was barely half-opened.

—Allí está, señora Blanquita —dijo Josefina muy quedito.

—Mire, seño, está mirando para acá, patrullando la casa . . . .

—Desgraciado, voy a llamar a la policía —dijo la señora.

—Sí, señora, péguele un susto antes de que nos mate.

Estuvimos espiando el peligro hasta quién sabe qué horas, porque Faustino y yo nos retiramos a dormir. Casi no dormí pensando en el enemigo que acechaba a la señora Blanquita. Oí las horas: las doce, la una de la madrugada, y ellas allí seguían, espiando los pasos del malhechor, para estar prevenidas. Menos mal que la señora Blanquita parecía muy arredrada. Lo mismo que Josefina y que Panchita. Con ese pensamiento me dormí.

—¿Ya desayunó, don Loretito? —me preguntó la señora en la mañana.

—Ya, niña.

—Hoy le doy su dinero, para que vuelva a Guanajuato. . . .

Y los días empezaron a correr y yo cada vez estaba más avergonzado. La señora Blanquita no tenía ni un centavo, y yo no podía hacer nada por ella, ni siquiera irme, porque la hubiera ofendido.

—¡Déjeme ir, señora Blanquita!

—¡Está loco, don Loretito!

Se reía, ponía música y bailaba. No se acongojaba por nada. Nunca salía, estaba muy amenazada. Por las noches espiaba la calle con sus criadas.

—¡Estamos enchiqueradas!

—Sólo Dios nos puede ayudar.

En el día Josefina iba a pedir fiado. Antes de salir se asomaba a los balcones. —Voy en una carrera antes de que llegue y me agarre.

—There he is, Señora Blanquita —Josefina said quietly.

—Look, sir, he's looking over there, patrolling the house. . . .

—The creep. I'm going to call the police —said the Señora.

—Yes, Señora. Give him a scare before he kills us.

We sat there keeping watch until who knows what time. Faustino and I went to bed. I could hardly sleep as I lay there thinking about the enemy stalking Señora Blanquita. I listened as hours crept by: midnight, one in the morning. So each hour passed, listening for the criminal's footsteps so that we would be warned. At least Señora Blanquita seemed intimidated, as did Josefina and Panchita. I fell asleep with that on my mind.

—Have you already had breakfast, don Loretito? —the Señora asked me the next morning.

—Yes, miss.

—Today I'll give you your money so you can go back to Guanajuato.

Days began to trickle by and I felt more ashamed. Señora Blanquita didn't have a cent to her name, and I could do nothing for her, not even leave, as that would have offended her.

—Let me leave, Señora Blanquita!

—You're crazy, don Loretito!

She laughed, played music and danced. She didn't let herself get distressed about anything. She didn't go out. Under threat, she spied at night on the street next to her servants.

—We are like prisoners!

—Only God can help us.

During the day Josefina would ask for credit. Before leaving she'd peer out over the balcony. —I'm going out to the street before he arrives and catches me.

Y volvía enseguida con las compras fiadas. Mientras preparaba la sopa de fideos y las quesadillas de flor de calabaza, cantaba. Tenía bonita voz la tal Josefina. Panchita también cantaba mientras tendía las camas y limpiaba los espejos. La señora Blanquita, tantito bailaba y tantito bordaba. Yo me hallé bien y ya no pedía irme. ¿Qué más quería? Tenía buen trato y buena compañía. A mi nieto lo dejaban jugar con el radio. De la ciudad ya ni me acordaba. Algún día la Divina Providencia nos recordaría y nos mandaría el dinero que necesitábamos. Entonces, con todo el dolor de mi corazón, yo me regresaría a Guanajuato. Y digo con todo el dolor porque me había engreído con esas tres mujeres: Es difícil hallarlas tan reidoras. Así pensaba yo, y así se me pasaban los días. Fue una tarde, cuando ya empezaba a pardear, cuando llamaron a la puerta. Desde mi cuarto alcancé a oír la voz de Josefina.

—Perdone, señor, pero no puedo agarrar el paquetito. . . .

—¿Por qué no? —era tamaño vozarrón de hombre.

Oí que Josefina cerró la puerta de golpe.

—¡Señora Blanquita, dejaron esto! —gritó Josefina apesadumbrada.

—¡Estúpida! ¿Por qué lo agarraste?

Oí que deshacían el paquetito.

—¿Ves? ¿Ves? ¡Mira! ¡Mira!

No me atreví a asomar la cabeza para ver que habían traído. Josefina entró muy disgustada.

—La van a matar . . . la van a matar. . . .

Al rato vi que Faustino estaba jugando con dos muñequitas rotas. Las dos estaban vestidas de novia y los vestidos blancos estaban hechos jirones, las mechitas güeras casi arrancadas.

—¿Dónde las encontraste, muchacho?

—Ahí estaban, en el suelo.

She would speedily return with the credited goods. While she prepared noodle soup and pumpkin-stem quesadillas she would sing. She had a beautiful voice, that Josefina. Panchita would also sing while she made the beds and polished the mirrors. Señora Blanquita would sometimes dance and sometimes do embroidery. I felt good, and I no longer asked to leave. What more could I want? I had a good set-up and good company. They let my grandson play with the radio. I no longer thought about the city. Some day Divine Providence would remember us and send us the money we needed. Then, with a pained heart, I would return to Guanajuato. I say with pain because I had become spoiled by those three ladies; it's hard to find women who laugh so much. And that's what I thought about, and how I passed my days.

One afternoon, as it was starting to get dark out, someone knocked on the door. From my room I could hear Josefina.

–Sorry, sir, but I can't take the package . . . .

–Why not? –An incredibly loud man's voice.

I heard Josefina slam the door. –Señora Blanquita, this was left for you! –yelled Josefina, sounding distressed.

–Stupid girl! Why did you take it?

I heard them untying the package.

–You see! See! Look! Look!

I didn't dare peek to see what they had brought. Josefina came into the room upset.

–They are going to kill her . . . they're going to kill her . . . .

At that moment I saw that Faustino was playing with two broken little dolls. Both were dressed like brides, their white dresses in shreds, their blond hair almost entirely ripped out.

–Where'd you find them, son?

–They were over there, on the floor.

Pedimos unas agujas y un poco de hilo y nos pusimos a componerlas. En eso estábamos cuando volvieron a llamar a la puerta. Me puse en guardia, para algo había yo de servir a pesar de mis ochenta y dos años.

—¿La quiere matar? —gritó Josefina.

—¡Para que floree su tumba! —oí el mismo vozarrón de hombre.

—¡Señora! . . . Señora Blanquita.

También yo salí a ver: Allí estaban regadas en el suelo, quién sabe cuántas rosas rojas.

—¡Las aventó, señora, cuando yo no las quise agarrar!

—Flores en el suelo de mi casa, ¡qué mal agüero!, ¡Qué mal agüero! —gritó la señora Blanquita.

Bien roja de mohina las empezó a levantar, abrió la ventana y las tiró a la calle. Josefina la ayudó. En cambio Panchita agarró una docena y la escondió en uno de los baños.

—Venga a ver, don Loretito.

La señora me llevó al balcón. Ya había oscurecido y las flores con la luz de los faroles, brillaban como confeti. Lástima que los coches les pasaran por encima. Nos metimos cuando vimos que todas estaban machucadas. Al rato volvieron a llamar a la puerta, pero esta vez eran golpes muy recios, como si quisieran echarla abajo. Me pareció que le daban de patadas o de cachazos de pistola.

—¡Yo abro, Josefina!

Vimos pasar a la señora Blanquita, como una centella. Iba embravecida.

Luego ya no oímos nada. Con precaución salimos del cuarto, en el suelo del salón había otro tanto de rosas rojas, y la puerta de la calle estaba completamente abierta.

—¡Se la llevó! —gritó Josefina.

—Sí, se la llevó —repitió Faustino.

We asked for some needles and a little bit of thread and started putting them back together again. As we did, there was another knock at the door. I stood guard—at least I could finally be of use, even despite my eighty-two years.

—Do you want to kill her?! —Josefina screamed.

—Let her tomb flower! —the same man's loud voice.

—Señora! . . . Señora Blanquita.

I too went out to look. There, sprinkled across the floor, were who-knows-how-many red roses.

—He threw them, Señora, when I didn't want to take them!

—Flowers on the floor of my house, what an awful omen! What an awful omen! —screamed Señora Blanquita. Red with annoyance, she began to pick them up off the floor, opened a window, and tossed them onto the street. Josefina helped her. Panchita meanwhile grabbed a dozen and hid them in one of the bathrooms.

—Come see, don Loretito. The Señora brought me over to the balcony. It was already dark out, and the flowers in the light of the street lamps shone like confetti. It was a shame to see the cars drive on top of them, and we came back inside when they had all been crushed.

A moment later he knocked on the door again, this time with forceful blows, as if to tear the door down. It seemed as if he were smashing the door with boots, or goring it with guns.

—I'll get it, Josefina!

We saw Señora Blanquita walk by like a flash of lightning. She looked enraged.

Then we heard nothing. With precaution, we left the bedroom. The living room floor was scattered with as many red roses as before, and the front door was wide open.

—He took off with her! —yelled Josefina.

—Yes, he took off with her —Faustino repeated.

Los cuatro nos vimos muy espantados. Sólo Dios sabía a dónde y si algún día la devolvería. Apenas íbamos a decir algo, cuando la señora Blanquita se nos apareció de nuevo. Venía bien revolcada, con el pelo lacio sobre la cara y su vestido blanco, roto.

—¡Me echó el coche encima! . . . dame un tequila. . . .

La señora se dejó caer en una silla de seda. Tenía las rodillas raspadas. Josefina le limpió la sangre de las piernas, le arregló el pelo y le pasó un pañuelo por la cara. Panchita nos dio a todos un buen fajo de tequila.

—Ande don Loretito, para el susto.

Con la señora Blanquita, va uno de sobresalto en sobresalto. Se bebió su tequila de un trago, se repuso, se levantó y se fue al teléfono.

—Haga el favor de venir a la esquina de mi casa. A ver si tiene valor de decírmelo en mi cara . . . . Lo espero en diez minutos.

Al rato entró a la cocina bien girita. Llevaba otro vestido. Nos sonrió, pero yo vi que estaba bien enojada. Buscó y buscó entre los cuchillos y luego escogió un martillo. Se lo puso bajo el brazo, con la cabeza para arriba, el palo pegado al cuerpo y lo sostuvo con el brazo. Parecía que iba desarmada. ¡Es ladina, y sabe muy bien lo que hace!

—Ahorita vengo.

Nos tiró un beso con la mano libre y se fue. Las muchachas se me quedaron mirando: "Viejo tarugo, ¿para que sirve?" Les leí el pensamiento.

—Voy a seguir sus pasos . . . nunca se sabe. . . .

Salí a la calle, que no había pisado en muchos días. De noche había tantos automóviles, como al mediodía, y sus faroles la llenaban de reflejos. A causa de ellos, no atinaba yo a ver por dónde andaba la señora Blanquita.

All four of us were terrified. Only God could know where he had taken her and if he'd ever bring her back. No sooner had we started talking than Señora Blanquita appeared in front of us, looking beaten up, her lank hair covering her face, her white dress ripped.

—He ran his car right over me! . . . get me a tequila . . . .

The Señora collapsed into a silk chair. Her knees were scraped and Josefina cleaned the blood off her legs, fixed her hair, and wiped a handkerchief over her face. Panchita gave all of us a good mouthful of tequila.

—Here don Loretito, to allay your fears.

With Señora Blanquita one goes from one fright to another. She drank her tequila in one gulp, regained composure, stood up, and walked over to the phone. —Do me a favor and come to my street corner. We'll see if you have the guts to tell it to my face . . . I'll be waiting for you there in ten minutes.

A bit later she came into the kitchen looking like new. She was wearing a different dress. She smiled at us, but I could see she was angry. She searched and searched among the knives and then settled on a hammer. She tucked it underneath her armpit, the head straight up, the handle tight against her body, held in place by her arm. It looked as if she didn't have a weapon. She's a crafty lady. She definitely knows what she's doing!

—I'm going now—. She threw us a kiss with her free hand and left. The girls kept looking at me. I could read their minds: *You old oaf, what good are you?*

—I'm going to follow her . . . you never know . . . .

I went onto the street, which I hadn't done in many days. At night there were many cars out, like during the day, and their headlights reflected images all across the street. As a result I wasn't able to see where Señora Blanquita had gone.

De repente la vi en la acera de enfrente. Junto a ella estaba un hombrón muy alto. Parecía que no se hablaban, nada más se miraban: midiéndose. Me metí entre los coches, y con mucha cautela, me acerqué.

—¡Sígame!

—¡Aquí no —gritó la señora.

El hombrón se volvió para todas partes, buscando.

—Debe tener usted a sus indios guardándola —dijo temeroso.

—Sígame.

La señora se echó a andar y el hombre la fue siguiendo, mirando, mirando para todas partes, desconfiado. A mí no me vio. ¿Quién se fija en mí? ¡Nadie! Nadie sabe ver a un pobre. Además yo sé caminar sin que me miren. Me lo enseñaron de chiquito. Nos fuimos metiendo por unas calles con jardines y sin gentes. ¡Muy oscuras! Yo me escurría entre los árboles y los pocos postes de luz. También me arrimaba a las puertas y a las rejas. La señora Blanquita iba muy adelante, caminando sin volver la cabeza, con los brazos pegados al cuerpo, escondiendo el arma, bien derechita. Dio vuelta a la izquierda y él la siguió. Yo me arrimé a la esquina y miré. El me daba la espalda. Ella se le fue acercando.

—A solas, repítame lo que dijo.

—¿Lo que dije? . . . ¿qué dije?— preguntó el hombre asustado.

—¡Repítame lo que me dijo!

—Eres mala. Muy mala. . . .

Y el hombre dio la vuelta después de dar su queja. Apenas le dio la espalda, la señora Blanquita sacó el martillo, lo levantó, agarrándolo con las dos manos y le dio un golpe seco sobre la nuca.

All of a sudden I saw her on the pavement in front of me, with a tall, well-built man. It seemed as if they weren't speaking to each other, only looking, weighing the other up. I hid between the cars and, with much discretion, inched my way closer.

—Follow me!

—Not here —yelled the Señora.

The man turned and looked all around, searching.

—You probably have your servants watching over you —he said, afraid.

—Follow me.

The Señora started walking and the man followed, peering, all around, wary, but he didn't see me. Who ever notices me? No one! No one knows how to see a poor man. And what's more, I know how to walk without being seen. I learned when I was a kid. We used to sneak onto streets with gardens, without people around. Very dark streets! I would slip through the trees and the few streetlamps. I would even edge close to the doors and the window bars.

Señora Blanquita kept in front, walking without looking behind her, her arms squeezed against her body, hiding her weapon. Walking in a straight line, she veered to the left and he followed. I stayed close to the corner of the street and watched. His back was to me and she approached him.

—We're alone now, so repeat to me what you said.

—What I said? . . . What did I say? —asked the man, who was visibly scared.

—Repeat to me what you said!

—You're an evil woman. Very evil . . . . And the man turned away from her, right after lodging his complaint. No sooner was his back to her than Señora Blanquita withdrew the hammer, raised it, and seizing it with both of her hands, delivered a sharp

La cabeza del martillo brincó sobre la acera y se fue rebotando hasta media calle. ¡Así de recio fue el golpe! El hombre dio unos pasos bamboleándose. A la luz de los faroles le vi los ojos en blanco. Luego, como borracho se fue a media calle y a tientas buscó la cabeza del martillo, la agarró y alcanzó a tirarla adentro de un jardín. Después se dejó caer al suelo y se cogió la cabeza entre las manos. La señora Blanquita se acercó a rematarlo con el palo del martillo. Pero el hombre se lo arrebató de un manotazo y lo tiró adentro del jardín.

—¡Traidora! . . . Das por la espalda. . . .

Estaba enojada de haber dejado vivo a su enemigo. Era valiente, porque el enemigo era bien fornido, le sacaba la cabeza y pesaba el doble que ella. Allí sentado, le vi tamañas manos y tamañas espaldas. La señora lo miró un rato y luego agarró el camino de su casa. El hombre se levantó para seguirla. Pasaron muy cerquita de mí, sin verme. Yo los seguí. "Mientras ella lleve la ventaja, yo no meto las manos. Es bien bragada y defensa no necesita", me iba yo diciendo, cuando llegamos a la última callecita, la que desemboca en su avenida. Allí ella se detuvo, pensando, ¡adivinar en qué! Cerca de la esquina había un estanquillo abierto.

—¡Cómpreme unos cigarros! —ordenó.

Me acordé que desde la mañana no fumaba, porque el Chino no había querido fiarle sus Monte Carlo.

—Sí, mi amor. . . .

Oí que contestaba su enemigo. Y con cautela, se paró en la puerta del estanquillo, para cuidar la bocacalle y que ella no ganara la avenida. Le estaba cerrando el paso. Ella lo miró y reculó muy despacito, muy despacito. Cuando el enemigo entró a pagar los cigarros, la señora Blanquita miró para todas partes,

blow to his neck. The head of the hammer skipped across the pavement and bounced all the way into the middle of the street. It was a hard hit! The man took a few steps back, swaying from side to side. In the glow of the headlights I could see the whites of his eyes. Then, as if drunk, he walked into the middle of the street and felt for the hammer with his hands, grasped it, and managed to throw it into a garden. Then he fell to the ground and placed his head between his hands. Señora Blanquita got closer, looking to kill him again, with the base of the hammer. The man snatched it from her with one swipe and threw it into the garden.

—Traitor! . . . Hitting a man from behind . . . .

She was angry for having left her enemy alive, and brave—considering that her enemy was heavy-set, a foot taller than she, and double her weight. He just sat there, and I could make out his large hands and back. The Señora looked at him for a brief moment, then headed down the street towards her house. The man stood up to follow and they passed right next to me without seeing me. I pursued them. *While she has the upper hand, I won't get involved. She's quite strong and doesn't need me to defend her,* I kept telling myself. When we arrived at the last little street that opens onto the main avenue, she stopped there, thinking, but one can only guess about what! Near the corner was an open grocery store.

—Buy me some cigarettes! —she ordered.

I remembered she hadn't smoked since morning, because El Chino hadn't wanted to give her Monte Carlos on credit.

—Yes, my love— I heard her enemy respond.

With caution, he stopped at the front of the store, to keep an eye on the street so she wouldn't make her way over to the avenue, trying to block her path. She saw him and inched back slowly, very slowly. When the enemy went in to pay for cigarettes,

buscando salida en la callecita oscura, pero no tenía más remedio que pasar frente a la puerta del estanquillo. Miró para el cielo y se halló con las ramas del fresno. Sin pensarlo, se trepó al árbol como un gato y desapareció en lo oscuro del follaje. El hombre salió con los cigarros en la mano y no la vio. Pero no se desanimó: alerta, fue calle arriba, mirando para todas partes, escudriñando los jardines, las rejas, las salientes de las casas. Luego, calle abajo. Luego otra vez calle arriba, buscando; luego otra vez calle abajo. Yo me senté en el borde de la acera, me bajé el sombrero y me hice el que dormía, mientras lo miraba: calle arriba, calle abajo. El árbol de la señora Blanquita estaba muy quietecito. Y el hombre seguía calle arriba, calle abajo, mirando para todos lados. "¡Condenado, sabe que no ha salido de estos andurriales y le anda cerrando el paso!" Pasó más de una hora. Cerraron el estanquillo y el hombre seguía calle arriba, calle abajo. De seguro la señora Blanquita lo miraba y por eso no se movía.

—¡Echeme un cigarro!—gritó de pronto desde las ramas del fresno. Siempre he dicho que tanto el hombre como la mujer siempre se venden por sus vicios.

—¿Dónde, Blanca, dónde?—preguntó el hombre dando vueltas como trompo.

—Acá arriba.

—¿Dónde?

—¡En el fresno!

El enemigo se agarró al tronco del árbol y le dio tanta risa, que a mí también me la contagió. Se reía tanto, que trabajo le costó tirarle los cigarros, porque ella no quiso bajarse.

—¡Lárguese, para que pueda volver a mi casa!

—¡Quiero verle la carita!

—No se puede. Sólo mis amigos pueden verla.

Señora Blanquita looked around, searching for a way out of this dark street, but there were no options besides walking right in front of the grocery store. She looked up to the sky and spotted the branches of an ash tree. Without thinking, she clambered up the tree like a cat and disappeared into the dark foliage. The man walked out with the cigarettes in his hand and didn't see her. He didn't get discouraged: very alert, he walked up the street, looking all around, scanning gardens, window bars, bulges on houses. Down the street, then up it again, searching; then down again.

I sat down on the edge of the sidewalk, lowered my head, and pretended to be asleep while I watched him: up the street, down the street. Señora Blanquita's tree was absolutely silent. The man continued, up and down the street, looking on all sides. *This damn guy knew she hadn't left this godforsaken area and he tried to block her from escaping!* More than an hour went by. They closed the store and he continued up and down the street. Surely Señora Blanquita saw him, and that's why she wasn't moving.

–Throw me a cigarette! –she yelled all of a sudden, from the branches of the ash tree. I've always said that both men and women end up doing themselves in with their vices.

–Where, Blanca, where? –asked the man, spinning like a top.

–Up here.

–Where?

–In the ash tree!

The enemy grabbed hold of the tree trunk and laughed so loudly that even I became infected with laughter. He laughed so much that it was hard to throw her the cigarettes, and she certainly didn't want to come down for them.

–Go away so that I can go back home!

–I want to see your cute little face!

–You can't. Only my friends can see it.

—¿Cuánto vale su carita? ¡La compro!

—¡Quinientos pesos!

—¿Los mismos que me pediste?

—¡Los mismos! Se los debo al zapaterito de Guanajuato.

Se me quitó la risa. El zapaterito de Guanajuato era yo, Loreto Rosales. Me agaché bien. No quería que nadie me viera la cara. Me dio vergüenza que yo, Loreto Rosales, pusiera a una señora en el trance de matar a martillazos al mal hombre que le negaba ¡quinientos pesos!

—¿En dónde está su zapaterito, para dárselos?

—En un lugar secreto y usted no lo verá.

En verdad no debía verme. Me fui hasta la esquina bien agachado. Pasé frente al estanquillo, que tenía las puertas cerradas. Di la vuelta, llegué a la avenida y gané la casa. Entré y agarré a Faustino y luego tomé el camino de regreso a Guanajuato. Hice once días, porque no hallaba la salida de la mentada ciudad de México. Me fui hasta sin despedirme, porque hay veces en que no despedirse es de más cortesía. En los once días de andada, me reconfortaba pensar que yéndome, libraba a la señora Blanquita de la cárcel. Hace ya siete días que llegué a mi casa. Pero no estoy tranquilo. Anoche soñé a la señora Blanquita, parada en el Hemiciclo a Juárez, buscándome. Tal vez me necesite. Por eso de buena hora agarré el camino de regreso a México. A buen paso, Faustino y yo llegaremos en nueve días, y allá veremos que es menester que hagamos por ella. Al fin que mientras ella lleve la ventaja, yo no meteré las manos . . . . Aunque con la señora Blanquita, nunca se sabe, nunca se sabe . . . .

—How much is your face worth? I'll buy it!

—Five hundred pesos!

—The same five hundred pesos that you asked me for?

—The same. I owe it to the little shoemaker from Guanajuato.

I stopped laughing. The little shoemaker from Guanajuato was me, Loreto Rosales. I ducked down. I didn't want anyone to notice my face. I was ashamed that I, Loreto Rosales, could drive a woman to the point of hammering to death a man who had refused her five hundred pesos!

—And where is your shoemaker, so I can give him this money?

—In a secret place, and you will never see him.

It was true that he would never see me. Crouched down, I made my way to the corner. I passed in front of the grocery store with its doors locked shut. I turned around, reached the main avenue and found my way home. I entered and seized Faustino, and then followed the road that would lead us back to Guanajuato. It took eleven days, because I couldn't find my way out of the damned city of Mexico. I didn't even say goodbye, because there are times when not saying goodbye is the most courteous way to leave. In our eleven days of walking, I was comforted in the knowledge that by leaving, I freed Señora Blanquita from confinement.

It's now seven days since I've been home, but I don't feel settled. Last night I dreamed of Señora Blanquita, standing next to the statue of Benito Juárez, looking for me. Maybe she needs me. For that reason, I woke up early and took the road back to Mexico City. At a steady pace, Faustino and I should be able to arrive in nine days, and we'll see what we must do for her. In the end, if she holds the upper hand, I won't get involved . . . although with Señora Blanquita, one never knows, one never knows . . . .

An Event in Summer

Reginald Gibbons

Something else in addition to his falling happened when Jake fell heavily to the floor. He tried to get up again, blindly, like an animal. Thinking about painting the porch, he had been standing at the open second-story window of the bedroom, and now he tried to pull himself back up, leaning on the sill because he did not seem to have any strength, and he was calling, crying, pitifully wailing in panic, for Lynette to come quick. Jake had only retired from the line at the transformer manufacturer four months ago. And now something was happening that would make everything forever different in him—what was it? what was happening? a stroke? He was terrified. But something happened in Lynette, also, who had been slumped in a weekday doze in her chair downstairs in front of the droning soaps. She had been wakened instantly by the loud far-out-of-the-ordinary thud that had been Jake on the floor, which for a few seconds she could not understand, till she heard Jake calling her frantically—he knew she was downstairs—calling and calling, she did not know why. And already she had two trains of thought running in her head—one in response to Jake's disaster (What was it?), and another in response to her own split-second self-questioning—

for here is the important thing: she did not rise to her tired feet and take the stairs as quickly as she could, which was not ever very fast. She hesitated. Jake was calling, "Lynette! Lynette!" She could hear the fear in him; he was given, anyway, to fears. And she did not move. Perhaps she waited only for five seconds. Or was it ten? But it was long enough to create within herself a breach—incomprehensible for now—with him, and with herself as she had been up until this very instant. First she heard the sound, then she knew that the sound was Jake falling, then she didn't move. Then she was hurrying toward him. While also shocked at herself—but already she didn't want to think about that. And she really was frightened. Was he all right? Would he be all right? He would not know about those five seconds. Or ten. She was already wondering what she herself now knew. Or did not wish to know. About herself. About her feelings for him. For anyone? After all the years of taking care of him, of the children, of him again. But she mustn't tell anyone, especially Jake, what she had just felt within herself. Or must not tell anyone that she had not felt an instantaneous, instinctive leaping to respond. That is what she should have felt, wasn't it?

Byron the Lyron

Richard Bausch

She was eighty-four and had lived a long, rich life, and she told her one son, Byron, that she was ready. Byron Mailley wept, putting his head down on her shoulder. Georgia's shoulder.

They were in her hospital room—the hospital wing of Brighton Creek Farm, the assisted living facility she had resided in over the last decade. She patted the back of his head. That had always been her most charming gesture of affection toward him—since he was nine or ten and learning the complications of being a bookish boy on a street full of rough characters. Her name for them. She had a way of setting all his problems in terms of the books they read together in the evenings, because he couldn't sleep. The books were all adventure: Hardy Boys, and Nancy Drew, Robert Louis Stevenson, Theodore J. Waldek's book, *Lions on the Hunt*, written from the point of view of the young lion. Byron the lyron, Georgia called him. It was their little joke, just between them. Byron the lyron had night terrors, panic attacks.

Fears of cancer, fears of madness, split personality, delusions, polio, tuberculosis, the atomic bomb, the death of parents. His father gone—first with the military, flying jets, then just gone. Remarried far away. Far away was good, actually, because Father had wanted Byron to be tough, and had worked to accomplish it: a drill-like discipline early; its looming displeased powerful presence early. Byron tried hard, and couldn't make the grade, as Father put it. There were fights between Georgia and the old man about the boy. The old man was gone but the panics started not long after he left.

Night was a terrible prospect. He'd sit crying, nine years old, and she, pregnant with the child she would lose, her husband gone away, sat up with Byron, patiently holding him, humming to him, patting the back of his head; then, on into the next year, the terrors recurring, and it was really just the two of them for good (her words). And she'd read other things to him: Dickens, the Bible–laughing and making fun of all the begots, and scoffing at the heavy seriousness. Language is fun, she told him. Play.

Let's play.

He had always felt that she was more friend than mother.

*

Now he wept, and she patted his head and murmured, "Stop. Stop."

So he stopped. Brave girl, he thought. But kept still.

"Tell me what happened," she said.

She meant this about Reese. "I'm not crying about Reese," he told her. But partly he was. The look in his own eyes, he knew, admitted it. She patted the side of his face.

"Just tell me."

He kissed her hand, and held it. "Georgia," he murmured. "What will I do?"

"Tell me about Reese."

Last week, after twelve years, Reese had announced tearfully that he was leaving–this just two days past a big surprise party, Byron's forty-fifth birthday. He'd invited every one Byron knew, going back to his school days. Even Ms. Evelyn Wasson, his seventh grade teacher showed up to read a wonderful tribute she had written about her certainty that Byron Mailley would make something of himself. Such a bright, look-right-at-you little boy, she said, with her endearing habit of using hyphenated expressions in her talk. She went on about Byron, talking about his work as a magazine photographer, his time in Rome, in his twenties, sending her post cards and pictures he had taken of the magnificent places and the wonderful people he had come to know. Reese stood there proudly, smiling during it all. He'd arranged everything. He led the applause and offered a toast to Byron for his generosity and his goodness. Nobody more kindly than Byron, taking Reese in at such a time in his life, offering love, nurture, tolerating his nightmares, his neuroses, his failures of love and sensibility. A true artist, Byron. Not Reese—who was in fact a fairly successful painter. But about whom, indeed, the flat statement he uttered next happened to be true: "My work is bunk," Reese, who couldn't really believe that, said. One lie leads to another. Reese said uncharacteristically self-deprecating things all night, praising Byron. He had put together an elegant panel show of some of Byron's photographs; and during the celebration several people rose to read from Byron's poems. They were political verses, clever, funny. Light verse. Byron liked the sensibility of the original, Lord Byron, with his insistence that poetry was just something occupational and fun.

His mother, ill, failing, already in the hospital wing, couldn't be there, but Reese made a tape, and took it over there the next morning and played it for her. She was listening to it when Byron came to see her that evening, not twenty minutes past the revelation, delivered in the upstairs hallway of the house, in a weepy sorrowful voice by Reese, that he must find his way alone for a time, and was leaving. Byron had been an emotional nursemaid all these years, surely Byron could see this, and Reese would never reach any kind of autonomy if he stayed any longer. "We can be friends," Reese said. "I so want that, Byron."

Byron suspected there must be someone else for Reese, now, though it was true that Byron had done plenty of nurse-maiding from the beginning. Reese had been Georgia's physical therapist; that was how they had met—Reese, a young artist, working for Blue Ridge Orthopedic Clinic to make enough money to put food on the table, had worked with Georgia after her knee replacement surgery, and Georgia had introduced him to Byron. Reese came over to see Georgia and to work with her, and then it was just visiting. They made each other laugh. Reese was sad a lot of the time and had other troubles, mostly having to do with confidence in his work, and confidence in general. There was a neediness in him, about which he often teased. It was charming, though like most teasing it hinted at the truth. Byron and Reese began going to see Georgia together, and everything went quite naturally to the next stage. They had lived together quite happily, it seemed to Byron, but then Reese had begun to do well enough with his painting to quit the physio-therapy, and there were, Byron had to admit, subtle changes.

The kindest way of seeing this now was that Reese was being honest in his own self-deluding way; he had depended on Byron so long, and now wanted to strike out on his own. Byron chose to look at it this way, suffering with quiet dignity through the whole thing, while also going through the anguish of his mother's last illness. He was by nature kindly, and this is not to say that kindness came easily to him: as we all know, kindliness is work. It was in all the details of his lived life. Perhaps Reese felt the necessity of the big surprise party and the tributes to salve his conscience for what he knew he was already in the process of doing. But the hundred-twenty townspeople who came to the party wanted to honor Byron. They all loved him, and for good reason.

Georgia reminded him of this, looking at him now, her still-dark hair spread so lovely on the pillow. "You know you could never hide anything from me. It hurts when someone leaves you. I felt it too, you know."

"I don't want to talk about Reese anymore," Byron said. "Let's talk about something else."

"Reese was here, earlier."

"Well, he's moving out."

"He wants to come see me tomorrow."

Byron shrugged. "I guess that's between the two of you."

"Tell me about your party," she said. "The good parts."

But she was drugged, and the drowse began to work in her. And he felt uncomfortably sullen, because she had talked so casually about Reese coming to see her. He spoke half-heartedly about Mrs. Wasson and her memory of him, writing to her from Rome. Try as she might—and she did try—Georgia's lids grew heavy; they closed and opened in that sluggish way, the eyes glazing over. Feeling the pressure to bring it up anyway, Byron went on to say that Reese had planned the party and seemed very happy doing that—deciding on the guest list, on the way it would all go. He drove a hundred miles west and south, to the Tennessee line, and bought five hundred dollars worth of fireworks, using his own savings account. Byron, seeing how much he apparently needed this, let him have his way about it. It was not in Byron's makeup to seek this kind of thing. He liked a party; he was gregarious and—people talked about it—he had wonderful ability as a raconteur and storyteller, could do any accent in the world, and would do so, telling a joke, so that the experience of it was positively dramatic. But in truth, he was also rather self-effacing. He had known so many punk jerks parading themselves during his time in Rome, and New York. All those years hustling photographs. His strongest sense of how life ought to be lived had always involved the old idea that one didn't let the right hand know what the left was doing. One was generous without considerations about who might know it. No telling how much can be accomplished if we don't care who gets the credit. Byron had performed all sorts of kindnesses, the source of which the recipients of those kindnesses never knew. No one ever knew. Not even Georgia, who knew most everything else.

*

She slept now. He adjusted the blanket across her slowly rising-and-falling chest, kissed her cheek softly, and stood there weeping silently for a time. Then he moved to the door and out. It would be soon, the doctors all said. A week, two weeks. The heart was so tired; it was giving out slowly. Byron went to the nurse's station and reiterated that he wished to be called if there was the slightest change. Each of the last five nights, he had left Georgia sleeping peacefully. She claimed no nightmares, no frights. It was all right. He held her hand and she went in and out of sleep, and when they talked it was nearly as it always had been—her interest in the world hadn't flagged a bit.

Outside, in the chill of early March, he walked to the car and got in. The street was windy; the traffic light wavered and threw its red light on the walls of the buildings at the first intersection. Byron drove there and waited for the light to change. The street looked empty, and the emptiness of it seemed itself a kind of anguish coming at him, not for himself, but for Georgia, lying alone in that room in the coming night. He turned around in the middle of the intersection, drove back to the parking lot, and hurried into the building. At the nurse's station the woman gave him a look. A past-visiting-hours look. He nodded at her and went on to Georgia's room, and took his chair.

*

The night of the party the fireworks went off into the trees, and there were hurrahs and shouts of excitement, and everyone had such a good time. Byron talked to Georgia from the bedroom telephone, and she sounded so chipper, so happy for him. He heard the weakness, and the slight breathlessness, but she had her wits about her, in spite of the medicine, thinking to ask if his next door neighbor, Mrs. Ewing, had brought her dog with her to the party—Mrs. Ewing being one of those people who treated her dogs and cats better than she ever treated any human being, including her own daughter, Marvina, who was a good friend of Georgia's, and Byron's.

Eight years ago, the three of them had gone to Rome on one of Georgia's whims. She had lived there briefly when she went to Europe before the war, and she said she wanted to be in the city with Byron, to see where he had lived and walked and been happy. One of her dearest friends was an opera singer who lived near the Pantheon. They all sat out on the Piazza Navona, drinking Compari and soda, and the opera singer, whom she called Umberto, broke into an aria, drunk and happy, leaning toward Georgia as if to serenade her. He was a big, florid man, who kept saying when will you come live here with me. It was all joking, because Umberto already had a companion, named Pietro, who had lost a leg in the war, and served as his personal secretary. Georgia kept saying that she wished Reese had been able to make the journey—but Reese was recovering from shoulder surgery.

Over the years, Byron often thought of returning to the ancient city, and he would trouble Georgia about it, believing that she was settling too well at Brighton Creek Farm. She knew this of course, and she would say "I'm happy. Really. I can go anywhere, just closing my eyes."

Marvina also talked about Rome, and she had done so more often recently, because her mother had shown up to take over her house, wresting it from the daughter in an act of pretended salvage, telling everyone that it was necessary because of Marvina's lack of practical skills. Marvina had been quite funny about all this to Georgia, and they both imparted some of it to Byron. There had been times when they all talked about Mrs. Ewing. Even Reese, who hated gossip—even the positive kind, and in fact seldom talked very interestedly about anyone but himself. It was something people tolerated because he could be funny, and at times his very vanity was comical.

He could be appallingly self-absorbed, and he had a way of supposing that, because he was an artist, people would understand. Perhaps for a Picasso, people would. But Reese was no Picasso—his paintings were all of boating scenes, harbors in sunset light, sail boats on a lake, reflections on the surface, houses at lakesides with little docks at the ends of the lawns; beach houses and white sand and fishing trawlers off ocean shores. About Mrs. Ewing, Reese was cruel, in fact. There wasn't anything funny or catty in it. It was serious and rather brutal. Mrs. Ewing represented all the evils of respectability, Reese said. He reserved this part of his opinion of her for Byron, who tried to argue that she was a product of her time and place, a little dull, perhaps, and even someone about whom one could make a joke, but she wasn't evil—certainly not deserving of the invective with which Reese spoke of her. Byron wondered, sitting in the chair by his mother's hospital bed, what, in other circumstances, Reese might have found to say about Georgia, who had come from her time and place. But Reese had been devoted to her, all these years, and she was one of the few people who could bring him out of himself. Byron recognized the thought as unworthy: his erstwhile companion would never criticize her for anything.

*

He stayed in her room until well past midnight. She slept, breathing easily, perfectly still, no slightest stress in her features. He nodded off, and shook himself awake; it happened several times. When he went home at last, he couldn't sleep. Reese had come in and taken most of his things. A row of his paintings leaned against the downstairs wall, with a note attached: he'd be by to pick this up in the morning. There were a few items of furniture, a few books, some bric-a-brac. It had always been Byron who did most of the collecting of things. Reese never kept many books; yet the empty places in the shelves showed.

The lights were on next door at the Ewing's, so Byron went out and walked the sidewalk in front of the two houses. A clear, cold night, with a moon and moon-shadows everywhere. If Marvina wanted company, she would see him and come to the door. This was how they had navigated socializing since Mrs. Ewing had moved into the house. Marvina had never been one to keep regular hours and was often awake all night. She liked to sleep in, and often took naps in the middle of the afternoons. Alma had attempted to put a stop to all that. Like most people concerned heavily with morality in others, Alma believed that early to bed early to rise was the most healthy way of living. Tonight Marvina was up—he could hear music—but she didn't come to the door, and finally he went back into his own house, and into bed. He could still hear her music–the Rolling Stones, and she was probably playing it loud to annoy her mother. Perhaps it was partly the music that kept him awake.

*

Early next morning, he heard Reese downstairs, collecting the last of the paintings, and realized that there were two voices. Byron buried his face in his pillows and tried not to hear anything, his heart hurting so badly he wondered if he were not having a coronary: how physical heartbreak was! He would never have believed it. He thought he had felt it before; but this was completely and awfully new. The rattling downstairs took a very long, bad time, but at last it ended. He took the pillow away, got up, slowly, rubbing his chest, and walked downstairs. Paintings gone. The house to himself. He sat at the kitchen table, with a cup of coffee, and wept quietly.

Marvina walked over perhaps an hour later to ask if there was anything she could do. He'd showered, shaved, and dressed, and he felt slightly better. It was just itself, the same pure pressure under the heart, the same band of deep aching. He had gathered some of the cards and letters that had come from Georgia's far flung friendships–many of these people were bedridden themselves, or housebound. They ranged as far away as India, and as close as next door (Marvina).

She wanted to bring something for Georgia to read. She was also contemplating a basket of fruit–Georgia had always loved Bosque pears, and they were particularly good now. But then she also had no appetite to speak of.

"What do you think?" Marvina asked.

"How late were you up last night?" Byron asked her.

She thought a moment. "I took a pill and went to sleep."

"Your music was on late."

"Did it keep you up? I meant it to keep Alma up."

Byron smiled. "Did it?"

"Alma's sleeping late," Marvina said.

They smiled. He was astonished that he could smile. It rose up in him like a breath, and he could feel it traveling along his nerves.

*

They went together to the small grocery store down the street. Marvina drove. They bought several pears, some apples and Clementines. She found a small straw basket in the little boutique next to the grocery. She bought it, and a linen cloth which she folded over the fruit. It looked enough like a gift basket. Georgia liked things homemade, this way. For her, always, something that took time to make was much more valuable and fine as a gift. Every year in early fall she began fashioning the things she would give for Christmas: knitted mittens and scarves, calendars she had made out of old photographs, cards with cutout trees on them, decorated frames, corkboards. Every gift had something of the person it was intended for—a theme or a special flavor reflecting her feeling for that person.

"She'll like the smell of the Clementines," Byron said.

"Some flowers?" Marvina frowned. "No."

They said little for the drive over. It was bright, chilly, windless; the little puffs of scattered cloud seemed utterly motionless in the wide, pure blue. At the hospital she got out first. Byron carried the basket of fruit. In the room, they found Reese sitting with Georgia, who was asleep.

"She hasn't waked yet," Reese said. His eyes were rounded with shadow. He didn't look at Byron, or at Marvina. Byron moved around Georgia's bed and took her hand. It was warm.

He squeezed it. There was the slightest squeezing back. Perhaps he had imagined it.

"Tell her I was here?" Reese said, looking sorrowful.

Byron nodded at him. Marvina and Reese went out, then, and he was alone with Georgia, and the basket of fruit, in this room that was so institutional and clean, with its dull art and its cheerful paint and its television. He went around to the chair and sat down, but the chair was still warm from Reese. He stood again, reached over and took his mother's other hand, and she opened her eyes.

"It's hard on poor Reese," she said. "I think he's confused."

"You were awake."

"For some of it. Some. He didn't know." She squeezed his hand. "He just sits there looking at me and trying not to cry. I didn't let him know I saw."

"I think he has someone else," Byron said.

She squeezed his hand again. "Maybe not."

Byron told her about the two voices he had heard.

"Could be a friend."

"I don't understand him," Byron said. "Does he not know I'd tell you he left me?"

She shook her head, but didn't speak. A moment passed, in which he thought she might have gone back to sleep. Then: "I'm so tired, son."

He sat down again, still holding her hand. "Marvina drove me over here. We brought you some fruit."

The little squeeze, again. He began to have to fight tears. He had so wanted to be cheerful, to get Marvina talking and gossiping about her mother. Georgia would like the idea of Alma Ewing sleeping late, having been kept up with Hot Rocks playing at volume. The dogs and cats would feel neglected. But Alma

Ewing would never give the satisfaction, as she saw it, of ever letting Marvina know that Marvina was getting to her. Alma Ewing was too proud for anger, or any display of temper.

After a time, when it was clear that Georgia was sleeping again, very gently he took his hand away and went to the door of the room. At the far end of the hall, two nurses stood talking. There was no sign of Marvina or Reese. He went back into the room and sat down, and took Georgia's hand once more. Just in time. She turned slightly, and looked at him.

"I smell Clementines," she said, and smiled.

He reached for the basket, but when he turned back around, she had gone back to sleep. He ate a pear, and waited, and began quietly to cry again, the tears running down his cheeks. When he heard Marvina talking to one of the nurses, he slipped into Georgia's little bathroom and ran water over his face, wiped his eyes, dried himself with one of those brown paper towels. His nose was running, like a kid's, with crying.

In the room, Marvina had opened the curtains wider to let in more sun. Georgia was still asleep.

"Reese is a mess," Marvina said.

"I don't want to talk about him," Byron said. "Really, Marvina." He offered her the chair, and she declined, standing there looking over the fruit, picking up a pear and setting it back, finally settling on a Clementine. When she opened it, the fragrance went all over the room. A nurse brought another chair, Marvina having apparently asked for it earlier. Byron thought of these humble practical arrangements in a kind of nightmarish light, as if their very ordinariness were a flaunting of the awful facts, the plain objective world brandishing itself at him, while his mother slipped away forever.

*

Georgia Susan Michael Townsend Mailley. The Michael was there at her father's insistence, after his younger brother, who was killed at the Marne River in 1918. A picture of this young soldier hung on the wall in her parents' house all their lives. Soft features, round eyes, small straight mouth—an innocent, intelligent face. Hard to imagine him being shot in the neck, bleeding to death on a barbed wire fence in the rain and sludge of a terrible May morning all those years ago. Georgia had kept the picture on the foyer wall of her own house for most of Byron's growing up. It had lain in a box of her things for the years she lived at Brighton Creek Farm. Byron, according to his grandfather, favored the long-dead uncle. Georgia had resisted the name for him, incurring her father's wrath. As she had often done. Head strong, willful, stubborn—all these terms her father used to describe his one daughter. He would talk about how she had confounded him at every turn—in fact, he had taken it upon himself to warn others about the difficulties of raising a daughter. He would call friends when their wives had children, to congratulate them if they had sons, and to commiserate with them if they had daughters.

Georgia married young, and then left that marriage after only a period of weeks; the fellow reminded her too much, she said, of her father—it was her father, though, who had it annulled. And in fact his frustrations with her over the years were tinged with admiration, no matter how dismayed he seemed. Georgia had done more in the world than all the sons of his friends and associates. After the marriage episode, which took place her last year of high school, she went on to Radcliff, graduated early, then traveled to live in Europe. She didn't return until just before the outbreak of hostilities in 1939. One of her favorite stories was how, in June of 1938, working for a foreign press service as a secretary and occasional feature writer, she had climbed part way up a lamppost to set eyes upon Adolf Hitler himself, a ridiculous looking little Chaplinesque man standing in the back of a big black automobile with one hand up in that farcical salute. She was later ejected from a café for imitating the Fuhrer's stance. She would laugh, telling the story. "I was young, you know. Only twenty or so."

Byron got his storytelling ability from her. He'd also gotten the adventuresome, generous spirit, too—though he would never attribute this kind of thing to himself. Others, who knew them both, did. Georgia was her own country, some said, meaning it as the highest praise. An empire, was Georgia, with her several careers, her loves and tumultuous friendships and loyalties. No one ever left her willingly except one—the second husband. The military man. He had flown for the Air Corps over Germany, and after the war he flew for the airlines, three years of that before re-enlisting. He was a retired Colonel somewhere out west, the last Byron heard, with a fourth wife and a pair of young twins. Probably ramrod straight, those twins, Georgia would say. She had outlived so many of her friends and companions, most of whom were older than she had been. There was something about her that drew people to her, from her earliest life. Who could imagine a girl nineteen years old traveling alone, employed by a wire service, to write about conditions in the new Germany? But she had done that. She had also been in plays off Broadway, and written a memoir that was published, about life in England just after the war—the rebuilding of London. And when she had Byron, from the Air Corps chap, as she called him, she settled in this little Virginia town to raise her son, her family. She thought she would have more children—hoped for half a dozen, anyway. But things changed rapidly: hostilities in Korea—and at home—caused her husband to go away, and she lost the second child unexpectedly, at almost eight months. Byron had memories of the long night when that happened, pacing in the too-brightly lit waiting room with his grandfather and several friends from the library where she had gone to work. He would never forget the look of fright on his grandfather's face. "I'm afraid we're going to lose her," the old man said.

*

How strange to think of that now. He held her hand, and wept a little more, trying to keep it from Marvina, who ate another pear and then called her mother to wake her. That was the announced purpose of the call, and she said it to please Georgia, who had opened her eyes long enough to nod and smile.

"No answer," Marvina said.

"Poor woman," said Georgia.

A little later, she asked Byron for a piece of paper. It hurt to talk. She signaled that her throat was sore and dry. Marvina got her some water, and she sipped it carefully, seemed to hold it a long time in her mouth. Byron was afraid she might pass out with it still there, and choke. But she swallowed it, and then wrote on the paper: Byron, I'm dying. He looked at it, and then at her face, with that strange peaceful smile. She wrote again: For a Clementine.

Marvina, reading over his shoulder, sobbed and said, "Oh, God. Georgia—if that isn't typical of you." She was laughing and crying at the same time.

"I'm sorry," Georgia said, rasping. "That was mean."

Byron shook his head and helped calm Marvina down. Georgia wrote another note, asking for some music—she had brought with her a complete set of the Sinatra-Dorsey recordings, and Byron put it on for her. She had two songs she especially liked from these years: "I'll Never Smile Again," and "Everything Happens To Me."

They put the music on, and sat listening to it. A nurse came in and worked on the I.V. lines for a time, then asked Byron and Marvina to leave so she could help Georgia go to the bathroom and take a sprits bath. They went together down to the cafeteria and had a cup of coffee. There were several other people there, all looking tired and worried, clearly wishing they could be anywhere else. At one table a pair of young girls sat with an older brother, and they had balloons announcing the birth of a sister. The balloons were tied to the chair in which one of the girls sat. They were eating pastries and ignoring each other.

"Guess I'll call Alma again," Marvina said. "Poor woman."

"Tell me about Reese," said Byron.

She shrugged. "He's confused. Sick at heart. You know how he feels about Georgia. And you."

"He's seeing someone else, Marvina."

"I think he was feeling smothered by everyone's love of you, Byron. No kidding. That's what it sounded like this morning, talking to him. He kept saying he didn't want to compete. He felt awful that we got there while he was visiting Georgia."

"How could he think we wouldn't come to see her?"

"He was leaving—you know."

"I don't want to talk about him."

Again, she shrugged. Then she reached into her purse, brought out her cell phone, and dialed Alma, who answered this time. Alma claimed she'd been up and around, had gone out to the store to buy groceries. She asked how Georgia was.

Marvina told her about the Clementine incident, winking at Byron. The Clementine incident would profoundly disturb Alma, who considered that the occasion called for somber music and long faces. Marvina said this, after disconnecting with Alma, and then seemed to catch herself. "God almighty, what the hell am I saying?" And she began to cry.

They returned upstairs, to find that Georgia was still being attended to. The door was closed. They waited at the nurse's station in the garish light, while people moved around them and past them. An old, old man walked by, slow, pulling his own I.V. apparatus with him. His slippers made a whispery noise, and Byron noted that he could hear the faintest strains of Georgia's music coming from the closed door.

When they were let in at last by the nurse, Georgia was falling asleep again. Movement of any kind, the nurse said, was exhausting for her. She had been a little sick.

"What a lady," the nurse whispered. "You know what she said? She apologized to me for being such a bore. Imagine it."

Byron wanted to embrace her. For a moment they all just stood there, appreciating the small, slender woman in the bed, lying so still, breathing softly, sleeping, it seemed, without dreams.

*

That afternoon, Marvina had to go home for a while, and Byron told her to go on. He'd stay the night. "Oh, I'll come back," Marvina said. "I would've been here last night only–" she shrugged. Her mother, of course. Alma, for all her talk about salvaging things for her impractical daughter, needed attention. And poor Marvina had to give it without actually seeming to.

Byron accompanied her to the elevators and hugged her.

"Can I bring you something to eat?" she asked.

"I'll get something downstairs."

She kissed his cheek and got on, and she was sniffling as the doors closed on her. He went back to Georgia's room, and found her awake.

"I had a dream," she said. Her eyes were blazing. "It wasn't a good dream."

He moved to the chair and took her hand again. "Tell me."

"It's silly. I was doing a calendar for someone. But then something went wrong with it. All the pictures kept dissolving, and I couldn't pick them up. It swept over me, somehow. It was just awful. It was just a calendar I had ruined, but it was terrifying."

He reached for her other hand, and they sat there for a time. He thought she might be going back to sleep, and he felt himself hoping for it.

"I'm scared," she said suddenly. "Oh, hell. I thought I'd dealt with this."

"I'm right here," Byron said.

She held tight. She was weathering it, enduring it; it swept through her in a trembling, her hand was so tight in his that he marveled at how strong she still was. She'd shut her eyes, but was not sleeping. No, she was trying to put something away from her, inside, trying to master herself. When she opened her eyes again, they were still rounded and too bright. "Oh," she said. "Damn it all."

He put his other hand over hers, then stood and leaned over, trying to embrace her—but she wouldn't let go of his hand. "I love you," he said.

"Read something to me," she said. But she wouldn't let go of him. So they remained that way until, at last, she seemed to let down, sighing, drifting a little, then jerking awake. Each time this happened, she squeezed tight again, and looked at him out of those brilliantly lighted eyes. There was something almost supernatural in the way they shone.

After a long interval, she let go, and he sat back down. She was still awake. She stared at him as if not quite able to discern who he was. Then she patted the bed and said, "I'm sorry. Read to me?"

So he read some of the cards and letters, all expressing the hope—the faith, really—that she would come through this and be her old self. One of them was from a priest she had known in Europe before the war.

"I miss the consolations of religion," she said, interrupting him.

"Do you—would you like me to see if—"

"If someone would take me?" She smiled, then. "Funny."

He was at a loss. He went on reading the letter, but then saw that she was staring beyond him, at the door. He turned, expecting Marvina, but it was Reese. Evidently he had waited until Byron saw him. He came forward into the room, with his own little gift of soaps and lotions in a basket. "For your hands," he said to Georgia.

She raised one arm so he could come be hugged and kissed. It was always the way they had greeted each other. Byron took his clumsy embrace in turn, and then they were both sitting there while Georgia opened one of the lotion bottles and put it on her hands, being careful of the place where the I.V. went into the back of the right one. Georgia looked from one to the other of them. There was still that unsettling brightness in her eyes, as if the fear were still climbing inside her and she was choosing to pretend it wasn't there. But then the nurse came in, and it was time for changing things again, and she shooed them out into the hall. They stood there, in the fading, early-evening light from the window at that end. Across from them several people were arranged around the bed of another woman, also old, and probably also dying; this was, after all, where they brought people from the assisted living part of Brighton Creek Farm.

Out the window was the building itself, where she had come to stay ten years ago. They were both staring out at it. Byron feeling the pain in his lower chest, wanting not to show it, wanting to be far away from Reese. Perhaps he would go down now to the cafeteria for something he wouldn't eat, having no appetite now. But Reese might go with him. Or stay and be alone with Georgia.

"Remember when we brought her here to talk to them," Reese said now. "That first time?"

Byron nodded, without quite looking at him.

"Who was that guy? I can't remember his name."

"Scottish sounding," said Byron, who remembered perfectly well the name, McCutcheon. He said, "Mac-something."

"I can't recall it," Reese said.

They were quiet. Georgia had sat patiently listening to McCutcheon talk about all the advantages of assisted living, and she had abruptly interrupted him to say, "Excuse me, are you quite serious?"

The man was stunned, and silent. He stared.

Georgia turned to Reese–yes, it had been Reese–and said, "This guy's an ass, isn't he?"

Byron remembered that now, and he knew Reese was remembering it, too. He almost said something. But the nurse opened the door again and came out, and they could go back in to Georgia, who lay with eyes closed, in fresh sheets, fresh nightgown. Soon they would bring dinner. But she would probably not eat it. She had eaten a little of the Clementine. Food was the one thing that had ceased to interest her particularly; it was such an effort to chew.

She opened her eyes. "Boys," she said.

"Sister," Reese said. That was what he had always called her.

"Tell me about it," she said, looking at neither of them.

Reese began to cry. Byron lifted himself from the chair and went back out into the hall. He heard Georgia say his name, and hesitated. But when he looked back into the room he saw that Reese was bent over the bed, holding her hand, and she was saying something to him.

Byron felt a rage working in him, and he went down to the cafeteria and ordered coffee. He sensed, with a small stab of regret, his own abruptness toward the slow lady behind the counter, who handed him the coffee with a lackluster shrug and went about cleaning the grill. He went to a table alone and sat there, hands shaking, sipping the coffee, which was too hot. He couldn't believe his own anger. And he felt it at Georgia, too, for accepting Reese's affection, knowing what she knew. It hurt him, at a level for which he was unprepared. How could she, knowing what she knew? But then, he remembered with a sinking at his heart, what she also knew. He couldn't decide what to do with his own emotions. He drank the coffee, which burned his tongue, and he sat there feeling childish. He actually had the child's thought, I'll go away and then they'll be sorry. "Stupid," he said, aloud. Then put his hands to his face and wept.

When he went back up to the room, he found the door open, Reese gone. Georgia was lying there staring out the window. He went to the chair and sat down. They had brought her a meal, which she hadn't touched—such meager fare: a roll, mashed potatoes, three slices of turkey, all of it looking like a frozen dinner. She'd had a little of the apple juice, which she had apparently asked for.

"You didn't eat," he said.

"Don't be mad at me, son. I'm unable to select anymore. Don't want to."

"I don't understand," he told her, because he didn't.

"I don't know what happened with you and Reese," she said. Then she took a deep breath, so weighted with exhaustion that he thought, with alarm, that she might pass out. "I don't want to send anybody away," she said. "Not now. Do you understand?"

"Yes," he said.

"I'm not convinced."

"No," he said. "I do."

"Byron, the lyron," she murmured. "You know I always meant it, that you were brave."

"I'm not brave," Byron said.

"Yes." She raised one hand, almost as if to wave at him. "I'll be the judge of that." It was automatic now, and she was falling asleep again. He moved the tray of food away, and then sat there watching her sleep. Marvina came back in at last, with her mother. Alma wanted to say hello. Marvina had brought cards, and when Georgia woke, the two of them played a couple of slow rounds of gin rummy on Georgia's dinner tray. Later, Reese came back and stood off to one side, watching the card game. Everyone was gentle, and in the pauses when Georgia slipped off to her fitful sleep, they were quiet, and quite still, almost as if frozen that way in a photograph.

They all left at the end of the evening visiting hour. Georgia was sound asleep. Very still, breathing very easily. Reese kissed her cheek. Marvina and Alma did, too. Byron held her hand again for a time, and then kissed her himself. Outside the room, he took Reese by the arm just above the elbow. For a second, it was almost impossible to draw in air. Marvina and her mother had gone a ways down the hall. "I'll be right along," Byron said to them. They went on. Reese was looking at him with a kind of resigned alarm.

"I want you to be here for her," Byron said, low. Managing to get it out. "She wants it, and I want it. No standing to the side. No hanging back. Please."

Reese nodded, his eyes widening slightly.

"I don't want any confusion about it. Nothing is changed between you and me if you're here for her. Only don't let her see you hanging back. This is about her bravery. Not yours, or mine."

"Thank you," Reese said, with a deep sigh. "You have always been–" He didn't finish. He just looked down and repeated the phrase: "Thank you."

Byron let go, and they walked side by side down to where the other two waited. He rode with Marvina and her mother back to the house. Reese had gone off to wherever he was staying now in the city.

When they got to the house, they saw that the Ewing's dogs and cats where setting up a ruckus. Marvina hurried her mother in, and then came back to where Byron was standing on his porch. He'd had the sense she wanted to speak with him.

"Reese is seeing someone else," she said. "I hope I'm doing the right thing telling you."

He bent slightly at the waist, from the pain. He turned from her, and looked out at the lights of his town.

"I'm sorry, Byron. And I think he's miserable."

He couldn't get enough air again. He faced her, breathless, all dark inside, a desolation–a man losing everything. Marvina walked over and put her arms around him. "I'm so sorry," she said. "Want me to stay tonight?"

He shook his head. "I told him to keep coming to see Georgia. She wants it."

Marvina shrugged; her expression seemed to say that it was hard to explain.

No, Byron thought. It wasn't really so hard to explain at all. Georgia had said to him, quite honestly and gently, what she required. It wasn't too much to ask. He could find a way to do what she wanted. He was Byron the lyron.

*

Georgia Susan Michael Townsend Mailley passed away in the middle of the night, almost exactly one week later. There was no warning; it happened quite suddenly and peacefully. Her son was downstairs in the cafeteria with Marvina, drinking coffee. Reese had left, with a promise of returning in the morning, first thing. Everyone had settled into a pattern of visiting with the failing woman, who seemed at the end to be growing stronger, and holding on. She was alert when awake, and herself right to the end. After her passing, the people who had stood with her at the edge of her darkness drifted to other lives, as people often do—Marvina took her mother's advice and sold her house. The two women live in a duplex in the old town section of Charlottesville, Virginia. Reese drifted out to California with his new companion for a time, and then came back to Virginia. He took a job teaching art in the local high school, and continued to make money with his painting. Byron moved to New York again and worked for a magazine there for a year or two, then settled in a little walk-up flat on a narrow street in Rome. He still lives there, and not always alone. Now and then he walks out near sunset and takes pictures of the old part of the city, those ancient buildings, with their long history, their beauty and complication, their tragedy and sorrow.

The Prayer

Paul Maliszewski

February 4, 2002

Dear President Bush,

This morning, Mr. Lambier called us all to a meeting in his office. Ted and I had been working out back, stacking pallets of stone gargoyles and, in between, taking breaks to discuss the odd ways of the human heart and our congenital inability to begin even to understand those ways. What I mean to say is I was discussing Nancy and her ways while Ted discussed his live-in girlfriend Rhonda. Rhonda is not so odd to me and Nancy is not so odd to Ted, so usually Ted can manage to come up with something to say to me that I had never thought of, and vice versa. Today Ted was telling me that Rhonda had taken recently to calling him "her baby bird" because of how when they kiss he often has his head tilted back and his mouth flapping open and shut in a desperate and needy manner. Ted wanted my opinion on whether he should feel a) offended, b) only lightly kidded, or c) the object of her unswerving endearment, that is the nickname was evidence that Rhonda loves him even though he looks sometimes like a hungry baby bird. I was describing for Ted my dream of Nancy sitting on the patio with her back to me. I had a hunch and put forth my theory that her back facing me the whole dream and the fact I could not see her face were not insignificant considerations.

Ted said, "Right. Right," as if he knew already where I was going with my interpretation. The fact was I didn't know where I was going with the interpretation. I'd just thought of it.

Lambier's voice coming over the loudspeakers interrupted our discussion. "Hello, employees. Good morning. This is Mr. Lambier speaking. All employees please report to my office for a ten o'clock meeting. All employees, my office, ten o'clock. Thank you."

"Wonder what this is about," I said.

Ted shrugged. "Maybe Lambier has an interpretation of your dream he wants to share."

Lambier came back over the loudspeaker. "Ten o'clock is in ten minutes," he said. "Thank you."

"Or maybe he has a theory about why you became such a prick," I said.

Ted said, "I didn't think that was still a mystery."

"Your mom and dad fuck you up, you mean?" I asked.

"My mom and dad," Ted said, counting off one on the index finger of his left hand. "Wasn't breastfed. Got sent to shitty public schools." He stopped to think, his middle finger bent back. "Poor nutrition," he continued. "Did you know we drank PET milk? Have you ever drank PET milk?"

I shook my head no and no.

Ted said. "And finally, I got no exercise. None whatsoever."

Ten minutes later Lambier began the meeting by saying that he had some good news and some bad news. I heard most everyone in the room exhale noisily, a collective sigh. Will there always and forever be good news and bad news? Will one always travel with the other, the vivacious and kindly aunt of good news never not arriving at our doorstep with her husband, the belligerent and opinionated uncle of news that is bad? Lambier told us that the warehouse was in trouble, what with the whole economy slowing, and his profits were shrinking by the month.

Lambier was sitting behind his desk, which is as large as a barge and bare of any of the major indicators of work. "So that's the bad news," he said. As he pronounced the obvious and spoke it slowly, making what was blatant also annoying, he raised his hands off the desk, palms up, as if he held all of the bad news before us, for examination.

"The good news," Lambier said, letting his hands fall flat on his desk, pushing his chair back, and coming around the corner to sit with one haunch on the desk and one leg dangling, "is that this weekend I discovered Jesus Christ."

His manner, casual, studied, relaxed, suggested he'd recently read an early chapter in a book entitled, *How to Make It Look Like You're Casual, Studied, and Relaxed When You're Anything But.*

I took Lambier's announcement as a cue to hang my head and study the tops of my boots. I was ashamed. I was embarrassed for Lambier and ashamed that I had in common with him as much as I did: basic things, things such as the English language, certain key snippets of DNA, and the shapes and alignment of all our internal organs. My boots were dusty, worn at the toes, and scuffed around the tops. Most of the wear resulted from working the pedals on the forklift.

It occurred to me that Lambier might interpret my bowed head as reverential or, worse, pious. When I looked up he smiled at me, nodding his head several degrees in an affirmative manner, and then got down off the desk. He opened his arms as if to embrace us all and said, "I'd like us to say a little prayer now."

The Two Bobs and a few others bowed their heads and joined hands. Some people grumbled. Ted kicked me to get my attention. When I looked at him, he only glared, afraid to speak but afraid also not to register his disquiet.

Lambier said, "Let's all join hands and pray."

Everyone joined hands. I held Ted's and Holly's. Holly's hands were clammy. Clammy hands are always unfortunate and hers were like slick pieces of unrisen dough, provided unrisen dough customarily wore lots of rings. The Two Bobs fell to their knees then, a bold choice to be sure. Lambier did likewise and a few others followed suit. Before long, we were all kneeling before Lambier's barge of a desk.

"Let us pray," Lambier said, as if he needed to ask permission at this point or there was any debate to the contrary. "Lord, please look after my warehouse and all of my employees as we work together and alongside one another to weather this most difficult and trying period in our lives. With growth last quarter lower than expected and earnings in the current quarter looking soft as well as a steady, if not alarming decline in the overall, inflation-adjusted value of new orders received plus renewals, we will need all your help and wisdom and guidance in the short-term. In particular, we will need your help in the ceramic planter and concrete birdfeeder divisions, divisions which this economic downturn has, for whatever reason, seen fit to take a harsh toll upon. Lord, the outcome of this fiscal year may well try our souls, but we do not doubt for a moment that if we maintain our love for you and, moreover, in you, that you will return our love ten-fold. Loving the Lord, we realize, produces the best return of all. Loving the Lord is an investment that pays out for all eternity, like an annuity except longer. I cannot speak for all people's love for you, or even all warehouses' love for you. I can only tell you about my warehouse and my people, because that is what I know. My warehouse operates according to Christian principles. All of my employees treat each other and all others with whom they come into contact in the Christian manner. It is for these reasons that we pray to you and ask you to lift up our productivity so that we may devote more of our productive lives to you, Lord."

As Lambier spoke, Ted tightened and loosened his grip on my hand. I wasn't sure if he was aware of what he was doing. Was it nerves or was he trying to tell me something? Sir, I have tried to believe. I have tried to believe in God and, on occasion, have tried to pray to him on my and my family's behalf, but I find, in the end, I just do not believe, or maybe do not believe passionately enough. It occurred to me then that I hadn't touched Ted's hand since shaking it on his first day of work. Now friends, we greeted each other with nods and waves, with our hands held up and then dropped to our sides. Most everything we agreed upon we did so without words or any formality.

Lambier was relating to God the specific numbers for each division in the interest, he said, of fully disclosing all of the business's particulars. I did want to believe. No, I didn't want to believe the way Lambier believed, issuing demands and then expecting results, like any boss, I suppose, but surely I did want to believe in something or other. From time to time, I felt belief might offer some comfort–it's supposed to, right?–though kneeling on the floor of Lambier's office was not doing the trick. If anything, I felt coerced, almost bullied, into kneeling, overwhelmed and then cowed by the sheer numbers of those kneeling around me. They were good people, I reasoned. And they kneeled. Why shouldn't I join them and, like them, kneel also? Maybe they were onto something.

Ted's grip on my hand acquired a dependable regularity, a short series of squeezes followed by a number of looser grips. Tight. Loose. Tight, tight. Loose. Tight. Loose, loose, loose. Ted had a good grip, a firm grip. It was firm without ever being too aggressive. Lambier continued reading down the columns of numbers, entering them into the Lord's memory banks, he said, so as to guarantee, he added, that he would acquire the best advice possible. I imagined then that Ted was squeezing a message through my hand. Perhaps it was Morse Code, an emergency plea relayed from his ship, lost somewhere at sea, to me, on shore, in one of those buildings with the big lamps in them that they construct on rocks. Perhaps it was an S.O.S. Or perhaps Ted was communicating to me in some new code of his own devising. Lighthouses, that's what those buildings are called. The signals ran from Ted through his fingers and into my hand. From there, the signals ran up my arm, and I came to appreciate what I took to be an emerging pattern. I started to transmit the message to Holly, squeezing her hand and then letting my grip go slack in time with Ted's grip on my hand. I didn't understand the message—I never would, Lord knows—but I sent it along anyway, intact and unaltered. The message passed through me and into Holly and from there, who knows.

Keep up the good work, sir.

Sincerely,
Harvey Strub

Tow

Morgan McDermott

Bruni took five years learning the tricks to mastering a blind dog. It took that long for her to understand the nuances of discipline, to realize that to officer is at once to love, and to limit. She has learned that it is essential to never let a blind dog lose sight of who is leading whom; a blind dog, after all, cannot read halfhearted gestures or mixed signals. Failing to train a blind dog properly is in itself an act of cruelty.

After five long years of learning that to love anything, or anyone, is to be George S. Patton at times, Bruni is confident she now has the skills to take on a young man.

The young man leans his shoulder casually against the bulletproof window in the tow office. He unwraps a stick of chewing gum thoughtfully, pondering his next words, as they may make or break him in the eyes of his girl. This is how the young man thinks of their courtship. He thinks of it as a horse race. He thinks that how he exits the gate means everything.

The tow office is an aluminum trailer with curved, reflective interior walls. A posting from the police is bolted into the metal, as official as the Ten Commandments. The curve creates a funhouse mirror effect, capturing those who enter, twisting them into freaks. There is nowhere in the shiny room that those who have come for their cars might sit, so Bruni stands against the wall by the door. The surface hurts her elbows, but she does not let it show on her face. She has been practicing not showing pain. Living with a sighted person soon, she will have to speak a whole new body language.

The young man chews three sticks of gum at once. It lends him the air of a wrangler, a bull-rider, a man who knows how to wrestle trouble with his hands. It is early in their relationship. She is still convincing him that she finds him handsome, and manly, and smart. He is still learning how to champion her. He is still learning which problems she wants him to solve, and which ones she only needs to talk about. He has decided this moment falls into the first category.

The young man leans close to the glass and asks Mr. Tow if Mrs. Tow is happy married to a hijacker. Mr. Tow shakes his head sadly, explaining this detail for perhaps the thousandth time. Through the circular metal speaker in the center of the window, Mr. Tow says that there is no Mrs. Tow, and in fact there is no Mr. Tow: the name is franchised, a corporate logo. Then he says if the young man wants the car, he must pay for the tow and the hourly storage like everyone else. Mr. Tow points to the sign above the window.

ALL VIOLATORS ARE EQUAL IN THE EYES OF MR. TOW the sign reads.

Bruni and the young man need the car to start their new life together. The car is roomy, an SUV with leather seats and a tow bar mounted below the bumper. They need it to carry Bruni's belongings from her apartment to what will be their apartment, once one is found. Bruni desperately needs it so they can move into a mutual space at the same time. She does not want to suffer the stigma of the space being his first, and only later one shared. She wants them to start this adventure on an equal footing, as equal partners.

That equality is now in doubt. This afternoon they were treated to the chilling sight of an automobile vanished. The street where they had left it had been swept clean of parked cars. Bruni knew at once that she now would not be allowed to use the car, that any footing she might have had in argument with her sister, any claim to adult privilege, had been towed away. She knew at once that her escape, perhaps even her courtship, was in trouble.

The young man asks if Mrs. Tow is proud that he is a pirate, that he chose privateering as a career.

Bruni checks her watch. Five minutes, and counting. The young man promised her that he could reason with Mr. Tow and have the SUV back in ten. She looks down at the newspaper she holds folded to the want ads: luxury townhouses are available next to the university campus, two and three bedrooms. Astronomical rent. She continues down the page.

Mr. Tow says his wife is proud that he runs a successful business, and thanks the young man for asking.

Her sister pokes Bruni in the shoulder, the poke she has when she has a question. Brynne has just entered the trailer from the parking lot, where she has let her blind dog off the leash to roam. She has missed most of the action. Whispering, she asks if Mr. Tow is tall. Bruni says the man is tall, yes, but not attractive. She says Mr. Tow is Abe Lincoln-tall. Brynne likes only tall men, and though she is blind, she usually does not have to ask. The speaker, and the curved walls, and the fact that Bruni is leaving her, are all throwing off her perception.

Mr. Tow says if the young man mentions his wife again, there will be trouble. He calls the young man Buster.

Brynne and her blind dog are present because they own the SUV. When people ask why a blind woman owns a car—and a car the size of Panama at that—Brynne claims she bought it for the dog. The chocolate lab was in the seeing-eye business, and is frustrated in its retirement. She tells everyone that hearing the dog bump into the furniture pains her, and that long rides with the windows open would be a tonic. It would be a safe way for the dog to enjoy itself.

Bruni knows the real reason. The real reason is that Bruni's driving terrifies. Brynne never liked being driven by her little sister, even before the accident, and now she wants an island of steel around her as a buffer. Five years of living with Brynne has taught Bruni that buffers, whether constructed out of steel, or bulletproof glass, or sharp words, not only protect, they keep others in step.

Mr. Tow tells the young man to grow up, that there is nothing personal in having a car towed. Mr. Tow says some people choose to believe only they can move their cars. They are fools.

At the auto dealership, Brynne told the salesman she had nearly died in a traffic accident, and insisted on only looking at the largest SUVs in stock. Bruni recalls how her sister selected the model by touching the machine front to back, measuring inside and out, rapping the sheet metal to gauge its ability to absorb a hit. The salesman grew excited when Brynne did not bother to look at the brochures. He was in the passenger seat for the test drive before he realized she was blind. Bruni remembers the look of deliberation on the man's face as he considered handing her the keys anyway, as he wrestled with the benefits versus the risks.

Brynne is an object of deliberation for many men. They weigh carefully her pros and cons, weigh the effort required to be with her against the softness of her golden hair, the smoothness of her skin, the timbre of her voice. Perhaps she does not have sight, but she has looks, and Bruni knows women who would think long and hard about that trade. The men who decide to court Brynne take her to the movies, where they love whispering details into her perfect ears. They take her to art galleries so she can breathe in the masters. Eventually these men grow comfortable enough to take her to dinner just so they can look into her luminous, decorative brown eyes and admire themselves without reservation.

It is about that point Brynne dumps them.

Bruni remembers how the salesman clenched his hand slowly around the keys, how he kept them hidden until Bruni stepped forward and offered to drive. She remembers how the salesman smiled as though he had won a hand of poker. Left to make the car-buying decision herself, Bruni would have told the salesman to tell his story walking. She would have kept the old Honda, its bodywork long ago hammered back into shape, its windshield replaced. She would have saved the cash and put the dog to sleep. But that would have sent the wrong message to her sister.

The young man kicks the wall gently as he speaks. He says if there is nothing personal, if no one should take offense, then why does Mr. Tow hide behind a bulletproof shield?

Mr. Tow eyes Brynne as the young man speaks. He eyes her legs. Mr. Tow gives Bruni the impression of a man who drinks most of his meals. He has the long face, the sad eyes, the pouty lips of a man who trained to climb a professional ladder but lost his footing and slid several rungs before halting. He looks like he is holding on too tightly to that ladder to drop any further, but also too tightly to pull himself up. Mr. Tow must know his is not a good look for a man in his post. Eyes on Brynne, Mr. Tow straightens up, thrusts his chest forward, squares his shoulders.

Bruni snorts. She gets a kick out of the preening men do around her blind sister, the adjusting of ties, the running of hands through hair, the discreet removal of wedding rings.

The young man says since Mr. Tow is in the ransom business, he should at least look the part: he should wear a vest, a hoop earring, a cloth around his head. He should wear an eye patch.

Mr. Tow says it is all funny until someone loses an eye.

Brynne grinds her teeth. Even at a distance, Bruni hears the jaw muscles click. It sounds like a coin striking pavement, calling for attention.

The young man says he is surprised anyone finds Mr. Tow funny. He is a man who steals for a living. He is a man who inflicts trauma.

Mr. Tow says he steals nothing. The cars go home eventually.

The young man asks about the mountains of cars stacked outside in the wrecking yard.

Mr. Tow says those cars are not displaced, they are disloved. He says all the cars that end up at his establishment suffer from some degree of dislove, from a lack of attention to detail that only comes from weariness with love, the wish that what was once an object of adoration would just go away already.

Bruni presses herself against the wall. She assumes the room was designed narrow to avoid mob action. With her and the young man and Brynne, the air is tight, and it puts her in mind of a tomb. The narrow trailer sits on a gravel lot stacked high with automobile carcasses, stacks that remind Bruni of Egypt, of the Sphinx and the pyramids. Bruni has not been to Egypt. Bruni has been nowhere, but she has cable television. Every time she suggests travel to Brynne, she meets resistance. When Bruni suggests they drive the SUV up to Montreal, or down to Memphis, her sister says she does not want to risk it. The way Brynne says risk, Bruni hears clearly the shriek of rubber on pavement, the crunch of glass as the crown of Brynne's head breaks the windshield. It has taken five years for Bruni to admit there is living without sight, and then there is living without vision, and that her poor driving inflicted only one of these conditions on her sister.

The young man tells Mr. Tow that love is not the issue in this case. He says the issue is his car was towed without fair warning. Tilting his head, catching the discrepancy, Mr. Tow says that when he first came to the window, the young man stated it was not his car that was towed, but a friend's. Mr. Tow's voice is stern. He is the victim of a lie.

Brynne startles them both when she interrupts, when she says that they are wasting her time. She steps forward and says the car does not belong to a friend of the young man, it belongs to her. She says she is not the young man's friend. He has stolen her sister's heart, and he is without a substantial job, and he borrows her car without asking.

Mr. Tow says it is the young man who should wear an eye patch.

The young man says it is a long story.

Mr. Tow says that he can see on Brynne's face, and on the young man's face, and on the face of the girl standing by the door holding the want ads, much of that story. He says the young man should invest in some bulletproof glass, as it helps everything appear more manageable.

As she listens to the men, Brynne's head moves as though spectating a tennis match.

She is a professional listener. She handles collection calls for the state child-support agency. The calls come to the apartment on a dedicated line, and between eight and four Chicago time Brynne confronts deception and insult and hard-luck stories. She reads silence the way a sighted person reads facial muscles. She reads a good lie like an oenologist reads a fine wine, reveling in the hints and blush of its heritage, appreciating the skill behind its crafting. She fits what a man tells her together with what he does not like puzzle pieces, assembling a complete picture of both the problem, and the man.

When Brynne is on the job, she will sometimes put her party on hold and describe to Bruni what the deadbeat is wearing. Brynne can tell a deadbeat's age to the year, and where he or she was born. She can tell if a deadbeat is rich or poor; fat or thin. She can tell who is healthy, and who is headed for the pine-box derby. While they are dating, some men assume Brynne has ESP. When they are discharged, many accuse her of being a witch. Bruni is not bothered by her sister's talent. She enjoys the details of people far away. It is a little like traveling.

Brynne turns to Bruni and says that the young man is going about this all wrong, that he does not listen. She says Bruni will be able to do nothing with this young man. She speaks loudly enough for the young man to hear.

Bruni concentrates on her reading: one bedroom, one bath, but in a high-rise building, with a pool and a heated garage, boosting the monthly well out of reach. She does not circle the phone number. Brynne presses on, says there is not one bit of give in the young man, that he will be dead of burst pipes and disappointment at a young age. She says Bruni has much to learn about disappointment in men. She says that it is like rust on a car. Disappointment eats away at a man.

Bruni fixes her eyes on the newspaper because she cannot look anywhere else without meeting a twisted face. She fixes on an ad for a three bedroom, one bath coachhouse, all utilities included. Just the word coachhouse makes her shiver, the thought of living behind a lakefront house, living servant-class, under scrutiny.

Living small.

Bruni has served the last five years under careful watch, learning that being visually able is not the same thing as being visible. She has learned her lesson. After the accident, she skipped going away to college. She lived with Brynne in the condominium bought with the insurance settlement and took classes at the local school. She was of use. She had been a precocious child, in possession of the precocious child's distaste with being young. She is over that now.

Brynne says Bruni does not have to listen. It is enough for now that she just hears.

Bruni tries hard to hear elsewhere. Outside, other tow victims stand on the gravel path to the trailer, waiting patiently to be fleeced. They are all neighbors, made criminals by arcane street-cleaning tow zones that appear and disappear with the seasons. Focusing on their conversations, Bruni is not surprised by the lack of grumbling. In this college town just north of the city, very professional, very educated people routinely toe illogical lines without complaint. Residents are accustomed to being soaked by taxes and fines and tickets. The civic abuse is the price they endure for the privilege of living along the lake. Bruni is not surprised by the festive air: business cards are exchanged, mutual friends are discovered, the names and telephone numbers of good baby-sitters float for all to hear. Those waiting in line were rattled when their heaviest, most expensive, most trusted belonging was snatched up by the undertow of civilization. They have lived in the wrong time and place for at least a moment. They have had a taste of Czarist Russia, or Oklahoma in the spring. They are relieved to be reminded that they are all Americans, and that to right their world requires only a credit card.

Bruni lets the tow victims' chatter flow over her like music as she scans the columns of print: one bedroom, one bath, near the lake, the rent a nice punch in the mouth. She marks it anyway, to bolster her resolve. She will look at it. She might not be able to afford many of the listings, but she also cannot afford to stay where she is.

The young man asks Mr. Tow to be reasonable. It is midsummer. There is no snow to plow. The SUV was parked neither in front of a hydrant, nor in a bus zone. No crime took place. Why must people suffer?

Mr. Tow says he takes no action out of cruelty; signs clearly command one not to leave a car where it does not belong, and when that commandment is broken, he appears.

The young man says that what happened to him is not fair. He says Mr. Tow should see where some people park: in front of hydrants, in handicapped spots, on sidewalks. Sidewalks. He says those are real sins. Mr. Tow agrees free will is often abused, but says he always catches up in the end.

The young man says Mr. Tow is wrong to claim he is not cruel.

Mr. Tow says he would not say it if he did not believe it.

Mr. Tow is saved by the bell, the cheerful *ting* of a microwave from the rear of the office. Mr. Tow turns, and is gone. The young man faces an empty window.

Brynne's head tilts as she tracks the sound of Mr. Tow's footsteps. The tension washed from the room for the moment, the air quiet, Bruni's senses come out from under cover; she notices that the room smells doughy and damp, of cheap frozen pasta. Outside, the dog is playing with the crowd, growling as it offers its toy, a hard rubber ball with a rattle inside. One of the dog's favorite games since going blind is tug-of-war. It likes to assert its physical presence, exercise its ability to push, and to pull. The lab is still young. When it had sight, it was docile, but it has found fire in recent years, found mischief.

She peeks through the doorway and sees one of the tow truck drivers playing with the dog, twirling in a circle and forcing it to turn in dance-step with him as he tries to wrestle the ball from clenched jaws. The dog and the man match each other, grunt for grunt, both of them accustomed to having say over direction. Short and thick, the driver wears threadbare gray overalls with a red and white patch over his breast pocket.

SOFOCLES, the patch reads.

The young man places his open palms on the glass, then a cheek, angling to see where his adversary went. Face to the glass, he tells the women that he has the tow guy on the ropes.

Brynne tells the young man to hush up.

Bruni looks from the young man, to her sister, to the advertisements. She pauses over a bold announcement: a vintage apartment, two bedrooms, two baths, located in an upscale neighborhood in the college town, renting for twice what she can afford.

Her pen hovers over the ad.

To earn money Bruni writes term papers on commission, twenty dollars a page. She writes papers on any subject, for she loves to learn. Her favorites are English and history, and currently she is writing a master's thesis on the mistakes that led to World War Two, the resentments and grudges. She is learning how the world can be torn apart when people refuse to let go of the past. Bruni figures that if she works another job, works retail or waits tables, she might be able to live a lifestyle advertised boldly.

The young man says the tow guy is buckling, that he almost has the car.

Brynne says this is a first for her, a man who knows nothing about women, and also knows nothing about men.

The young man's shirt is open at the collar, and as his skin flushes, as he reddens, Bruni catches sight of the scars at his neck, scars that trail like latticework down his chest. Her young man is a survivor. He has survived a shooting, and more importantly he has survived its healing, has avoided the cruel demeanor that can come from regarding oneself as a victim. She is still learning the scars by sight and by touch, still learning his landscape. Bruni lowers the newspaper and says they parked her sister's car poorly, she and the young man, and they can take responsibility. They can pay the fine. They might have acted poorly, but they are not poor.

Brynne says that if Bruni marries this man, she will have to clean up after him coming and going.

The young man tells Brynne to keep her mouth shut if she cannot see the big picture.

Bruni wants to kiss him. All her boyfriends have been partly in love with her older and stronger and more beautiful sister. Bruni knows that to be in love with such a woman is partly to be afraid of her. But this young man is not cowed by Brynne. This young man does not flinch.

Brynne says that the young man is miffed because he knows she has his number.

The young man says Brynne may have his number, but he has Bruni.

Brynne tells the young man that her sister will grow bored with him. She says that like Jean-Paul Sartre, her sister will always have an eye somewhere else.

As Brynne speaks, the young man steps away from the glass to stand at Bruni's side. He tries to put his arm around Bruni, but he comes too close and steps on her toes. Bruni is wearing sandals and the misstep hurts magnificently, but she does not show it. Her practice is paying off. To hide her grimace, she turns away, looks out the door. In the lot, the chocolate lab is toying with the crowd, walking away slowly enough to be pursued, ball in mouth, tail wagging in defiance. The driver stands with his hands on his hips, calling to the dog in Spanish. The animal continues toward the automobile graveyard. The driver claps his hands, trying to be sweet, to no effect. He knows none of the tricks.

Brynne advances on the spot where the young man stood just a moment before. She stands sideways to Mr. Tow's window. She faces the emptiness in such a way that an observer could not help but conclude she has made a mistake, that she thinks the young man stands before her still. Brynne faces her distorted reflection on the far wall and, next to it, the legal disclaimer posted by the police. Bruni has seen Brynne do this when denied her way. Bruni has seen her sister look high over the head of someone in order to put that person off balance, or let her head sway back and forth when she wants to shame an opponent into silence. Speaking into thin air, Brynne accuses the young man of being so immature that he assumes to sleep with a woman is to know her. She warns the young man that he will regret carrying her sister away the minute he realizes how much of a woman is composed of secrets. She addresses the wall and its posted notice vehemently, her usual cool manner carefully, expertly disassembled.

YOU HAVE THE RIGHT TO AN APPEAL reads the notice.

Bruni feels the young man's grip fade around her, his resolve ebbing as he confronts a handicapped woman lost without her sister, literally not knowing which direction to turn. His hand falls to his side. Bruni takes hold of his arm, the same way she holds her sister when crossing a busy intersection.

Outside, several of those waiting their turn are whistling for the blind dog, calling to it, some calling it Girl, some calling it Boy.

The young man slips Bruni's grasp without a word, steps through the door into the lengthening shadows of the late afternoon. Bruni watches him stalk toward the flattened and stacked autos, the American pyramids, ancient ruins of the modern world. She knows he will fare no better than the truck driver. The dog will dodge him. It frustrates the young man that the dog does not listen. He assumes the dog does not listen because it does not like him. He has not yet learned the trick to commanding a blind dog is to earn its respect, to acquire its trust while breaking its will. Bruni is debating whether or not to teach him.

As soon as he is gone, Brynne turns to Bruni, facing her dead on.

"You'll see," Brynne says.

Bruni returns to the newspaper: two bedrooms, one bath, hardwood floors and lots of light, but only a summer sublet, a temporary solution. Bruni writes a question mark next to the ad. There is a shuffling in the back of the office. The aroma of wet noodles has faded. Brynne turns to the window, gathers her hair behind her head, then lets it fall evenly, fan out over her shoulders. Brynne's nose sweeps the air, and Bruni realizes her sister has been following the steady disappearance of Mr. Tow's food, that she has been timing the moment the man's break will end, collecting herself for her presentation, marshaling her forces.

Brynne knows all the tricks.

Stone Boat

William Kittredge

The Mexican steers were shades of orange and blue, even green, color like rock moss over their tight, shorthaired hides. Twelve hundred and seventy-four came down from the Northern Pacific railroad cars, quick animals with horns like opalescent hooks, gathered off the Sonoran deserts. They had been nine weeks in New Mexico because of the wartime shortage of railroad cars, before being shipped north to Oregon, then been in the cars a week, only unloaded twice, watered in Fresno and Redding.

Sonora lay south of Arizona on the boy's creased, heavy-paper *National Geographic* map, an area colored pale yellow and almost empty. Damon Booth, who owned the steers, said yellow was the color for Mexico. Orange blossoms had smelled yellow at twilight. Children played between thick-walled adobe houses. At the Booth Acreage, an unpainted shiplap building on the Klamath Marsh, on an alkali knoll beside a horse corral, timbered mountains blue off in the distance, Damon would squat on salt grass in the midday silence, a few flies moving, and talk of Mexico. The summer was dry as the worst years of the thirties, the creek empty but for the holes where frogs survived. The peat cracked in rifts wider than a horse could leap. Summer Mallards circled and flew on.

The Indian, Hazzard Beal, claimed the cracks led down to an underworld. The Klamaths and the Modocs, Hazzard said, laughing as he talked, maybe to hide his seriousness, or maybe, as Damon claimed, covering up for lying. Hazzard claimed the cracks were always there, waiting to be opened by the spirits on bad years when the world was evil, the spirits coming up to cause burnt grass and no water birds. Indians stayed away from the swamp in dry years. The boy, knowing it was silly, imagined his dead grandfather haunting the world into this war.

His mother hadn't let him look when the men brought his grandfather's body back to his elaborate house, surrounded by yellow-barked pines, far up the swamp where Blueback Creek came out of the timber. That house had been sold. His mother had taken him over the Cascades to the rainy Willamette Valley. They lived in a little brick house with vines on the walls and she taught English in University High School in Eugene. He wished he'd been allowed to look when his grandfather was brought home, dead of what was called an accident with a rifle, because his father had been killed during the invasion of Tarawa. He dreamed of his father, the dark shape of a man walking toward him. If he'd seen his grandfather's deadness he might have been able to think his father was dead instead of just gone.

"No accident about it," Damon said, talking about the grandfather. "Done it himself." The boy was unable to see how being dead would be something you wanted. Yet his father had gone to war when he might have stayed home with an agricultural deferment. His mother locked herself in her room, crying before she walked down the hill from the brick house to church in Eugene.

"Their war," Damon said. It was evening, the cool air carrying the odor of manure from the corral. Damon rolled a smoke, snapped a kitchen match over his thumbnail, wandered to the well-house and came back with a dripping cold beer. "The idea is to not be a fool who can't live his life." The boy heard his uncle clank the iron stove lid as he laid the fire for morning.

On the morning when they unloaded the Mexican steers, the train jerked, creaked, and the engine flowered steam, frightening the steers into banging at corral fences. The men sat their horses in the jack pine shade alongside the road heading toward the marsh, horses sweeping their tails at the flies. "They're going to scatter," Damon said. "Clear as anything. All to hell."

The road to the marsh was not fenced. On the sides stretched miles of open Forest Service and Klamath Reservation timber, impassable jack pine thickets overgrown with brush and scattered with rotting logs, the aftermath of a fire that had burned off the flat fifty years before. If the steers broke and ran there was no chance of heading them off. They'd be rounding them up a few at a time, over the summer.

Damon stayed away from the war and yet always went full out in the timber. It was a thing the boy thought about in the night while recalling the timber, holding his breath, clutching at the saddle-horn and waiting for his horse to catch its forefeet and slowly cartwheel forward. He rode with his feet out, letting the stirrups beat on his shins, ready to cast off if the horse went down, ashamed. "My log-jumping horse," Damon had said, grinning at the boy while saddling a long-legged gray gelding before sunrise, teasing the boy. They were going to be riding the timber.

Hazzard Beal was grinning under his black hat. Half his front teeth were missing and his smile lopped to the left, but he wasn't foolish. In sixty years he'd come to own nearly six hundred good Hereford cows and the land to run them on. During the depression,

Hazzard had traded cattle for land, the increase of his herd for more acres, living almost without money, eating venison, and vegetables from the rambling garden behind the shed of a house where he lived with his fat, silent wife. During the dry years, Hazzard had pumped water with a pitcher pump from a hand-dug well on the edge of the timber, carrying the water in buckets on a pole across his back to irrigate his garden when the creek stopped flowing and the swamp dried up and cracked. Hazzard cocked his head to one side. "Be noon pretty quick," he said.

"You going to help?" Damon asked, nearly shouting. Hazzard grinned. He heard perfectly, and had heard the same things many times.

"Not much of a horse I rode this morning." Hazzard was not bothering to excuse himself for having ridden a sorry horse from his herd of fifty some.

"Boy tells me they're going to head straight out," Damon said.

"Them boys don't know nothing," Hazzard said. "But that's all right."

The black steam engine went on jerking and clattering as the cars were moved forward to the unloading chute. Dry, hungry steers went on milling the corrals until they were entirely unloaded and the gates opened. Then they shouldered through, jarring posts, gone in a ground-shaking run, escaping. The boy followed Hazzard in clouding pumice dust, horses in a hard-jarring run. He could see only the stragglers, and hear the drumming sound of their running. He kicked his horse through an opening, hanging on, ducking the whipping branches and clamping his knees tight to avoid having them jammed against black-barked jack pines. Dust hung between the trees. Abruptly he saw the open meadows of the marsh. They were almost to the gate into the fields when his horse went down in soft footing around a burn-blackened Ponderosa stump. His leg trapped between the ribcage of the horse and soft pumice, he was trying to get away from the floundering animal when the horse rose, forelegs first. The boy was still in the saddle and not frightened. He kicked the horse into another run in which they turned onto the slick grass of the meadow to confront the fence.

Steers were charging through the gates into the field, soundless and dustless on the sod. He had ridden the timber, and fallen, and now, as the steers passed into the meadow, he looked back and could see the glacial summer snow atop the peaks of the Cascades.

Posts on both sides of the gates went down. Steers floundered into tangled wire while the others were slowing, fanning out toward the creek. The steers coming out of the wire were streaked with cuts. When the last of the herd was through the gate, he began to feel scratches on his face, the aching in his knees.

"We was lucky," Damon said. The lead steers were almost across to the creek.

Hazzard Beal laughed. "That boy was right."

Damon left the boy guarding the gate and trotted off after the steers, making sure none were badly cut up in the wire while he had some help.

"Sit tight," Damon told the boy. "I'll be right back, and we'll rebuild the gates."

Shadows reached across the meadows like fingers as Damon came back with his team of Belgian geldings, the man and horses far off as the steers trotted the fence-lines. Damon stood on the stone boat, a low sled with runners of skinned jack pine, a conveyance named for sleds used to haul loads of free rocks from meadows in stony country. This one was loaded with tools and posts.

Dinner was canned Spam, a red and white box of soda crackers, and half a case of Acme Beer, bottles damp from the cold water overflowing the artesian well. "I guess you earned a beer," Damon said. "You done the finest you done so far." He twisted open the Spam, and cut slices with his knife while the boy sipped the cold, bitter beer. Then they began replacing the broken posts, digging in the dry soil, dropping the posts into fresh holes and tamping around them with shovel handles. The boy was sweating and had not even finished the first set of holes for the brace posts when Damon was done untangling the wire. He handed the boy another beer and took the shovel. Raw blisters glistened on the boy's palms while he drank. Head swimming, he helped set the final posts and stretch the wire. The steers wandered the half-shadowed meadow. "Full of water and looking for Mexico," Damon said. "Going to be at it all summer."

Riding on the stone boat, leading his horse, the boy imagined steers scattered through the timber like bits of colored cloth, searching for Mexico. He remembered his room in Eugene, maps and pins and ribbons on the walls to mark the progress of American troops through France and Germany to the Rhine, pictures of broken-topped palms, bodies floating on shallow Pacific tides. Somewhere in sun-warmed water the bones of his father were being absorbed into coral. He'd read about it.

The boy opened a beer, and handed Damon the bottle. Damon smiled after sipping at it and handed it back. It had to be noon over some island. The night air was growing chilled by the time the horses were rolling in the corral dust. The boy dreamed of Sonora, and blossoming orange trees, a land he could only imagine. Back in Eugene, he fell in love, fathered children, grew old, told them this story.

Swan in Retreat

Mitch Wieland

Despite years among the tumbleweed and sage, Ferrell Swan hates the wind as never before. He imagines the howling gusts as a perpetual soundtrack to his downhill life, a bleak accompaniment to those nightly dreams of Ohio and his youth long past. In his waking hours the wind pervades his very thoughts, as if to scour his mind clean of all memory and regret.

Today Ferrell is moving the last of his sheep, the most thankless chore he's ever known. He purchased the stock soon after buying his retirement retreat in southwest Idaho—one hundred acres of high desert scrub, an outpost from the civilized world. His thinking seemed right at the time: combine hot rainless land with the durability of sheep. He recalled Old Testament shepherds peacefully guarding their flocks, angels from above blessing animal and man. But the beasts turned out more stupid than the colleagues from his teaching days, and between the coyotes and the scorching sun, he lost more lambs each year than he took to the sale yards in Caldwell, where hundred-pound lambs brought just thirty dollars, more highway robbery than business transaction, if someone asked him.

Ferrell circles the barn with his face turned from the blowing grit. At his side pasture, he opens the gate and sends the dog wide. His border collie flanks the herd in a fluid curving arc, lambs and ewes turning with their single mind. The collie reverses direction, wheeling back in another sweeping turn, then aims the flock toward the holding pen. When the last of the sheep has flooded through the gate, Ferrell closes it behind them.

The man had called last night from Meridian, asking if Ferrell had sheep to sell. Ferrell couldn't make out much, but he heard the words Bosnia and Sarajevo and the rest he could figure. Some of his rancher friends near Letha sold lambs to the local Bosnians, getting twice what the sale could offer. The Bosnians, he was told, would arrive en mass—husbands and wives, kids and grandparents, distant relatives twice removed—and would butcher the lambs right on the property, skinning and gutting with patient inefficiency, leaving hours later, content and happy, in their mini vans or station wagons, the blood on the ground bright as fresh paint.

"You still going to do this?" Rilla says, coming up behind him in her English riding get-up. He knows she's heading to the endless BLM, those ten thousand acres of public land bordering their property, her basic plan to miss the day's events.

"I guess."

Rilla glances to where her sorrel mare waits at the fence. Last night she'd argued bitterly about the Bosnians, yelling every obvious thing she could muster: how she couldn't fathom a retired history teacher taking up sheep killing, why the hell he moved to the Wild West in the first place. She described in great detail how his selfish act of buying a chunk of desert led directly to their divorce and all the pain involved. Ferrell could only shrug. Rilla's specialty had always been to move any argument from its immediate particulars to the larger topic of Ferrell's general failure as a warm and loving man.

"I can't believe you want holy sacrifices on your land, Ferrell," she says, taking up where she'd left off the night before.

The flock mills about the holding pen, bleating latent reassurances. The poor beasts have already calmed down, the ordeal of the dog fading from memory. In the bright sun they look wise and serene, though Ferrell knows there isn't much wattage in the dark caverns of their skulls. Beside him, the dog sits wild-eyed and trembling, his work ethic way too strong to suit Ferrell. He knows the dog could herd all day and still not be satisfied. It makes him tired just thinking about it.

Ferrell glances east to a caravan negotiating the long lane, dust plumes blown sideways with dramatic effect. Rilla huffs and walks off, and Ferrell has to admit that for fifty-five she still looks mighty fine in her tight English riding pants. She's aged better than him, he believes, in both her body and her head. He watches her leg-up into the saddle, adjust her riding crop to her left hand and straighten her black helmet. Without visible signal she moves the horse into a walk. As the cars and vans park beside the cabin, Rilla canters the horse along the edge of the drive, then moves her into a run, each hoof raising small explosions of dust.

When the caravan has parked, Ferrell waits but nothing happens. He stands buffeted by the wind, perhaps a dozen pair of eyes trained in his direction, then doors open and slam and he finds himself surrounded. An older man dressed in white steps forward, the designated spokesperson, Ferrell assumes.

"We come for sheep," he says, the voice from the phone. "I am Javad."

Ferrell points to the holding pen, deciding directness and simplicity is the way to go. "Take your pick," he says.

The visitors crowd the fence, as if in reverence. Ferrell guesses four generations stand before him, a single bloodline reaching from the toothless man leaning on the gate, to the babies bundled in their young mothers' arms.

"How many do you want?" Ferrell says when the leader has looked the sheep over.

"All."

"You want to buy every sheep?"

"Yes, all." The man studies Ferrell as if he were slow-witted and forgetful besides. "We take seven today and then come back. We take all by two week's end."

"That's twenty head," Ferrell says. "What will you do with them?"

"We cook and eat in the park. We have many family and blankets on the ground. We eat and have drink as we have always done. In Bosnia, we do this. So here, of course, we do this."

Without discussion, three of the younger men enter the pen and wade into the flock. The man named Javad speaks to them in their own language, points and gestures. At last one of the moret bucks is singled out and cornered. The men wrestle the lamb out the gate and onto the driveway.

"Here?" the leader asks.

Ferrell notices for the first time the sets of long knives the women carry. Javad slides his finger across his throat in a way that doesn't warm Ferrell's heart. He pictures Rilla riding down the blood-soaked drive.

"Behind the barn," he says.

*

On bad days Ferrell wonders where his life has gone—an age-old inquiry, he well understands, but knowing his thoughts are timeless doesn't help his mood. His flesh and bones may be sixty plus, but his eyes still see with the same crying ache as ever, as if acute yearning were the natural order of things, as if his smoldering heart were about to catch flame. An old song on the radio, a cherished passage from one of his books, and Ferrell still goes all tingly, like he's swooning for the first time. At dusk he still gushes at the setting sun like some Hallmark poet, like some lovestruck boy with heart and pecker utterly linked. Though he's witnessed sundowns into the thousands, each one comes as a glorious surprise.

This morning the melancholy clings to Ferrell like a second skin. Overhead is nothing but blue, the sun a great gold star, yet Ferrell walks through this Eden in a dark gloom. He ponders the source of his unease, not sure why he feels so rattled. Perhaps it's yesterday's knives and those horrible last gasps, perhaps it's the blood now black on the ground. He pushes these thoughts from his mind, a puzzle he'll reserve for his evening shots of single malt, the only time of the day he ever tries to figure out his life.

Ferrell spends the morning avoiding chores around his homestead. He's never been all that fond of work, which partly explains why he went into teaching in the first place—pacing before a class in his creased trousers and tie, nary breaking a sweat in thirty some years. His father and both grandfathers, his multitude of uncles, all worked their butts off in fields or factories, in garages beneath scores of grimy cars. At first, when he built his log cabin and barn, he liked the newness of having actual work to do—setting fence posts beneath the blazing sun, tossing hay bales around, shoveling out the pungent stalls. But after seven years in Idaho the novelty has worn off, and Ferrell knows why he wasn't a farmer to begin with: busting your ass gets old, however noble the calling.

In the forenoon Rilla saddles up without speaking a word. Ferrell is pumping water into the trough beside the barn, but he might as well be invisible for all Rilla notices him. She hasn't spoken since the Bosnians. She returned from her ride yesterday and seemed intent on avoiding his very face. She stayed on the porch while he cooked dinner, her anger bringing an early dusk to their desert land. After he'd gone to bed he heard her finally in the kitchen, the chink and tap of flatware the loudest sounds in their entire hundred acres.

Now Rilla canters out into the vast nothingness around the cabin, riding with a purpose he wishes he shared. She looks for all the world like she isn't coming back. Ferrell watches until she and the horse blur into the wavering horizon, a final scene from a western he once saw.

With Rilla physically gone, she gallops back into his head. He thinks of all the other times one of them has stormed off mad, the decades of tempest and turmoil they've shared. Married seventeen years and divorced three, then seven years of living in sporadic sin—they've shared much and little at one and the same time. For a long while, raising her wild son Levon kept Rilla and him busier than they ever wanted, but then he was grown and gone, leaving them alone with too much time to reflect. Over the years Ferrell had always thought it would get better, that they would reach some state of grace in which to move about, as if in a fine white light. Against better sense, Ferrell rose each sunrise believing this would be the day they got their lives on track.

Growing up, Ferrell often heard his own dad promise to be a better man. "Tomorrow is a day of monumental change," he would announce at dinner. "A new me from now to goddamn eternity. I'm turning over a new leaf. Just watch me shine."

But to Ferrell, his father only got worse with each passing day. His old man nourished his aloneness like it was the key to salvation, his mood storms coming with greater frequency and duration. When his father finally left, Ferrell and his mother kept their relief unspoken. Ferrell was fourteen at the time, on the border himself of wild mystery and change. On the bus to school he could feel his father's curse harbored in his blood, encrypted in the very circuitry of his cells: those inexplicable angers and festering grievances, against loved and unloved alike, that distinct lack of passion and joy. He'd watch the fields slide past, the corn as tall as the grown man he was becoming, and wonder if willpower and sacrifice alone could thwart the dictator seeking to rule his heart.

*

Late afternoon Rilla rides through the gate, dust-covered and sweaty, an English princess abandoned on the American frontier. In her eyes is that look she gets when she rides long and hard—as if she's had a few words with God and has some inside news.

"That was almost worth it," she says.

"How far did you go?" Ferrell says, surprised she has spoken. If he can keep the conversation in gear, they'll be headed to another temporary reconciliation.

"Far enough."

"Did you see any coyotes?"

"No."

"Mustangs?"

Rilla gives him the evil eye. "I'm an ex-counselor, remember? I know prompting when it comes my way."

"We can change, Rilla. Do better."

Ferrell toes the powdery dust with his boot. He hadn't planned on blurting things out, especially tired lines from daytime soaps, but the words had leapt before his lips could block the way.

Rilla stops in the drive, legs braced. She looks truly surprised at his invitation to enter the fray.

"Oh, hell, Ferrell, it's been hit or miss for years. You want to be alone more than you want someone around. You want the nasty when the urge strikes—and god bless you for that—but beyond sweaty sheets you don't need or want much else."

"At least we're not co-dependent."

"If I wanted absolute freedom, I'd have stayed in Ohio. Alone, I wouldn't have to put up with your foul temper and moody disposition. I'd have all the perks of going solo, and none of this extra work."

"But you like it here."

"Ferrell, it's like living on the goddamn face of the moon. For awhile you're Neil Armstrong, getting inspired over all the distance and space, that view of your planet so far away. But then, in short order, you miss your home."

Rilla touches him lightly on the sleeve. "I miss seeing things grow," she says. "I miss the smell of rain."

"What about your riding, all those acres of desert to roam?"

"Riding the open range has been seriously overvalued. Anymore, I get out there and feel all shrunk down, like the planet's too big or I'm just too small. Maybe both."

"When are you leaving?"

"Dammit," Rilla says, stepping close. "Don't always accept me leaving like that. Beg me to stay this time, or beg to come with me. For Christ sakes, beg for something, anything."

"Okay, stay."

Rilla takes his face in her warm hands. In her eyes he sees neither anger nor pain, just something he can only describe as an exhausted calm. "Let's get the hell out of Dodge," she says. "Move back home with me."

"I'll think about it."

"You and your damn head, Ferrell. I wish you'd just run on pure want for once."

"I can try."

"You don't fucking try to want something, Ferrell." Rilla starts toward the cabin, then turns to face him. "We weren't raised here, you know. These stark rhythms aren't in our blood. Our brain isn't used to just dust and wind."

*

Friday noon, the caravan returns. Ferrell steps onto the porch as the unloading begins—an invasion, he can't help but feel, of his secret desert fortress. As before, Javad approaches Ferrell alone, dressed in his perpetual white. On their first visit, as Javad drew the knife across, one of his sons had lost grip on the forelegs, the head and chest of the lamb heaving from the ground, splattering the man in his pristine clothes. A few red drops arced gracefully onto Ferrell's boots—blood not at all his own. He had gone inside to wipe them clean.

"Mr. Swan," Javad says. "Today is my daughter's date of birth. We will need your best ram for this, and two others, if possible."

"You know what I have," Ferrell says.

Javad signals to another of his sons, a tall skinny boy just out of his teens. The whole mob turns as one and moves toward the barn. Javad steps forward and climbs the porch steps, a place he's not yet been. He takes out a small leather purse and counts the money into Ferrell's palm.

"How many children do you have?" Ferrell says.

"Ten in all, from the ages of eight to twenty-one."

"That's a lot of mouths to feed."

"As well as many strong hands."

"My stepson wouldn't lift a finger when he was home. He ran off at seventeen. We hardly see him now, mostly just to handle the trouble he finds."

"I had such a son. My Sali would not expend himself for anyone. He also refused to share our roof, once he came of age."

"Where is he now?"

"We buried him before we left Sarajevo. He did not last on his own two years with all his reckless ways." The man gives Ferrell a long look, seeming to Ferrell to regard him as a mythic fellow traveler, not a man selling sheep. They have moved from a transaction older than Moses, from something other than just the exchange of Roman coins.

"I'm sorry," Ferrell says.

"When it came to Sali, everyone was sorry. Even the police who shot my son were very much sorry. They knew him well and do not want to pull their triggers." Javad looks toward where his extended family has disappeared around the barn. "We all still wake expecting Sali to come home. We open our eyes and think we hear him shouting and stumbling about."

"Our Levon always seems confined in his own skin."

"Confined?"

"Held captive, like a prisoner."

"Ah," Javad says. "Yes, a prisoner. I, too, feel like a prisoner without having a proper place to rest my head."

"But you're in a new country," Ferrell says. "A new home."

"New country, yes, not home." Javad motions to the distant

mountains before them. "This is where we live, but Bosnia is home."

"Will you go back?" Ferrell says, not sure why he wants to know, only that he does.

"God has not told me, but I hope he allows my bones to sleep beside those of my son." As if about to fall, Javad reaches for the porch rail in front of him. He holds on tight with both hands, his eyes raised to the sky. Ferrell feels he's witnessing yet another siege in a prolonged war with anguish and despair. With all we endure, Ferrell thinks, it's a wonder we ever get out of bed.

Someone shouts for Javad, and he nods once to Ferrell—all the communication, it seems, he can offer for now. He starts down the steps, raising his hand over his shoulder in silent farewell. Ferrell watches him go, the man's shoulders slumped in the attitude of defeat, feeling he is somehow watching himself.

*

In the days that follow, Rilla calls the airlines, digs out her battered suitcases from the chaos of her closet. Despite his feeble attempts at love and affection, Ferrell fails to win her back, believes she's already left in her heart, the most absolute separation he knows. He has long understood he needs to respond to the call before she loses faith in him, not in the smoking ruins after.

At high noon on Sunday, the Bosnians come for the last of the flock. Rilla keeps to the house, refuses, actually, to even leave the bedroom. Ferrell himself keeps a low profile as the Bosnians go about their tasks. After Javad pays him in straight twenties, Ferrell sits on the porch with his evening whiskey, despite the high altitude of the sun. He's had his fill of sheep death to be sure, wants no more of the flowery scent of their blood, of those smooth shiny organs revealed to the air. He keeps the amber bottle on the porch boards beside the rocker, the scotch whiskey incandescent, as if lit from within. He holds the whiskey on his tongue before sending it down, waits for that good low burn, that lovely fusion of bitterness and sweet. Rilla once told him it was like drinking smoke, but he knows she didn't give single malts a chance, didn't come close to understanding the miracle of Lagavulin. He tried to explain the way his taste buds leap and frolic as the whiskey hits home, but she didn't want to hear it.

Javad climbs the steps when all is done. "If you have more lambs, please use the telephone."

"No more sheep," Ferrell says, shaking his head. "Just that horse there is all I'll be caring for."

"And your wife."

"She hasn't been my wife for years."

"And still she stays."

"Comes and goes, more like."

"Your ways are different from ours."

"Same problems, though," Ferrell says, letting the whiskey decide which words he'll use.

"Your way offers no solution to your troubles."

"Are you some kind of priest?"

"In my country, I was the operator of a truck. What is your occupation?"

"I was a teacher," Ferrell says. "History."

"You are very special, then," Javad says, reaching out to shake his hand. "You understand all that has come before. You know more than the common man."

"Not even close," Ferrell says.

As the Bosnians drive off for the final time, Ferrell raises his glass to their dust trails in the air. The screen door slaps and Rilla stands at the porch rail, her back to him.

"It's done?" she says.

Ferrell's not sure if she means the sheep or them. "There's no one here, but us."

"That's never been enough, has it?"

"Sometimes it has." Ferrell can feel the bravery of the whiskey in his blood. True courage or not, he'll take what he can get. "You must have nothing but regret, Rilla. I mean all this time spent on a man who always lets you down?"

"We're too old for self-pity." Rilla reaches down for the bottle, refills his glass. She takes the glass from his hand like an offering. "This stuff any better than it used to be?"

"Besides you, it's the one thing that gets better with age."

Rilla ignores his lame remark, sips whiskey instead. "Jesus Henry Christ," she says, wiping her eyes on her sleeve. She gives him the gunfighter staredown, a long look of cool intensity he'd like to escape.

"What gets better, Ferrell Swan, is our ability to spend time apart."

"That's better than nothing, I suppose."

Over the distant Owyhees the sun hovers low and smoldering. Rilla hands him the glass, and he drinks his share of the communion they've begun. "We'll make love when it gets dark," she says. "Right here, on the porch."

"I thought we didn't plan?"

Rilla takes the glass again, drinks and doesn't sputter. She delivers it back to his hand. "We'll do things in your honor tonight. Drinking and fucking."

Ferrell doesn't speak, just looks at his ice cube islands in their sea of gold. He can't even rally enough enthusiasm to protest her hurtful remark.

"Okay," she says, "that was low and mean. Undignified, too."

"Probably true, though."

"Oh hell, most things are true about most of us most of the time."

"Where's that from?"

"I just made it up." Rilla takes her turn at the glass, eyes shut. "I'll leave the horse, decide what to do with her later."

"She'll be here when you come back."

"I'm not sure I'll be for a while."

"Then I'll drive her back to Ohio on the Swan express."

A long spell of quiet falls over them, and Ferrell knows they've reached rock bottom in their pitiful stockpile of words. He watches a lone red tail turn on the late afternoon thermals, circling high above the sageland, wing feathers fanned as if caressing the air. As the hawk passes directly over the cabin, Ferrell studies the undersides of those tremendous wings, the intricate design fired in the last of the sun.

"I'm looking forward to missing you," Rilla says after even more time has passed. "To feeling those good feelings once again. Isn't that something–to look forward to missing someone?"

"I guess I look better from a distance."

Rilla drinks yet again, as if taking the bitterest of medicine. "We're stuck, aren't we, Ferrell? I mean, so many of our friends and family dead and gone. It's like we are the last people on the planet sometimes."

"Or the first."

"No, it's more apocalyptic. Much more end of the world than its beginning." Rilla sets the glass on the porch boards. To the west the sun is down, leaving behind a blazing sky of neon red. "No more talk," she says, rising from her chair. She settles into his lap, runs a hand over the smooth dome of his head. She takes his face in her gentle palms, brings her lips to his own in a long kiss of goodbye.

"I'm dying, Ferrell," she says when the kiss is done.

"What?"

"You are, too."

"You mean bit by bit?"

"I mean no matter how you cut it, we are running on fumes. The clock's running, our time's expired, the ride's about over. Lord, I can feel the cold breath of mortality breathing down my neck as we speak."

"Then don't speak."

They drive out at midnight beneath those billion stars, the domed sky blazing white, the pale mist of the Milky Way arcing up and over. As they drive, dying stars let loose in fiery streaks, blaze imprints upon Ferrell's eyes. Rilla stays turned from him, staring at the black desert miles as if she expects some savior to appear. Near two, Ferrell crosses the Snake and stops for gas just past the bridge. The station sits high above the river, and as Ferrell pumps the gasoline he searches for the water slithering off into the distance. Rilla comes back from the restroom and climbs into the cab, a stranger he is taking to the airport in Boise, some hitchhiker picked up along the deserted highway. Ferrell marvels how slow their progress has always been toward peaceful coexistence, yet how fast they can reverse direction—become separate at warp speed, unknown to each other and themselves.

Ferrell pulls back onto his dusty lane around mid-morning. He parks in the drive and shuts the motor down, staring out the bug-splattered windshield at his barn of faded red, at the side pastures now empty. From the corral, Rilla's horse watches him intently. Chroma knows Ferrell's the new keeper of the hay, wants him to get the message loud and clear.

As expected the house isn't the same inside, just walls and a ceiling, a few mute rooms. He feels his tiredness like a drug, as if his bones have gone hollow, his head full of nothing but air. Without Rilla his hours ahead loom uncharted and full of rocky shoals. He feels inclined to take to bed and skip the daylight altogether. Outside again, Ferrell stands at the fence, his arms folded on the top rail. He stares at the mountains heaved straight up from the desert floor. He notices the air is absolutely calm, so tender and delicate, the still leaves as if painted on the trees. By the early heat, he guesses it will be hot, an honest summer day at last. He wonders why it's always this way: too little, too late, the day perfect and Rilla half a continent gone. With this hallowed day unfolding, Ferrell does the only thing he can. He gets the scotch whiskey from the kitchen, clinks two ice cubes into a glass, and takes to the porch for the slow desperate fall of the sun.

He's into the smooth second third of the bottle when he sees the dust–a car on his long washboard lane, Rilla somehow returned. But he knows it can't be Rilla, not with her airborne so many hours at six hundred miles per. The car parks beside his pick-up and sits idling, its dark tinted windows nothing but threat and menace. Has violence found him at last, he wonders, sought him out across the wide expanse? When the door opens, the old Bosnian steps out like a messenger from afar. He's dressed in white, as always, yet no entourage follows him from the other doors, just Javad strolling alone to the steps of the porch.

"I come for lambs," he says in some weird desert *deja vu.*

"You bought them all," Ferrell says. "Their mamas too. I told you there'd be no more."

"People change ideas. You may have birthed more lambs."

"Without any ewes?

"One can hope for anything."

"One can hope too much."

Ferrell hears the scotch call his name, but he doesn't want to drink under the scrutiny of another man. Javad glances at the empty glass in Ferrell's hand, then at Ferrell's feet, where the bottle sits waiting, a faithful companion.

"You are celebrating?"

"Opposite, more like."

The Bosnian stands patiently in the sun, and now Ferrell can't help but see a holy pilgrim come a long way for truth.

"Oh, hell," he says. "My ex went home again." He reaches for the scotch and pours himself three fingers, plus a few extra for good measure. "Can't live with 'em. . . ."

"With whom?"

"Wives," he says and raises his glass in a toast. "I've had three myself. Lord bless them, everyone."

Javad folds his arms across his chest, but looks less perplexed than intrigued. "You have two glasses?" he says.

"What?"

"A second glass?"

"You are a fan of the demon rum?"

"Is that not Lagavulin whiskey?"

"Oh, Lordy," Ferrell says and gives the man his best grin, very much deserved.

*

By dusk Ferrell has a new best friend, the two men bonding, he knows, in ways only two bottles of the finest scotch can ever achieve. Beside him Javad rocks in Rilla's rocker, sipping from a shot glass her son Levon stole in Vegas. From their porch, the scrubland extends without end and Ferrell has the distinct impression they sit before a vast empty stage. He believes them waiting for the start of the world's greatest show, though what that show will be he won't guess.

Sunlight fans into long sweeping columns, spotlighting the barn and corral fences, the horse prancing for her evening hay. Ferrell spies the low level of Javad's glass and pours scotch to the brim. In the past several hours they've discussed sheep raising, their boyhoods, and the weather in Sarajevo. They're men speaking with a lot of time between their sentences, men doing more thinking and drinking than anything else. To Ferrell's dismay he notes the sun will indeed set, and darkness will flood off the land as if to wash the cabin from its foundation.

"Won't your wife be worried?" he says. "Sun's going down."

"Worried, yes. Angry too."

"Will you be in trouble?"

"Oh, very much trouble." Javad holds his glass up, then drains it like a gunslinger. "Sari will yell and break some things, perhaps slap my cheeks. She is a very vibrant woman."

"Then what?"

"Some things are private, even between men."

Ferrell lets loose a good full laugh. He reaches out and pats Javad on the back, thinking life will never, not ever, make a lick of sense. "So how long under the yolk?"

"If you mean wedded bliss, thirty years and still not parted." Javad winks with elegant flair. "You think I should have instruction for you? Wisdom of pearls?"

"Well?"

"Sari and I have no more harmony than the governments of foreign nations."

"You must get along?"

"In God's name, no. Fights, grievances, indiscretions never forgotten or forgiven. Sari harbors angers at words I spoke when we were young and without common sense. Yet we stay. We battle, we rest ourselves. We threaten and shout loudly, we love-make with great vigor. Always we wake with our wedding bands still on our fingers."

"Hallelujah," Ferrell says, hands raised to the gospel according to Javad.

"All big joke, men and women seeing eye to eye. My idea is God is more mischievous. He makes women so nobody gets bored. God has much humor in his heart. He has laugh lines around his eyes."

Ferrell feels his own heart go expansive toward all creatures, great and small. He welcomes sudden benevolent love for the stranger at his side. "Amen."

"Do you know how to ride that horse?" Javad says.

"Never been on her."

"When I was a boy, I was often on a horse's back. My father had much land, and many horses. Now I don't own even the small space beneath my family's feet, nor the roof over their heads."

Ferrell stands to lean against the porch rail. He surveys the darkening horizon, the earth curving down and around to come back behind them. He understands at once what they are destined to do.

"Follow me," he says.

In the corral, Javad slips on the bridle and saddle with ease. An evening wind picks up, blowing the daily dust and grit. The coolness jolts the horse like a shock, her head swinging up and down, her feet sidestepping as if she cannot contain her elation. Javad puts his foot in the stirrup and swings gracefully onto the saddle. He reaches down an open hand.

"Grab," he says. "We'll ride."

Ferrell extends his arm and is pulled right up. He scrambles to sit behind the cantle, his arms encircling Javad's hearty middle, then the horse's complex musculature goes alive beneath him, a tremendous flex and release that Ferrell feels through his jeans, the intricate muscle groupings like wave swells from his thighs to his bony butt. When all is said and done, the acute physicality of the movement, its intense intimacy, sends his heart to racing. The horse clops across the corral and Ferrell goes all giddy inside. In some dreamy physical memory, he is on a merry-go-round at the fair, laughing with pure kid glee at the lift and drop of the brightly painted pony, the wind against his face, his doomed father blurred with rushing movement.

Javad heads for the big double gates, each step of the horse signaled back to Ferrell in that fantastic play of bone and muscle. He looks over Javad's shoulder to watch the horse head guiding them through the world, those ears like radar searching. Before them is a Wild West landscape of distance and sage, of mountains shadowed in the failing light. He is for once and all time a cowboy of the open range, a rider of the goddamn purple sage, John Wayne in the flesh, off to save the world. He wishes old Rilla could see him now.

At the gate, Javad unlatches the hook still mounted on Chroma's back. The horse is beside herself with the call of the desert dusk, and Javad can barely hold her from breaking into a canter. When they reach the place where the BLM runs far and deep, Javad reins up short, the two men studying those ten thousand acres as if they've never been crossed.

And then they are free, with nothing but the ground beneath them and the first bright stars above. In this open territory, Javad lets the horse have her will, and she trots then canters then gallops flat out, leaving Ferrell hanging on, wild with delight. He clings tight as Javad steers toward the sunset flaring in all its glory, toward the Owyhees looming black against the molten sky. Chroma runs like no sun will ever rise again, her legs driving for all the speed she can summon.

Ferrell leans close as gravity pulls. He hears Javad's breath blowing from his lungs, feels the man's clanging heart beneath his hands. He thinks, against his will, of his lonely father, so long in the terrible ground, feels that black curse still alive in his veins. He pictures Rilla in their quaint hometown, unlocking the door to an empty home. Levon out in LA or Vegas, Jackpot perhaps, hunting trouble down. Javad's own son, finding too much as the bullets fly. Ferrell's no sheriff in pursuit, he understands, but the one pursued, a damn misfit like the scores that have come before, hiding out in the badlands because there's nowhere left to be. He sits up tall, an outlaw of his own design. He imagines he and Javad as desperadoes without hearth or kin. Butch and Sundance, on the run. His heart rides high, and he yells because he must, yells into a world both damned and saved.

Good Hands

Robert Dawson

When I was ten, my grandmama took me to be baptized in the Ouachita River. Ten was too young for us Free Will Baptists, but Grandmama was sure I had a craving for Jesus, so she took me to the revivalists and fibbed about my age. Daddy would have been mad as hell, but he was in Korea. My mama was working in Chicago, which nobody considered a fit place for me to be brought up.

A few days later I came down with a delirium. Grandmama doused me with willow bark and castor oil and put me to bed. During the night, I woke up screaming how God was wanting to kill me. Grandmama wrapped me in quilts to break the fever. She blamed herself for her spiritual presumption. In the morning I couldn't move my legs.

The doctor said I was a rare one. Polio was a white youngster's sickness, and he'd never seen a colored child stricken and couldn't be much help. The only hope, he said, was to convince a white doctor to treat me. Grandmama held a lot of hard feelings toward white folk, and anyway we were poor as weevils, so I lay with my body in a coma for three days until Mama swept home and carried me to the army clinic in Pine Bluff. Mama always said the military doctors there paid me no more heed than a possum on the roadside. They let a colored nurse come feed and wash me, and puzzled why my lungs kept pumping while my limbs were paralyzed. It wasn't until I started to recover spontaneously that they took notice of me.

Grandmama and Mama took shifts sitting by me and rubbing my legs and arms, hour after hour. That was Mama's idea. Otherwise she figured the blood would go stagnant, and I guess she was right because after three weeks I could move my shoulders a little. I remember thinking, "Shoulders, move!" and a few seconds later they would twitch like I'd sent them a postcard from afar. After that, the doctors started wheeling me to physical therapy every day. A white woman would jostle my limbs back and forth until she felt my muscles tense against her. As soon as I could wiggle my toes at will, they plunked me in a pool of warm water—the same pool as white patients used—and walked me to and fro. Meanwhile the war in Korea ended, and Daddy came home. When I could stand by myself, Mama took me to Pittsburg, California, near Camp Pendleton where Daddy was stationed. Grandmama stayed in Arkansas. I never saw her alive again, which goes to show how often we traveled home. Daddy thought Pittsburg was Heaven, and I reckon it was, after Korea. He said he'd live there till he died, and he did. With any luck, I will too.

Eventually I recovered full use of my limbs. I suppose it took ten months or more, since I remember stumbling around like a fool my first year of school in Pittsburg. Being laughed at made me work hard at rebuilding my body. Daddy had climbed the ranks to sergeant. He took me to where new recruits got basic training and hollered me through the drills like a half-size soldier. He didn't have a word for weakness, my daddy. When I could do five chin-ups, he clamped his hands over mine on the bar and ordered me to do ten.

By high school, I was a stack of muscle. I played offensive tackle on the Pittsburg team that whipped Oakland 42 to 6. Would it be bragging to mention that I also made the honor roll, the only Negro out of a forty percent "colored" high school? My daddy used to say that a white man was just a black man with less to prove. He also said you were only as black as you let people paint you. Well, let it be. Football and good grades sent me to USC instead of Vietnam.

But old Mr. Polio didn't let me off scot-free. For one thing, I was never much of a sprinter. I didn't have that explosive quickness coaches expected from a black athlete. White boys with half my musculature could pitch 20 mph faster or throw a football twenty yards farther. My fingers were slow, too. For a while, in high school, I wanted more than heaven on earth to play the saxophone like Dexter Gordon, but I couldn't get past the eighth notes. I had the worst penmanship and the best spelling in every grade, and I never mastered touch-typing. Teachers told me my hands were muscle-bound, but I knew it was the virus lingering.

My son had the hands I should have had. I could tell when he was just thigh high. I could toss a tennis ball at his face from any distance and he'd catch it. Pretty soon he started flicking the ball back right through my guard, at my nose, and we had to find another game. By the time he was ten, he could catch a football over either shoulder or throw a pass into a bushel from thirty yards. You can bet I didn't take him to be baptized. He had a future in my mind that didn't depend on the Hereafter.

*

Dad scared hell out of me, calling from the hospital. He caught me on my cell phone just before I crossed airport security. They were keeping him for observation, he said. His right leg was acting funny and the doc in emergency was worried he might have had a stroke. How do you mean, funny, I asked him. Stroke was the scariest word he could have spoken, since my granddad died of one at age forty-nine. Well, it just won't move quite when I tell it to, he answered.

I phoned the Contra Costa Regional Medical Center from O'Hare while the ground crew scuttled around beneath my wings. A Dr. John Lee informed me that the CAT scan had ruled out cerebral hemorrhage, that there was no indication of cardiac irregularity, but my father was experiencing some neurological distress and would need further testing. Naïvely, I assumed those tests would be completed by the time I downed my bird at San Francisco Airport and drove to the hospital in Martinez. In fact, he had just been gurneyed from emergency to the ICU. Already his right leg was too weak to stand on, and his reflexes were compromised on both sides.

Dr. Lee had a lot of questions for me about my father's medical history, but I had almost nothing to tell. My dad, who hadn't missed a practice or a game in twenty-three years, was an iron man, the head football coach at McClymonds High, the roughest school in Oakland. He didn't smoke. A fifth of Southern Comfort lasted him a year. What do you know about his polio, the doctor asked. What polio, I asked back blankly. He'd never mentioned being sick as a child.

Dad's skin is lustrous bittersweet. Mine is milk, Hershey. When I fly into Lagos or Dakar, I feel transmigrated into a kind of wer-white, but he could pass for Nuba. Against the hospital pillow, however, his face looked like cold toast. Why'd you never talk about having polio, I frowned.

Oh, he slurred, I don't hardly think back on it.

You weren't paralyzed, were you, I asked.

I wasn't in the iron lung, if that's what you mean.

But the doctors said you had polio.

They never were too clear as I recall. I might've just had a lasting fever from swimming in the Ouachita.

I told him I could take family-emergency leave, but he commanded me not to. I'm in good hands, he said.

Driving home, I called Arkansas. My Grandma, his mama, had never liked California, so when Granddad died she took the excuse of caring for her ailing sister to rush back to Calion, where all our folk were born before me. Your daddy caught a dreadful fever, she told me on the phone, and lay delirious over a week. The army doctors said he had all the symptoms of polio plus a few, but he got well almost as sudden as he fell sick. Took him most of a year to get his strength back, though.

The doctor here wants to know if he was vaccinated with the Salk vaccine.

Gracious, young man, that was forty-some years ago! But I believe they said at school not to risk it since he'd been exposed already.

Grandma wanted badly to hasten to her oldest son's bedside, where she could massage his strength back, but she was burdened with two of my cousin LaTroya's babies while LaTroya was dealing with substance abuse. I was logged for Frankfurt the next day, but I spent the early morning in the hospital. Dad was worse. His speech was slurpier, both legs were immobile, and he said his hands were starting to tingle. The nurses had him prepped for something called a nerve-conduction test. Dr. Lee seemed puzzled by what I told him of my Grandma's recollections. There were lots of misdiagnoses back then, he said, but everything seems consistent with what we call abortive poliomyelitis. Unfortunately, there've been reports lately of recurrences in adults who had polio fifty years ago.

Thirty-two thousand feet above Manitoba, my copilot Chet offered another diagnosis. Chet is a piece of aviation history, a relic of the Right Stuff, complete with Chuck Yaeger drawl. Your pa get the flu vaccine this year? he asked.

How should I know, I replied. He keeps his own council.

You oughtta find out, he said. There's been all kinds of side-effects, includin' several cases of Guillain-Barrè syndrome which the medical establishment don't want to acknowledge.

Chet rambled on about arsenic in the food chain and the role of Jewish dentists in the fluoride conspiracy all the way over Greenland and the North Atlantic. Something stuck in my mind, an article in *Newsweek* or some other lounge magazine about FDR being rediagnosed as not having had polio after all. Hi-tech Chet gave me a Web site to search—*hothealthnews.com*—and the name of his chiropractor in Livermore. He fixed my wife's PMS, Chet volunteered, when all the medicos could do was feed her Paxil.

The cockpit lounge at *der Frankfurter Flughafen* has internet hook-ups with Qwerty keyboards. I tapped out a Google search for Guillen Barrè and sure enough, up popped thirty-some sites. One was Chet's *hothealthnews* and another was the Homeopathy Help List at *lyfeforce.com*. I surfed the whole batch, hopping over the flakiest. Several links took me to the same page, a subscription newsletter edited by a foxy lady chiropractor with big hair. The best of the bunch was a sports medicine site called

4thegame.com, which at least offered some case histories with an eerie similarity to my dad's. Frankfurt, by the way, is the dullest town in Deutschland. The big sport is growing cucumbers, if you're lucky enough to have a garden patch.

What puzzled me on Google was the absence of any academic or NIH pages. Everything from autism to asthma—crossing the Barrs Epstein and Guillen—was being blamed on inoculations, yet so-called "western medicine" offered no defense. I phoned Martinez as soon as the time zones meshed, and, surprisingly, I got past the advice nurse to Dr. Lee. GBS is a distinct possibility, he said, though it's vanishingly rare. It usually follows a viral infection with high fever, which I suppose might be consistent with your father's childhood episode. I'll go ahead and order a spinal fluid tap to get a secure diagnosis.

I told him what I'd found and hadn't found on the Web. That's odd, he answered. Why don't you try again under 'acute ascending polyneuritis,' which is a stuffy medical name for the same thing? Or I can have our librarian run a search and zap the results to you.

Whatever you've heard about hospital run-arounds and faceless physicians, I have to give Dr. Lee credit: he wasted no time. Eight hours later, after my regulation Frankfurter nap, my e-mail included a four-page download from *mdconsult.com* titled "All about Guillain-Barré syndrome." I shot back a reply immediately, noting the spelling variation which had one crowd of bloggers and spammers fulminating against the other crowd of public health pundits, without any cross-indexing. My dad would love it, as soon as he felt tough enough for irony again. He always said that if I could spell the white man's language better than the man himself, I could knead the system in my hands like clay. He taught American literature at McClymonds, by the way, as well as football.

*

The future I had in mind for my son wasn't what he turned out wanting, and I'm still ashamed of myself for being disappointed. My heart was set on him becoming the first black quarterback in the NFL. He had the tools. I coached him myself through three undefeated state varsity championships. Then he chose the Air Force over USC, where I played, or UCLA. Hell, he could have gone to Stanford. Their recruiter damn near begged him to apply. But he wanted to be a pilot from the first time we flew to Little Rock for my grandmama's funeral. Otherwise, no man ever had a better son. Lucky for me, since it came out he was my only child.

His mother was a light-skinned woman. A light-hearted woman, too. She left us when he was twelve and didn't bother to keep in touch with him. I tell him he was lucky to get her looks and my brains, instead of the other way around. This weakness here has set me doubting if I shouldn't have married again. If I die, he won't have a soul closer than his welfare-sotted cousins back in Arkansas. I reckon he's got lady friends inside ten miles of every airport on the map, but he won't ever forgive his mama enough to love one of them. A man never loves a woman anyway, like his own blood. He just craves her, and after the craving fades the only feeling left is how a bird feels when another bird sits too close on the wire.

*

Guillain-Barrè is good news, since eighty-five percent of patients achieve nearly perfect recovery, says Dr. Lee. Polio seldom fails to destroy when it has a second chance. It's not a virus, he assures me. It's an auto-immune mix-up where the body's own defenses attack the insulation of the nerve cells.

What becomes of the other fifteen percent, I ask.

He flinches. Understand, these numbers are based on relatively small samples, he says. Perhaps ten to twenty percent suffer chronic fatigue, abnormal tingling or twitching sensations, loss of taste, constipation, muscle aches, reduced coordination. Less than twenty-five percent ever need to be put on a respirator.

His percentages add up to more than a hundred, but I trust Dr. Lee and don't need to challenge him. Dad is uncomfortable. He says the bed sheets burn his feet, yet when he bangs his elbow on the bed frame, he shows no sign of feeling it. The heart monitor constrains his movements, he complains, and his voice has slunk down to his thorax like the scat bass in a gospel quartet. He's been in the ICU six days now, while I've logged Frankfurt and back twice.

You still enjoy your flying? he rumbles, as if he heard my thought.

Yes, sir, I answer dutifully. All but the ground time.

That's something to be thankful for, he intones, when a man respects his own work.

I know he wishes I'd followed his footsteps and become a football coach. Sometimes I wish so, too. Flying has become as routine as delivering mail, though I still draw anxious gasps from passengers who've never seen a black pilot. The whole truth is, I only ever loved the cruising at high altitude, when most pilots doze. The higher I get, the higher I get. Elijah in his chariot. I felt it the first time in the plane that carried me to my grandmama's funeral, when I was a motherless child. So high, I won't ever have to die.

Dr. John Lee looks like a man who couldn't help tapping his foot in church. He has the Virginia slouch and freckles of someone whose ancestors owned slaves, but I get no racial vibes from him, not like some of my cockpit cohorts who see only blackness when they look at me. Your dad is still in the progressive stage of GBS, he tells me in the hallway, but we've started IVIg, which should speed up his turnaround.

I know what IVIg is from the printouts: *intravenous immunoglobin*. I've read about the Dutch study: daily doses of 0.4 g/kg resulted in strength improvement in fifty-three percent of patients versus thirty-four percent on the placebo, and earlier recovery, twenty-seven days average versus forty-one. Twenty-seven days! Thirteen flights to Frankfurt and back!

How about *plasmapheresis*, I question Dr. Lee.

We could start with that, he nods collegially, although the studies don't support any significant advantage from combining therapies.

Plasmapheresis is the extraction and separation of red and white blood cells, with the red returned to the patient. I read all about it on *uptodate.com*. But the real question is, what the hell business do I have jabbering with the good doctor as if I understood such things?

*

My own daddy was discharged from the army at forty-six. He had all his teeth and hair, and he thought he and I could retrieve our boyhoods together by going fishing. He never much cared for football or baseball. I can't recall when we ever played catch. I was in my first years of coaching JV at McClymonds. He came to every game, but scarcely knew when to cheer. I wasn't much better at casting a plug or feeling a bite on a slack line. Then one Sunday—he was waxing his car—a blood clot lodged in his neck and he hit the ground dead.

It's a sore disadvantage, not being a praying man, when you're laid out stiff in a hospital bed with tubes in your veins and a seismograph taped to your breast. Guess I'll leave all my prayers in my son's hands. He's got a thirty thousand foot start toward heaven on me.

This foot massaging business must be doctor's orders. We've never been much for touching each other in our family, but each time he visits, my son peels back the sheets and rubs my sorry old soles. He says it's for the circulation, same as my mama said when I was stricken in Arkansas, but I know it's the L-word. Who am I, to be twice blessed with such knowledge?

I used to thank my daddy for dying without warning—without muss nor fuss, without the pain of apologizing to either side. Now I'm not so sure. I'd give a lot to go back and rub his feet.

*

Thirty-two days after checking himself in, my father is discharged from the Contra Costa Regional Medical Center with only a slight gimpiness—what the therapists call "foot-drop"—in his right leg. He's eager to walk, but insurance regulations pin him to his wheelchair till we exit the building. Dr. Lee escorts us out of the ward. Make sure he comes to rehab, he admonishes and shakes my hand. I have a surprise for Dad, which I deliver as he stands up from the wheelchair outside the hospital: two tickets to Miami to see the Eagles battle the Ravens in the Super Bowl. The flight is gratis, but the game is costing me four trips to Frankfurt. Still, it's worth the price to watch Donovan McNabb, the quarterback that lard-ass Limbaugh said was only playing because he's black. The dude my dad wanted me to be.

Chuck the Terrible, Chuck of the Deep

Oliver Broudy

Privacy was nonexistent on a 33-foot boat. A mere curtain separated the V-bunk from the main cabin, and the thin door of the head didn't lock. Chuck tried regardless, a couple times, while they were underway, but there were the waves to reckon with, the boat busy with its own paroxysms, and there was always the possibility that his father might ring the tack bell, meaning fifteen seconds to stow the lust in the sea locker, de-mast the hard-on and hustle topside to man the jib (his sister claimed to be too weak to crank the winch).

There was no escaping his parents. They loomed, overfriendly, insipid, like the billboards at the entrance to Yellowstone Park—last year's vacation, before Dad's computer job. This year it was two weeks sailing in the Virgin Islands. And Chuck was beginning to think he wasn't going to survive. As long as his parents were around, distracting him with their parental vibes, he could never achieve the mathematician's concentration that was necessary to pursue what, at age twelve, was pretty much his sole interest.

How are you feeling today, Chuck?

How's your sunburn, Chuck?

What would you like for breakfast, Chuck?

Are you okay in there, Chuck?

They were provoking him, hoping he'd snap and say something awful. It was all part of a demonic plot to shatter his mind.

In such a small space, everyone necessarily hovered. His parents especially, as they were predisposed to hover. Hovering became the primary mode of being. It replaced all others. Sitting, standing, lying down—all became forms of hovering. They became expert at it. His mother, for instance, could hover at a distance. She could be at one end of the boat and Chuck could be at the other and her hovering would not be in the least bit impaired. Compared to her, Chuck's dad was a novice. But he was learning quick. And he was taller, which meant he might eventually be able to use his hovering skills to more devastating effect.

Chuck furiously immersed himself in the single piece of reading material he had brought, a tattered Daredevil comic. But sometimes even Daredevil couldn't deliver him. He'd find himself fixating uneasily on the wet hair plastered against his father's calves. With a shudder he'd shift his gaze, only to encounter, voila, his mother's bunion. Another twitch and he'd be caught in the valley of her breasts. Each of these visual misfires visited instant chaos upon that fairytale realm of honey-legged gals and golden-armed honeys that Chuck, a fledgling lecher, had only recently begun to devise for himself. He parried as best he could. And then a hard-on would arrive, knocking like a salesman. Chuck declined, declined again, expressionless, grim. The smell of coconut suntan oil was everywhere, lubriciously suggestive.

Then there was Kay, Chuck's sister. Early on in the trip she had taken a crap in the head, and it must have been a huge crap, because it clogged the flush tube as she tried to pump it out. Dad switched the valve and pumped the rest into the holding tank. Since then they had been reduced to schlepping their offal around in a big yellow bucket, crapping right there on the cabin floor, since there was no room to squat in the head. For Chuck, it was a terrible indignity. The last circle of privacy had been destroyed. Worse, however, was the sudden and unwelcome awareness of familial excrement, released from the ritual confines of the head now, and impossible to ignore. Despite his love of scatological humor, or perhaps by way of explaining it, Chuck had always been painfully squeamish about certain bodily functions.

At unexpected moments, lying on deck, for instance, lost in bikini reveries, a horrifying image would flash across his mind: Dad, squatting hairy-assed, or Mom, emerging from the companionway, lugging the bucket. It was then that Chuck hated Kay the most. It was because of her that the momness of Mom became tainted with intimations of fecality. He didn't want to know what was in that bucket. He didn't want to think about it. But then Dad called out "Leeward, dear!" and he couldn't help listening as the contents hit the water.

Sleeping was difficult. It so happened that the holding tank was right beneath Chuck's bunk. Even with the hatch open and all the roof vents agape he could still smell it. And whenever the odor seemed to have disappeared, he was overtaken by a strange compulsion to find it again. Yup, still there, thick, tawny, blending with the woodwork, claiming all brown as its own. Lying in his bunk at night, staring coldly across at Kay (they slept in the main cabin, parents in the V-berth), Chuck failed to comprehend how she could still look haughty, even in sleep, staring down her nose at the moon. Especially since she should never have pumped the crap in the first place, as it was considered bad manners to flush into a harbor, even a simple anchorage such as this.

"Well what am I supposed to do?" Kay had said, voice pulpy and raw. "I have to go!"

At the time, Chuck had been jubilant. Kay generally carried on as though she didn't even have an asshole.

"So much for my night swim," he said, pushing his rare advantage.

The sunset that night was particularly glorious (for once Chuck agreed with his mother), the air pungent with spiced rum and decaying vegetation and sororital feces. The sun flattened cat-like against the horizon. Patches of pink—flowers and rooftops—spotted the densely green hills rising up on either side of the bay. The long-suffering donkeys stood on the shore and allowed themselves to be absorbed by the gloom. The anchor lights were motionless at the mast tops, decoys to bring stars. And for a moment Chuck was happy. He was sitting across from his mother in the cockpit, having invited her to join him for a round of rummy on the "poop deck." Dad had given up on the head for the moment, emerging from the cabin with bruised hands and an expressive sigh. Kay meanwhile remained pouting in the cabin below, reading a physics textbook, momentarily vanquished.

"The air's a little better up here, Kay," Chuck called down solicitously.

*

A weird kind of suspense had followed this win and lasted until they reached Lameshur. They stood on the bow as the Pearson glided into the bay. The sails were down, the jib rolled behind the forestay and the main lashed to the boom. The inboard clunked into reverse and they released the anchor, watching it sink through the deep, clear water, its twin blades coming to rest against the sand. Kay leaned over the pulpit rail to give the line a tug, and for perhaps the millionth time, Chuck resisted the impulse to shove her in. Of course he knew that she was doing it on purpose, flaunting her inviolability. In the event that he did shove her, she'd do the drowning shtick. She was an expert swimmer, of course, and it seemed impossible to drown in such clear water, but none of this mattered with such credulous parents.

There was no competing with Kay. Resistance was sporadic, hyperbolic, doomed. Scat jokes were an effective weapon, up to a point. Ever since Kay imploded the head, though, Chuck had felt strangely enervated, as though his boundless appetite for toilet humor had been definitively satisfied with that single, terrible flush. The problem was that Kay would always be a degree more cynical than Chuck. It was a few years ago that Chuck had first realized the extent of his parents' gullibility, their willingness to be fooled, and right then he had almost given up: on justice, on truth, on the explicable, on all the values for which Daredevil bravely fought. But honestly he couldn't have given up even if he had wanted to. He just wasn't programmed that way. This was his weakness, and Kay knew it.

Kay's weaknesses were never so grand or obvious. Sometimes, though, they were deliciously evident, like her eyelids. In preparation for the trip she had visited a tanning salon, lying between two banks of lights wearing only a bikini and a pair of opaque goggles. Beneath the goggles, her eyelids had remained white, and by the end of the first day under the Caribbean sun they had burnt sizzling red, so that she mewled with each blink. Chuck had taken care not to show any signs of exultation. He had learned: you can get away with almost anything, so long as you don't let on that you enjoyed it. There was an interesting corollary to this: you haven't necessarily lost, so long as you don't acknowledge that you've lost. In the world of Kay and

Chuck, the rigorous pursuit of these tenets would eventually lead to colossal displays of thespianism: one pretending to be innocent of enjoyment, and the other, with B-movie nonchalance, pretending not to be in pain, each upstaging the other until someone (Chuck) became disoriented and/or nauseous by the spiraling make-believe and had to gallop for the exit.

Banished to his room following some impulsive transgression (shaking pepper into her hair, launching a snot from his knuckle), Chuck would vainly endeavor to console himself. Poor Kay. She thinks she has won. And perhaps she has, in a way. But what's the point of winning if you can't spend what you've won? Kay spent nothing. She took after Dad, a born miser, a saver of ketchup packets. When milkshakes were at issue, Chuck would be noisily guiding his straw around the base of the cup (seconds away from a rebuke), while Kay still had half to go. "It's best to finish it before it melts," Chuck would declare, unconvincingly.

On the other hand, Kay had never known and probably never would know the thrill of kicking a hole through an enemy's bedroom door. The crunch of hollow wood splintering. The two-count of criminal seconds before the snowball hits. The secret knowledge of a rival's burning breakfast after having tweaked the toaster timer. The glory of revolt, of resistance, of revolution—all these things, she would never know.

What did she know? The drone of dominance, where win followed mindless win, without triumph, without joy.

The Danforth dug into the soft sand, the line tightened—a perfect hypotenuse rising from water—and Kay tied it off at the cleat. Slowly the boat began to swing around into the wind, still huffing softly from the southwest. The stern faced the shore, a few steep yards cobbled with smooth blue stones the size of babies' feet. Beyond that was green wreckage, a mass of hibiscus and oleander, gossiping leaves and the occasional bone-white tree trunk, salted by the sea, devoured by island flowers. Scarlet racemes spun like pinwheels amidst the paper flutter of yellow genip blooms. Here and there a century plant met the sun with its own green rays, shooting upwards from the tropical bracken. At either corner of the beach dark mangroves plunged their roots into the shallows.

The guidebook said that Lameshur was favored by hawk-billed turtles, owing to the delectable grasses which grew on the sandy floor. Kay wasn't interested in turtles, or at least pretended not to be. She had wanted to stick to the original itinerary and proceed directly to Cruz Bay, where they were scheduled to meet up with Tina, a friend of the family, the following morning. But Chuck had leveraged his rare good-standing and won the day.

"I'll do what Chuck wants," Kay said, from the three point line. Both parents smiled warmly.

The day was bright and gorgeous, which meant nothing to Chuck, who disliked abstractions, as well as classical music and games of concentration. He stood in the cockpit, getting his gear together and responsibly applying suntan lotion to those portions of his back within reach (a red snake's head would later hiss between his shoulders). Kay had surprised him by jumping in almost immediately, and he was afraid that she would find the turtles first and scare them all away. Still, not giving her the flippers had been a tactical error. But he had merely been observing a basic principle: so long as you have something that she wants, the advantage is yours, and you should do what you can to preserve it: he dallied as Kay churned water; he put away the other flippers, the ones Kay had taken by accident; he dug slowly through the cockpit lockers.

"Just give me my flippers, Chuck," Kay said, weaving the water with her outstretched arms.

"I'm looking, I'm looking."

Finally he withdrew a pair, a pair he knew weren't the right size. But even before he handed them down Kay was saying, in a voice that, despite her exertion, still managed to project a tone of heroic patience, "Dad, could you get my flippers for me please?"

"Give her the flippers, Chuck," Dad said, floppily recrossing his legs like a ventriloquist's dummy.

"Chuck, don't be difficult," Mom called from inside the cabin. There was a rhythmic squeaking as she pumped the fresh-water pedal, rinsing dishes.

It occurred to Chuck that Kay had probably taken the wrong flippers on purpose. She knew what he would do. She knew he would bungle it.

"I thought you didn't want to swim," Chuck said.

"Chuck–I changed my mind. Can I please have my flippers?"

Chuck was overtaken by a sense of fate. A sense of his own nature. Did you know that the puffer fish can inflate to more than twice its normal size? That one of the defenses of the sea cucumber is to turn itself inside-out? Did you know that the trumpetfish will use the parrotfish as a blind, when hunting small wrasse or other algae grazers?

"Here are your fucking flippers," Chuck remarked and threw them over the side, where they began to sink.

"Hey!" Dad barked, standing up.

But Chuck already had his mask and flippers in hand. The ridged fiberglass grabbed at his bare feet, and then he was over. Despite everything he smiled as he tumbled into the silky water, bubbles streaming past his neck. He knew Kay would let the flippers sink. One was near the surface, and he grabbed it as he pulled on his own. The other, a blue triangle, was falling samara-wise towards the ridged sand below. Chuck propelled himself downward with quick kicks. His lungs had begun to ache by time he was able to grasp the fleeting fin, ears popping, and turn upwards, where he could see Kay's skinny legs steadily treading, and the bald bottom of the boat. How puny she seemed! How is it that she had enslaved him? Him! Chuck the Terrible! Unsinkable Chuck! Chuck of the Deep!

Nearing the surface, he began to expel air. His head throbbed and his lungs were burning. Sea water flooded his fogged mask. Ah! If only he could hold his breath like the hawk-billed turtle, and just glide away into the turquoise obscurity!

Resurfacing he handed the flippers to Kay.

"Sorry," he said nasally. He pulled off his mask and emptied it.

"I said I was sorry," he called to his father, frozen on the foredeck with his chest out like a prison guard.

Chuck didn't wait around for a rebuke. He bobbed next to Kay for as long as it took to suck a lungful of air, and then plunged back down into the blue.

Dad's irascibility could be partly attributed to the fact that they were on vacation. He wanted them smiling one hundred percent of the time, just to get his money's worth. The thought that a single moment might be "wasted" bickering drove him crazy.

Skimming the floor of Lameshur Bay, Chuck trailed his fingertips with picket-fence pleasure across the sculpted sand ridges. There was grass, pale green and swaying, but—predictably—no turtles. Eventually he aimed towards the reefs of the bay's western spur, gliding above outlying blobs of brain coral and diving to check beneath them for spotted lobsters. A procession of three gray angelfish disappeared like a geisha's smile behind a huge green sea fan. All the fish looked alert, as though just having heard that clever coloring had not prevented an acquaintance from getting gobbled. Peddling back into a cloud of orange and blue tangs, snorkel woggling, Chuck was utterly absorbed in his freedom.

By the time he returned to the boat, the daily afternoon downpour had commenced, pocking the surface. He lingered in the warm water, diving beneath the boat and studying the rain from below. The rain tickled his back when he surfaced, and he dove, and dove again, feeling wonderfully remote, and strangely dry. It almost made up for not having seen any turtles.

"Did you see them?" Kay said, as soon as he surfaced.

She was sitting cross-legged in the cockpit with her algebra book. Mom was writing postcards, Dad scribbling in the ship's log and chewing an unlit cigar. He had strung a bright blue tarp across the tail of the boom, covering the cockpit entirely. It was alive with the rain's rhythm.

Chuck dumped his gear in the dinghy and clambered up the transom ladder, suddenly wet and miserable. Mom handed him a damp towel and he stood shivering, water dripping down his forehead and off his eyelashes.

"There were two," Kay said. "Hawkbills. They came right up to the boat."

She stared at him expectantly with her lizard eyes.

"Yeah," Chuck lied. "I saw them."

*

The sun didn't come out again that day, and by the time dinner was prepared, the air was still bulging with moisture from the afternoon rains. Reluctantly Chuck took his place next to Kay at the fold-down table. The smell of dinner (franks, beans) was making him nauseous, and beneath everything else—the sweat and the coconut oil, the gasoline and the rotting fruit—the faint stink of feces bloomed. For four days now it had been jostling around in the holding tank, incubating darkly. It was inadvisable to comment on it, but privately he wondered if it were possible for shit to go bad.

He was beginning to regret that he had insisted on Lameshur, since now he would be cooped up in the boat all night, whereas in Cruz he might have been allowed to wander. Looking around at the faces, red and swollen in the lamplight, he felt the first twinges of acute claustrophobia. A plate of something brown was put before him, and he began breathing through his mouth. Amazingly, none of this discouraged another random stirring in his groin, which he quickly trapped and throttled between his legs. Meanwhile Kay kept bumping him with her thigh, with a ticklish prickling of fine hairs, until finally he asked if she would please stop touching him. He meant to say it coolly, the way she would say it, but instead it came out strangled.

Dad glared at him, a drop of sweat hanging from his long nose. Chuck clenched his legs together tighter and waited for the drop to fall. Maddening! Why didn't he wipe it away?

"I don't see why you kids can't try harder to get along," Mom said, and then the drop puckered loose and wobbled down into the beans. Chuck repressed a surge of hysteria, closing his eyes and picturing turtle grass soothed by invisible currents. The calmness, the immense blue volume, that big-eared ray he had seen, listening to whispering sand. He had heard tales of the mind games prisoners played in solitary confinement, in order to keep themselves sane. One guy had trained his imagination to the point where he could sit back and watch it, like TV. With relief, he felt the blood beginning to drain from his groin.

Then Dad had to go ruin his concentration by breaking wind. Instantly Chuck toppled over in a fit of giggles. In his mind he could see Kay rolling her eyes, his mother's tight mouth—but it didn't matter: the supplicating, two-toned dissonance of the sound, the profound counterpoint of it in relation to those humorless, sunburned faces, and its defiant issue, like some sat-on truth refusing to be censored, left Chuck helplessly giddy. To his ears it was not vulgar but heroic, or heroic because it was vulgar, which was the only sort of heroism left, outside of comics, that is. There was no flatulence in the world of comics, but then there didn't need to be, so long as conflict remained a matter of knives and knuckles.

"You're excused, Chuck," Mom said coldly.

Chuck lay on his side, convulsed and debilitated, picturing Mom's stern face, saggy and drawn without her usual make-up. Ah, it felt so wonderful to laugh! Glorious, heliotrope laughter! A bright school of Chuck chuckles, a white-spotted guffaw, the yellow-headed yuk!

Finally, with a massive effort, Chuck managed to choke back his hilarity and lever himself upright.

"I don't get it," he said, still smiling, wiping his eyes. "I'm not the one who—"

"Out, Chuck," Kay said.

At this Chuck almost burst out laughing again, but he captured the snort in his sinuses and slid out from behind the table with elaborate dignity.

"Right," he said in a deep voice. "Out, Chuck. Forgive Chuck. Chuck go out."

With this he went above-deck, where, under the hollow night sky, his merriment drained quickly away, and his mood turned cataclysmically black.

*

The next morning, Chuck tried to get out of going ashore. When the extra jostle from the wake of passing cruisers was sufficient to cause arousal, the situation was indeed dire. He sat miserably on the bow, afraid to move, the vibration of the inboard slowly throbbing its way into his lap. As they rounded the last point, and were met by the xylophone halyards of Cruz Bay, he crossed his legs and despaired. In his embattled skull, a hopelessly outnumbered party of decomposing corpses were steadily losing ground before a vast legion of nude nymphs and sexpots.

He had actually gone for a swim before leaving Lameshur, with the intention of taking care of the problem subaqueously, and was floating there, making ripples and furiously chewing his mouthpiece, when he happened to open his eyes and notice, yup, a hawk-billed turtle hoving into view. It glided almost directly beneath him, gently levering the water with its swept fins, shell doubly patterned with the sun's mesmeric parquetry. Chuck froze, hooting softly through his breathing tube. The turtle fixed him with a tiny, knowing eye, then banked and planed away, following parallel trails left in the sand by a caravan of sea-bound conches. By the time Chuck had caught up with the critter, and thoroughly spooked it in the course of trying to touch its shell, it was time to weigh anchor.

Over in Cruz, Chuck hooked the mooring and ran the line through the chock and then picked his way back to the cockpit. He sat down glumly on a sail cushion as Dad switched off the engine and went through his usual round of brow-bent gauge-tapping. Kay sat on the bench opposite, pulling on a pair of sneakers.

"I wanna stay here and read," Chuck said thickly.

"Read what?" Kay said, not looking up from her laces. "You don't read."

"Homework," Chuck replied.

"Yeah, right."

Chuck waited for Dad to say something. There was no way they were going to let him stay. Not in a million years. It was like trying to get out of a street gang. There was perhaps a slim chance with Mom; she was the most understanding, and was prone to occasional, utterly unpredictable acts of mercy.

"Get a shirt on, Chuck," Dad said, finally.

Bent over fetching life vests from the locker, his face was hidden behind his shiny blue rear, and his flat tone suggested nothing. Was he mad? Mildly impatient? Indifferent? Chuck's paranoia peaked. He glanced now at his sister, busy squirreling the binocs and winch handles below deck. No doubt she suspected his real reason for wanting to stay. How could she not? It was impossible to believe that his bright lust could remain undetected by her crow's eyes. But then again, Kay always looked like she knew something. That horrible knowing look of hers.

"I said I'm staying," Chuck said.

Kay looked at Chuck and sighed. "I'll get the hatches," she said, with routine exasperation.

Just then Mom emerged from the cabin, strangely garbed, all of a sudden, in meretricious shore gear. She even wore earrings, and had stacked make-up on top of her sunburn.

"Everything okay?" she said, glancing between Dad and Chuck.

"Chuck doesn't want to go ashore," Dad said, groping in the locker for the dinghy oars. Mom stood in the companionway with her chin on her forearm, eyeing Chuck somewhat seductively, trying out a shore pose.

"C'mon darling," she said kindly, rattling her coral bracelets. "We'll have lunch with Tina and then walk around and see the town. It'll be fun."

"Jesus Christ, Mom, I just want to stay here, okay?"

Even before the locker slammed and Dad had grabbed his arm, Chuck knew immediately that, once again, he had blown it.

"Time for a talk, huh," Chuck said, as his father yanked him towards the bow.

The "talk" was of the usual variety. Poetic, in a way: short stanzas of reflective rhetoric interspersed with dramatic caesuras. The caesuras were the worst, for they brought to mind the thought of his father thinking, trying to unravel this simple puzzle, to which even Chuck, a mere seventh-grader, knew the answer. Chuck looked away, anything to avoid that suspenseful face, stuck like a dying man's between fury and confusion.

Throughout, Chuck could see his mother, smoking a long cigarette and looking somberly out to sea. Perhaps answers lay there, over the ocean. Kay sat at Mom's side, trying to cheer her up with bright tidbits from the guidebook ("The white settlers were so outnumbered by black slaves that they enacted harsher and harsher measures to keep them in line: flogging was common, as was branding, and even amputation!"). Occasionally she turned her head and fixed Chuck with a bland stare.

In these moments, the man holding his arm was like some vaguely familiar stranger, like the drugstore clerk who once caught him shoplifting, or the father of a friend, daddish in stature, possessed of that brutal authority—but the beard didn't click. Who was this man, this tall man with yellow teeth and hair on his stomach, continually jangling his arm? Chuck had no idea—just that it was best to go limp, and that eventually he would be left alone.

"Is that what you want? Well?"

"No, that's not what I want," Chuck said, surfacing briefly from the rain-pocked water.

"Okay, then I'll be looking for a marked improvement in your behavior," the man said. "You can start by giving your mother a full apology."

All this was rote, and Chuck did his best not to pay attention. His apology was brief, routine, like those grammar exercises where elements used in an earlier sentence to form a question are reorganized to produce a statement. From afar, the next boat over, say, a pretty ketch with wine sails at its ankles, the scene must have looked vaguely ritualistic: little boy standing with bowed head before a woman sitting erectly. Man and girl bear witness.

Chuck bowed slightly to his mother, and then again to Kay for good measure. It didn't hurt. He was far beyond all that, far beyond himself. He stood still, waiting for what was next, mindless as a sea cucumber, turned inside-out.

Perhaps the most baffling, the most awful thing, was the way Dad brightly concluded the ceremony, and began loudly reminiscing about his last visit to St. John's, and then about Tina, a Greek expatriate, a painter, and so on—so cheerful, so mindless, as though everything was normal, as though nothing had happened.

How could he do that? How was it possible to bawl him out one second and grin like a newscaster the next? This was something different, a new genre of duplicity, brasher than Kay's, more willful. Adult.

Chuck focused on the buckling rubber of the Zodiac's floor, ignoring his father's offer to let him pilot the return trip, sinking down, down, as after some glittering artifact vanishing in the cold dark.

*

The cab was little more than a pick-up truck with a kind of canopied palanquin welded (one hoped) onto the back. They sat on facing benches, feet sliding on the sandy metal floor as the driver rounded hairpin turns, grinding gears, yanking in his mirror whenever cabs passed in the opposite direction. "Ho ho!" Dad exclaimed heartily, neck bulging. Reggae music and giant palm leaves luffed in the island breeze, and the shit-rich reek of vegetation was almost overwhelming. Mongeese skittered across the road, and the cab slowly toiled towards the center of the island, where Tina supposedly lived.

Chuck sat next to his mother, holed up in himself like a bank robber. She kept telling him to turn around and look at the ocean. "There's a huge catamaran out there," she whispered, knowing Chuck's love of catamarans. "It's up on one pontoon!"

Chuck hunched over further and said nothing. The stink of the island was incredible, like fumes from a burning manure load. He clamped off his nasal passages and breathed through his mouth. The rough touch of the wooden bench on his thighs was unbearable to him, as was the peripheral trembling of his mother's breasts. The cab shuddered on the uneven road, and when he felt the familiar tickling in his groin, along with a constricting wave of claustrophobia, he almost began to cry—but crying was out of the question, as impossible as speech, which he had abandoned like an overrun outpost. Everything, in fact, was out of the question. It was no use resisting. He had been outmaneuvered at every turn. There was nothing to be done except hold as still as possible, and hope for an opening—a window, a door, someplace to run.

He hadn't actually seen this woman yet, Tina, the friend of the family, of his grandmother to be exact. He hadn't seen her face. He saw the tiles of the airy entrance hall, felt the wretched breeze, heard it rustling among the sea grape trees. He saw bony, sandaled feet sticking out from loose cotton slacks. He saw a half-inch of water in the saucer of a flowerpot by the door. He heard her strangely accented voice, which, to Chuck, sounded like, "*Eet eez nize* to meet you."

Saw a thin, spotted hand extended, which he took and shook once.

Then his father's voice, with anger audible behind the sonic smile, "Say hello, Chuck."

And Kay intervening, "He's being dramatic."

Chuck said nothing. He studied the tiles like a chess player, lower lids swallowing his pupils. His throat was twisted shut.

As they moved towards the terrace his mother affected that strange, slow-motion way of speaking as she complimented the won-der-ful house, the beau-ti-ful view. She held her arms akimbo and rotated her head as though underwater. The family made their way by different routes among the furniture.

"Eh, it's not bad," Tina said airily, sliding open a glass door. "The only worry is the hurricanes, but I am high up enough so I don't get washed away, but I perhaps get blown away, from the wind. But if I do, so what."

She had a tendency to flatten her words, so that "wind" became "weaned" and "washed" became "west," the "s" soft and whistling through loose dentures. Even in his dark and shriveled state Chuck found himself positively disposed towards this woman, a batty old broad on a mountaintop. She was sincere, he could tell. At her age, with nothing to lose, she had no reason not to be. She was the opposite of him. She could say anything; he could not speak at all.

Lunch was served on the terrace, looking out over the northwestern bays and the cays that stepped towards St. Thomas. Chuck ate nothing, kept his eyes on the edge of the table, and prayed that no one would talk to him. He passed the time devising an elaborate escape plan, which commenced with him going to the bathroom—but it would never work, because it required that he use his voice to ask to be excused. And so instead he concentrated on strengthening his fortifications, in anticipation of his mother's next catamaran ploy. Which was inevitable. He was ready for it. But then he kept getting distracted by Tina's voice, so airy and petite.

"She must come here," she exclaimed lispily of Chuck's grandmother. They were discussing her various medical conditions. "Live in the wind with me and the parrots. I send her a postcard. Do you think she come?"

Behind her, a wall-clinging lizard held preternaturally still, as though there were a murderer in the room. Chuck refocused, fighting off the affectionate breeze, the playful tinkling of the silverware. A diabolical dog appeared and began to lick his knuckles. Everything was a betrayal, a goad. His fist and every other part of him was clenched. And then, as he knew she would, his mother attempted another sally.

"Chuck just got in some snorkeling this morning, over at Lameshur Bay," she said stagily.

Chuck braced himself, tense and impregnable. There was nothing she could say that would dislodge him. This alone he was sure of. This alone kept him calm, and convinced of who he was, Chuck the Terrible, Chuck of the Deep. His fortifications were strong, his back was to the mountains, and with archers at the crenels and a well-provisioned cellar he figured he could hold out for days.

Alas, he was mistaken, for he had disregarded Tina. "Oh?" she said innocently. "How you like the fishes?" but with her accent *fishes* came out as *feces*. A long silence followed, as though everyone were weighing the question. At his end, Chuck conjured a screwdriver-wielding psychopath to keep his hilarity at bay, and on the wall the lizard suddenly twitched ninety degrees, as though sensing his presence.

What was funny was that Tina had asked precisely the right question, the one question of all questions that he could actually see himself answering. And the answer was no, he cared not for the feces. Except that feces, he was beginning to realize, was family. Chuck was briefly stunned by the deepness of the thought, and wondered where it arrived from. It put the whole trip into perspective and absolved them all of their various failures. As he raised his head to share these revelations he felt a new benevolence blooming in him, and even his father with his horrid whiskers didn't seem so bad, nor Kay so miserably mean. Like him they were in it up to their eyeballs. They would understand—his mother, too. All he needed was a minute to explain.

Little Deaths

Aryn Kyle

There is the rest of the world and there is Maisie. In her circle, Maisie is the one who must be thought of in advance and planned around at parties. She does not drive at night, does not watch movies that take place in New York City, does not eat anything red. It's an inconvenience, certainly, but she is delicate, with small dimpled hands and a high light voice. Her fussiness is indulged. "Someone has to pick Maisie up," her friends remind each other. "Remember that Maisie doesn't like Mexican food."

Her family has money—she could have gone to a good college. But she wanted to live out West. So she came here. Her father says that Maisie is out of her element, that she should come home where he will get her a nice apartment in a good neighborhood. She should take walks in the park and help her mother organize symphony benefits.

Sometimes at parties, she begins crying and can't stop. Other times, she takes her clothes off so that her friends can see her muscles. Strange little Maisie: they squeeze her biceps, admire her flat stomach. When people ask, she says she is glad she came to college here. She likes the sky and has made very good friends.

Maisie's best friend is Ellen, who is also from the East and looks just like Maisie, only taller and thinner. "Where are you from?" bartenders ask Ellen when they go out. They offer to show her the mountains, the rivers, take her cross-country skiing. These same bartenders run their fingers over Maisie's ID, hold it up to the light. "Sorry," they say when Ellen vouches for her. "You're just so little."

Afterwards, Maisie calls her other friends and asks if they think Ellen is prettier than she is. Her friends say that Maisie is every bit as pretty as Ellen, prettier because she has an interesting personality and Ellen does not. Yes, Ellen is tall and skinny and has very graceful hands, but Ellen tells boring stories about boring people. Maisie should be glad she is not Ellen.

Her other friends do not worry about the same things Maisie does. They worry about college ending soon, about finding jobs and dental plans and paying their own car insurance. At parties, they drink beer and smoke cigarettes and sit with their legs looped across their boyfriends' thighs. Maisie sits to the side with her knees together and watches, holding her big beer glass with both hands.

With the men who love Maisie, she is weightless, foam and rubber. She sits on laps, rests her head on shoulders, claps her hands when they kill a spider, change her light bulbs, cut her meat for her. Her last boyfriend was Josh. The first time Josh saw her naked, he pressed against her and came, hot and sticky, in the small of her back. "My God," he whispered. "You have the body of a twelve-year-old."

*

Maisie has trouble sleeping. It began when she was a child, before there were commercials about insomnia, before everyone had trouble sleeping. Maisie listens to people on television share their stories and she feels stingy. Nothing belongs just to her. Ellen used to have trouble sleeping too. She says that if Maisie stops eating sugar and starts taking yoga classes, it will change everything.

Maisie feels lonely. Her restlessness is not food-related, not chemical, not trendy. At night, she sits on her balcony and stares at the empty street. Windows darken and, one by one, her neighbors disappear into other worlds, leaving Maisie behind in this one.

In the afternoons, Maisie runs on the track at the high school by her apartment. Let Ellen have her yoga. Out here, the sun is an enemy, as are the wind and the rain. The sky is open, raw and endless. Maisie runs until her joints swell, until the pads of her feet bruise. *Stop*, her mind begs. But Maisie does not stop. She runs until the pain throbs through her, until there is no sound, no scent, no thought. Her body is not her own, not a body at all. The world runs wet around her, blurring in smears of green and blue, earth and sky. But still, the body goes on, a muscle of pain until that moment when her heart explodes behind her eyes and everything goes dark.

She lies on the grass, limbs twitching as the sky spins circles above her. This is what moments before death will feel like, the body giving up, giving in, giving over. Whatever comes next will be better, fuller, simpler than this. Maisie will float into the wide western sky and there will be nothing but silence.

Only, it will not happen today. Today, like yesterday, like the day before, her breathing slows, her heartbeat quiets, the world reshapes around her and she settles back into herself. These collapses, they are only little deaths. Maisie always recovers.

Afterwards, she sits on the empty bleachers beside the track. Inside her head, she hears traffic, horns and sirens, the grinding machine of a city. Somewhere, a child is crying. She peeks through the slats of the bleachers and there he is, huddled in the shadows. He is thirteen, fourteen at most, with thin arms and big knees. He sits, crying into a backpack the size of a boulder.

"Do you need help?" Maisie asks.

He hiccups into the crook of his arm."Get lost," he says.

*

"What will you do after college?" Maisie's friends ask and she does not know. She supposes she will go back to the city, to the nice apartment in the nice neighborhood her father has promised her. Heads tilt when she says this. Eyebrows lift. What must it be like to be always taken care of?

*

Maisie is still on the ground beside the track when the trouble starts. The boy from under the bleachers shuffles along the side-walk, the blade of his spine curving under the weight of his backpack. Behind him, a group of bigger boys whoop and whistle. *Fag*, they shout. *Pussy*. A rock is thrown, then another. He begins to run.

Maisie's chest is aching, her face chapped with sweat and wind. But she stands as he runs towards her. The twigs of his legs bow, pitching his body forward. He is yards away and still Maisie raises her arms. She reaches as he falls.

The backpack splits open when he hits the ground, books and papers exploding across the grass. The bigger boys cheer and clap, pumping their fists through the air. By the time Maisie reaches him, they have gone.

Notebooks, pencils, loose paper—Maisie uses her feet to keep everything from blowing away. The boy sits on the grass, his backpack lying beside him like a gutted animal. Maisie's arms spill over with history notes and ink drawings. When she crouches beside him, she sees the streaks, tears and dirt, down the sides of his face.

"Don't," he says. "Don't look at me."

She sets the pile of papers on the ground and leaves him there, crying into his broken backpack.

*

Maisie is sitting down when Ellen calls with news. "Are you sitting down?" Ellen asks and Maisie stands before she says yes. Ellen has met someone. He is perfect, smart and funny, and looks like Robert Redford in the Gatsby years. He could be the one. Maisie says she is very happy for Ellen and that of course she will be a bridesmaid.

Maisie's other friends say it will never last. Ellen is Ellen. She lives in a fantasy. They give it a month, tops. Maisie should be glad she is not deluded like Ellen.

*

Beside the track, Maisie crawls on her hands and knees, shaking and gagging into the grass. There are strings of bile, saliva, chunks of wheat toast she ate for breakfast. When she looks up, he is there. His backpack is misshapen, held together with strips of duct tape. Maisie cranes her head, searching for the boys with rocks.

"They took off," he says. "While you were puking."

Maisie wipes her mouth with the back of her arm. When he reaches to help her up, his hand is soft and damp in hers. "I've never seen anyone run like that," he says. "You're supposed to stop before you fall down."

He pulls a water bottle from his backpack and drinks twice, then hands it to her. The water is warm and tastes of plastic, but she holds it on her tongue before swallowing. "Why do they chase you?" she asks and he shakes his head at the ground.

"You're a pretty good runner," he says. He lifts his eyes, and they linger on the scabs of her knees, the grass stains. "You're the toughest girl I've ever seen."

*

Maisie looks at herself in the mirror and for a moment she is pleased. Her legs are hard, her arms tight. But then she sees it. Between the curtains of her hair, something has shifted. Hidden within her own face is another, older face. A woman's face, it stares, mean and ugly, through her eyes. I am coming, it whispers. I am here. Someday it will speak louder. Someday it will scream. Someday, even men who love children will stop loving Maisie.

*

The last pink of daylight is draining from the sky when Maisie walks across the high school parking lot. He is already there, sitting on the bleachers, the points of his knees poking out through his blue jeans. "Your parents don't mind you being out?" he asks.

"They're in New York," Maisie says.

The field lights buzz, then snap on above their heads, an oval of false moons. He smells of soap and earth and nacho cheese. When Maisie kisses him, his mouth is dry, his tongue heavy. She can taste the newness of him, the fear. He tries to touch the side of her face, but his hand is shaking and she pushes it away.

When she steps back, Maisie can see the flutter of heartbeat through his T-shirt. She lifts the hem and his jaw quivers. "Stop," he whispers and Maisie feels him shrink before her, a boy with thin legs and large feet, a boy without friends.

When she does not stop, he raises his arms, holding them rigid. Obedient. The fabric peels away from his damp skin, catching on his ears, mussing his hair into stiff tufts. His chest is white and hairless, his ribs smooth and slender. There is no sound except the tremble of his breath, the hum of the field lights. Maisie cups her hand over the hollow of his chest, the shivering muscle of his heart, and it pulses against her palm—light as a bird's wing.

The walk home will be long and the pain will creak through Maisie's joints beneath the small glow of the streetlights. Her breath will be soundless, her heart slow and sleeping. In her apartment, Maisie will turn on lights and close curtains. She will sit. She will wait. But right now, there is dark sky and wet grass. The world is a tiny living animal against her palm. All she has to do is close her hand around it. All she has to do is squeeze, and it will crack into a thousand pieces.

The Mugging

Paul Maliszewski

June 17, 2002

Dear President Bush,

Last night I dreamt I witnessed a mugging. I was wandering around inside a giant parking garage, walking from its upper reaches to the lowest level, and I had good reason to suspect that I was nearing the bottom. The parking garage was built in the fashion of a dungeon. Its walls were made of rocks stacked one atop another, and the rocks were covered with moss and lichen. They were damp to the touch. Water dripped and pooled in places. Rats with large hips waddled in and out of view. The floor was cobblestone. The lights were standard parking garage lights.

Down the ramp and around a corner, I heard a muffled shout, then some scuffling, like shoe leather skidding on stone, then nothing. I took cover, crouching by the base of the wall, and tried to calm my racing heart. I did what I always do in order not to panic: I pronounced my name and told myself everything will be okay, Harvey, everything will be all right, everything will work out just fine in the end. That's when I discerned two shadows cast on the wall. The shadows were men, one tall and the other short. The tall shadow had his arms raised up high in the air. The short shadow threatened him, lunging repeatedly in his direction, then attacked his middle with his fists and threatened him once more. The short shadow attacked the tall shadow again, and the tall shadow buckled. As the tall shadow collapsed, the short shadow brought his knee up, and then the tall shadow was upright again, staggering back. The struggle went on like this for some time, sir, and I am ashamed to say I did nothing to stop it. Instead I remained in the dark, watching the shadows play across the walls.

When the short shadow struck the tall shadow across the face, I made a break for it. I ran back up the ramp to the level above, and I did not stop running until I was almost directly above the scene of the mugging. I stopped to listen, to see if I was being pursued. I bent over double, palmed my kneecaps, and gasped for air. I feared the worst, but was too tired to run any farther. I let a length of spit dangle from my between my lips then broke it off.

When I stood up again, I saw before me, on the wall, two new shadows. They were roughly equal in size and engaged in another life-and-death struggle, one mugging and the other being mugged.

This second mugging played out much as the first had: one shadow menaced the other; the second shadow raised his hands high up in the air, and the first shadow set to pummeling him; the second shadow collapsed until the first shadow brought him up again, sharply, with a knee to his chin. Just like before, I did nothing. I did not try to cry out. I did not seek to create a distraction. I did not attempt to intervene. I simply cowered in the dark until the time seemed most opportune, for me, and then I ran back up another level.

That night there were many muggings, more than I can count, one on every level of the parking garage, and I witnessed them all, and after witnessing them, I ran. There were subtle variations among the participants, just as there are said to be varieties of tomatoes or models of cars. They came in all sizes and shapes, the muggers and the mugged. I felt sure some of those shadows getting mugged were women. And some of those shadows doing the mugging were children.

The end of the night neared just as I emerged onto the roof of the parking garage. Day began to break, faintly first as a smidgen of watery pink on the horizon and then as a thin piece of an orange's rind. The air was cool, the moon looked like an errant toenail clipping lying on a black marble floor, and I folded my arms across my chest and hugged my sides for want of a better coat. The parking garage brightened, the shadows vanished, and, in the light, I guess I must have become briefly emboldened. I decided to go back down to the scene of the most recent mugging, which had involved a child mugging a child.

I found the mugged child's body lying crumpled on the ground. The child–it was a he–was breathing. As I looked down at the child, I wanted to ask him, "Are you Jesus?" It was an important question, but it seemed rude just to come right out and ask like that. I didn't want to pry. I shook the child awake and said, "You all right?"

The child sat up, shook his head from left to right, then let it hang. His shoulders slumped.

I said, "You got mugged."

The child nodded.

"Pretty bad," I said, "You got mugged pretty bad."

The child nodded again.

"I saw it happen," I said.

The child nodded once more.

"That's how come I know it was pretty bad," I said.

The child nodded, and as he nodded, he examined the cuts and bruises on his arms, the tears and rips in his clothing, and the abrasions on his legs. As he went about this grim accounting of his many injuries, I thought of all the mugged figures on all the levels of the parking garage, and I saw them all raise themselves up just then, almost as one, and begin to study their bodies for where and how their bodies had failed them. The ways a body may fail a person are many and various, sir. All the mugged bodies shook their heads then, as if I had asked each one, "You all right?" As if I said this a hundred times—You all right? You all right? You all right?—and heard in response one hundred answers "no." Then they all hung their heads. There were at least a hundred of them, perhaps more, I don't know. Their shoulders slumped in a close but inexact sort of unison, and I felt the air in my lungs take leave of my chest and saw myself as I almost never do, clearly, and as others see me, as an utter heel.

Keep up the good work, sir.

Sincerely,
Harvey Strub

Absolute Numbers

Karen Ackland

I'm not offended at being known as a number by my bank or the IRS, but I see no reason for my own mind to be stingy with words, which is why I'm confused when I find myself repeating 150,000 at odd moments through the day. If 150,000 is a sign, I want to know what it means. Why not repeat something useful like, "Money comes to me in unexpected ways"?

I hope the number is positive, although the way things have been going lately it probably points toward loss. Visually it's not interesting, with only two numerals on the left and a string of zeros. Count them. Husband: 0. Boyfriend: 0. Job: 0. Immediate prospects: 0.

There are, of course, the positive numbers. House with pool: 1. Occupants of house: 5 (daughter, sister, two dogs, and me). A daughter and a sister, fortified with a pair of dogs, should add up to more than the lack of a man and the loss of a job, except when I multiply, and then the result is always zero.

*

I'm trying to view this time as an opportunity to explore different options. I consider taking a trip with Victoria, my daughter. I imagine us lying on the beach in Mexico or laughing as we climb the steep pyramids together. We'll eat fish tacos and shop for embroidered blouses we'll never wear at home. This could be a chance to really get to know each other.

"Don't you need a job?" Vicky replies when I suggest the trip over dinner. "Why did you lose yours, anyway?" Vicky is eating deep fried tofu with plum sauce. I keep forgetting she recently declared herself a vegan. I'll need to rethink the tacos.

"Vicky," my sister cautions. Dolores's conflict monitor has a hair trigger. I wave her off. A family needs to have these discussions.

I look at Vicky and shrug, emphasizing the uncertainty of life as an adult. Trying to build enthusiasm for my vacation idea I call to my sister. "Dolores, why don't you come to Mexico, too?"

Dolores has already left the table and is rinsing the dishes. She turns on the garbage disposal.

"We could rent a condo south of Cancun and spend part of our time exploring the Mayan ruins and the rest on the beach," I continue once it quiets down in the kitchen.

"Andrea's family invited me to go to Disneyland with them this summer," Vicky counters.

"Aren't you too old for Disneyland?"

"You're never too old for Disneyland."

"You may need a job this summer," I suggest. Vicky leaves the table and slams the door to her room. Dolores comes back with two cups of coffee and a plate of almond cookies.

*

"Disneyland makes me grumpy," I say. Usually, a weak stomach is sufficient to explain a dislike of amusement parks, but when I tell people I don't like Disneyland, they respond as if I'm un-American and unable to have a good time.

"But Vicky likes it," my sister replies. Dolores reverts to the safely obvious under stress. "Mama would have loved it, too."

"Maybe the Disneyland gene skips a generation," I concede. It's true our mother would have admired the cleanliness of Main Street, the friendly young blond attendants, the oversized cartoon characters. She no longer recognizes either of us, although I suspect she'd know Mickey Mouse. "It's a hard age."

"Vicky's or Mama's?"

"Ours."

*

Percentage total has always been my favorite function on the calculator. Percentage total can be woven into a narrative such as, North America accounts for 73% of the unit sales and is supported by 60% of the advertising budget. When new management arrived at the company where I'd worked for twelve years, talking about maximizing synergies and conspiring computers, I knew I wasn't going anywhere. Still, I thought I was safely part of the furniture, utilitarian if no longer showy, and was surprised to be called redundant.

At home, the percentage total function is not proving useful. 87% of the soda in the house is consumed by 33% of its human occupants. Frankly, no one cares.

*

Hanging around home all summer, I feel adolescent. You'd think this would give Vicky and me something in common, but it hasn't worked that way. I ask Dolores if she feels the same, but she's six years younger and it may take her a while to catch up.

"Adolescent? I don't understand."

"You know, the need to start again from the beginning. Feeling clumsy and misunderstood." I'm not sure what I do mean.

"I've never considered you clumsy."

I try another angle. "I can't imagine going back to the same job."

"They called and want you back?"

"No. I meant the same type of job. Are you listening to me?"

"Of course. I didn't think you could afford to retire. What with

Vicky and all." Dolores includes herself in the "and all." She has been living with me since her husband left her five years ago.

Although Dolores has a part-time job with the school library, her real vocation is cooking dinner. Last month she went through an Asian phase, and now we seem to have moved on to Morocco. Judging from the large bottle of pomegranate juice in the refrigerator, we may be here for awhile.

I don't identify with adolescents because I'm without a paying job. I identify with adolescents because I feel petulant, an emotion that is unattractive enough in the young where it can be forgiven, but in the middle aged it is like a fleshy back of the knee exposed in a skirt slit too high. I'm learning to keep my mouth shut at home. And I've no where else to go.

*

It doesn't help that even our dog doesn't recognize me. We got Nathan a year ago. The idea was to keep our twelve year old golden retriever Hannah company while Dolores and I were at work and Vicky at school. Nathan was Vicky's idea, although Dolores is the one who takes care of him.

Nathan is handsome, but dumb. Each morning he barks when he sees me through the sliding glass door. "I own this house," I tell him, "I buy your dog food." He isn't persuaded. Around 10:00 he quiets down and accepts my presence. Until then, I play computer solitaire in the back of the house. Is a need the same as a want? I need a black nine, but I don't know what I want.

*

I haven't mentioned a job again to Vicky so I'm surprised when she announces over dinner that she made forty dollars.

"Good. How'd you do that?"

"I sold some concert T-shirts on eBay."

"Someone wanted them?"

"Sure. They're good groups."

As if that answers my question. "How much is the shipping?" I ask, attempting to teach a gentle lesson in economics.

"They pay the shipping. I get forty dollars."

"For t-shirts?"

"I don't wear them anymore. Do you have anything I can sell?"

The next morning I clean out the hall closets. I pull down videos, old photographs, board games, and stuffed animals. There is a fisherman's sweater that is several sizes too small for me, and embroidered hand towels I know I'll never iron. This is important, I decide. This deserves my attention.

Each morning I clean a closet or cupboard, and each evening Vicky rummages through the plastic bags I stack in the hallway. Most of it she stuffs back into the bags, but some she takes to her room and drafts a description for eBay. She asks if I want to split what she makes for selling my things.

"I've got very high ratings," she confides.

I tell her she can keep the money.

*

Vicky's industry surprises me since I seem to have lost my own. I've two weeks of severance pay left, and I'm not looking for a job. I should be worried, but can't even muster the energy for that. Earlier in the summer, I thought it would become obvious what I should do next, but it hasn't.

As part of my outplacement service, I had a networking dinner with two women who described themselves as having high levels of testosterone. I found this amusing, like bragging about a Type A personality. They were both broad-shouldered, slim-hipped women and were probably correct about their hormonal levels. I usually associate math with men and wonder if repeating 150,000 might be evidence of more testosterone than I normally give myself credit for.

*

On Saturday while Vicky and her friends lounge by the pool and Dolores is grocery shopping, I decide to tackle the attic. I pull down the ceiling ladder and climb up. It isn't really a room, barely larger than a crawl space, but if I sit cross legged I can sort through boxes of old files, stuffing papers into black garbage bags which I drop to the floor like bombs.

I thumb through a journal I kept when I was getting divorced. I no longer have the impulse to keep a journal, and I'm not interested in renewing my acquaintance with the woman who did.

One of the boxes contains a folder labeled "Affirmations." Years ago I read a book that suggested writing positive affirmations in support of my goals. The memory of my earnest efforts is embarrassing, but when I open the folder I note how appropriate many of the affirmations remain.

I read through the old list. "Everything turns out exquisitely." OK by me. "I believe my future needs will be met." That one's still appropriate, too. "My family loves and believes in me." When I wrote it twenty years ago I didn't expect my nuclear family to consist of a sister and teenage daughter, but it works. I wouldn't change it.

At the top of the list I write, "150,000 is a positive number." If I'm going to repeat it, I should make sure it's going in the right direction. I look at the number and realize that if I lose the 1 and the 5, I'd achieve a perfect zero. Or, I could add a 5 and a 1 at the end and create a palindrome. Consider 5 goldfish and 1 guinea pig; 5 T-shirts and 1 designer jacket; 5 lamb kabobs and 1 dish of pistachio ice cream. It's easy to throw things away. Perfection no longer interests me. What I need are a few more odd numbers. A few more odd numbers should be enough to last me a lifetime.

The Way People Act in the World

Justin M. Kramon

As a child, Clara Shore awoke every morning to the sound of her father's voice calling her from the doorway of her bedroom. He spoke softly, and it sounded as if he were a great distance away, but Clara would hear him even at the first click of her name. She stayed in bed, though, with her eyes shut, listening to him say it again and again. Sometimes he said it six or eight times before she rose and said okay. She just loved listening to him call her. When she got up, her father would be standing in the doorway in his suit, his hair greased back, his breath smelling of cherries from the tablets he chewed to settle his stomach. He was thin, her father, and his figure had hardly more presence in the room than a shadow. He didn't say anything else to Clara; he just kissed her goodbye and walked away.

For breakfast she was left to her own devices. She ate cold cereal or crackers with jam or bread and butter because that was all she knew how to prepare for herself. Sometimes she concocted bizarre arrangements for variety–cereal with jam in it, cracker sandwiches. She ate quickly and messily, slopping food on the table, on her clothes and hands. When she turned papers in for school they were often decorated with greasy spots, or else they stuck together from sugary red pools.

She never saw her mother until she got home from school. Clara's mother was a gorgeous woman, always handsomely made up, stylishly dressed, never untidy. Clara had heard people say that she looked like Jackie Kennedy. Her mother had a way of entering rooms, as if in a wave of rosy smells and gentle words. In the afternoons she greeted Clara with cookies and soda and cake so sweet it made her teeth hurt. Clara ate everything without guilt, stuffing herself until her stomach ballooned and her body lulled to a lazy warmth. After her snack Clara climbed the stairs to her bedroom and collapsed on her bed in a tingly sort of happiness.

Once Clara asked her mother why she was never there in the mornings.

"Oh, Clara," her mother said with a pained expression. "I hope you don't miss me then. I'm just sleeping, honey. Your daddy spoils me and lets me sleep as long as I want. And it's so lovely of you to let me sleep, honey."

Clara was used to this, to having all of her questions answered with compliments.

Why don't we ever play together?

You're so independent, Clara. It's wonderful. You can entertain yourself for hours.

Why don't you pick me up from school?

Oh, sweetheart, that's such a long walk. And I'm so impressed that you can do it every day.

She understood what her mother expected, that she would be proud and praiseworthy, and Clara assumed that role to please her. She walked home alone and played by herself, took long naps in the afternoon.

There was a time when Clara needed to buy an outfit for a play she was in at school. It was the fifth grade's fall production.

The play was about the different classes in England and it took place a long time ago. There were peasants and merchants and kings and noblemen all on the stage at once. Clara had the role of a beggar who was to sit at the side of the stage and ask the actors for handouts as they entered and exited. She didn't have to learn any real lines. She said things like, "Can you spare some change?" or "A little food, ma'am?" or "Have a heart. Would you help a poor beggar?" It didn't matter which one she used, only that she alternated the way she begged and did not become a nuisance on the stage from asking the same thing in different words, again and again.

Clara didn't like her part, but she wanted to play it well. She wanted tattered clothes, black make-up to streak her face, stockings with holes in them. She asked her mother if she could borrow some of her clothes and make-up for the part.

"Oh, I don't think I could just have you tearing up my clothes, sweetheart. But I think it's fabulous that you're in a play. I'm so proud of you."

"Then can I buy them?" Clara asked. "I need something to wear."

Clara's mother dropped her off at the shopping mall with twenty dollars and told her to buy whatever she needed for the play. She said she would be back in two hours, after she had her nails done, that she would meet her in front of Macy's. Clara took the money and jammed it into her pocket, thanking her mother as if it were a kindness she did not deserve.

She was terribly free. Without her mother there to watch over her Clara bought gloves, a hat, a meal of nonpareils and sugar wafers. She bought all she needed for the play. She rode the escalator up and down, and even went down the up one when no one was looking. It was a sneaky thing to do, a sort of gag that Clara would perform more often as she got older, in order to frighten or impress her more timid friends. Later she would learn to slip candy into her pocket when the store clerk wasn't looking, to smoke cigarettes behind the school during her classes. She loved the slyness of it, the control she had to take and do what she pleased, the way her friends always wondered what was in her pockets.

She got outside fifteen minutes late and her mother was not there. It was almost five o'clock, the time when the mall closed on Saturdays. In the parking lot families were walking off to their cars together, toting colorful bags crammed with their purchases. The weather was cool. The sun dipped low, gathering reds and yellows as if claiming them before slipping out of the sky.

Clara had the idea that her mother must have been there and left. She must have waited and become angry, drove off with the other cars in the lot. Or else she came early. She went inside to look for Clara and saw her on the escalator, running down the up one. She was appalled. She left.

By five-thirty the parking lot was empty and Clara began to whisper what she was thinking. Please come back. Please don't leave me here. It was getting dark.

Her mother pulled up soon. She was driving quickly and the wheels squeaked when she stopped. Clara got in and both she and her mother spoke at the same time.

"I'm so sorry," they said.

*

Clara's father sold suits. While she was growing up he had a store in Pikesville, in one of the strip malls by the beltway. On Saturday mornings he would take Clara to the store while her mother slept. She would roam the aisles of jackets, brushing the coarse fabrics with her fingers. She liked to hide behind a row of them, sitting on the carpet in the dusty darkness, the stale smell of wool in her nose, and watch her father with his customers. He could not see her there, she thought, and for that reason what she saw must have been more real, closer to the way he acted when she wasn't around.

Her father had a charming, easy way with his customers. He greeted them like friends, with a smile and a handshake, and he wasn't afraid to pat a man on the shoulder. He spoke to them in a quiet, measured voice about the news, about their lives and his, and he never took his eyes off of them as they spoke, as if he had nothing better to do than listen to their stories. Clara could see how the men looked back at him, almost the way children look at adults, as if his presence were some kind of a gift. When he sold a suit, Clara's father didn't make a production out of it. He simply thanked the customer. Then, as the man was leaving, her father would toss something out from their conversation. And good luck with that water heater, he would say. Or: Have fun at the Cape, all right?

Once Clara saw her father interviewing a young man for a position working behind the counter in the store. The man was tall and awkward looking. He bent over as Clara's father spoke to him, squinting a little. Clara had snuck behind some coats to watch. Her face itched from the fabric.

"Yes," the man kept saying, nodding his head as her father talked. "I see. No problem."

Clara's father was explaining refund policies, employee discounts, lunch breaks.

"Good," her father said. "Then the last thing we have to do is fit you for a coat. You'll wear that whenever you're in the store."

"Sure," the young man said.

Clara's father ran his hand along a row of slightly-weathered black sports jackets. He looked the man up and down once. "It looks like you'll need a–this should work."

He plucked a jacket off the rack, and held it open for the young man to slide his arms into. Then, as he helped the man into the coat, Clara's father pushed a dollar bill into the pocket, without effort or expression, the way a man scratches his own chin. The action made no sense to Clara. It was a gesture from that adult world her parents lived in–like her mother applying eye shadow or her father opening doors for ladies–and, as in those times, Clara could only watch in amazement, marveling at the things she didn't understand.

"There. Take a look at it," her father said.

The man turned to face one of the mirrors on the wall.

"What do you think?" Clara's father said. "How's the length in the arms?"

"Fine, I think. It'll do fine."

"Very good. Then we're just going to have you fill out some forms. I hope you don't mind."

"Not at all," the man said.

"And you can hold onto the coat. You'll need that for work. In fact, try it out. Walk around in it. I'll be right back. I have to get those papers together for you."

Clara's father left the man standing there while he went into his office in the rear of the store. Clara saw the man begin to pace. He buttoned up the coat while he waited, stuck his hands in the pockets. Then his expression changed. His mouth jumped and he wrinkled his forehead. He looked around the store, back towards the office where Clara's father had gone. The young man slipped the dollar bill out of the jacket, hiding it in his palm, took a look at it, then shrugged and stuffed it in his pants pocket.

Clara's father came back out in a minute with some papers in his hand.

"Here you are," he said, handing them to the man. "I'm going to need the jacket back for just a minute, though. I need to mark it off the inventory. Why don't you go get yourself a cup of coffee and start working on those papers?"

When the man left, Clara saw her father stick his hand in the pocket where the dollar had been. His expression didn't change at all. He folded the coat over his arm and walked to the back of the store. Clara never saw the young man again.

When she was older Clara remembered all of these details about the young man her father tricked. She recalled expressions, hints of what he was feeling, what she never saw as a child watching her father. She didn't even really know it was a trick until she was in high school and she began to tell stories about her past to make people laugh. She thought it was business, the way people acted in the world. And later she thought it was stupid of her to think that.

She would also begin to wonder what the man did when he got out of the store. He probably thought back on how things happened and realized that he had been tricked, that whatever excuse Clara's father had given for not hiring him, the truth was that he lost his job over a dollar. And what could he say to that? How could he approach Clara's father to get another chance? How could he admit to his mistake? The best thing was to take the dollar and accept the bargain he had made.

*

By the time they had begun living together, when they were both well into their thirties, Clara always drove when she was in the car with Steven. She said it was because of that time Steven nearly hit a man riding a bike. They had been driving at dusk, searching for a restaurant in the faint outline of an unfamiliar street. Neither of them saw the biker turn.

"Watch out!" the biker screamed. His voice was muffled by the window. He pounded once on the glass with his fist. Clara could see that his bike was inches away from the curb.

"Move over!" Clara said to Steven.

The biker slowed, and Steven pulled away from him. Clara looked back at the man's gray shape, careening in the half-lit street.

"Watch where you're going, idiot!" the man yelled, and Clara took it to heart. She had not been watching. She had trusted Steven to guide her, and it was a mistake.

They had met at a party in Baltimore, but not one Clara had been invited to, at least not as a guest. It was an office party for the accounting firm where Steven worked. Clara had been asked to videotape it. She ran a small business that recorded events for people and edited them into polished montages of singing and cake-cutting. She interviewed guests and set their words to appropriate music: jazz for happy events, violins for sad. Her customers liked the tapes. She knew how to pare down a rambling speech, how to smooth over awkward moments, find romance in the most uninspired anniversary party. She thought of her job as making stories out of a clutter of images, as giving order to memory, as showing people the way they wanted to be seen.

Steven's boss had asked her to make a video of the annual office party that he could send out to all of his employees as a holiday present. The party was held at a restaurant in Little Italy, in a large, shadowy room with a deep red carpet and scenic oil paintings on the walls. Most of the guests were seated with their families, dressed in formal clothes and smiling at the restless children who tugged at their collars and skirts and kicked each other under the table. The conversation was soft and polite, and Clara thought it would be a peculiar challenge to make something out of this.

She took some shots of the food, of kids stringing spaghetti into their mouths, of portly men in business suits waving to each other. It was boring. She hated to think of the people at the party watching themselves and remembering how boring it was. She would need some interviews, some thoughtful words she could hustle up into an emotion with the right music.

Steven was alone, chewing on a piece of bread. When Clara approached him with the microphone he stopped chewing and stared at the camera with his mouth open. Later Clara would tease him about their meeting, saying how foolish he looked, how he would have lost his job if she had kept the camera running.

She asked him if he wanted to say a few words to his coworkers.

"Sure," he said. "What should I say?"

Clara didn't hesitate. "You could say something about how much you enjoy working with them. You could say what a nice dinner this is. Whatever you want."

"No, I think I like what you said. Can you write it down?"

"Sure, I'll tell you exactly what to say."

"And make it straight from the heart."

"I'll tell them exactly how you feel."

"Good. I wouldn't want them to get the wrong idea."

They talked for a while, poking fun at Steven's coworkers, the restaurant's decor. Mostly they agreed with each other, and Clara liked the feeling of sitting outside of things with someone, of whispering wise comments in the shadows. They continued to talk about people—on the phone in the evenings, and then in other restaurants, and finally lying next to each other at night in Clara's apartment. He told her about his family, his friends, his coworkers, his clients. They speculated on office feuds and imagined affairs. And Clara described the birthday parties she filmed, the Bar Mitzvahs and weddings. They decided how long each marriage would last, whether the bride would make a good wife, whether the in-laws would be a problem. She was never more than half serious, always ready to grab onto some comment and toss it around like someone's dirty underwear.

"We're terrible," Steven said to her once when they lay together, naked and whispering in the sheets. "Can we do anything but gossip?"

Clara shot out her laugh. "I love it," she said with that devilish feeling, like when she used to sneak things in her pockets. "It's so much fun."

"But don't you feel a little guilty? Wouldn't you hate to think of other people talking about you like that?"

"It's what people do. It's natural. And besides, I don't think they'd have a lot to say about me."

"How could they not?" Steven said.

"Why? Am I such a spectacle?"

"Hey, no, it's just that you make an impression."

"I'll give you an impression." She pulled the sheet over his head.

"I mean that in a good way," he said.

"You better."

"I do," he said. He poked his head out of the sheet and kissed her. "The best possible way."

Then Clara rolled on top of him, laughing. She straddled his body and pinned him down with her hands on his chest. He played along, pretending to struggle beneath her, protesting loudly. He thrashed around and kicked the sheets.

"It's no use," she said. "We're going to talk about people whether you like it or not."

So they did. They talked while they made love—Clara on top, holding him down, forcing the secrets out of him.

Tell me about your boss.

What's his wife like?

Do you think he cheats on her?

What about that secretary?

Steven gave short answers, nodding in agreement when Clara offered her theories, pausing when their breathing became too urgent. At the end he let out a sigh like she had finally won.

When they were finished in bed, Clara played some of the tapes she made at work. They sat in front of the television, pointing at faces and gestures, telling stories about people they didn't even know, and Clara loved the world they created out of almost nothing.

*

She was a terrible actress. Everyone who had tried out had gotten a part, and Clara had the role of the beggar only because it was the easiest. But she couldn't do it. During the scenes her mind would wander off. She would think of some stupid thing she said in class or wonder whether anyone had heard her flush the toilet twice during recess. She became nervous, imagined consequences, missed her lines. Or if she said them they came out too quickly, as if someone had kicked her in the rear and told her to speak. On stage she was abrupt and clumsy. She spoke louder than she should have. All of it was forced. She hated being put in the role of someone who has to ask the same questions again and again. She would have preferred to play a nobleman, the sturdy, competent, heroic type. But all of those parts went to boys anyway.

They rehearsed in one of the classrooms after school had let out, pushing the desks and chairs into the corners. The blackboards were still decorated with equations and spelling exercises. They were doing dress rehearsals now. Clara wore the clothes she had bought with her mother's money. She had liked them while she was in the store, but now they felt cheap compared to the polished boots and neatly sewn shirts her classmates displayed. She noticed that her socks were not white, but a funny yellowish color, and that her shirt was baggy under the arms. She looked untidy, even for a beggar.

Ms. Feinman, the drama teacher, had a way of saying Clara's name every time she made a mistake. It was a soft, motherly sort of way, as if she were waking Clara from a nap. Ms. Feinman said other things, too. She told Clara to relax, take a deep breath, pretend she was alone. She called Clara "honey." She stopped the rehearsals and babied her. Clara, honey, just remember to say your lines now. Years later Clara could still recall her whispery voice, the painted lips, the saccharin smell of perfume that flowed around her body like a gown.

The few times Clara actually said the right words at the right time, Ms. Feinman would break into applause, interrupting the rehearsal. She would glow with pride, clapping and marveling at Clara as if she were a toddler taking her first steps. The humiliation was relentless. She felt the way she did when her mother would hug her in the street or hold her hand when they were walking in a store.

The others didn't hesitate to screech and giggle. It was like a trick being played on Clara, as if they all knew a secret she didn't and they were watching to see if she would catch on. And she kept blundering, encouraging their laughter like a clown pretending earnestness.

The rehearsals left her in a sour mood. She came home and stamped around her room, slammed doors, grumbled to herself. She was quiet and sullen at the dinner table. She picked at her food and spent hours alone in her bedroom. And her parents didn't say anything about her behavior. They must have noticed, but thought it was too silly to mention. It was the type of thing adults wouldn't want to hear about, Clara thought, a childish drama. Often she would lock her door and lie with her face pushed in a pillow, her breath warming the fabric, the blankets pulled over her head, and when she would finally emerge to brush her teeth or use the bathroom her mother would tell her how well-behaved she was being.

At one rehearsal Clara was having a particularly hard time, tripping over her lines all afternoon, gathering a fuzzy, sickening anxiety inside herself. It was like falling in the mud over and over again, worrying that she'd never be able to wash the dirt from her clothes.

One time she said, "Have a change. Could you spare some heart?"

She was so nervous she didn't even realize she had switched the words until someone let out a squeal and the others started to laugh. She tried to think of what she did, and she imagined an open zipper, a giant tear on the seat of her pants.

One of the boys repeated what Clara had said, distorting his face and throwing his voice into a grating nasal pitch that made Clara shudder at herself. They carried on for a while with the laughter, squeezing their lungs out and then filling them up for another round. They looked at each other for encouragement, stirring up their own hilarity, building Clara's little slip into a gigantic, tumbling belly flop.

Clara thought she would cry. Then she thought she would throw up. She hoped she would pass out and wake up somewhere else. But she held on and watched with a brutal consciousness.

Ms. Feinman shushed them. She lifted one hand and put a finger to her lips. She flipped the lights on and off in the classroom. "Students," she said. "Children." The flashing lights made Clara even more nauseated.

When they quieted down Ms. Feinman rushed to Clara as if she'd been injured. "Honey," she said, brushing back her hair, "don't worry. It's just a little mistake. Everyone makes them."

For a moment Clara thought she would hug her teacher. She imagined giving herself over to Ms. Feinman, collapsing in her arms and chest and being wrapped up in that warmth and honeyed odor. But then she had another thought.

"Bitch," she said.

It was a word she knew from the movies. Actors said it and it won them a chorus of approval. She expected yelps of laughter, hooting and applause.

But instead she got silence. No one moved. They stared as if they were looking at dinosaurs or magic. She had hit something more serious than she thought. Ms. Feinman looked like she had been slapped.

Clara started to apologize. "I—"

Ms. Feinman grabbed her by the sleeve and tugged her out of the room. The others kept quiet. Over her shoulder Clara saw their faces mooning at her, their eyes and mouths wide. They appeared the way she must have, as if everything they saw were new and they had no idea what was coming.

In the hall Clara tried to speak to her teacher, but Ms. Feinman held her lips shut and shook her head. She kept pulling Clara forward and every so often she winced and pursed her mouth, like she had been dealt a fresh blow. Her head continued shaking back and forth as if measuring Clara's mistake in some unknown units. She pulled Clara past all the lockers and the classrooms, past the cafeteria and the gym.

At the end of the hall there was a pair of doors that let out onto a field behind the school. It was where the boys kicked the ball or played catch at recess. Now it was empty. Ms. Feinman pulled Clara through the doors and into the field. They stopped there, planted in the grass, Ms. Feinman still holding Clara by the sleeve. The sky was a dazzling, cold blue. They faced each other.

"Clara, honey, why did you do it?" she said. Her lips were trembling.

Clara didn't have any words for this. She knew the question was big and that Ms. Feinman was asking for more than an answer.

"I'm so disappointed," Ms. Feinman said. "I thought we were friends."

Clara began to apologize again. She reached inside herself for an explanation. But her voice stopped in her throat. All she could think of was the silence in the room when she said it. That wasn't at all what Clara had expected. And this wouldn't do for Ms. Feinman. What would she care about the way those children reacted?

Ms. Feinman was asking for more, so much more from Clara, and this kind of intimacy was something Clara had not experienced. As an adult she would become used to it, when her female friends confided in her about battles with their parents, divorces and failed marriages. It was a way women had, when life planted its heels, releasing an unbearable burden, when men took it on themselves, turning inward, a way of letting it all topple over for a moment, of collapsing onto someone else. Then they would gather themselves, these women, with a strength they could have only learned as children. They would plan what to say next, laugh, cope.

Clara never learned this way. She held these women as they sobbed, always wanting in words to comfort. Now she waited for Ms. Feinman to finish, to suspend her or slap her. The punishment would come as such a great relief, because this was the worst part, this waiting and never knowing the right thing to say.

But Ms. Feinman didn't hit her. She stood there and held Clara's sleeve.

"I liked you so much," she said, as if it were already in the past.

*

When Clara went out with Steven it was usually to the movies, and they alternated who chose. Often Clara didn't choose the movie she wanted to see; she picked movies that she thought Steven would like, not so much to please him as to show him that she could pick a good movie. And she was almost always right. They would leave her choices arm in arm, laughing over the conclusion or puzzling out the details of the plot. In the car, as she steered them home, Clara would begin to recount her favorite parts, and eventually he would join her, nodding in agreement, recalling his own favorite lines, praising her choice until she couldn't help but feel a certain warmth, an affection like the one she had only known as a child, lying in her bed, stuffed with her mother's sweets and hidden from the world.

Once Steven picked a movie about a man who had lost his wife and had to raise his daughter by himself. It sounded awful, and Clara had teased him about the sentimentality of his choice.

"Is that the one where the mother's killed by a hunter?"

"What can I say?" Steven said. "I've got a romantic streak."

The movie turned out to fulfill all of Clara's expectations. Everything the man did was fake. As she watched the movie Clara was storing up material for afterwards, scenes that came off as particularly cloying and which she thought they could get a good laugh out of. Like when the father put on the dress in the store. What a fool! she imagined saying to Steven. Or when the daughter got scared at the circus and they left and got ice cream. I would have tied her to her seat if I had paid for that ticket. The ending was obvious and mawkish. Clara groaned at the credits.

As the lights came up she got her expression ready. She stuck her tongue out like she was choking and turned to look at Steven. He was crying.

On the way home, from the passenger seat of the car, Steven said that he thought the father in the movie had played his part beautifully.

"He was gentle and real," Steven said.

"You thought so?" Clara said. "Because I didn't. I didn't see him that way at all."

They were driving under streetlights and the inside of the car pulsed with flashes of light like heartbeats.

"I thought it was so subtle," Steven said, "the way he showed his affection for his daughter. Like when he put on that dress. He didn't care how he looked. You know? He wasn't thinking about himself."

"You call that subtle?" Clara turned towards Steven for a second, but he was looking out the window. "That little girl was a spoiled brat."

"Interesting," he said, like she had pointed at a landmark outside the window. "She didn't strike me that way. But I guess I could see that. What I really liked was the father."

"No real father would act like that."

"I don't know. He seemed very genuine to me. And he was so tender, like in that scene at the circus."

The car went dark for a second and Clara shook with rage. Words like tender had that effect. She squeezed hard on the steering wheel, as if another word like that might send them hurtling off a cliff.

"People don't act like that," she said. "They don't just get up and leave any time some little girl has a problem. He'd be changing seats every five seconds if he listened whenever she complained."

Clara thought she had done it, clipped the conversation. The car went light and dark and the swish of wind and hum of engine filled the air like voices, louder than their own.

"I don't agree," he said after a moment, and his face flashed in the light of the window, a defiant reflection. "I think people do act like that, or at least they can."

Something rose in her, some deep and disgusting pool of memory. It stuffed her and choked her at the same time. In the window the lights seemed to come faster now, beating like a mad heart.

Before she knew it she was screaming, "I understand people!"

Steven tried to say something, but her words thundered inside the car, louder than anything: "I know how people act!"

*

Ms. Feinman didn't tell anyone what Clara said, at least no one Clara ever found out about. The next rehearsal was almost normal, except now when Clara stuttered and bumbled, Ms. Feinman let her alone. Sometimes it would take several tries for Clara to get a line out correctly, but she received no encouragement.

Ms. Feinman just watched her blankly, like a movie or a television program. She had been hurt, and even then Clara could recognize it. It was as if Ms. Feinman had offered her a hand, and instead of holding it Clara had chosen to bite it.

During the rehearsal Clara watched the door of the classroom. She thought about how she would leave at the end, how she would rush from the room before all the others. As she stammered out her lines, Clara imagined the path she would take, the release of neatly slipping from view. She thought about where she would go, about roller skating or eating an ice cream cone at the pharmacy. She was the first one out of the room.

But she went home. She walked straight home because she didn't want to go anywhere by herself.

Outside it was warm for fall, one of the last warm days. The morning had been windy and now Clara wore a jacket and a sweater. The sweater itched and the heat made her feel lightheaded and slightly sick. Her mind was full. She was remembering, hearing again all the lines she bungled and her own painful awkwardness. As she walked, Clara hummed to herself. She made a tune and sang her lines from the play. She heard certain words—please, change, heart—and the rest were like the sibilant sounds of a river, a soft and steady current that lifted the important words to the surface again and again. The lines came easily now, and she sang loudly to herself, imagining an audience, Ms. Feinman, the kids at school, her father. She belted the words until they broke from her with the force of an honest request: "Could you *please* spare some *change*! Would you *have* a little *heart*!"

She continued her chanting as she walked up the path to her own house. The front of the house stared down on her like the face of some exotic creature. Clara sang back at it: "Would you *have* a little *heart!*" She imagined the words themselves striking, cracking against the ugly face in front of her. She barked them with such force as to expel more than just the words. The sound of them was ringing louder than anything now, louder than all of her pathetic blunders, than that disgusting word she had blurted out the day before. She was singing over her thoughts, and it was as if a wave were washing over all the terrible words and images that cycled in her head.

Inside, Clara's mother had a plate of cookies ready for her. They sat in the kitchen together, her mother filing her nails, Clara eating the cookies one after another. For a long time neither spoke. Clara watched her mother sawing away at her fingers. She was waiting for her to ask something about school. Then Clara would tell everything. She would repeat that word she had said the day before and her mother would slap her, or else send her to her room until her father came home to punish her.

Clara finished the cookies before her mother said anything. She looked down at the empty plate, spotted with chocolate. Her head was buzzing from the sugar.

"We had rehearsal today," Clara said. "For the play."

"And how was that, honey?"

"Okay."

Clara waited for her mother to ask more, but she was concentrating on the file.

"Something happened," Clara said. "At rehearsal."

Her mother looked up. She held the file against the tip of her finger. "What happened?"

"It was because I messed up," Clara blurted out. "The thing that happened. It's because I can't get my part right."

"I don't understand, sweetheart."

"I called her a bitch. The teacher. Ms. Feinman."

"That's a terrible name to call your teacher," her mother said. "I'm disappointed in you, Clara."

"I'm so sorry I did it. Am I going to get punished?"

"I'll have to talk to your father. But right now I'm just disappointed. I can hardly believe that you would say something like that to an adult. Go to your room until your father comes home."

Clara got up from the table. She wiped her hands on her shirt.

"I don't even know where you picked up language like that," her mother said. She dropped the nail file on the table. "I don't even want to know."

When her father got up to her room later, Clara was sitting on her bed, facing the door. Her father stepped just barely inside the room, the way he did when he woke her in the mornings. He pushed the door closed behind him, but it stayed open a crack, and Clara could see the shadow of her mother in the hallway. This was something Clara would remember for a long time, the way her mother was there, almost in the room with them, and yet not there at all.

"Your mother told me what you said to your teacher," he said.

"I'm so sorry," Clara said.

"That was a truly awful thing to do."

"I know it was terrible. I feel terrible about it."

"It's embarrassing for us—for your mother and me—to think that our daughter says things like that to people."

Clara didn't like the way he said us, the way he said your mother and me. It was as if he were holding her mother off in a corner while they whispered things and pointed at Clara.

"We don't want you to grow up into someone who says words like that," he continued. "It reflects badly on us."

She thought he would hit her now. He had done it a few times before, when she had made him late for an appointment or broken a glass in the kitchen. He never did it very seriously. He didn't seem committed to beatings. They were always just tough enough to let her know he was in charge. She expected this now, the satisfying clap of skin on skin, a moment of contact.

But all he did was shake his head, as if he were appraising her in those same foreign units Ms. Feinman had.

"What's my punishment?" Clara said.

"Your punishment is that if you keep saying things like that nobody is going to want to talk to you. Everybody ends up paying for their actions in the long run."

"I mean, from you. What's my punishment from you?"

"I don't have a punishment for you, Clara. The punishment is that if you keep doing this you're going to end up alone."

He turned to open the door, and Clara got up off the bed to stop him. She didn't know what she wanted to say, or what she wanted him to say, but she knew she couldn't let him go. She ran and grabbed onto his arm when he was halfway out of the door. Her mother was there, too, just outside in the hallway.

"Wait," Clara said. "Please wait for a minute."

"What else do you have to say?" her father asked.

Clara remembered the silence again, right after she had said the word. For a long time that would be all she could think of when people asked her these difficult questions about herself.

"I don't know," Clara said. "I just thought there would be more."

"What else is there?" her father said.

Clara let go of her father's arm. She craned her neck, trying to catch a glance from her mother. That would help. At least she would know her mother was watching. But Clara's mother turned away. She started walking down the hall. Clara reached for her. She stretched her arms out to grab her mother's dress.

But her father held her. He picked Clara up under the arms—it seemed like nothing to him—and put her down inside the room.

Then he closed the door.

*

In her adult life, stories became a way for Clara to deal with the past. She told them to co-workers, to family, to lovers. Usually they were short, punchy tales that left people smiling. Among her friends she was known for outrageous anecdotes, for saying things that no one else would say, and for making them funny. Many times, when she was dangling on the verge of tears, Clara would lock herself in her room, unhook the phone, and staring into silence she would pluck out the words to make it funny. It was how she knew she had won, and how she knew she could get on.

It was what she did when Steven broke things off with her. He ended it the night they had fought about the movie.

"You're right," he had said, finally, when they were in the apartment and still arguing over the movie. "You're right about everything. But that doesn't change how things are. And I don't like them!"

She had nothing to say to that, so he continued. "That's the problem, Clara. I don't like how things are with you. With us. I just don't think it's going to work out."

She didn't cry. She wouldn't let herself. It took her six months to make a good story, and when she found it, she tried it out on her friend, Maureen, over coffee.

Maureen was an attorney. She was small and tough, and she had developed a man's way of meeting the world from living so long in a world of men. She dressed in blazers and slacks. She used words like theory and moral compromise. She gave firm handshakes and was always the first to laugh at jokes, and usually the first to tell them. Seated in a restaurant with Maureen, Clara felt waves of confidence swelling beneath her and lifting them over the other talk around them. Maureen's hardiness was like an offering from her world, one that had served Clara with only occasional affection since she was a child.

"My last relationship was so serious it broke up over a movie," Clara began, and she knew how to smile in just the right way, how to soften and invite, how to tease and lead her friend to the conclusion, all without effort, the way a woman scratches her own chin. She knew these things the way others know how to cook or to sing in tune, as habits learned in childhood, habits so long practiced that descriptions like right and wrong no longer applied. These, among others, were the gifts of the past.

What she didn't say was that her relationship with Steven was her most serious relationship with any man, that she thought she loved him and would marry him. She didn't say that after he left she had started to tremble—to actually tremble—she was so afraid of being alone. She remembered losing control of her body, watching it shake as if it were in a different world. She held herself, almost like a child, shivering and wild with fear. She didn't say things like that in her stories. It was too much information, had nothing to do with the point of the story, and it wasn't funny at all.

The story about Steven went over well. Maureen laughed with Clara, nodding her head and biting her lip as if she felt sorry for him, and Clara had an image of herself and Maureen, like two gigantic birds, towering over Steven and cackling to themselves. They had finished lunch, and they sat stirring cups of coffee by the window in the small cafe. Some customers had left, but the music of conversation still twittered around them. An old woman at the table next to theirs was wrapped around a steaming cup. She blew into it and the smoke rose to her face. She closed her eyes and breathed deeply to herself, as if it had reminded her of something warm.

Outside it was windy, and people on the street gripped their collars against the searching air. Every once in a while the wind would strike up and whistle by the window. It blew papers and dust in the street. Even a man's hat rolled by. It was a black bowler, old and elegant, blown in from another time.

Seated in the cafe, Clara felt again that funny affection, like when she was a child and she would stuff herself with her mother's food. Only it was a little sadder now. Something was filling her, a feeling she didn't understand, maybe the success of her story, of watching and laughing, or maybe the comfort of bathing in the late-afternoon sunlight from the window, a little warmth in this cold world. She didn't want to leave; she wanted to stretch the afternoon like the sunlight, reaching its arms in the window and pawing her with its long, balmy strokes.

It was like the way she used to lie in bed in the mornings, cocooned in her thick blankets, listening to her father call from far away. She thought of his shining hair, the straight shoulders of his suit, his cherry breath, and these images of him bloomed in her mind, fuller than they had ever been while he was alive. He had died years ago, while Clara was in college. An employee found him pitched over on his desk in the back room of the store, his head resting on the inventory books. Clara's mother had called him several times that afternoon, and he hadn't picked up the phone. At the luncheon after the funeral, Clara overheard someone making a joke about her father. His head was always in the books. She had repeated the line dozens of times to her friends, whenever she told stories about her father.

Now Clara started telling Maureen about her mother. She wanted to talk and it gave her something to talk about. Clara's mother was still alive, packed into an apartment near the interstate with all of her jewelry and clothes and late husband's things. Clara would visit on the weekends with sweets from the bakery and only a touch of irony, but mostly love. They talked about family, and Clara told her mother about the videos she made, the functions she attended, the events in other people's lives. Her mother liked the stories. They would talk late into the evening, softening as night pressed harder against the windows, until the whole apartment, her mother's entire life, seemed like a whisper in the dark. They would watch television, and in the caramel light of the room Clara would look over, hushed and bleary-eyed, with a tender affection for that old woman nodding in a chair, drifting into her dreams while Clara held on in this world.

Maureen sipped her coffee and clanked her spoon around in the cup as Clara spun out all of these details about her mother's life. She watched Clara as if from a distance. She was waiting, Clara saw, for her cue, that touch of guidance that comes at the end of stories, a gesture to imitate.

Clara stopped talking. She didn't know what the point of the story was or how it would end. She stared back at Maureen, a little helpless now. There was a space she couldn't fill with words. She remembered her mother, standing in the hallway outside Clara's room, both with her and not, waiting for it all to be over. The memory was soft and small, like a feeling, like a tiny voice reminding her of something.

Winter Dogs

J. T. Barbarese

Two twenty-foot wide porches, detached twins with twenty feet of two- to three-foot deep snow up to the steps, yellow porch lights and strings of Christmas lights on the gutters. A snowy hell. It was impossible to run.

So they met me in the middle of the street. I just stood there facing them in the full glare of the snow under the streetlight and a man came to the door, as I hoped he would. He cracked it open and looked out. "They yours?" He had only his head out the door, turning to look in both directions.

"No," I said.

"Don't do anything sudden."

"Are they yours?"

"I thought they were yours."

"They just came up," I said. I did not move. I held my arms stiff at my side. The walking and breathing in the cold air made me sound short of breath.

"They hurt you?" I could see something in his hand now. He was eating an apple.

"They just came right up." I looked at the dogs and then back at his door. He had come all the way outside and leaned over his porch wall. "They look a little scary."

"One of them looks pit bull," he said, completely out of his house by then. He kept shaking his head as if in amazement. "Would you look?" There was an overhead light on his porch and his head shone bald and white, and yellow light bounced off his glasses. He wore a lumberjack shirt and khakis, and leaned well over the porch rail, the bitten apple rising as he made a point.

"No sudden moves. One of them was just on my porch." The dogs heard his voice now and sniffed his way. "Nothing sudden," he said again. He took a big chew out of the apple.

"You have a gun?"

He leaned further toward me. I figured I was about a house length from him, maybe fifteen yards.

"Have a what?"

"Do you have a gun?" It was so silent that my voice echoed through the street.

"No," he said. He was smiling. It was a bad moment, the dogs sniffed up at him, then back at me. It could have gone either way. He leaned back toward his front door as if about to reenter it.

I lurched. The dogs paused, as I knew they would, then leapt after me, through the snowed-in lawn and up to the wall of the porch where they had to stop. He helped me, pulled me up and over the wall while the dogs barked at me. They raced around to the steps, but by then, and before I could ask, he had me in his house.

He closed the outside storm door.

"Safe," he said.

The dogs sniffed, wagging their tails, moving back and forth.

"I just called the cops," he said. "They ought to be here soon." He was in his fifties. His hair was white, where he had hair. His glasses were smudged. His house smelled of putty and wood and smoke and hot food. There was another smell behind it too, of bodies washed and unwashed, of things left out. He held out his hand. He was tall and doughy, maybe three inches taller than me and had teeth missing and an old scar over his eye. His face had that marbled look of kid acne.

"Charlie," he said.

I gave him a name and my hand and thanked him.

"No problem," he said. "They nearly got you."

I looked around. It was a moderately furnished place. I saw pictures on the mantle and heard a radio somewhere. A set of door keys hung on a hook by the door, a foot from me.

"I called, like I said, but in this snow who knows. The cops could take forever." The dogs were still sniffing, wagging their tails, snuffling the door. "Wagging those tails all the time. Which is why I didn't think they were a threat. I heard something out there and noticed the one, the boxerish-looking. . ." He pointed and tapped the door and the dogs sniffed up at him together. "See the brown one is a boxer. Nice-looking mutt. But I didn't see the other, the pit bull. So I'm halfway outside before I realize there're two, and the other one enough of a pit to scare me."

I made a sound of agreement.

"Now what they should do is they should arrest the owner. Instead they'll lay down the dogs. Both of them." He *tsk-tsked*. "That brown one has got to be a boxer." He made a certain sound in his throat. "That white there is a pit. Look at that flat face."

"A pit, yes."

"Friendly, too, but you can't be too careful."

I made another sound of agreement. Their snouts were right at the lower panel of the glass door, smearing it with their breath.

"You get weather like this, they get loose. I've seen this before. They get out and go native," he said.

"Feral," I said.

"You get a winter like this one. Long and brutal. I seen this years ago when we had that last big snow. Ice storms, brutal cold. Packs of feral dogs. Those ice storms, about seven years back."

I nodded.

"Turns you into cavemen. Where were you walking?"

"To my truck." I pointed at the van.

"How far?"

"I don't know." I kept pointing. "That way."

"The drugstore lot?"

"The lot." I lowered my arm.

"Them dogs, wow. Something in winter turns them. Normal domesticated canines. If there is a domesticated pit bull. . . ." He shrugged. "They'll probably lay them down even if they find the owner. Then they should fine the bastard. Hang him." He was hard in concentration, staring out the door now, hardly minding me. "Cops should be here."

He turned to face me and smiled.

"Get you something? Coffee, glass of water?"

"I'm good. How long ago did you call?"

"Just before I saw you standing out there. Not more than five minutes before. I was watching my show and I noticed the brown one and went out. With all this snow, it could be a while. You want to use the phone?"

"I'm okay," I said. I was standing behind him.

"Phone, facilities, whatever," and he disappeared around a wall. I heard a chair scrape the floor. Old hardwood furniture, scratched and pawed, probably painted in the upstairs rooms. No bank account but probably cash, maybe a certificate.

He reappeared with a portable phone. "You can make a call if you want." I was listening for the *whoop*, tensed for headlights racking across the houses. "How about an apple?"

The dogs had not moved far. They wagged their tails and sniffed and one of them barked. Every now and then they would find my range and stop moving completely and stare in at me and the boxer would bark once. "I might in a minute," I said.

"I was middle of my show and about to do me a beer. How about you? Do you a beer?" He was already seated in an old corduroy chair. It looked like it might have been an heirloom. It looked like the sort of chair that was special to people like him. A retirement chair with wheels, green corduroy with matching covers on the arms and big leather buttons. There was an old brownish stain on one cover. It would smell of farts and old clothes. He sat back and I saw him poised with the lifted beer bottle, smiling. He rocked back and forth on the wheels. He loved this chair.

"A beer, maybe," I said finally.

He leaned forward and pulled himself up and crossed to the kitchen. He made a grunt as he got up. The chair rocked forward on its front wheels, followed him and rocked back. The chair knew his body, fit his ass and thighs. Between the cushion and the arms you could see things—popcorn, a pen, a cable guide stuffed in there. On the television a man in a black shirt was telling three women that their departed mother was in heaven and praying for them. The sound was lowered. The room adjoining the kitchen was filled with boxes. The one piece of furniture was a dining room table. There was a chandelier and the lights were dimmed. The television looked like the most valuable thing in the house, and it was pure dimestore. It anchored the room.

He came back and handed me a bottle. "I'd offer you a glass but I'm out," he said. "You want a glass?" He lifted the glass to me and to the light at the same time. He arched his eyebrows in an important way. "Gotta run the washer. If I can find the detergent."

I took the bottle in my gloved hand, not drinking.

"She hides the detergent." He said this more to himself than to me.

"Looks like you're moving," I said.

"Her stuff," he said. "She's moving. Or has. As in has moved out." He had his back to me, staring at the boxes. "You married?"

"Yes," I lied.

"Widowed or divorced?"

"Yes," I lied.

"Which?"

I acted like I hadn't heard him.

"Either is hard, but widowed is hardest. Take it from me." He lifted his bottle. "Cheers."

"That's too bad," I said.

"I'm just widowed."

Now he walked into the room with all the boxes and reached for something. The chandelier dimmed, then brightened. I could see the boxes now, more of them than I had realized at first. On the wall was an oil painting of NFL linebackers tackling mushroom-shaped Vietcong in black pajamas and an illustration of a country doctor on horseback. On the far wall, there was a framed discharge.

"You go up my second floor, looks just the same. Three rooms, two empty, and boxes, boxes." He looked at the floor.

"I have one box alone filled with her stuff. Shampoos, soap, hair stuff. There's stuff up there, was up there, from motels fifteen years ago. You know those little soaps." He had his back to me. He kept waving his free hand over the boxes. "A music box." He turned a key. Nothing happened.

"Ask me how I feel and it's like the loss of a limb. It's like asking, how do you feel about your right arm?"

I thought I heard something up the street and looked out, but it was wind gusting and blowing the snow horizontally, harder. The dogs stiffened.

"Got her heart attack at work and died in the ambulance, on the way to the hospital." He took a big swig of beer and his eyes teared. "We have, which is to say I have, one car. She had it when she left, her last day. The car is, God knows where. I don't know where she parked it. Next thing we get this." He meant the snow. "I'm not sure I'll ever find the car. Maybe in the spring." Something in his chest made a sound and he tapped his sternum. "She died Monday." He looked up and around. "Monday. Tuesday it started snowing. What's today?"

"Friday," I said.

He leaned over and lifted a page of a newspaper from the floor. "I never called the papers. Tuesday I went for the boxes. I couldn't hardly get out." He lifted his bottle and drained it and looked at me.

"I'm okay," I said. I hadn't touched the beer. "You need one."

"I definitely need one." He walked out. The boxes were unmarked and not taped, their flaps folded over. They had come from the supermarket and they were all different. I took a step toward the dining room and smelled produce and fish and a mix of other smells, clothes and shoes and candles. There was the smell of leather and old sweat. He came back in with another beer.

"Cheers," he said. "You're sure now, they ain't your dogs." He was smiling at me.

"Absolutely."

"You're sure now."

"Never seen them." He was starting to annoy me.

"The cops will be here any minute. Is it ten minutes? So you're headed where?"

I pointed to the corner.

"Right. Cheers."

He raised his bottle again, his head back and his eyes shut on the room, and he drained it halfway. "Now all I have to do's figure out how to spend the rest of my life." He raised the bottle to finish it, shutting his eyes and gulping hard.

*

Peter and Paul met me at my van. Peter was smart, but Paul was a genius. Peter sniffed my left cuff as I unlocked the van. He sniffed, smelling, recognizing. Paul, the genius pit bull, sniffed and blinked but did not move. He stared up, pure menace, hanging back, sniffing, then pulled his mouth back in a way that would be a smile if he were human. Then he lowered his eyes and jumped in. I had heard a whoop and could see the light rack's red reflection in the clouds, but I was a block away and I had four-wheel drive and chains and I knew where I was going. I patted my right pocket. I had taken the keys that had been on the hook. I would never be back, but you never knew where you would be. I held the beer bottle between my legs and the engine turned right over and the tires crunched the fresh snow. I love that sound.

Runaway

Richard Lee Zuras

It was the day my father got thrown in county lock-up that Mom finally split. I didn't blame her either. My father was not, outside of his uniform, what anyone would call an honorable man. It was not uncommon for us at the high school to clue each other in on whose parents were sexing it up outside their marriage. No matter who you were, or what your grades were or who you hung out with, eventually your father's name came up. You only hoped your mother's did not. There were far fewer mothers involved, and those who were involved were always new to the area, passing through on fixed assignments. Or, of course, it was Sharlene, the latest wife of the Rear Admiral who ruled most of nearby Portsmouth.

My mother's name never did come up and that didn't surprise me one bit. My mother was fond of telling me she was a virgin when she married my father. I asked her if that meant she expected the same teen-age celibacy of me, and she said, "Well, of course not."

I figured the day my father got put in lock-up was just the last straw for her, but later it began to make even more sense: my father was changing.

The Navy somehow got him out and had the charges against him—whatever they were I never found out—dropped without consequence. When my father and I came home we noticed a few things missing, my mother's truck and her record collection among them. I had, of course, risked driving to the jail on just my learner's permit. I expected my father would ream me for it, but he didn't say a word. When he came out of the station he got right into the passenger side. The only thing he said to me was "stay there." So I drove home, well under the speed limit, half expecting to be smacked up-side the head for driving his cherished 1972 Chevy Nova.

The next day he went into the attic and pulled out the boxes of records I guessed had belonged to him before they'd gotten married. Buddy Holly, Elvis, Eddie Cochran, Chuck Berry, Les Paul. There were some other records too, mostly on drumming techniques, and what must have been country and western. Records with names like Buck Owens and Roy Clark, people I'd never heard of. He put them into the empty built-in shelves where my mother's records had always been. For years, my mother had listened only to dance music. Waltz, bosa nova, flamenco, it didn't matter as long as there were steps she could learn. She would order the plastic templates of the steps from the back of the albums or make them herself out of yardsale Twister games. She would learn each dance to the point of perfection—and always by herself. My father had banged his knee on a door shaft in a submarine years back, and couldn't, he said, take the stress of dancing. He had served tours on practically every type of vessel known to man, supported operations all around the world, even taken fire atop an aircraft carrier—and yet his lone injury came from stumbling around a sub after an all night peace-time poker game. It was the one endearing thing about my father.

That first night we spent alone he put a stack of maybe six of his records onto the turntable and lit a cigarette. He watched me eat the last of the apple pie Mom had baked the day before she left. Then he said, "That's the last of that." He pointed his cigarette at my plate and made smoky circles to make sure I knew what he meant.

"She'll be home again," I said.

"No," he said. He tapped his cigarette onto his plate.

"She's left before," I said.

"When? She's never left me, Jake," he said.

"Well, she's wanted to," I said.

"When?"

"I don't know," I said. And I didn't. It just seemed like something to say. In my world people's parents were always splitting up. Cheating. Divorcing. Separating. It honestly seemed inevitable. None of us truly believed in sanctuary. Our fathers were always off to support battles most people didn't even know we were fighting. My great-grandfather, in fact, died fighting in South America in a war you won't find in history books. By the time we turned ten or twelve, we began to see our fathers as casualties. They were there, sometimes, but also they felt gone. At school, we began talking to one another about our troubles adjusting to their time at home, rather than their time away.

My father and I did begin to fall into our own routine. I would come home from school and try to do some of the cleaning Mom would have done. Every couple of days I vacuumed the living room and the bathrooms, went through and separated the mail, washed the dishes. My father came home earlier than usual, or later, and he would sit down in his chair and rifle through the newspapers.

After a while he began to hit the bottle. I had never really seen him drink. For awhile, years before, Mom had taken to downing a few glasses of red wine with dinner, but my father had stuck to coffee. If it was ninety-five degrees out, which it was for weeks at a time, he still stuck to his habit of strong, black coffee.

It was more than a week after our brief dinner conversation that he even said two words to me. I was in the shower when it happened. He came in and he took a piss and then he put the lid down and sat on the toilet. I stood a half a foot back from the shower expecting him to flush it, but he only sat there, his face in his hands. When I finally stepped out he handed me a towel and watched me as I dried off and combed my hair. "You aren't shaving yet, are you?" he said.

"No," I said, though I had been shaving under my nose for about a year. My father had more than once spoken of ungroomed facial hair as a weakness. I didn't really know what he meant by that, but I knew enough not to let him spot that weakness on me.

"Look, Jake. I want to ask you a question and I want you to answer me." He flushed the toilet and looked up at my reflection in the mirror.

"Okay," I said. I put my clothes on and used a hand-towel to dab at the counters where I had dripped.

"Did you, did Mom ever leave before?"

"How do you mean?" I said. It was a phrase he hated and one I seldom used. For some reason, it came out then.

"When I was gone," he said. "At sea."

"No."

"Did you two ever leave?"

"You mean to take trips?"

"You know what I mean, Jake," he said. He banged on the side of the commode. "This damn thing," he said.

"I don't know what you mean," I said.

He stood, lifted the tank lid and looked into the workings of the toilet. It was making a metallic, hissing sound. "I mean, Jake, did you two ever leave with the intention of not coming back."

"No," I said. Then without thinking I said, "Only Mom's jokes about going to Vegas." I couldn't see his face, and I didn't need to. I was putting one and one together for myself. I felt a sense of relief in knowing where she was. I figured she'd be back when she ran out of money, or got sick of the people or the endless neon lights.

When my father turned around, he was still holding the ballcock. "Fix this damn thing," he said. He slammed the bathroom door as he left, and in a minute I heard the sound of his car starting up. It was the last time I saw him for over a month.

It was difficult, at first, to get by without admitting to anyone that my parents were gone. The few friends I trusted, I told. Most of them managed to sneak me grocery bags of food from their houses. All of them had paranoid fathers who believed in overstocking basement racks with non-perishable foods. I paid the bills as they came in, signing my father's name for awhile, until it dawned on me that Mom wrote most of the checks herself. Forging her name was the one thing I had to do that made me feel like shit. I almost began to think she wouldn't be coming back.

I let the machine get the phone, picking up only when my friends left long-winded messages. I made up lies when I had to, told the truth when I could. After a while, I barely noticed the difference. I went to the beach to kill time on weekends. For a moment or two, I almost thought I could become one of the runaways you saw down on the strip. I had seen a local newscast not long before focusing on the high numbers of runaways in Virginia Beach. One girl, right around my age, answered the newsguy by saying, "If you were a runaway in this country, wouldn't you hitchhike to the beach?" He just smiled, but I don't think he really got her. I did. I remember wanting to go down to the beach and look for her, but it wasn't something I could really do. Like the rest of my friends, I avoided the beach and had rarely gone into the ocean. Our parents didn't understand, but it seemed absolutely reasonable to us.

But with no one around to judge me, I drove down there and just walked around the boardwalk. I felt too much like a phony to hang out with the runaways. What happened was I started going into the arcades—when it rained the runaways always gathered in the arcades—and what I did was I dropped dollar bills behind them. If they didn't see them right away I'd tell them that they must have dropped some money. It was after one skinny, filthy, green-eyed girl thanked me and called me "sir" that I stopped hanging around.

My father eventually called on a Friday evening just after I had washed the week's dishes.

He said into the machine, "I'm in town, Jake."

There was a part of me that wanted to avoid picking up the phone. But there was a part of me—deep inside me—that wanted nothing more than to talk to my father. What I said when I picked it up was, "Why haven't you come home?"

"I've had some things to take care of, Jake."

"What things?"

"Just things, Jake. They don't concern you."

"Where have you been, Dad? Where's Mom? With you?"

There was a bit of static then, and some clacking noises I assumed were coming from pool tables.

"I'll be home later," he said.

"When?"

"When I get there," he said. "That's when."

When I hung up the phone I realized how little I had been doing while they were gone. Mail was scattered all over the house along with newspapers and some sports magazines I had been buying to pass the time. Half-full glasses of Coke sat on the mantle, empty TV dinner trays on the tables. I had no idea when my father meant to be home, but I thought maybe I could at least try to clean the place before he got home. More than anything I didn't want him assuming I hadn't been able to get by.

By the time he did get home–well past eleven–I had managed to finish the vacuuming and get the garbage out. I hid several trash bags behind the garage so he wouldn't realize I'd forgotten to get the cans around for a couple of weeks.

He came in laughing so hard I assumed Mom was with him. I did, in fact, flash an image in my head that my parents had renewed their wedding vows at one of those little white chapels you always heard about. Maybe they had even decided to have another kid. When I came out into the living room my father was all that I saw. He seemed bigger than when I had seen him last, and I could smell his breath from across the room. In his one hand he held his keys, in the other he was holding what looked to be our doorknob.

All I could say was, "Hello."

"Damndest thing came right off. Right off."

"I'll fix it," I said.

He tossed it onto the couch and then sat down beside it.

Then I said, "Where's Mom?"

"What the hell are you asking me for?" he said. As he spoke, he drooled a bit on his uniform. In the bright light of the living room, I could see spots and what might have been bloodstains. He sat down and unbuttoned his jacket. I could see him scanning the room, looking for something to criticize.

"I'm sorry," I said.

"For what?"

"The house," I said.

"Looks fine to me," he said. The doorknob he had been spinning on his palm fell, and he gave it a light kick across the room. When it hit the fireplace gate, it gave off a noise that seemed to startle him. He stood up, reached behind himself, and pulled out a black pistol. For a moment I thought he might shoot that doorknob. Instead, he simply laid the gun down on the coffee table, pulled off his jacket, and sat back down.

"Where's Mom?" I asked again.

"Gone," he said.

He pulled out a cigarette and lit it.

"I know that," I said.

He shot me a look and blew smoke in my direction.

"You do, huh? What do you know, boy?"

"I know you've been gone." Then I said "Sir."

He stubbed his cigarette out on one of my sports magazines. "You've been reading a lot, I see," he said.

"Trying to keep busy."

"Could have done a bit more housework."

"Yes. Sir."

"Doesn't matter now," he said.

"It doesn't?"

Then he wheeled my way and looked past me, toward the kitchen. "Do you love me, Son?"

"I guess," I said.

"You guess?"

"I mean yes. Sure I do."

"Do you think I love you?"

I shrugged.

He turned back toward the fireplace and picked up the gun. He popped out the cylinder and peered into each hole. One by one. Then he slapped it back into place. "I do love you," he said. He held the gun out in front of him and cocked the trigger. "You need to know that."

"Okay. I do." I thought through every possible thought. His brains over the fireplace like a painting. A bullet in my chest and then one in his. A game of Russian Roulette. It seemed completely possible. All of a sudden, it seemed inevitable.

"You want to know where your mother is?"

I couldn't answer. For a moment, I thought of running.

"Get the doorknob," he said. "Put it back in the door."

"Is Mom coming home?"

"Just do it," he said. He placed the gun at his side. Everything inside me started to burn. I cleared my throat and felt an acid on my tongue. My chest heaved and before I knew it, I had thrown up in my mouth and onto my chest. I wiped at my face with the backs of my hands. "Put the doorknob in the fucking door," he said.

I started to walk toward the fireplace, afraid to show the weakness that had come over me. And I didn't like turning my back to him. I picked the doorknob up and placed it onto the mantle. "I'll need some tools," I said.

"Sit down," he said.

I turned toward him and sat down where I was. He didn't seem to care that I'd thrown up.

"Here," he said. He patted the sofa cushion next to the gun.

"No," I said. "I'm fine here."

"Suit yourself," he said.

I noticed the gun was pointed right at me. "Maybe," I said, "I will sit next to you." I took my place next to him and for a moment I thought about grabbing the gun.

"Let me tell you," he said, "where your mother is." He picked the gun up and put the trigger at rest. Then he tossed it onto the table. "You ever heard that saying, Son, that if you show a gun you better be ready to use it?"

"No," I said.

"Have you ever fired this gun?"

"No."

"Good," he said. "That's good." He picked it up and fingered the barrel. "A gun like this," he said, "it stays hot a while after it's fired. A good long while."

"I wouldn't know," I said. Then I said, "Mom?"

He stood up and walked over to the fireplace, putting the gun back in his pants. "Your mother," he said. "I tracked her down in Atlantic City."

"Not Vegas," I said.

"No, not Las Vegas." He pulled out another cigarette and lit it. He smoked as he talked to me about how he tracked her down. How he'd found a private investigator in the yellow pages. About how he'd had her tracked through her gas station credit cards.

I couldn't pay attention to the details. He went on for awhile, maybe it was half an hour–then he said, "That's where I caught up with her."

I tried to replay his conversation in my head, to get to the point he had arrived at. I couldn't.

"She was working in one of Trump's casinos," he said. "You know? She was slinging drinks at 5:00 AM in a little skirt. Your mom. I haven't seen her in a skirt in years." Then the phone rang and before the machine could pick up, he lifted the receiver, then dropped it onto its cradle. "She said she was never coming back to me," he said. "To us."

I started to wonder if it was her on the phone just then.

Then he said, "So I shot her." He looked me right in the face and added, "I killed her." There was a dog's bark suddenly audible in the side yard. A truck caught a pothole in the street and I could literally hear its contents shift. "I'm sorry," he said. "I truly am."

All I said was that I didn't understand.

He said, "The police will be here any minute."

"Mom's alive," I said. "That was her on the phone."

"Sure," he said. "That was probably her calling to check up on you. Right? It's okay, Son," he said. He put his hand on my head. "You don't need her and you don't need me either." Then he stood up and said, "Well, I'm not going to stay here for the cops to catch."

"You're not?"

"No."

"Well, I'm not staying here," I said.

He said, "I can't think of any reason why either of us should." After a moment I stood up and walked past him into the parking lot. "Here," he said. He pointed at a lime green Oldsmobile. I went around and got in. The stereo was missing. "Believe that?" he said. "First somebody went and stole these folks' radio and then I come along and steal their whole damn car!" He turned the key several times before the ignition caught. The car smelled of something foul. There was a plastic statue of the Virgin Mary on my side of the dashboard. Part of her lower half was chipped off.

"Let's go see Mom," I said.

He looked at me and then back at the road. His right hand went absently for the missing radio and then came back to the steering wheel. "You want me to take you to your mother?"

"Yes," I said.

"Right now?"

I nodded.

"So be it," he said. "So be it."

We drove what seemed to be the back-assed way around to wherever we were going. After two lefts we hit a wall of lights, and I could see a policeman talking to a woman holding a microphone. He stopped the car and lit a cigarette. I sat a minute watching him before I got out of that Oldsmobile. I passed the news van, under the yellow line of police tape, and walked into the spectacle everyone had come to see.

Behind me a car door slammed shut. Then I heard the turn of his motor. Nothing. And again. The sound of his transmission finding reverse. One moment to turn and point at my father. One moment to let him go. In the distance I could see a policeman sliding the cover off my mother and another man taking photographs. His camera's bright flash against the pulp of her head. White on red. A blinding flash, her eyes closed, flash, and then the sweep of my father's headlights across the scene, and the cover was back on her.

In some of the newspapers, I'm in the background of the shot. Standing right there, off to the side. If you look hard, you can almost see me.

A History of the Ghosts of Judy, Tennessee

Michael Poore

Vonda Stewart stands between railroad tracks and says a secret word three times. She is fourteen. She quivers in the November chill as she stares down the tracks, east into twilight, waiting. When nothing happens, she stomps off into the woods to smoke a tiny joint snatched from her mother's ashtray.

After a while, she is joined by her friends, Ashley and Jill, who have taken the long way around, crossing the tracks behind the Starvin' Marvin because they are afraid to go near the underpass. Vonda is the only kid in Judy, Tennessee who crosses there, because the underpass is where Odie Clark got killed. If you cross there and say the secret word three times, you can see him sometimes, a headless mist in the dark.

Ashley and Jill bring hot dogs from the Starvin' Marvin. The three of them smoke the joint before they eat. In their bellies, supper is transformed.

The hot dogs, Ashley says, will give them Strength.

The onion rings, says Jill, will become Magical Powers.

Vonda says the ketchup, red like a heart, will be the Perfection of Love.

*

When Vonda thinks about Odie Clark's ghost, she gets the shivers a little, but not as much as when she thinks of Odie alive.

In fifth grade, Vonda remembers, Odie Clark was this smelly kid with a huge Band-Aid over his good eye. The Band-Aid was meant to force the other eye to grow stronger. If you walked up on Odie's left, or if a kickball bounced up on that side, Odie would cock his head around like a chicken, so that he seemed always to stagger sideways through the halls of the school.

A tendency to fall asleep further lowered his stock. He'd fall asleep in the middle of spelling, in the middle of kickball, in the middle of peering around to see if anyone was sneaking up on him. Sometimes, back in fifth grade, Vonda and Ashley and Jill used to have a great time going to the library to look up all the things that were wrong with Odie Clark, and then teasing him with fancy words. "Narcolepsy!" they'd shout at recess, running up on his blind side, "Narcolepsy Boy!" Odie's head would peck around, and his other eye would do space-loops in its socket.

Odie Clark's eyes are one reason Ashley and Jill won't cross the railroad tracks by the underpass. They could stand to see a ghost, they say, but a ghost with a lazy eye was more chilling, somehow. If the ghost of Odie Clark walked up to you and pulled away the giant Band-Aid over his good eye, what would you see?

"Something deeper than deep," whisper Ashley and Jill, and they go around the long way, drawing crosses in the air.

*

Judy, Tennessee has other ghosts too.

Zion Calder, according to Ashley, is the oldest, the ghost who haunts Judy's drinking water.

Back in the Depression, says Ashley, Calder was the most stubborn man alive. He lost an eye in a sawmill accident, but wouldn't admit it. He stuffed the socket with a cottonball and went around for the rest of his life that way, one eye normal, the other a flash of bad lightning. When Renfro County exercised its right to build a road across his property, Calder simply refused to believe in the road. For years, if you drove out that way, you slowed to a crawl because you might find Calder drinking coffee in the middle of the road that wasn't there.

"It wasn't the sawmill or the road that made Calder a ghost, though," says Ashley. "It was water. When they built the Little Turkeyfoot Dam, he didn't believe in that, either."

*

Around Thanksgiving of that fifth grade year, Odie Clark did something that launched him from outcast to cult status in the space of a single afternoon. Right in the middle of arithmetic class, he screamed, "Dog balls!" at the top of his lungs. Then, during the pandemonium that followed, he fell fast asleep.

For a week, Odie's desk was empty.

"Tourette's," announced Jill, conferring with Vonda and Ashley at the library. "He can't help it."

When Odie returned, he still cocked his head around like a chicken. He still smelled. Now, however, he had become the center of a universe of expectation. His classmates developed chicken habits of their own, ears tilted in Odie's direction, ready for his next eruption, the next chapter in his legend.

It didn't happen often. Like his sleeping problem and his smell, the twitch of obscenity in his brain was not offensive enough on its own to ensure a constant state of catastrophe. When he did go off, though, the effect was like a Christmas,

Halloween, birthday and Valentine's Day party rolled into one bright shock. "Pig shit!" Odie would shriek, his war-cry interrupting filmstrips and reading circles, rising in wild glory above the roar of the cafeteria. "Butt licker!" he wailed at fire safety, jumping-jacks, room mothers, and Benjamin Franklin.

The response was always the same. The principal would fetch Odie, walk with him to the farthest reaches of the playground, and stand there with him until the fit had passed.

After their initial chorus of joy, Odie's classmates would watch the playground from the corner of chicken-cocked eyes, observing the figures of Odie and the principal across the intervening distance. Through six hundred feet of the mist—which seemed at all times to haunt the valleys and low places of Judy—the old man and the boy with the lazy eye seemed to vanish and reappear, or to hover halfway in-between, like shadows turned inside-out.

*

According to Ashley, Zion Calder was so stubborn he had to die twice before he could become a ghost. The first time, he died because he had a huge blind spot due to his cotton eye. He wandered into the path of a moving hoist and got knocked into the chipper, a monster of a machine which took in whole trees at one end and spat out chips at the other. Somehow, Zion Calder went through the chipper and came out the other end without a scratch. No one could believe he'd survived, least of all Zion Calder.

"Well," he sighed, "that's done it. I'm dead." He marched himself off to the graveyard, built a little shack there, and nothing anyone said could convince him to come home.

Not that anyone said much. There was something patently miraculous about the way the old man had gotten through the chipper in one piece, and a lot of people tended to treat Zion Calder as a sort of accidental holy man after that. They scribbled their most urgent prayers on scraps of paper, then crept out to the cemetery at night to tack them to his door. Whether Calder read the prayers was unknown, and probably immaterial. The door of his shack fluttered with a thousand paper wings.

In 1939, the Tennessee Valley Authority decided to harness the Little Turkeyfoot River with a dam. Much of Judy, Tennessee, would be lost underwater, but what remained on higher ground would have electricity. Zion Calder's graveyard sat right in the middle of the proposed reservoir. Calder, naturally, declared "there ain't no such thing as a TVA," and locked his prayer-bedecked door like a fortress.

The dam got built anyway. The waters of the Little Turkeyfoot began to swell and rise, and men from the county engineer's office came to move the cemetery. Calder advised them to go ahead and move whatever they wanted as long as they left his shack alone. This advice was rendered over the barrel of his squirrel rifle, punctuated by the flashing white of his cotton eyeball. They didn't bother him again.

All summer long, graves were opened and coffins pried loose. The diggers wore perfumed handkerchiefs over their faces, and were glad to move on to other work when the cemetery was finally tucked into high ground in the next township. Pilgrims stopped tacking prayers to Calder's door, and by mid-July the old paper scraps had disintegrated in the humidity, leaving only bare wood and a forest of tacks.

*

Sometimes Odie Clark showed up at school with bruises, and everyone knew it was because his mom liked to hit. She wasn't like the people at the school; when Odie yelled "Butt licker!" at home, the consequences were less than gentle. Sometimes he had bruises on his arms, sometimes in places you couldn't see. One time he had a great welt on his neck, and for a whole week he couldn't cock his head sideways and got beaned with the kickball four times. By the end of January, Odie had gone from outcast to hero to object of angry pity. And then, too fast for the minds of his schoolmates to follow, he became a ghost.

One day, his mother grabbed his hair and punched him in the ear for yelling "Pig fucker!" while she was on the phone. Odie went out to cry and rub his ear. He went out, like he often did, to put pennies on the railroad tracks, to lower his undamaged ear to the rail and listen for approaching wheels.

He fell asleep with his head on the rail, and vanished into legend.

*

Zion Calder, Ashley said, sat alone in his shack amidst rows and rows of empty graves. As the water table climbed, the graves slowly filled until they resembled rows of mirrors.

The water table rose, inch by inch, swallowing the basements of abandoned houses, filling the caverns and hollows and valleys, forcing the coal mines to close. At last, one morning in late October, Calder stepped out to find the Little Turkeyfoot River lapping at his toes. He tipped his hat to the water, slipped back inside and waited behind his locked door.

By mid-November, Little Turkeyfoot River had become Little Turkeyfoot Lake. Its winter-gray surface swallowed Calder's shack, the cemetery and the houses. The lake, like Calder, denied everything.

*

Sometimes Vonda wishes her mother were more like Odie Clark's. Even a mother who hits is at least a mother who does something. Vonda's mother goes to work and gets tired. She comes home and sits, or disappears into her room at the end of the trailer and goes straight to sleep. She's a ghost who isn't dead.

*

Vonda goes out alone sometimes and puts her ear on the railroad tracks, right where Odie Clark became a ghost. She tells Jill and Ashley that if you go to the tracks at midnight and cover your left eye with your hand and say "Butt licker" three times, a ghost train will come moaning through, a ghost train that's just a headlight and a wind that tosses your hair, followed by the headless ghost of Odie Clark staggering along with his head under his arm, bleeding from the ear where his mom hit him.

Sometimes, too, she tells about her father, pretending to remember him. "He went by a fake name the whole time he lived with my mom," she says. "Now he's really famous. If I told you who he was, you'd freak."

"Who?" says Ashley, says Jill.

"You'd freak," repeats Vonda, nothing more.

*

"The winter Little Turkeyfoot Lake was born," Ashley says, "Tennessee got unbelievably cold." For the first time in living memory, the temperature dipped below freezing and stayed there for three months. The new lake froze solid from shore to shore. People got in the habit of walking out onto the lake and wondering aloud about old Zion Calder sitting down there in the dark, wondering if he was stubborn enough to breathe underwater.

With the spring thaw, three fishermen decided to give the lake a try. They were floating around out there in the middle when Calder's shack, half-full of air, finally let go of the ground and came rocketing out of the lake, near their boat. It hung gracefully in the air for a moment, then landed on its side, more or less whole, floating cattywampus in the water. Nearby floated its builder, truly dead at last, and minus his head.

'Eaten by fish,' some speculated, regarding the head. 'Raptured,' said others. Either way, no one wanted to go out on the lake until Calder's head was accounted for.

The sheriff used dynamite, trying to shock it to the surface. The head failed to rise. What did rise, to the displeasure of the valley residents, were parts of old houses and old trees and the mortally wounded steeple of the First Redemption Church.

But that wasn't all. Something like a wooden submarine splashed to the surface, and bobbed darkly in the water. A second submarine followed, then another, and another. Coffins. Apparently the engineers had been less than thorough in their efforts to clear out the cemetery and move on to other, sweeter-smelling tasks.

Like Zion Calder before them, the people of Judy, Tennessee turned their backs. 'Lake? What lake?' they'd say. "My own grampa," claims Ashley, "will get up and walk out of the room if you so much as mention the lake. He will, I swear to God."

*

When Vonda gets tired of her mom being tired, sometimes she goes over to Jill's house, which is a real house, not a trailer. Jill has a real dad, too, not a story-dad, even if he's not famous. Jill's dad keeps an electric train in the basement, a huge layout with little towns and hills and lakes and tunnels for the trains to go through.

Ever since they were in grade school, he would sometimes sit at the controls in a high chair, like a bar stool, wearing an engineer's cap with dark blue stripes. He would let the girls sit in his lap and open switches, telling the trains where to go. If he were drinking beer, like he did at times, his lap seemed to change shape under them. When that happened, the girls would bite their lips and avoid each other's eyes.

The summer Vonda and Jill both turned fourteen—the same month Vonda started stealing roaches from her mother's ashtrays—Jill's dad added a new track to the miniature railroad world. The new section had woods and a perfect model of the haunted underpass.

"Shit," breathed the girls when they first saw the tiny underpass. It seemed kind of sick, even made them feel sick, but they couldn't look away. Jill's dad stood behind them, watching.

*

Ashley isn't the only girl in Judy, Tennessee who talks about Zion Calder. His name floats stubbornly down the years, whispered by citizens of all ages. The ghost is not the ghost of Calder's body, just the ghost of his teeth and his long, gray hair, the ghost of his white cotton eye—a ghost like lightning, or prophecy. He haunts Judy's waters like a fish, like a bad movie that floats in puddles, glares from dishwater, kiddie pools, toilets, and shot glasses. His bloated lips curl, cursing the TVA.

*

Jill says that when they are old, they'll be the wise women of Judy, Tennessee. People will come to them, mostly children, wanting to know about the ghost of Odie Clark. They'll tell how they knew Odie Clark when he was alive.

Jill says it's important to keep the blood moving in stories like that, so one day when Jill is sitting in her father's lap, opening and closing switches with a numb look in her eyes, Vonda grabs a toy whistle off the worktable. The wooden whistle makes a noise like an old-fashioned train. She runs upstairs with it and hides it at home in her dresser.

Sometimes Vonda takes the whistle to the real railroad tracks and blows on it, and the idea is that maybe someone will hear it and look and see nothing there, and they'll know, they'll know in their souls, that it's the ghost of the train that nailed Odie Clark. And they'll get the shivers.

She steals a joint before she goes and smokes it alone, since Ashley and Jill fear the underpass. Sometimes a train comes, as if summoned by the stolen whistle—a real train, although all trains are ghostly by moonlight.

Vonda climbs the right-of-way and stands as close as she dares, while the air fills with a wild diesel throb. Rust and steel rocket by in the dark, inches away, shedding mist like a caul. She lifts her eyes, spreads her arms, swimming at the edge of balance, and wishes—the wish coming from every part of her, rising like fire, like smoke. She doesn't even know what the wish is, but she wishes it real, real hard.

I've Looked Everywhere

Susan Jackson Rodgers

I lost my cell phone yesterday. This afternoon I heard it ringing faintly from deep inside its hiding place: a totebag, purse, kitchen drawer, pocket? I tried tracking the sound—first it seemed to be coming from the bedroom, then the study—but just as I thought I was getting close, the battery must have lost power, or else the person hung up. I went through the possibilities. Not very many people have the cell phone number. You, my sister, my ex-husband, my massage therapist, my housepainter who is also maybe my boyfriend, though maybe not. I called them all, all except you and the ex-husband, because he'd only call in case of an emergency and he'd try the land line first for that; and the housepainter, because I've called twice this week, and I don't want to appear desperate.

I decided to go to the library, to return the overdue books, but remembered that they are lost too. Three of them, checked out two months ago, and the fines have almost exceeded the value of the books. One was a book of poetry that I used to keep by my bed, because after you left I discovered that reading poetry before I went to sleep produced interesting, poetic dreams. The other was a biography of a child actor; I love stories about people doing drugs. And the third I can't remember.

I'm losing confidence, but not weight. I'm losing my glasses, my mind, my sense of balance. In yoga class I used to be able to do the Stork and now I can't, I topple over like a badly constructed block tower. Everyone pretends not to notice because they're practicing their serene yoga faces. I'm losing estrogen, instant recall, the ability to spell words I have always known how to spell. The stocks I own are losing money, have lost money, are worthless. The country I live in is losing wars—against drugs, fat, violence, stupidity, invisible forces we can't name, enemies we've only imagined who now rightly despise us. I'm losing faith. Altitude. Ground. I've lost two husbands—one to heart failure, and one to a twenty-year-old—and children—one to her dreaded Peer Group, and the other to a cultish mentality about a particular heavy metal band that shall go unnamed. I lost my name, twice, and now I can't get it back again. I'm losing elasticity, skin and otherwise. Losing perspective. Losing my appetite, but not for food. I've lost my mother's recipe for honey cake. I've lost the receipt to the beige dress I bought for my daughter's high school graduation that she said made me look like a matronly cow so I decided to wear the purple rayon pantsuit instead. Without the receipt, I'm stuck with the cowsuit, which hangs in my closet with many other articles of clothing my daughter has forbidden me to wear.

I've lost my taste for older men, because really, how much older can I go? I've lost my yen. For transatlantic travel, for driving a stick-shift, for falling snow, loud dinner parties, loud noise of any kind except certain rock bands from an entirely different era, late-night phone calls. I've lost the left shoe from my favorite pair, the black sandals for whom I get regular pedicures in the summer, the sandals that I bought three years ago in Italy—you were with me. Do you remember the sandals? Where in God's name does a single black leather Milanese sandal go? Is it at your house? Under the bed, perhaps, or in your closet, with your shoes?

Old friends. The desire to be first in line. The desire to go at all. The need to fit in, to do what I'm told, to accept second best, to fight the good fight, to be quiet. I've lost the remote control—forever this time, my car keys, a pair of $200 sunglasses I promised myself I would never lose, three skin cancers off my back, the directions to your sister's summer house, the children's baby teeth, many important documents that I'm certain I had signed by a notary public but did not, apparently, store in a safe place, a charcoal sketch of my childhood home, and the Maxime Le Forestier album I bought in Quebec in 1975. On the list of lost things also is the list of things I keep meaning to do, and the list of things I'm sorry I did—though when I wake up at four in the morning, there they all are, crowded around my bedside like eager dogs, pawing my hand, begging me to scratch their ears.

I've lost my place in the book I'm reading, the negative for the picture of us I wanted to enlarge (standing on the stone steps, the lake behind us), the phone number for the acupuncturist my neighbor recommended. Both parents and a brother, six dogs, eight cats, four hamsters, three birds and, I'm not kidding, a pear tree which died of blight. The instructions to the Cuisinart, the breadmaker I got for my second wedding—and you tell me where a breadmaker could possibly be hiding. The extension cord I swore I bought last week, this week's *TV Guide*, my favorite pen.

I've looked everywhere.

Every day there's something else, things dropping away like the careless removal of clothing or make-up after a party, like the diamond earring that slips from my fingers into the bathroom sink and down the drain, disappearing so quickly it seems to have planned its daring escape. We both watch it fall, incredulous, as if this kind of thing never happens. You kindly take apart the pipes underneath the sink (still wearing your handsome evening clothes, crisp white sleeves rolled up to your elbows) but the earring is gone. You straighten, unroll your sleeves, pluck the remaining earring from my palm and drop it into the drain just like that, without looking at me. And I can't read the gesture or the expression on your face; can't decide if what you mean is, See, it doesn't matter, it's just a *thing*; or, Now the two earrings will be together forever; or, Through your terrible carelessness, your inability to watch what you're doing, your consistently wretched sense of timing, you've sealed your fate, and mine.

There! Did you hear that? The phone—it's ringing again. Three rings, four. Now is the moment when I realize I could have just dialed the cell number myself, and tracked down the phone. "Dur," my oldest daughter would say. I stand in the middle of the room—six, seven—the afternoon light fading now, the shadows lengthening across the woven rugs. The rings stop. It must be later than I think, the way the light falls across the floors. The day must have gotten away from me, as it does sometimes. Does that ever happen to you? The day slipping by? Who knows where it goes. But it's late, in any case, it's starting to get dark, it's getting dark a lot earlier now, and in the mornings when I go for my walk, there's a chill, a dampness. Sometimes I wear a sweatshirt, my favorite one, faded blue, extra large, soft from many washings. The one you must assume, by now, that you've lost.

The Dark Between Them

Shann Ray

NANCE,
THANKS FOR
THE LOVE YOU GAVE
TO THIS STORY. YOUR ART
IS A LIGHT TO ME. —SHANN

EARLY MORNING, April 4, in the small square of their bed room a thin light opened the dark. When light became stronger, he emerged and imagined the sunrise on the edge of the world. The sun shone to the city and struck the sidewall of the trailer–a singlewide shortbox, late sixties, early seventies. He felt the light, and the stiffening of her body. She was awake and trying not to wake him, and he thought he would let himself come fully up from sleep to behold her. But he was unable to wake himself, still in the clarity of the dream, the clean line of reason. The great lighted neural pathways made everything crisp and alive, and he slept the sleep of the dead. She lay on her back staring toward the ceiling, her body straight under the covers, her arms to her sides. Watching her, he felt pressure in his chest.

Born in the same year, they were thirty-three.

Beside her in the yellow light, he took her hand and brought her fingers to his lips. Before he'd fallen asleep last night he had done what was asked of him, sung the song she wanted, her favorite song, a love song whose words now, in the dream, eluded him. Holding her hand he felt her bones and the tightness in her body. He was trying to soften her, hoping his head was wrong, but her voice became shrill, alarming him. Before they met she'd cut off the tip of her ring finger at the sawmill in

Ashland and her mother said she never uttered a word, just went to the hospital in Lame Deer with a straight face. This is no good, he thought. "Water," she said. "Washcloth."

He slid from the bed, ran down the hall to the kitchen. His body seemed ethereal, caught as he was in another world, and as he returned he didn't know what to do. In the bedroom the shades formed dark rectangles, white-blind at the edges, linear and numinous. He held the glass of water in one hand, the wet washcloth in the other. The star quilt her mother made was thrown from the bed, the slip-sheet coiled around his wife's lower body and entwined with her legs. The crazed sounds from her mouth intensified, and she knotted her fists on the hem of her nightshirt—sleeveless gown, yellow pastel and calf-length, and of the rayon blend she liked. She opened her hands, bent them upward to the hair at her temples, and entangled her fingers in her hair, made more fists.

He felt dumb. He stared at the glass in his hand. He leaned down and touched her face with the glass and she took it from him, drinking hastily. He gave her the wet washcloth.

"Let's go," he said.

She shook her head, warding him off.

"Please," he said.

She didn't move. Her voice hitched like that of a broken animal, and he saw the noises she made, grey-colored, ascend from the line of her mouth in dark spirals to the ceiling where they mixed and formed a black band above her head. She won't give herself permission, he told himself. When had he dreamed of her ring finger, elegant and tan and perfect? He freed her legs from the sheets and lifted her in his arms, surprised at his own strength, and as he held her it seemed she was there as a calf or a lamb, she was that small.

*

He was on the reservation, walking an open field in the morning of a new snowfall. The snow fell slow and big in the grey sky. A white veil covered the ground. He was six months into his life on the rez. The night before, he'd been tired and drunk enough to sleep where he was, so he had lain down on the sidewalk outside the Boys and Girls Club at two a.m. A few hours later the cold came and he woke, deciding he would walk to warm himself. The blood to his legs felt better, the movement, and he blew heat into his hands, forgot about the cold, and kept walking.

He found himself three miles from Lame Deer in an open field that ended on a thin forest of jack pine. Still below the line of the world, the sun had started its burn, red-gold, far off among the trees. Snow filled the sky, and it surprised him, the loud hush of it among the timothy grass and young sage. His shoes were soaking wet.

He thought of himself as a child, and of his father. A slight wind carried the damp, pungent odor of the sagebrush, the smell of grasses, the wet smell of dark soil. In a rage, the old man had thrown a cue ball at him, striking him on the skull behind the ear, knocking him out. He was ten years old. Walking, he felt the heat of it even now, a ridge of pain at his neck and up into the bones of his head. When he had come to, he couldn't see, and he felt warm blood on his skin. He was in his father's arms, hanging limp. He didn't know where his mother was.

The sun crested and flared long gold beams through the trees and out over the field. He decided to enter the forest and walk into the light, in through the deadgrowth to the end of the treeline. From there he could look down to where the sun had come from, and then he would head back to town. He had started that way, nearing the first line of the forest, when something drew his attention—throaty sound, far off on his right. In the distance, in the curve of a draw, he saw a rust-colored form. He made it out to be a cow on its side, bawling and straining its head and neck upward. He thought of killing the cow, getting some steak for himself, cooking it and eating it and drinking some milk back at the house where he was staying. He was on rez land, fenceless, without bounds. Stranger things had happened, like back when a big 18-wheel pig truck overturned on the highway and everyone cut school or left their jobs to kill pigs for supper. No one would care, he thought.

Yes they would.

He was white and he felt it.

He moved toward the sound, the cow's noise loud over the plushing his tennis shoes made in the snow. It took him some time to get to the animal, the sage grown tight in the draw, and the cow being farther off than he imagined. When he reached the cow he saw she was a heifer, and she had given birth to a dark brown calf. The mother lay on her side, the glistening calf curled in a ball between her front and hind legs, up against her stomach. She licked the calf, cleaning the nose and mouth, the sleek fur of the head. Keeping his distance, he sat cross-legged on the snowy ground and watched the scene. His head felt watery from how drunk he was. He liked the feel of the soft earth, bendable as clay beneath him. He liked how the snow soaked through his jeans. The mother nuzzled the calf's face. Seeing the simple, expectant look in her eyes dismantled him and he put his face in his hands.

*

He carried her through the bedroom door, bumping his shoulder on the doorjamb. His actions all felt literal, his choices predetermined. I could be a good father, he thought. In the hall, he hit her knee squarely on the wall. She winced and struck at him with her nails. He jerked back and forced the anger down, fearing something darker in him would awaken, something unalterable. Near the front of the trailer, he crossed the main room, bracing her to his chest, cradling her so that he wouldn't harm the bulb that was her stomach. He couldn't decipher the dream from reality. He pressed his face to hers and whispered I love you. He pushed the door wide, emerging into the day as from a cave.

On the tan bench seat of the Impala he set her down, then ran to his side of the car and drove. She moaned and curled fetal on the wide vinyl, her head on his thigh, her feet on the passenger door. He drove blind, spinning from the square lot of trailers, down the straightaway on 51st, descending the down ramp until he merged blatantly with the traffic on I-5.

He hardened his face and made his vehicle a fist. The other motorists, equally aggressive, rode their engines, forcing the fast metal of their cars. He heard the high whine of the tires. In the air ahead a thick bloom of exhaust belched from the back of an old truck. The fumes in oily charred clouds came on, rising before they went vaporous and disappeared behind him. He smelled the road smell, his wife's perfume, the sweetness of her sweat. He was free, speeding from space to space, then blocked in again. He jammed the break, punched the gas. The ocean, the blue lie of the sound and its bays, and out far the Olympics shrouded in white, the grid of concrete and wires, Seattle: all of it was as nothing to him.

On the seat beside him, he saw what he needed to see. Sara's head was pressed to the right front pocket of his jeans. Her nightgown, tucked at her feet earlier, was up near mid-thigh now. Her hands touched the gown at her crotch and he found in that bunching of hands and gathered cloth precisely what he hoped he could dismiss. In reality no blood showed, yet he imagined her body a river. She was a small woman with small hands, and he watched her fine-boned fingers, slender, translucent, nearly hueless. He envisioned again a real ring on her finger, not the thin one he had given her, the one bought in Billings, used, simple as a band of copper. He saw her finger healed, not stunted from the saw blade, no absent last knuckle making her hand alien, and deformed. In his mind he saw a very fine ring, graced by diamonds. Only what's real, that's what we need, he thought. That's all. But driving, he couldn't remember a single thing he and she had ever talked about, or why they might have pressed their faces to one another as they had, why their hands would be locked together in his dreams, in the dreams of his own creation, his own discord. In every dream.

He remembered at the start he had exerted so much energy fighting the idea that he needed her, finally killing it and succeeding in not needing her, then staring into her ashen face with his own expressionless eyes so that she'd know he'd overcome her. He'd felt ill about himself then, and now he felt out of sorts again. His mind kept warping things and the distortion felt familiar like kin, or the way mescaline bent his thoughts and sent him undulating. A run of meth could unravel him. He hadn't slept for days.

She sat up, staring out the windshield, out over the hood to the roadway, to the push of cars. If there is blood, her hands cover it, he thought, they cover where it must be spotting her gown. He convinced himself there was blood down beneath where her fingers had dug in, and he felt his thoughts constrict and he couldn't shake them. She was silent. He kept looking at her to be sure and each time, though he knew his own head was bent, his bulky zigzagged mind ruined things and his thoughts flared. He was lost by how she sat there so quiet.

*

They met in the alley behind Lucky Lil's, the modernized gas station/casino in Lame Deer. January, southeast Montana, Northern Cheyenne reservation: Zebulon Sindelar and Sara Runs Too Far. His family called him Zeb, but she called him Z and it was the first time he liked his name. He wished everyone would call him Z, the sound as smooth as he wanted to be.

"Ha ho," she'd said when he sat down next to her, "Cold, enit." He had nodded. "Will you get me some more?" She tipped an empty styrofoam cup his way.

He walked around the building into Lucky Lil's to get two coffees. From the start he loved how she said enit, an affectionate word, a connecting word that everyone on the rez seemed to use. The two of them sat with their backs to the wall of the gas station, knees in their arms. They held the Styrofoam cups in their hands and steam lifted from the small round openings, up into their faces. Keep warm, he thought, let the alcohol burn down. She was Northern Cheyenne and, he decided, not as ugly as him. Her looks weren't much, but her frame could be attractive. She was tiny, a descendent of Chief Morning Star, she said.

They started liking each other. They talked a lot and did little, and in late September, they married on a cutbank above the Powder River, a drunken priest officiating. Sara's mother, her brother, and her uncle Benjamin were present. Her dad was knifed in the throat behind a bar when she was three. On the bank, Zeb cussed under his breath at Sara's uncle for trying to take over the wedding. The uncle had done some smudging with sweetgrass and used a gold eagle fan to waft smoke in their faces. Sara stared at Zeb, but kept silent. Zeb's own family knew nothing.

*

"At Colstrip," the health teacher said, "fifty percent of girls on the rez are sexually abused." Zeb had grown up in Colstrip, a white town, thirty-five miles away. They sat on the sidewalk in front of Lucky Lil's, feet in the street. They'd been married six months. Beaters drove by, trailing plumes of exhaust, broke down boats from the seventies or early eighties. They'd seen Matthew Bird's old Lincoln Continental, Blake Big Head in his Monte Carlo, and twice Jonas Woodenthigh's white Cadillac Eldorado, rusted at the sideboards and wheel wells, cruising. Jonas rode low in the front seat with only his forehead and the black shock of his hair visible.

"White numbers, Custer," she said. Then she thought about it, looking off. "Probably higher, really." She looked at him. "Sad, enit."

"Crazy," he said.

She looked at the houses across the street and he followed her eyes, seeing the dirt yards, the clear glass of the windows. The houses stood curtainless but for a bed sheet in the living room window of the house one down from where they sat. The sheet hung off kilter, likely put up with tape or nails. Set randomly on the slant of hills up and back from the road, the houses looked like square Easter eggs. In the late morning the buildings seemed sleepy. Beyond them, outhouses littered the hillsides. The outhouses had no doors, and from where Zeb sat the openings were dark rectangular holes. Passageways to somewhere else, he thought.

"Four suicides in one month last year," she said. "Two of them good friends of mine."

"Girls?" he asked.

"Men," she said. "Bobby Hanson. Buster Three Moons. C.L.

Beloit. Lester Standing Elk." Her face was matter of fact. "They used guns."

*

Like him, she felt the need to get out. Lame Deer, no good jobs, the miscarriage. They decided on Seattle and bought a '79 Impala with her rez money. Before leaving, though, she said her mind. "Z, you need to be at peace with Benjamin." They were in her mom's house, in bed watching a video animated with talking animals, a bright-lit land, a symphony of sounds and grave words. He told her he didn't know how. Two nights later, past midnight, Zeb observed Benjamin leaning over a sleeping child. There were still fifteen or twenty people downstairs, all in the living room around three separate card tables, losing money playing poker or black jack, some playing cribbage. A gambling cult flick showed on the big TV, the giant box Sara's mother had won at bingo. The lead actor, about man-sized on the huge screen, had set up his friend on a card scam, cheating him behind his back with a group of cops so they both ended up getting their faces beat in. From the portable stereo in the kitchen, guitars burned clean and wild. Sara's mom stood over a vat of oil, making fry-bread tacos.

With the plumbing out, Zeb had gone upstairs to relieve himself out the side window of the bathroom. When he emerged he saw Benjamin down the hall to his right, kneeling over one of his sons. The boy was his second born, a five-year-old asleep in the hall and Zeb hadn't noticed him before. The boy lay on his stomach, one arm tucked under, the other extended, face to the side. Benjamin lay down next to the child. He smoothed the boy's hair and stared at his face. He kissed the boy's cheek. When Benjamin stood up to go back downstairs, he noticed Zeb and smiled.

"Ha ho, Dirty White Boy," he said. "Any more money for me to take?" He'd already taken Zeb for more than a hundred.

"No," said Zeb.

"Too bad," said Benjamin, laughing, putting his hand on Zeb's shoulder. "White money is always the best, enit. How bout we get some fry-bread?" Benjamin motioned with his lips down toward the kitchen. The smell of the hot bread made Zeb's mouth water.

"I'll follow you," Zeb said.

"You done that all night, enit," said Benjamin, chuckling as he walked downstairs.

Zeb nodded and laughed. He was good and drunk and it felt good to laugh, to see Benjamin with his son and be given a second chance. He reached and touched Benjamin's shoulder, and they paused on the stairs.

"I'm sorry for how I was at the wedding," Zeb said.

"It's nothing, Z," said Benjamin, looking him in the face. He play-punched Zeb on the chest. Then he laughed again, shook his head and said "Dirty White Boy, enit."

*

Topping eighty on I-5, Zeb cut a line between two semis to the outside lane. He looked at Sara, still upright, head back, eyes closed. He watched the road. He wasn't sure she was real. Reaching for her arm he touched a sheen of sweat that made him shudder. I don't know her middle name, he thought, or why she parts her hair down the middle, why she slips her braids in front as she does, tied at the end in two-colored cloth—turquoise and black yesterday, orange and red the day before. Nothing today. Why that face, and why above her forehead the high abandon of her hair? Luminous like a woman made of filament, or fine glass. Backlit from the light of day, her body a fluted vase, her hair like fire, jet-black on her head, the shape of it plumed, not flat with the usual raven-like texture, not parted, not braided. She'd pulled at it making the root line at the temples pink and raw. The bones shone in her face: her jawline and cheekbones, the orbital bones around her eyes.

She needs me, he told himself. He liked her face, and it came to him how living in Seattle, because of their drugging and his own evasiveness, he knew her less, but found her more beautiful. The second miscarriage came a year ago. She's too thin, he thought, her head tipped back on the seat, arms slack, her skin grayish and pale. He imagined her eyes behind the closed eyelids, the black minute disks of her irises, the darker black of the pupil at the center. He was struck by a sense that a song, or a prayer, or something sacred should be done, but he had nothing. And she had nothing, he thought. Or at least he'd never heard of what she had, or never asked. The sweat on her had started to dull, and with the noise of the engine, he couldn't hear her next to him. She was no longer crying. He reached and touched her arm again. The skin was cool. He took his hand away. She looked straight ahead.

"She's dead," she said.

Her voice, disembodied, overly loud between him and the glass of the windshield, shocked him. It's the way I've angled myself, he thought, and he moved some, leaning forward more, shifting his weight so that he glared over the wheel, out at the dividing lines. It scared him, the power she held. He lost something of himself. He saw his mother's face. He pictured Sara next to him on the bank of the Powder River the day they were married. They wore the ribbon shirts her mother made, purple shirts with long pink and gold ribbons sewn to the shoulders and chest. In the wind the ribbons trailed behind them.

"The colors of earth and sunset," Sara had said.

"Yes," he'd answered.

"The baby's dead," she said now.

He said nothing. He stared at the road.

The hunger came, ravenous, like a disease.

With his left hand he drove. With his right he rifled the glove compartment, the crease of dash and windshield, under the seat. He wanted to leave and come back from somewhere else. He'd emerge from a place of dirt streets, from the hot space behind the middle class houses back in Colstrip on post-Independence Day, where the food from the alley barrels could be had for the taking. From there he would succeed in rising back to where he needed to be, back to the driver's seat for the April 4 drive on I-5 where the words remained like two loud claps, the twice-formed flowering of blue-yellow flames from the barrel of a gun alive in the dark.

It was what she said. He disliked words. He hated them. He wished he could be deaf. Everything is confusion, he thought, everything a dream. No one escapes. An urge swelled in him like a helium balloon. He felt the reach, the pulling upward. He considered his own death.

"She's dead," she said again.

"How do you know?" he said.

"She doesn't move," she whispered.

He stared at her. Her body had no luster. The muscles looked undefined: oblong shapes rounded downward at the calves; the flat oval of triceps on the back of her arm, above her elbow, below the line of her armpit. Vague decisions are the slaying of things, he thought, the cutting off of her or me, and the end of something, the beginning of what will not be reversed. The car felt brittle, like he might snap the wheel in his fingers or slam a hole in the floor with his foot. He thought of weeping, and wanted big tears on his face like mercury, thick and slow in the pocks and dents below his cheekbones, cresting the jawbone, running down his neck.

He wished she would say something.

She opened her eyes and looked over. He looked away.

He sped down the off ramp, the route on Third Street among the square tall high rises with clouds moving among them. Up ahead he saw the circle entrance of the Good Samaritan, the rectangular jut of hospital against sky. Through the electric doors he carried her. She seemed smaller to him now, and boneless.

His grandmother's porcelain-faced doll lay on the bed at the ranch house outside Colstrip, its curled blond locks and blue eyes under the white bonnet. White blouse and fine-flowered dress, white stockings and tiny black shoes. He was five years old. It fascinated him, the play of the arms, the graceful feel of the body and the legs, the face so exquisite and hard as stone. He remembered he had never asked Sara what she played with as a child, or with whom, or what fears she might have had.

The doctors knew. They were as certain as she. He'd scream at them, he decided, throw cursewords until his head blew. Say, "How? How do you know!" He'd say nothing. Stand as a stuffed man with no mouth or ears, his arms and body so elongated that the shoulders narrowed straight to the neck. He'd pack cotton bunting into the back of his own head to fill the space inside his face. No mouth or ears, but eyes. Black buttons from his father's first suit. In the silence he thought of men who abuse women, men with sisters, wives, children. He thought of himself as one of these men, empty and consumed by greed, given over.

*

He didn't know anymore what was real; the car idling a few feet from the front porch at Sara's mom's house in Lame Deer;

he and Sara leaving for Seattle? It was late September, the sun past the zenith. He sat in the driver's seat, waiting. The house, a two-story tower, set a slight shadow off east of itself. He heard Sara crying, and felt nothing. He was always shut down unless drunk or high, and then he broke wide open. He hated this about himself. She sat upright on her knees in the entryway. She clutched two of her nieces to her chest, a seven-year-old, and a four-year-old. They touched her eyes as she cried. The younger one looked confused. The older appeared curious and she kissed Sara's cheek. "Salty," she said, and smiled.

Zeb watched the scene, glad to be free of family, not hers so much, but his—his father especially, the way the old man burned every bridge.

Sara took her time, and Zeb thought it brave, how hard people have to work to make something new. He'd left Colstrip at fifteen and hitchhiked to Lame Deer thinking he would be white and weird, but largely unthreatened, as he had been in the summers, working the fireworks booths at Jimtown near the rez line. And people had taken him in, parents or uncles or aunts of friends he'd made at parties or at the odd jobs he held—fireworks in early summer, driving swather or shucking bails through August, pumping gas in the dead months of winter. Most of his host families didn't seem to care if he came or went, white boy walking from the bright HUD houses. They hardly noticed, and Zeb had preferred it that way. Dirty White Boy, the older crowd called him, after the Foreigner song from "Foreigner 4." He liked that. But being white, and not pretty, he'd had to guard his own back when he was out late and the drink and drug reached full tilt.

Sara kissed her nieces hands, sat down cross-legged, and took both children on her lap. She began singing them a song.

Please, he thought. He sighed, and settled back in the seat.

He looked up. The sun traveled soft and white and high. Early on, he had thought of her only rarely. He'd heard she and her mom were back from living ten years on the Sioux rez in Wolfpoint. He'd seen Sara in town, but she always ran with Clifford Rides Horse, a Crow boy she'd met in school at St. Labre. Then Clifford got shot in the face and killed at a party near Busby. Zeb's father had died the same year and Zeb mentioned it to her when they had coffee that first time. Montana Highway Patrol found the old man dead in a ditch on a dirt road five miles south of Colstrip. No one but Zeb's mom attended the funeral.

"Did you like your dad?" Sara had asked him.

"No," he'd said.

"Did you care if he died?"

"Fine with me," he said.

"Really?" she asked.

"I don't know," he said.

*

On the drive west, she spent the first five or six hours crying or sleeping. She'd turned herself from him, and he couldn't see her eyes, but he envisioned the dark sockets, the eyes burned out. Her body leaned into the armrest. She rested her cheek on the bumper of the side window and stared away north. So petite, he thought, so full of sorrows. She sat this way for a great while, looking over the long white bench of the plains, over the rise of the land, the mountains.

Nine hours in, he said, "We can go back." They had crossed the Great Divide near Butte and were past Missoula, on the upswing of Lolo Pass. Seattle waited, still only a dream. In the dark before Idaho, the high beams of the Impala shone pale as bones, pale as the open moon. To their left, the span of forest was endless. He pictured Tamaracks among the greater forest;

he'd seen them in the light before dark, firing the land with their bright burnt orange. They passed high dark pines at the roadside, lodgepoles, eerily individualized, bands of onlookers peering over, looking in.

"I'm just sad," she'd said.

But the first day in Seattle she had looked in the paper, made a call, and landed a cheap rental off I-5, close to downtown. He'd brought her here for opportunity, though what they found was hardly better: him at the Vietnamese market up 51st, her taking the bus to Pike's each morning to sell bracelets she wove from colored thread. They threaded things with television, alcohol and the drugs they could find, mostly mescaline, speed, and methadone. Easy to be invisible, he thought, so many people in the streets, a thousand vagabonds for every ten miles of city, most of them Anglo and hollow-eyed. People stare, he told himself, but I'm less conspicuous, though he knew he looked polar white and pocked up, his face grey-dented as the moon.

Two years in he found himself in the hull of the trailer at night, in an easy chair a short reach from the television. He liked the chamber dark, the length of his body encased in the bloom of light from the TV. "Too loud," she'd say from the back and he'd click the volume down with the remote.

He liked her voice, an edgy voice from down the hall, weary from the day, and drifting off. It reminded him of the acidic, hateful way she came at him back in Lame Deer when he walked on her. It didn't matter if they were in private or public, she'd tell him to shut up and curse him until he backed off. She'd call him Custer, or Evans, or some other white idiot from the past. Scratch his face, grab a fistful of hair. She'd jump on his back if she felt she had to, but mostly only when she was drunk. He would pull her off, and she'd calm if he'd get soft and say he was sorry. It was a mess if he resisted. Once he had thought he might have to kill her. It hadn't happened in a long time and he missed her quick anger, her fire.

He'd turn the volume down, and when he heard the sighs of her breathing again he'd push it back up. Broke, but they had cable. Had to have cable, he thought, to stay human. He'd get suspended in the globe of light the TV emitted and the thoughts would get him, images of Lame Deer and her family. He hated it but he'd go back to it, like a woman wearing long sleeves over the wounding she's done. Draw the sleeve back and make it bleed; hide when others draw near. The memories pierced him like that, opening his skin, making him feel something akin to love, but more the shadow of love; a promise consumed by emptiness; a self to which he felt he had always been bound, lonely, embittered, at enmity with all; the question for which he'd found no answer; the old sorrow come again to make a home in him.

The mixture of how she loved children, the lack he felt inside, and the visions he carried of her and him, of what they might be as parents, kept him going despite the walls he'd found between them. Three years worth. Two gifts gone. One lost here, one back on the reservation. Two deaths, though he reasoned they were only miscarriages, and early ones. And now she was pregnant again, and nearly full term, five months further than they'd gone before, and carrying the child they called Rachel, the child of their patience, their peace.

He saw the doctor's head, the mouth moving: I'm sorry, sir, the baby's dead. We'll have to deliver it. Wait here. We'll tell you when the procedure's over.

Zeb viewed the man through the heightened vision that came with doing speed. The doctor's slick black hair in a pointed widow's peak. The dark main shock swept back from the forehead, the silvery smooth sheen of the sidewalls in a pronounced C around the ears. Spit glistened on the doctor's lower lip. His teeth were grey, and Zeb thought: I should kill this man.

From the front pocket of his jeans Zeb drew a gun, easily, fluidly, as if his pocket was substantial and made of silk. The gun was obnoxiously large but Zeb's hand felt sure. He lifted and held the weapon high and read the print engraved on the stock: .38 Special. He lowered the gun and held it to the doctor's chest and the doctor smiled. The doctor pulled the gun forward and brought it close, compelled before being shot to read the words for himself. .44 Magnum this time. Nice, Zeb thought, and he let his arm come even. He breathed out, pulled his index finger gently and the gun banged and sent his hand to the ceiling, the shot like a small bomb in the hallway. The doctor smiled again. Zeb lay on the floor, a hole the size of a cereal dish in his own left chest, a star of red around the circumference, and people were running.

"She's grey," Sara said.

They were running down white tile floors with big-volumed words and the words were unwieldy and Zeb got caught in them while his wife was wheeled, white-sheeted between silver swinging doors. Before she disappeared he saw how thin her face had become, how the lines in it had gone dark and straight and the skin looked tight, almost iridescent.

He wasn't with her again until it was over. The white coats walked her down the hall and dropped her off with him in the lobby, assuring him the bleeding had stopped, her heart rate had come steady. She stood beside him, vacant, almost weightless. He put his arm around her. Everyone had gone. She leaned her head into his chest. He felt blank and dark.

He looked at his right hand, the gun stuck like an unwanted appendage there. His left hand was full of blood. He walked the hall and no one spoke to him. He had no hands. The tiles came to an end and he walked over the precipice and fell full and far before he rose with his arms in the shape of an eagle's wings, precise, powerful, his body elegant and refined, the body of a boy in an alley asleep between two dumpsters, a wedge of small stones piled against the windbreak his head makes.

From a hole in the half-world came a reverend—Mr. Reyes, the half-Cheyenne, half-white man he'd seen only once in the green hall of the clinic back in Lame Deer after the first miscarriage. His face, his words. "Son, this from God to your child. "Into the silence. "Arise, shine, for your light has come." The great expanse of a deep gorge among high mountains, the closeness, the vastness of all things. In the black of morning, Sara's form curved into him, her back to his chest, her legs matched neatly to his. Her hair smelling of dry sweat, and faintly of lilac. How utterly I have failed you, he thinks. He kisses the back of her head. "You are my beloved," he whispers. She clutches a braid of sweetgrass to her chest and he sees the plains to the straight edge of the alien world with nothing in between, the sun a dull white orb behind the grey sky. Caught in a crease on the horizon, a glow of light is the bright rim of all that lives and moves.

"They took her from me," she whispers. "She was grey."

The room is shadow. People never break free, he thinks.

The sound of the street, the electric circuitry of the industrial machine, the speedwire of technology, the light of the moon from the bedroom window, the shape of their bodies under the star quilt, the stillness, the proximity of their faces. He finds himself again. Born to this world. Shine. Early morning, April 4, his wife lying in bed beside him, holding something. "Wake up, Z" she says. "You're here, with me."

In the dark between them he sees the child. She is on her side, small, slender, elongated, helpless, her form a tiny keepsake they carry like an amulet surrounded by the heart-shaped angles of their bodies, their legs and arms, facing one another in the soft hope of their bed.

It is Sara's mouth that speaks the words, it is her body, the alluring movement of her hip beside him, and the way his hand must hold the sliver of her ribs to know the breath that resides there, the rise and fall not of her whisper, but of the engine from which her whisper moves. Not the pale cross of her collarbones more reminiscent of Christ than Valentino's fine lines, but that down below the bones, the beating and drumming of the heart and the uncertainty from which her confidence lifts and opens the night. He sees the soft beginnings of her smile, then bright and turned to him, her eyes, pools in the wilderness he calls his own. Finally, he sees the ring, so insignificant, so lovely on the wounded hand. He places his hand under hers, and she turns her hand to hold his, the fingers small and warm in the grooves of his own, the imperfection is a grace to him, he thinks, a strength he has needed all his life.

"Where are you?" he asks.

"I am with you," she answers.

In the half-light he beholds his daughter's face, the sweet smell of vanilla quiet in her breathing, the sounds she makes, cooing as she drifts sleepy in her mother's arms, and he sees that this then is the song to which every dream is tethered, a light divine and holy that gathers all hope in his hands, and he reaches out to his wife and cradles her head, and traces her lips with the tips of his fingers, and to them both before he sleeps he whispers, My darling. My love.

Ted

Paul Maliszewski

June 24, 2002

Dear President Bush,

It was break time at work, and so Ted and I drove our forklifts over to the far corner of the lot and made ourselves unavailable and hard to find. The lot changes over time, and forklift operators like Ted and I do the changing. We shift pallets. We unload trucks and stack the merchandise high. We move things around. Product comes in, and product goes out. Sometimes we have a lot of rectangular terra cotta planters on hand. Sometimes we have a lot of ceramic pots. One month it'll be stone cupids wherever I look; the next it'll be gnomes or frogs or peasant boys walking hand in hand with peasant girls. Whatever we have on hand, whatever the merchandise, we call it "shit," as in "Move that shit off that truck and over to section C," or "That shit over there's been marked down," or "I told you to get that shit ready for pick-up at three."

Today Ted and I sat on a piece of shit that resembled a large fountain. We sat on the rim, which was encircled by several large fish cast in concrete. The fish had swollen lips that were parted in such a way that the lips seemed almost human and the fish capable of speech. The fish were made to spit water in high arcs when the fountain was turned on.

Ted unwrapped a candy bar and offered me part. I shook my head and said, "No thanks."

Ted stuffed the wrapper into the mouth of one of the fish and started patting down his pockets, looking for his cigarettes.

"You okay?" he said.

I didn't know if I was okay or not and said as much. How does anyone know really whether they're okay or not? This was the day I woke up from all those mugging dreams I told you about, sir. I'd lived through a whole crime wave in my sleep, and so I felt jumpy, startled by noise, out of sorts, basically. Being awake offered no measure of solace, as ordinary objects and everyday occurrences had, in the night, while I slept, acquired an air of distinct menace. Even the fish on the fountain, with their empty eyes and open mouths, possessed menace.

"What gives?" Ted said.

"I just had all these bad dreams last night," I said. "No big deal."

Ted took a nibble from his candy bar and looked out across the lot as he chewed. "What sort of dreams?" he said.

"I don't know," I said. "It's really not a big deal."

Ted finished his candy bar, looked at his fingers, glanced around for someplace to wipe them, and then ran them back and forth over the legs of his pants. "Are we talking you had yourself a lot of gay sex or something?"

"No," I said, "we're not talking."

"I mean, against your will, of course," Ted said.

I didn't say anything. The fish looked on, their mouths hanging open, their eyes blank, their expressions dumb.

"As in you were forced," Ted said. He shook a cigarette loose from the pack, stuck it behind his ear and then started searching in his pockets for his lighter.

"I was in this parking garage," I said.

"Sounds gritty," Ted said. "And urban."

"There were all these muggings. It was like every time I turned a corner somebody was getting mugged. And I watched it happen a while," I said. "Because I wasn't sure what was going on, you know?"

Ted nodded.

"I knew I should step in," I said. "I knew I had to stop the muggings from happening."

"Right," Ted said.

"So I stepped in," I said. "I basically stopped them from happening."

"Those don't sound like bad dreams," Ted said.

"I dreamt of this awful place with all this violent crime," I said. "That's no way to spend the night.

"Right," Ted said, "but you were the hero."

I shrugged my shoulders and gripped one of the fish around the middle. It was loose, and I knew I could have shaken it free. I could have yanked it right off the fountain, but instead I just rocked the fish back and forth. I heard the underside of its body, its belly, start to crumble and turn to dust.

"I got beat up pretty bad," I said. "There were cuts and bruises on my arms. My clothing was ripped and torn. I had abrasions on my leg. And contusions–"

"What are contusions?" Ted said. "I always wondered about that."

"They're like bumps," I said. "Bumps deep down in the skin, close to the bone, I think. I don't know, Ted. I don't know what contusions are, exactly, but I'm sure I had them."

"You shouldn't have tried to stop the muggings," Ted said.

"I had to do something."

"They say you should always call for help. Don't get personally involved, get the authorities. Let them handle it. That's what they always tell you to do."

I asked Ted if it wasn't time for us to get back to work.

"My grandmother got mugged one time," he said. "I was young. I was in junior high school, I guess, and we were visiting her. It was the summer. My family always visited my grandmother in the summer. This was my mom's mom. She lived in New York State, outside of Buffalo. Anyway, it was evening and she wanted to take her walk—she took a walk every evening—and she asked me if I wanted to come with her. I had to say yes. The truth of the matter was I didn't want to go for a walk. I'd much rather have sat in her living room and watched television. My grandmother got Canadian channels. She had a big antenna on her roof, and you could make it turn by adjusting a dial on top of the television set. The dial was mounted to a console—it took up most of the top of her television, and her television was not small. Today the whole thing—console, dial, everything—would be like two tiny buttons on your remote. But anyway, the dial was marked around its perimeter with all the different channels, and mostly they were clustered in a couple of directions, southwest and due east. What I liked to do was sweep the antenna through the empty space on the dial. That's how I found the Canadian channels. There were four of them in all, six if you count the ones that didn't come in so well. My grandmother painted the numbers of the new channels on the console with her nail polish. Her nail polish was pearl-colored. The console was brown. It was made to look like wood—you know, the way all plastic used to be made to look like wood. I would have loved nothing more than to watch television. This was during the height of Canadian television comedy. A lot of famous comedians come from Canada, originally. I forget which ones are Canadian. I forget all their names, but they're a lot of people I'm sure you've heard of.

"My grandmother walked the same route every evening. She started off headed toward town, which was like a block or two from her house, then she went around the park in the center of town, past the firehouse, where she always stopped to say hello to the firemen. My grandfather had been a fireman for a while, and so my grandmother always did reserve a special place in her heart for them. She called them boys. When she baked us a pie, she baked an extra pie and brought it to the firehouse, for the boys. Sometimes she called them her boys. Everybody loved my grandmother's pie. It was the best, really. From the firehouse, she walked past the university, by the church, and then back home. All told, her walk took over an hour, or a little more than two Canadian comedy programs. It was a long walk. It felt long to me, and I was a kid. Time is nothing to kids. Time isn't even a consideration.

"We were somewhere between the university and the church when the mugger appeared. Old oak trees grow there on both sides of the street, and a line of tall bushes, firs, I guess, grow on the other side of one of the sidewalks, if you can picture that. We walked on the sidewalk, with the oaks to our right and the tall, bushy firs to our left. The mugger must have been hiding in the firs, waiting. My grandmother was holding her pie out before her. The firemen hadn't been in the firehouse. Nobody had been in the firehouse. The boys were at a fire, presumably. Nobody was manning the station. I was trying to walk with my grandmother in a way that made it seem to her that I was accompanying her while suggesting to everyone else—people who might drive by or jog past, say—that we weren't related, that we just happened at that moment to appear to be walking together, but that in the next moment we were just as likely to separate, as I sped up or my grandmother, inevitably, slowed down. The trick was I didn't want my grandmother to realize I was lagging behind her out of embarrassment. She had caught me before, plenty of times, in fact. She asked, 'Don't want to be seen walking next to some old coot?' My face flushed, turning red as much from her choice of words as the accuracy of her insight. So I lagged behind just a bit and feigned an interest in small bugs and a fascination with even smaller rocks. I let my mouth hang open in what I imagined to be a look of perpetual wonder, but which really just made me look retarded. I was my grandmother's budding naturalist, and she indulged my curiosity for the most part. When she got too far ahead, she called out my name. She said my name in a kind of singsong, so that Ted had two syllables: Te-ed. That's how she sounded.

"I had fallen behind on one of my fake explorations of the natural world when I heard my name. My grandmother's voice sounded weak, almost strangled, and I looked up expecting, I honestly believe, to see my grandmother dying, pressing her palms against a tree and leaning her full weight against its trunk. Instead, I saw the mugger waving a knife in front of her face. In the next few seconds—I don't even know if it was that long—I sprinted until I was even with my grandmother. Then I stopped, and then I stared. The mugger waved the knife in front of my face. I hadn't thought of what I'd do next, after running. In my mind, I hadn't got that far. I had no other move, so I did nothing. I looked at my feet and dropped my hands to my side and then reached one of my arms behind me, and held my other arm by the elbow. It's a nervous thing, I still do it, I don't know why.

"The mugger said to my grandmother, 'Give me your purse.'

"My grandmother still had her pie. She held it in front of her. She was clutching it, practically, with both hands. She said, 'I don't have any purse.'

"The mugger said, 'Don't give me that shit.' Then he must have looked and realized that she wasn't carrying a purse, or even a pocketbook. My grandmother never carried a purse when we walked, though I hadn't been aware of that until just then.

"The mugger said, 'This is fucking great.' Then he turned to me and said, 'Give me your wallet now.'

"My grandmother said, 'The boy doesn't have a wallet.'

"The mugger looked at me. I said, 'I don't have a wallet.' Then I added, 'I'm sorry.'

"I glanced at my grandmother. The pie looked like a gift or an offering in her hands. It looked all wrong.

"The mugger said, 'Jesus fuck, what's with you people? What are you, some kind of freaks? Don't any of you carry any money?'

"I felt my testicles tighten then and my penis shrink. I'll never forget that. It was such an odd feeling. My dick retracted itself up into my body like a turtle's head.

"My grandmother said, 'You can have this pie. I baked it.'

"The mugger looked at the pie and then at my grandmother and then at me. 'Is this some kind of joke?' he said.

"My grandmother and I didn't move or say one word. We were frozen, my grandmother offering her pie to this stranger, and me with my hands behind my back, wringing them, as much for the comfort of holding them as the raw energy of my nervousness.

"'I don't want your pie,' the mugger said. 'I'm not out here'—he waved the knife wildly—'I'm not out here hiding in the bushes with a fucking knife because I want some pie.'

"The mugger said, 'I mean,' but never completed his thought. He sputtered and spit and turned so mad he simply could not speak, though he did try. He jumped back into the bushes at the place where he had emerged and, just like that, he was gone.

"For a few seconds I heard nothing except the sound of his footsteps receding. He was running. Then I heard nothing. Then I heard the traffic, the cars and trucks and bikes and, of course, people, as if they all had miraculously paused for our entire ordeal, out of a sense of decorum, like an audience at a play, but then resumed their activity once our drama had concluded. Then I heard my grandmother sobbing, and I had no idea what to do. She stood there, still holding the pie out in front of her. I touched her arm tentatively, half expecting it to be very cold or very hot.

"'We should go home,' I said.

"After a moment my grandmother said, 'You're right.'

"And so, we set off walking, just as we had before. We didn't have much farther to go really.

"My grandmother said, 'I'm sorry you had to see that, at your age. I'm so sorry you had to see that.'"

Ted dropped his cigarette and ground it out with his boot. He looked over at me and kind of shrugged, as if to say, "What are you going to do."

Sir, I considered telling Ted how I had actually behaved in my dreams, how I intervened in no mugging, how I crouched behind walls and watched the crimes transpire from afar. I thought it might be some comfort to him, for me to own up to my gross inaction and propose to him then that we might now form a confederacy of the frightened, the timid, and the inappropriately silent. But I did not tell Ted. These things I kept to myself. These weaknesses I would sooner bury deep in the ground inside a metal box with a complicated lock than share with my friend.

Ted pried the crumpled up candy bar wrapper out of the fish's mouth and squeezed it in his fist, compressing it as tightly as he could. When, a moment later, he opened his hand, the wrapper expanded to its original size. Ted looked at the wrapper as if it were the most fascinating object in the world. I didn't guess he was pretending. He squeezed the wrapper again, and again, when he opened his hand, the wrapper expanded. He did this several more times, and then we resumed the workday.

Keep up the good work, sir.

Sincerely,
Harvey Strub

Search and Rescue

Gladys Swan

No moon and dark as the back of a mirror. Ahead was roiling black pitch except for the foam of the white caps. Joel checked the time: 21:30. The man they'd come in search of had been in the water for over three hours now, somewhere out in the Gulf of Mexico, drifting in a wind-driven sea. It was a puzzle, the incident that had put him there at the risk of his life: he had jumped overboard.

"That's a good one," Joel said to Martin, who'd organized the search. "Jumped or was pushed?"

"Jumped—that's what the captain said."

The captain of a shrimp boat had radioed in for help. He'd been asleep and hadn't discovered the missing crew member until he woke up, ready to begin the night's shrimping. "Where's Cochran?" he asked the crew. Overboard, they told him, apparently unconcerned.

Something had come up between him and one of the mates, who had gone after him with a knife. He'd thrown a few things together in a plastic bag and jumped overboard. Apparently figured he'd drift to shore. Only the wind had reversed.

"Right now, Martin said, "he's drifting toward Texas. I hope it's a comfort to him."

"Must have been pretty ugly if he was willing to jump."

"So I figure."

Joel had come as soon as he'd gotten the call. Fifteen minutes later he was down at the dock where Martin and Alex were waiting for him. They were to take Martin's boat out. "Alex, let Joel up here by me," Martin had said. "He's got the best pair of eyes."

"That's for sure," Alex said. "When I was in the army, I had as good a pair of eyes as anybody—I was a crack shot. Now I can't see worth shit."

They arranged themselves in Martin's boat, Alex taking in the lines as Martin started the motor. Joel couldn't have said exactly why he had to go on these occasions when called upon by the Coast Guard Auxiliary, this time interrupting a canasta game with their pleasant neighbors whom his wife, Ellen, had invited over.

"I hope it's worth it," she said when he kissed her, about to depart, and reminded him he was no youngster.

A sense of mission propelled him. Even the risks seemed some part of the compensation. He didn't speak of the possible dangers, some you could hardly predict. Before his time, a couple of the rescue missions had tangled with drug runners; in one case, the rescuer had been lured into a trap, had his boat stolen out from under him and was drowned for his pains. You couldn't just approach a boat without suspicion any more.

No, he didn't have to expose himself to this sort of risk. Yet something compelled him even more than a strong sense of dedication. Enough to bring him out in any weather and take him through all the rounds of study—rules and regulations, the intricacies of navigation. Often he wasn't in bed till past midnight. But the effort gave him satisfaction, got his mind into a discipline—definite ways of doing things, intricate calculations. He liked knowing things, though it wouldn't have occurred to him to think of himself as a man looking for knowledge. He saw himself as a practical man who enjoyed challenges.

So here they were together, the three of them bent on a simple common purpose—to take their know-how and save a man from drowning. He watched as Martin navigated the unmarked channel through Stump Pass, with caution, though he knew the way with sure instinct. Joel admired the way Martin knew things. Alex was a good one to have along—just tell him what to do, and he'd do it. Right as rain. But Joel's hat went off to Martin, a born leader, the natural choice to head up their flotilla. Theirs was the only one whose boats went out at night. There was nothing Martin couldn't tell you about handling a boat, and what you might expect in the bays and canals, along with shifting channels and reefs. He was in his late sixties, six years older than Joel, with a craggy, weathered face, but still quick-moving and agile. He lived alone now that his wife was gone, and spent most of his time around the dock, talking, gossiping, offering information and advice to novices. Occasionally, he gave himself a holiday and went out to fish, gave away the fish afterwards. He seemed to know everybody up and down the west coast of Florida who owned a boat.

"I think we're going to be in for some rain before it's over," Martin said. "See those clouds moving in over there?"

"Won't be good for our man if it storms," Alex said.

Nor for us, Joel thought. "So why does it have to be you?" he could hear Ellen saying. "You could just say you're busy—there are others."

True, he could have passed, but it wouldn't have set right. He'd have brooded over it, maybe even felt a kind of betrayal.

He felt some remote kinship to those who didn't know what was out there–or who'd had bad luck. Even to those who toyed with and tried to ignore things that he and Martin and the others knew deep down couldn't be trifled with. The ones that had to be saved from themselves.

Like the couple that got hung up at Stump Pass. "Well, here's the famous scene," Joel said, as they skirted the reef.

"Dumb idiots," Martin said. "Think they can do anything. Like you don't have to know shit."

Rich enough to think they could buy their way through any danger, apparently–the couple from Tennessee, newly retired to Florida. They'd put big bucks into a catamaran. No previous sailing experience. They'd just headed out into Tampa Bay, near sunset at that, to sail down to Manasota Key to visit the woman's sister. As well as facing the darkness, they had to steer through Stump Pass, the unmarked channel Martin took such caution in, part of local knowledge but dangerous for newcomers. They'd missed the channel and beached 500 yards south. Broken the rudder. Weather turning ugly, waves three to four feet high.

What a scene when Joel and Martin arrived: the woman beating on her husband, yelling, scared shitless, literally. Joel figured he had the tougher assignment, getting her back to land while others merely had to work to get the catamaran off the reef and back to the dock.

They were now out in open water. In the distance, a streak of lightning cut across the sky. "Boy, he certainly picked a great night to be drifting around the Gulf," Martin said. "Let's hope we can do something fast."

They'd set the Global Positioning System, figured the time and course the fellow must have drifted. Martin set his course in that direction—to where he'd be . . . If there was anything left of him to find.

This was Joel's first real search and rescue mission. And though he'd done various services to boat owners whose motors had stalled or who'd run out of gas, somehow the image of a man drifting in hostile waters brought back to him another image with unequaled vividness. In another sea under a brilliant sun when their landing craft had been shot out from under them in the Marianas. The explosion ripping things apart—and there they were, he and his buddy, Graham, with how many others lost. But all you could do was keep moving—toward the destroyer that had waited in the distance and was moving toward them. That was what they had to get to—close enough to be spotted and picked up. Exhausting, swimming in those waves. Now and then he'd paused to catch his breath and look back to see if Graham was with him. Only Graham, lagging behind, hadn't made it.

Now it was a question of whether this man would be lost or saved. They were in the vicinity, ready to begin the search course. Joel went to stand in the bow of the boat with his search light on the water, Martin steering, Alex was on hand to do whatever was needed—to throw the man a life line, if they found him.

"See anything?" Martin yelled over the motor.

"Just waves," Joel yelled back. Three-foot waves now. They hadn't been that high when he and Graham were swimming for their lives. How long could a man survive in these waves, this wind? Intently they searched the water.

Something caught Joel's attention. He couldn't be sure, but the light had glanced on something bobbing in the water. "Hey, hold it there. I see something in the trough of that wave." Joel pointed down.

Martin squinted. "You've got a helluva pair of eyes all right."

While Martin manoeuvered the boat, Joel took the net from Alex, reached out and scooped up a plastic bag. Inside were three packs of cigarettes and a plug of Copenhagen.

"Looks like we've hit the territory," Martin said. He radioed the shrimp boat." Your man a smoker?"

"That's right," came the answer. "GPC Cigarettes."

"He doesn't exactly go for class," Martin said. "But he's got the necessities." Then he radioed the Coast Guard cutter and reported their position and what they'd found. The boat would be on its way.

"We can do a little looking till they get here," Martin said. "Think I'll cut the motor for a minute or two."

Joel continued to shine the light on the water as the boat drifted. By now there were five miles out in the Gulf. It was 22:30, and the sky was leaden. Suddenly there he was, hardly a hundred yards away, waving his arms, yelling for all he was worth.

Martin started the motor, and they approached him slowly. When they were close enough, Alex threw him a life ring, and they hauled in the line. While Martin kept the boat steady, they pulled him over the side.

Gasping and dripping, the fellow sat leaning against the side. "Mighty grateful," he kept saying. "Mighty grateful." He was a thin, wiry man, with a fringe of dark hair around a bald spot, and sharp, unshaven face. There were only a handful of teeth in his head, a snaggle tooth in front. "Cochran," he said, extending a hand to all of them in turn, "J.R. Cochran. I do mighty appreciate it."

"You're a lucky man," Martin said.

"Don't I know it," the fellow said. "I figured I was a goner when that wind shifted."

They were looking down at his bare legs. He'd pulled off his pants to inflate them. They lay to one side like bedraggled wings. It was heavy shark water. Probably the three-foot waves had been in his favor. But if the sharks didn't get him, he'd have been done in eventually by hypothermia. "You just beat the weather," Martin said. "It looks like a storm's coming in from the south."

They were more than glad when the cutter arrived. They'd put a blanket around the man, but he couldn't stop shivering. He didn't have enough teeth to chatter. Martin pulled up alongside the cutter, and Alex took the line to link them together. Joel and Martin helped the fellow mount the ladder while Alex took the wheel.

"You've done a helluva job," the captain told them, when they'd come aboard. He was a young man, in his mid-thirties perhaps, strongly built, spiffy in his uniform. "You've saved a life. You'll get a citation for this."

One of the crew helped the fellow inside the cabin and another went off for dry clothes.

They stood by while the captain radioed the shrimp boat. "We've got your man—you want him back?"

"I would take him," the skipper radioed back. "I'm shorthanded, God knows, but my crew won't have him."

When the fellow returned, in dark pants and sweatshirt, he'd perked up a bit, tried to joke a little. "Well, at least I wasn't shark bait this time."

He was luckier than he knew, Joel thought.

"Man, I don't want to go back," he said, when the captain gave him the skipper's message. "Hell, I don't want to have to do this all over again."

"Where do you live?" the captain asked him.

"Don't have no address," he said. "Come over from west Texas—come down here to get me some work. Shrimping's not my line." He grinned.

Must have been in a few brawls along the way—so it looked. Or else he'd managed to avoid a dentist all his life. Joel wondered how often he'd been in such a fix, on the borderline, right where you could step over the edge. Here was a man, he figured, who'd always squeaked by, each time getting thinner pickings, and emerging a little worse for the wear. Like some wharf rat.

"You can just put me ashore anywhere. I won't give you any more trouble."

The Coast Guard would take him in. Martin and Joel returned to their boat, where Alex was waiting for them. The cutter took off, and they were free to head back.

"I think we'll just beat that storm," Martin said.

"Won't be in bed till after 1:30," Alex said. "But we got him."

"Yeah," Martin said. "We saved his worthless hide."

"Must be some kind of drifter," Alex said.

"It figures," Martin said, "considering where we found him."

"Wonder why he had to jump," Joel said. "Did he cheat somebody at cards? Try to put the make on one of the crew?"

"Doesn't matter," Martin said. "Just check 'All of the above.'" Did you get a good look at him? That man's never done a decent thing in his life. Probably tied tin cans on dogs' tails, beat up his wife every night and screwed his kids—both sexes. The sharks might as well have had him."

"But we did the job," Alex said, refusing to lose sight of that. "We did the calculations, pin-pointed the spot, and, by God, we found him. That's something."

For a moment Joel felt it as well—they'd saved a life. Gone out to the edge where life hung in the balance and snatched somebody back. They'd get a citation. Then he remembered the last time he'd turned around and seen Graham waving to him, "Goodbye," he yelled and went under. Joel had hung there in the water, unable to move, they'd been swimming so long.

It had preyed on him for years. He'd never been able to get rid of the sense he lived on the surface of another's death, as though it had become the reference point for everything he lived, doing it as much for Graham as for himself. As though there were a debt to be paid. Marriage, the kids—all of it. He hadn't been able to escape the sense that he wasn't alone in his life.

"You certainly have a high opinion of your fellow man," Alex was saying to Martin.

"Hell, you could see it in his eyes. They spelled trouble."

"I wonder if they'll check to see if he has a record."

"I'll wager he doesn't," Martin said. "There's a kind of cunning that can sneak around the law. Oh, well—all in a night's work."

"More than that," Alex insisted. "We figured it out—we did it right."

Joel took over the wheel—he could see Martin was tired. He himself was wide-awake and excited. You've saved a life. They'd done that. There on the edge, they'd snatched somebody back. We saved his worthless hide. The sharks might as well have had him. He began to feel a curious letdown as he steered through the dark waves.

Was this what he'd been aching to find out all these years? That the man who'd stood before him was not, could never be, any substitute for Graham, and that he'd never be any closer to the answer—why one man lived and another perished.

Just call it dumb luck. Like the luck that had saved him once on gangway watch. Graham had come up to replace him, and he'd handed Graham the forty-five automatic, the issue they carried. Graham had gone through the usual procedure: pressed the magazine release, pulled back the slide and moved the clip. He looked into the action, pushed back the slide and held up the gun, pointing right at Joel. "Suppose it was loaded," he said, pulling the trigger. A bullet whizzed past Joel's head, missing him by an inch. A single bullet had been in the chamber, pulled off by the extractor. Graham hadn't looked in the chamber. Afterwards, Graham sat and trembled for half an hour.

It had happened so quickly Joel hadn't had time to react. Then he laughed. Pure nerves.

Even at the outset, they'd been bound to one another by matters of life and death. As were the three of them here. Anything could have happened, could happen still. A high wind, the storm dropping in on them, an error of calculation. It was exactly this, the tension on the border that drew him. Drew him toward those with the same unspoken predilection.

Now he couldn't wait to get back. He wouldn't be able to sleep that night. He'd be replaying the whole venture, going back over every detail a dozen times. He would see the shadowy figure drifting there in the dark water, waving his arms in the face of rescue, just when his chances had all but gone bad. Nothing in sea or sky to give him the slightest heed, except the sharks. Waiting, holding onto whatever would allow him to exist, to live, while that other shadow hung in the background unable to die.

Postcards from the Flood

Paul Griffiths

NOAH:

When the Lord comes to you and says, I am about to put an end to all flesh for the earth is filled with lawlessness, how do you respond? It's not like you've asked for this information. The only reason you came outside was to have a smoke; your wife, asleep after making love, has a sensitive nose. You're just being courteous, a good husband—it's the Lord who interrupts.

Do you answer, Yes sir! Oh, very good. That's a fine idea, sir. Shall I be perishing as well? You love the people of this town. You are well-respected in their eyes: a judge, landholder, and father of three. Hearing this news sends the pipe tumbling from your mouth; your face grows wet with tears. To picture everyone dead—the corpses stinking to high heaven—well, it just rips at your heart.

You might plead, There must still be ten good people in the world. The Lord insists, I am surely going to destroy them.

If you can't talk Him out of it, why is He bothering to say anything at all? A chill runs up the back of your legs. You are the Lord's chosen instrument, favored in his sight. Perhaps he will carry out his punishment through you. If the Hidden One—who must watch men fouling men, men fouling beasts—if He sees evil lurking in human hearts, how much worse a torment might He devise?

So you beg for your wife. She is tender, kind, dim-witted but sincere. You have experience with the law; you make your case, Surely one person cannot administrate the whole earth. It is not good for man to be alone.

You remind the Lord of your three boys: Shem, skilled with hammer and wood; Ham, who can navigate the waters of the Tigris blind; Japeth, the youngest and your favorite, a shepherd without equal—the flocks have nearly doubled under his care. You are their father, having obeyed the decree to fill the earth, unaware this reversal lay ahead.

Yet even as you are talking, your mind begins to wander. You imagine a world of only your family. You imagine your sons—lonely, virile—watching their mother, the last woman on earth, rinse her clothes by a stream. Their red-rimmed eyes follow your wife's hand pouring water over her head to cool herself . . . so you beg for the boys' wives. They're whores, really. Hookers purchased for an evening who stayed on because your fields were high with grain in a year of famine. For these three—not your flesh but the very target of the Lord's anger—you plead, even for them.

And, when you have finished? As the last words leave your lips? The night is still as a frozen lake. You watch the slow drift of the stars turned by unseen hands. The fire has gone out; its smoke, tinny with the odor of green wood, traces a path as it disappears into the sky. Your ears ring with the sound of your own shallow breath.

When the Lord says, Build yourself an ark of gopher wood, you fall on your face. You pour handfuls of dirt down your throat. You bloody your knees in supplication. You can't ask for everyone.

What you do is show gratitude. And weep.

HAM:
He was a drunk! It wasn't something we talked about. You have to understand. We were meant to be a model family. But the old man couldn't go a week without a tipple. On the third day of the deluge, he passed out on the ark's up-most deck. We had barely begun to lift him off the ground and already the backs of his legs were darkened with shit—at six hundred! A grown man!

I washed him off with a rag, then rinsed the floor. And when he sobered up, did he thank me? No, he was embarrassed I had seen him naked. He sent me deep below, shamefaced, to sweep the stalls of the pigs.

So by the time we landed and got the first good harvest and I found him asleep outside his tent, I was cautious. My wife was with me, she can attest to this. Our plan was simply to shove him into bed—my mother couldn't do it by herself anymore. This was the first bender he'd been on in months; he was drinking to forget. Every night on the ark—his room was next to mine—he would cry himself to sleep.

When we rolled him over, we discovered his robes were open. My wife first noticed Dad's member and let out a little gasp. I didn't want to look, but my wife made me clean off the old man. And do you know what the fool had done? He'd clipped the skin of his own root. It looked like a thumb with the fingernail torn off, bloody, swollen. The sharpened rock was still in his hand.

My wife had once seen a man so trimmed. He was from the very end of the earth with skin the color of baked clay. He would visit her, cover her face with veils and address her in unfamiliar tongue by an unknown woman's name.

"This isn't right," I said. I refused to put him in bed. I wanted to show my brothers, Here's another of our father's delusions. I was trying to protect our family, you have to understand. The old man was getting reckless. His character had grown weak. Soon, I feared, he'd be taking the knife to us.

YHWH
(Declined to be interviewed.)

JAPETH'S WIFE:
Noah's wife rounded up the girls and I, the partner of her favorite, she gave the worst of the lot: the unclean beasts of the field. (The boys certainly weren't going to touch them.) "I don't even know what they are!" I cried. It was no lie. I was from a good clan up north.

Mummy made me fashion a net out of my prettiest scarf. "You won't need it where we're going," she said with a snort.

"There will still be parties," I said, between tears. My birthday was coming up, for example, before the rain was due. Surely they wouldn't forget?

"Useless," Mummy said. She spit into the dust.

I was lonely before we left. Shem had an ox for a wife; she couldn't appreciate the fine texture of silk. She spent her time cooking and eating. Shem devised a fake wall in the ark to store her dried meats. Ham's wife, who hated me as much as Shem's wife did, starved herself thin. All she ate was the attention of men. The idea that we'd be the only ones left alive! Well, she ground her teeth in her sleep. Soon she would become the most beautiful woman on the planet, but who would care?

I put the animal-catching off and invited my friends over for tea. We spent the afternoon applying rouge to our cheekbones. It was all the rage in town. Bunny was braiding my hair when I let slip about the ark.

She laughed it off. "My father says it's impossible. He can see the rains are coming too, but to cover the whole earth?" Her father was the high priest of a very important temple. "Who would the gods get to serve them? They need meat, honey, wine. They're too greedy for that."

I rubbed some cream over my hands. She didn't understand the Lord. I didn't either, exactly.

"Besides," Bunny continued, "We have the fishing boat and our house in the mountains." She checked a nail. "It'll be fine."

From my window, I could see the sky darkening.

I spent days in my bedroom, crying about my lost friends. My husband Japeth, the goody-goody, was no help. He had tender hands and a woman's pretty face but when you got right down to it, he had the same cold heart as his brothers.

"It's not like they don't deserve it," he said, trying to comfort me. At our wedding, we had a receiving line that stretched out beyond what the eye could see. It two took hours just to say thank you to all the people who attended. And the gifts? To think they would be destroyed too! I was inconsolable.

The day before the rains began, Mummy came to me in a fit of rage. "You greedy little girl," she cried. "You haven't gathered a single animal!" She grabbed me by the ear and dragged me out.

I could see the rotting teeth in the back of her mouth. She said, "If you don't get them on the boat, I will leave you to die."

I couldn't help it. I wet myself with fear.

"You fool!" She hit me upside the head. "They'll smell you coming now!"

She pushed me toward the thicket where my brothers-in-law felled game. I had to find something, quickly, to curry favor with the woman. I was desperate—I didn't want to die! My throat was raw but even still, I cried out the name of every god I knew. "Please, please, please, send me unclean beasts!"

Then I heard a rustle in the brush nearby. "Hello?" I said. "Who's there?" I stepped over a fallen tree and saw a beast I could not name. It appeared to be one long muscle: a green worm, except stronger, larger, with eyes that fixed on me, almost in recognition. How curious! It was making an odd noise, *pitter-patter, pitter-patter*, as if a child whistling.

Its tongue darted in and out of its mouth, but that didn't account for the sound. I leaned down and put my ear by its lips. Yes, they were words, gentle words. The beast was speaking! "A gift from the gods!" I cried. "They answered my prayers!" And to think, foolish Mummy wanted me to get the unclean animals. Well, I decided not to tell them about it right away. Why give them the satisfaction? But I knew—I was absolutely sure—such a marvelous creature had to make onto the ark. How boring would the new world be without it? Yes, I decided, I would keep it for a pet and surprise them all.

The Mistress of *Leche* Island

Melanie Conroy-Goldman

It takes Doug a half an hour to prepare Ella for lovemaking. Make love, take care. The words rhyme in their bed. Before they can proceed with their coupling, he must shim her, strap her, shift bone into careful alignment with bone. But, he has had practice. He's had two years to learn which kind of bending injures, and which she can just manage. And now, he completes the operation with all the confidence of his study. It is a bright morning, the sun already pressing its heat against the drawn yellow curtains. Lying perfectly still beneath his precise, surgical thrusts, Ella allows herself a tiny, private smile. His confidence is well-earned: she feels almost nothing.

She used to like a fast fuck, skirt around her ankles, shirt pulled up to the neck. She liked the force and mimed urgency of it, the adulterer's thrill. But also, she liked its efficiency. At twenty-five, she'd come to see sex as a service she performed for her body. The need was there; she could not dispense with it altogether. But she could finish with Doug, could be back at her desk in ten minutes. Doug would have preferred, she knew even then, a different sort of love. He was languorous and picky, partial to excruciating foreplay. Now, he gets his way. Ella can do nothing quickly. Even her lightning temper has had to become measured and awkward.

Though technically still newlyweds, Ella and Doug keep no wedding photos. Ella feels—how would she put it?—that such objects belong to a different sort of marriage. Before the injury (car crash, Ella's fault), she had been something of an itinerant. She followed jobs to unlikely places, picked up lovers as convenient, on her way to bigger things. Already, at twenty-five, her column was in limited syndication, and she fielded regular inquiries from as important markets as Chicago or D.C. Doug, like the newspaper gig in Scottsdale, would be a fine way to spend a few months, maybe a year. And he had understood his position. As he understands now: if it hadn't been for the accident, they never would have married.

Doug had been a dreamier sort of person than Ella; the things he tried to do went mysteriously wrong. Twice by the time she met him, Doug had gotten himself fired, and days into their relationship, he quit a third job. He was a man who could disappear for weeks, cease opening mail, bloat and gain weight. When he finally wrested himself from such a depression, it would be with a sudden burst of activity, so that he seemed constantly behind, constantly struggling to catch up. Now, it is different. Now, it is Doug who is always first, Ella who lags.

Her eyes shutter open just as he finishes, and she captures a brief frame of him. Taut, glazed with sweat, then gone. She can't turn her head to follow his movement. Always, the pain hovers at the edge of her. Ella knows it would be less intense if she kept up with her physical therapy, but she has never been good at being bad at things. She knows there's a trick to it, failing. Other people can bowl at sixty or bang into a bumper without trauma, but Ella has never had this ability. At least now, no one asks her to go bowling. They find other things to want from her.

"Was that better?" Doug asks from beyond her field of vision. "I think that was better." He means because he's ejaculated. These days, he often doesn't. Which makes sense. No amount of kindness can manufacture pleasure and her atrophied legs and loosening flesh can do little to inspire him.

"Maybe that was it," she says. "Maybe we've done it."

Theoretically, they are trying to have a baby. The doctors have cautioned them. Even if Ella is still fertile, paralysis brings countless complications to pregnancy. But Ella doesn't worry. She has an instinct that they can't do it, and this makes it possible for her to agree to try. And, in the meantime, the slim chance she's wrong adds a measure of uncertainty, a little palpitation of warmth to their sex life.

"Do you want to sit up?" Doug asks. "Get dressed?"

"You shower," she tells him. "I'll manage."

He looks surprised. The physical therapists insist that minor pain is salutary, that Ella should push. But until very recently, she has largely ignored this advice.

"I'm fine," she tells Doug, but she doesn't protest when he shifts her torso up to the wall and places a pillow beside her.

Between the chair and the modified car, she has a tiny portion of independence. If she arranges ahead of time for her doctor or her editor to meet her on the curb, Ella can keep an appointment. But without such planning, the only place she can go by herself is the Coffee Corral, an unremarkable café set in the parking lot of a strip mall. The Corral offers a mediocre cup, but also Sheryl, a charity-minded counter girl who is strong enough to heave Ella from the car to the chair. Scottsdale, Doug frequently reminds Ella, is the most accessible city in America. But Ella dreads the averted faces of commuters as a wheelchair bus slows, the unramped corner where she would have to beg rescue from a passer-by. Still, two years after the accident, she cannot bear to ask for consideration from strangers. Perhaps, if she had been the kind of person who gave help before, she would feel differently. But she believes that most people share her former impatience for the bus's deflating tires, or the cane-tapping woman at the elevator.

Ella has managed to dress herself and get herself into the chair by the time Doug emerges from the shower. He still thinks of himself as that flabby twenty-something, but he has become strong lifting her, aged well in the Arizona sun. It's her secret, his body, one of the few pleasures. She tugs at his towel as he passes, and he yanks back, shaking his head. "You," he scolds, bending to kiss her. And there it is, even now, real affection between them, something besides dependence and duty.

He touches the chair, her buttoned shirt. "You have an appointment? I didn't remember."

"Physical therapy," Ella answers, "And then, also, Sheryl gets on at one. I might write for a while." This last is a question, sort of. Doug does not like that she spends so much time, does such good work elsewhere. And Ella cannot explain why she prefers the little shop, how even his silence distracts her. But Doug also has to agree to any plan that involves a hospital visit. He attributes her sudden use of therapy to their pregnancy efforts, a desire to be strong for the baby.

"If that's OK," she says.

He squeezes her shoulder delicately, re-tucks his towel, and unlocks the door. "You good to the lobby? You want me to call Pedro?"

"I'm good," she says. "Thank you."

"Love you," he answers from behind the closing door.

*

Saguaro Junction is a battered complex of faux-Tudor buildings that fan out from a small, green pool. It is not, obviously, a hospital, not a doctor's office. And it is not the sort of place the Ella of two years ago would ever have found herself. Indeed, there is part of her that feels surprised when she turns off the highway as if the left were involuntary. But then, she navigates the identical units with confidence, and recognizes the man waiting outside #14. She pulls into his driveway, lets her mock incredulity and false confusion fall away.

The man is Louis, a balding, fleshy person in a pale blue running suit. He ducks his head in greeting, then scurries round to Ella's side of the car, pulls open the door before she has even stopped the engine.

"Emma," he says. "I thought you wouldn't come."

"You always think that," Ella answers.

Louis does not know her real name. Sheryl, who had introduced them at the Coffee Corral, had been nervous, had known from the start that the two of them meeting was a bad idea. But Louis was Sheryl's boss, her husband's boss, and in this economy, you couldn't afford to be a difficult employee. So she'd made the mistake, given Ella's pseudonym—the one she used for her books— as if a slip of the tongue.

"Just as well," Ella told her. And now, Ella is grateful for the extra layer of protection, the wall of an error between Louis and the rest of her life. When, eventually, Ella ends her visits to Saguaro Junction (as she should have already; why has she not?), it will be as if Louis never existed.

Today, as on previous occasions, Ella leaves her wheelchair in the car. Inside, for the things they do, she will have no need for the chair. Louis carries her into the apartment, sets her on the sofa, and Ella pretends not to notice the sweat breaking on his forehead, the momentary stagger. He stands back, catches his breath.

"Do you want a drink?"

Ella is not supposed to have alcohol, because of the medication, but with Louis she likes to have something strong. "Make sure it's cold," she says.

He takes a few steps towards the kitchen, but stops suddenly, as if reaching the choke point on an invisible leash, then he's turning, kneeling in front of her, pushing up her skirt.

"God," he says, as though stunned with wonder. "God."

Her legs are pale, flaccid, but slim, the thickness of an ordinary person's arms. And, though they are whole, there is something unfinished, truncated-looking about them. Ella thinks of a sculptor she had once modeled for, the way Ella had looked in wet gray clay. Still, even now, it is hard for her to believe something she can't feel is her, shares the same blood that reddens her lips.

For a moment, Louis remains mesmerized, but then he sets upon her, as if she were edible, as if trying to break through to some core. He pops a button, tears a seam, breaks the clasp of her necklace. The glint of aquamarine and gold is lost in the Salvation-Army brown of his sofa. And then, his half-erect cock, soft flesh against flesh, the searing pleasure.

With Louis, there is no brace, no care taken. Ella aches for hours after visiting him, her spine a shot of pain, her weak arms numb. The doctors tell her to stop anything which makes her lose sensation. The tingle could become paralysis, and she could lose the remaining limbs, too. But with Louis, she will not stop. She may cry out. He likes that, the little note of fear. Though she only makes noise when he reaches her. She will never fake the hurt for Louis. Faking is for her husband.

She could fit the conversations she's had with Louis onto one side of a cassette, but she thinks she's learned what she needs from objects in his apartment. On top of the TV is a stack of pornos, a pile of rinsed frozen dinner trays. To these he has added a collection of Ella's books, a pink box containing the lipstick-printed napkin, and hairpins that have lodged in his sofa during her visits. What this tells her is that Louis is a man satisfied with very little, with other people's trash. Which suits Ella nicely.

Afterwards, Ella has Louis carry her to the car. He lingers beside her open door, watching as she fixes her lipstick, pins closed a busted seam. In less than a minute, she can snap their afternoon shut. She gives her lover a distant, almost polite smile, and reaches out to slam the car door. It catches. Louis is holding it open.

"But I need to ask you something first."

Ella pulls on the door again, releases it, then turns the key. "Can't it wait?"

"About Buzzy," Louis says. "I wanted your advice."

Buzzy. Out of context, the person attached to the name eludes her for a moment, and then she thinks: the Coffee Corral. Sheryl's husband. He is a big, good-looking guy whom Ella has encountered occasionally as he ferries milk and paper cups from the warehouse store. He'd been hired as a stop-gap measure, after each of the accounts with the three local distributors had lapsed. More often, Ella encounters his absence in the form of rinsed paper cups, of reconstituted powdered milk, and of Sheryl, pleading quietly on the store telephone.

"I've never had an employee, Louis. I'm sure I can't be very helpful." Ella is much smarter than Louis, usually an advantage. But today, his murky logic is eluding her. What is he angling at?

"You're probably right," Louis says, but he keeps his hand on the door. "I'm almost decided on firing him, anyway."

Ella is visited by an image of Sheryl after closing time: literally on her knees, bleaching down the floor. It is on this scene that

Louis will sweep in, empty out the register, on his way to the Indian casino. And the next morning, Sheryl will be the one to face the vendors and their bills. It's nowhere near worth the eight dollars an hour. Sympathetic customers offer her work in their real estate offices, medical parks, on a regular basis. More money, half the grief. But with Buzzy's salary, the money is almost a living, and this is why they're stuck. Unlike his wife, Buzzy couldn't get a job elsewhere. His petty crime–check kiting, or something equally benign–earned him just eight months in the pen. But since an ugly murder three years earlier, regular background checks are standard practice in Scottsdale. And no one hires thieves.

"Yeah," Louis repeats. "I think I'm going to fire him."

"Don't be ridiculous," Ella says. "If you fire Buzzy, you'll lose Sheryl. You know you can't run the shop without her."

"You want me to keep him?" Louis says. "Because you know I'd do what you told me. I'd do anything you said."

Ella almost laughs. Louis is trying to manipulate her.

"Oh, no. Don't put this on me. I'm not involved."

He steps back a fraction, grip loosening on the door handle and Ella, seeing her advantage, slams the door. You don't take favors from a man like Louis, not on someone else's behalf.

Later, she will think back to this moment, to her non-hesitation before his offer. It will seem to her the map of what came after, the tunnel point to a story about her which she will have to tell later. Now, however, she only turns the key in the ignition, and gives him a dismissive little wave.

"I'll see you soon," she mouths through the closed door.

By the time she reaches the Junction gate, she has stowed the afternoon away in a secret fold of her brain. It is not only that she believes she will never see him again, but that she no longer believes in him at all.

*

"The Mistress of Faraway Island"

All afternoon, Belinda kept making excuses to be near the customers at table four. They were both tall, blond, and dressed in crisp linen, a typical Los Angeles couple. What could they be doing in White Station?

"Maintaining an affair is simple, really," said the woman to the man. "You must close your mind to it. When you arrive at the motel, it must be as a surprise to you. When you leave, you must forget it utterly. Keep this in mind, and you will never be discovered."

"Easier said, my wife, than done," the man replied.

Belinda gasped and dropped her eyes. How could a woman speak that way to her husband? Her response must have been audible. When she looked up again, they were both staring.

"Come over here, my dear," said the woman. "No, don't worry about your boss. Come sit down."

*

It is dim in the Coffee Corral. Scott, the new counter boy, chats with the only other customer in the place, a thin adolescent who covers her mouth when she smiles.

Sheryl wheels Ella to her table, and then, to Ella's dismay, pulls up a chair and sits down. Sheryl is wearing one of her church retreat tee-shirts. Life is Fragile–Handle with Prayer. It is stretched at the waist, where her fast-food stomach bulges. Her face, as usual, is flushed with the heat. An angelic sheen of sweat lights her brow. "You're late today. You know my shift is almost over."

"I like it in the afternoon," Ella says. "It's so quiet."

Sheryl glances around the empty shop, then lowers her voice to just above a whisper. "You've been with Louis, haven't you?"

"And you don't have a break now. You just took one."

"So what?" Sheryl's voice settles back to its ordinary tone of dull peevishness. "Scott left a sinkful of dishes and the decaf bin, like, totally empty. I spent an hour and a half, during the morning rush, getting ready to open. I deserve a little extra."

"Then I'm supposed to get my own coffee?"

Sheryl looks around, as if she's surprised that Ella is without her cup, then shakes her head. "See? This is what Pastor Sam is always talking about. The slothful habits of the mind. Laziness leads to anger. So, two minutes. Then, we'll have our chat."

Sheryl is still the closest Ella's come to friendship since the accident. Perhaps, since before. Ella has never been much with women. But Ella likes how Sheryl handles her—professional, nurse-like. It had been this manner that, six months ago, had allowed Ella to first accept Sheryl's help. It had been the day of her last real doctor's appointment, an appointment in which Ella had fallen. She'd landed face down, tasted tile, but the asshole doctor had just stood over her murmuring, *You can do it,* refusing to help her. As if falling were a matter of stubbornness only. As if she were a child refusing to eat greens. As if he did not know about the pain. Eventually, he'd called his assistant in to right her. He himself, he implied, could not be bothered with a person as difficult as Ella. *Only you can make you strong. We'll try again next week.*

He was pretty fucking arrogant for his Cayman Islands medical degree, and Ella told him so, but she was crying at the same time, already quaking in front of him. And in the car, she thought, there is nowhere to go. There is Doug, and there is the doctor, and there is driving in between. The pain shot—a thin metal pike—through her spine. She gripped the wheel, started the engine, and began to drive. For an hour, she drove in increasingly tighter circles, gas gauge sinking towards empty, engine temperature rising, until the throbbing in her shoulder had become unbearable. The Coffee Corral had been the next place she'd seen. She pulled into the parking lot, thinking only to rest, and then recognized the place. It was somewhere Doug had gone as a student, a place he'd done homework and played chess. He'd taken her there when they were first sleeping together, a man to whom cafés still seemed urbane. So, she had had a moment to suck in her breath, to wipe the moisture from her face, before the flushed, stocky girl appeared at her window. Without direction, Sheryl had understood how to touch Ella, had instinctively located a table where Ella's wheelchair could be unobtrusively stowed, and, after bringing Ella a coffee, had left her alone to work.

As far as Ella was concerned, this constituted the parameters of the perfect relationship. And so, of course, it has not lasted. At first Sheryl only asked little, nearly unrefusable favors: that Ella mind the shop for ten minutes, for the loan of forty dollars, and, increasingly, to talk. "Our Chat" is the culmination of this trajectory of tiny demands in which Ella's acquiescence has somehow become presumed, owed almost. The shift, if it can be marked at all, would date from around the time of Sheryl's introduction of her boss to her quiet customer, though Ella still isn't sure whether Louis was the actual cause. The culprit might be another event, with which the start of the affair nearly coincided. Ella had made the mistake of showing Sheryl her novels.

Sheryl had been dropping hints—how good she'd been in English back in high school, for example, how she'd managed to read almost the entire Sue Grafton alphabet just standing in line at the grocery store—but Ella had hesitated. Her stories were simple enough for a check-out reader: mysterious stranger whisks ingenue bored wife to exotic locale for sexual initiation.

Ella has written six of these and really, nothing changes from one to the next beside the names and, of course, the featured sex act (oral, multiple, girl-on-girl, etc). It was hardly Sunday-School fare. And then Ella thought, why not? Educate the girl a little, surprise her. Ella's amusements were few enough these days.

But it had been Ella who was surprised. Sheryl had approached Ella a week after the gift, blushing, to be sure, but also in a kind of awe. She asked Ella to sign the book, and then hurried out to purchase the other five Emma Fawkeses.

"I didn't know there were people like this," Sheryl said.

"There aren't," said Ella.

"No, not with the private planes or anything, but who do this stuff."

And that had not been the end of it. Sheryl wants to talk now about what she reads in the books. Today, sweet Victoria Lavoisier and sinister Vincent Drake are on her mind as she returns with Ella's steaming coffee. She wants to know if they will stay happy after the story is over, or whether they curdle with guilt somewhere in the blank end pages. She asks about their souls, whether there was church in their childhoods.

"It wouldn't be much of a fantasy if I made them suffer the consequences. Absolution is a privilege reserved for fictional characters."

"And you." Sheryl's broad, midwestern face takes on a crafty light. "You're as cool as a cucumber. And you were just with him."

Ella isn't fooled. It's not the salvation, but the sex–fictional and real–that interests Sheryl. Her Christ, it turns out, is still the badly-drawn blond man of her Sunday School readers, vague and convenient. He seems willing to buy (though Sheryl's pastor might not) that Sheryl's forays into pornography are a kind of anthropology of sin. Much of what she does seems to fall into this same pattern: conceived as a kind of sacrifice, Sheryl's actions nearly always work out to her own advantage. Ella wonders by what logic precisely Sheryl justifies her adulterous match-making between her pervert boss and his crippled customer.

Ella sets the mug on her writing paper, making a fat brown ring. It's the only use she'll get out of her notebook today. She should make a rule never to overlap dependencies. This is a way a cripple could survive. Count on a lover for thrill, a husband for longevity, a coffee girl for getting you in and out of vans.

Sheryl leans towards Ella, flips her stringy hair from her eyes. "He came in when we had customers, you know, yesterday."

"Who did?"

"You know–" Sheryl drops her voice. "Lou-is." She pronounces the name slowly, with distaste.

"He's got every right to. He owns the place."

"Well, I know that, but I thought..." Sheryl glances around the empty shop "...Well, OK, there was a blind woman in here too. He kept looking at her. Moved tables, even, to get closer, until she finally, like, sensed him there. She probably could hear him breathing. Anyway, all of a sudden, she went, 'What do you want?' Only, she did it the creepy way blind people do, not looking where she was talking. Louis just sat there, pretended like he didn't know she meant him. I mean, absolutely shameless."

Ella feels a tremor of something nasty. It is a feeling she gets when writing the more lurid scenes in her books, the ones where it comes to blood. "That's quite a story."

"But, no." Sheryl's voice takes on its churchy tone again. "Doesn't it bother you? Don't you ever feel weird?"

"Often." Ella moves the coffee cup from her pad and flips open a page. She imagines how the mysterious stranger would respond. *My dear*, she'd say. *Sometimes you must explore what repels you in order to discover what draws you. Disgust and eroticism often lie side by side.* The mysterious stranger was always saying, *my dear*, to the ingenue bored wife.

Sheryl keeps her hands on the table. "It makes me think he likes you for that, you know? Because you're differently-abled, not, you know—"

"Despite it?" Ella snaps.

The door chimes jangle in the quiet shop. Neither woman breaks her gaze.

Sheryl pulls her head back. "OK, yeah," she says. "Yeah, that's what I meant."

"Sheryl," someone calls. Ella and Sheryl look up to see Buzzy, swaying in the open doorway with a half-gallon of milk in each hand. He has an old, greenish black eye, and it may be just the heat, just the dizziness of working in the hot sun, but he also might be drunk. "Sheryl, doll. Come here."

His wife glances at Ella, as if hoping to catch a reflection of what this husband looks like to an older woman, a woman who knows the secret things book people do, but Ella's face is as blank as paper. Sheryl stands slowly, but then she is on her feet, scurrying after her husband, and Ella is left alone, finally, to write.

Ella can look like she is doing nothing at all. It is hard to move her pen, hard to hold her back straight enough that her spine does not begin to contract. Following the accident, she had tried the various software and technologies available through the government, from her Occupational Therapist, but the programs were so cumbersome that she lost her thoughts before the ends of her sentences. For a time, she had been sure her career was over, that she would never write an article again. And, indeed, she hasn't. But, as her writing ceased, her fantasies had developed into scenarios so rich and elaborate, she could nearly hold them in her head, could nearly compose without instruments. Transcribing her first Emma Fawkes, though painstaking, had essentially been a lark. She hoped it might also serve as practice, get her back to journalism. But the skills have not turned out to be transferable. In time, she has only become more slick at pornography. She makes enough money now, under the pseudonyms, and delightfully under government radar, that with Disability, she can afford her medical bills, plus hers and Doug's expenses. What she cannot afford is help, which would free her from others, from Sheryl and perhaps even Doug.

A baby would mean impossible complications for the delicate balance of her life. But Doug gets angry when she talks in financial terms. He calls it mercenary. And she's let the subject drop, counting on her body, for once, to protect her. The fact is, it is even harder to contemplate what would happen if Doug left. Public assistance, some cripple motel, a retard for a roommate.

*

> *Afterwards, Belinda lay on the bed, dizzy, shocked, and naked while the couple from the restaurant–Mr. and Mrs. Cartwright, she reminded herself–began to dress.*
>
> *"Explain it to me again," Belinda said.*
>
> *Mrs. Cartwright sat beside Belinda and drew the girl's hand to her tanned breast. "We're not monogamous creatures," she said. "Neither Mr. Cartwright, nor I. It's what we have in common."*
>
> *"But, then, what's the point of being married?" Belinda asked.*
>
> *"An excellent question," said Mr. Cartwright.*
>
> *"One we asked ourselves," Mrs. Cartwright concurred. "A marriage is an agreement. For most people, it's*

an agreement of monogamy. But for us, it's not cheating, so long as we do it together. That's our marriage."

*

Just as the voices cease, Ella becomes aware that she's been hearing the sounds of argument from the parking lot. Someone guns an engine. Then, brakes screech. There is a simultaneous thud and splatter: a sound like a trampoline-sized water balloon bursting on concrete, then the overpowering smell of milk. Ella can hear a man—Buzzy—laughing. A truck careens out of the parking lot.

A moment later, Sheryl, obviously crying, slips through the door. She pauses, glancing in the direction of Ella's averted face and then retreats into the back of the shop. Behind her, white, puddled footprints mark her path.

Ella understands that she is meant to follow, but also that it is not too late to flee. She places her notebook in her handbag, slings it onto the back of her chair. She jerks the wheels, snags on the carpet, and then thrusts herself towards the door. Other people's marriages, like their jobs, are not things Ella makes her business of.

In the center of the parking lot are the split and leaking gallon jugs that have leapt from Buzzy's open van as he stopped short. The edges of the puddle are drying so rapidly that the liquid seems to be a giant frying egg, the jumble of plastic its colorless yolk. Ella manages to navigate around it, but when she gets to the van, she stops. She is still sitting there, trying to figure out how to lift herself into the van when Sheryl comes swinging through the café doors.

"You have to talk to him," Sheryl says.

Ella turns her head away from the girl and jams the keys in the lock, hoping that if she avoids eye contact, she can pretend she hasn't seen the red face, the streaks. "I'm late for something, Sheryl. The afternoon has been a wash. I've got to get home."

Sheryl grasps the handles of the chair and spins it so that Ella faces her. "You knew, didn't you? You knew when you came in the shop today."

"Knew what?" But, of course, Ella does know, has known, in some way, from the moment Buzzy appeared in the door.

"Louis. He fired Buzzy. You have to talk to him." Sheryl's hands grip the armrests of Ella's chair. Ella tries to imagine the acrobatics that will allow her to escape.

"I'm sorry," says Ella. "You could try talking to a lawyer."

"No," Sheryl shakes her head. "No, you have to understand. Louis can't fire Buzzy. Because of me. He's said so. He can't run this place without me."

"He'll see that, then. He'll change his mind."

"No, you're not listening. It's because of you he fired Buzzy. To impress you or something. It's the only reason."

"That's absurd." With pain, Ella tries to wrench her chair from Sheryl's grip.

Sheryl tightens her grip. "I need you to promise you'll talk to him."

"Are you going to hold me hostage?" Ella asks.

Sheryl doesn't move.

"Put me in the van, Sheryl. I can see about it."

Sheryl nods heavily and slips her arms into their familiar place. When she lifts Ella, the two women avoid each other's faces, but Ella can feel the captured sobs heaving in Sheryl's chest. Ella listens to Sheryl folding the chair, and when the other door opens, Ella turns to look at the girl.

Sheryl meets her gaze. "Louis asks me things about you, you know. When you're not around. Where you live, things like that. I always just say I don't know." Sheryl's face has turned white, her voice thin, but clear. "I couldn't do anything bad to you." If she were a different sort of girl, one less intimate with Jesus Christ, Ella might almost think Sheryl were threatening her. But Ella dismisses the thought. It is absurd to think that a girl like Sheryl could ever best a woman like Ella.

"Maybe I just don't have your conscience, my dear. Maybe I lost it in a car accident." Ella slams the door closed, and shifts the hand control to drive.

On the way home, Ella notices other coffee houses, peers through their smudged windows, wondering which might harbor another bored ingènue.

*

> *When Belinda arrived at the hotel room the following afternoon, she was shocked to see the Cartwrights' suitcases standing packed by the door.*
>
> *"You're going?" she asked, more anxiously than she intended.*
>
> *"Not immediately," said Mr. Cartwright, helping her out of her soft sweater. "You didn't think we'd stay in White Station, did you?"*
>
> *Belinda shook her head dolefully and Mrs. Cartwright laughed. "Oh, we can't leave her here. Not when she's so delightfully forlorn. Can we fit her on the boat, do you think?"*
>
> *Mr. Cartwright's hand dipped into Belinda's silky panties. "She's not so big. And won't the tropics agree with this pretty Spanish skin?"*

*

Doug is waiting for her in the living room, his face lit with a manic glow. A little box lies on the coffee table, but she can't examine it. Her neck has become numb, a result of an afternoon she refuses to remember in Doug's company.

"Why didn't you say anything?" he asks.

She considers the things she hasn't said, her secret store.

He begins to smile queerly. "Or didn't you know?"

"Know what?"

"Oh!" Doug claps his hands together and picks up the box. "Oh, delightful."

It is a pregnancy test.

"You're late, aren't you? I didn't realize this morning when we were making love. But then I decided to finally put away the Easter decorations, and I realized. You had it just before. Do you remember? We made love on Easter morning?"

"Are you sure?" Ella asks. But she knows he is right.

"Sure, I'm sure." He places the package in her lap. "Do you need help, or can you manage?"

Ella looks for the loophole, the escape, but sees none. "I'll manage. But don't get your hopes up. You know I'm not regular."

He nods, but his hopes beam from his face. "I have a feeling. I have a feeling about this."

In the bathroom, she breaks her own rule. She thinks about Louis. She is nearly certain they have used a condom the six or seven times she's fucked him. Nearly, but not entirely. She thinks about the doughy creature such a mistake would bring into the world. A miniature psychotic, with a wheelchair mom. The directions on the box call for her to insert the absorbent end of the test stick into the stream of her urine. If she is pregnant, a tiny cross will appear like a blessing. If not, one vertical line still darkens, a measure to reassure the skittish that the test has worked, or perhaps to stymie would-be fakers. But Ella is undaunted. She pisses on a Q-Tip, paints a thin line of piss over one pale axis in the test window. For good measure, she runs the tip of the wand under the faucet to make it look wet. There remains only to dispose of the second test, which the kit includes for those idiots who manage to botch the first, and this Ella stuffs into an unused box of tampons. Then, face expectant, she wheels out to wait with Doug for his bad news.

How strangely satisfying it is to watch him crumple, to have him reach for her like that. He drops his head into her lap—the only part of her that has improved since the accident—and she strokes his hair.

"Shh," she says. "They're not reliable unless it's first thing in the morning. We'll try again. Shh." She thinks of how different this scene would have been before the accident. Once, she hated the weakness which quivers through his body. Now, it makes her feel triumphant. And so, she thinks, this too is true, that she loves him, in her crippled way.

*

Ella wakes at 4:30 A.M. to the scrape of teeth grinding, the sound of Doug's deepest sleep. She manages to unfold the chair, to shift herself into it with a minimum of noise and pain. This is the quietest hour in Scottsdale, Arizona. Still, the swamp coolers hum, the occasional truck spatters through the puddles left by nighttime sprinklers. All over the town, lights flick on for the insomniac elderly, and the occasional liar working her craft. Ella is not surprised to find she is pregnant. Not at this hour. She does not think of the things she should, how her body may not sustain the vomiting, much less the creature in it. How obscene a secret this will be to keep. Instead, she feels a terrific rush. A baby. Or not. It is in her power.

*

Holding a silver tray aloft, the houseboy approached Belinda and the Cartwrights. When he reached the shade of the palms, he posed before them, jutting his hip out insolently. Belinda could hardly believe this was the same shy boy who had greeted their boat a week before. She looked away from his laughing eyes, but Mrs. Cartwright wasn't impressed.

"Put that down, Tomás," she said. "If we need anything else from you, we'll ring."

Three tall glasses of frothed piña colada ringed a circlet of pills in the center of the tray. Belinda drew back.

"Are those drugs?" she asked.

Mrs. Cartwright laughed. "Here on our island, my dear, there are no laws. So you can do what you like, and then return to your respectable life without any consequences. No one is going to punish you."

"Which isn't to say," Mr. Cartwright said, "that there aren't rules."

"One rule, darling. Just the one."

*

Not once during the following week does Ella miss the coffee shop, nor does she find herself drawn to the gates of Louis's sad complex. These days she even leaves the house; she goes to physical therapy. The doctor, a man who seems now shockingly young, utterly forgivable, is surprised when she actually appears. "The prodigal returns!" he says. "Miraculous." He clucks over her softened muscles and shakes his head when she tumbles from the big green ball. But she waves away his help, and hauls herself back upright with her own paltry strength. She does not mention the pregnancy.

Doug gets no work during these days and so is usually at home when she returns from these sessions. But she finds now, she can write with him around. The baby inside her makes a shelter of privacy that Doug's shuffling and care cannot invade.

More than once during this week, the telephone rings.

Sheryl's messages are brief. She does not identify herself, only pleads, *call me. You promised. You owe me*. Once, Doug hears one of these strange monologues, broadcasted through the machine's speaker. Ella shrugs it away. "Wrong number," she says. "It's sad to think that the intended person will never hear the message." Ella feels no sense of danger in these messages, though in theory any one of them might reveal a secret. Ella is filled with a keen delight.

*

On the eighth day, Ella wakes to find Doug gone. It takes her a few groggy minutes to remember the early-morning phone call he had answered, and still longer to guess that he must have gotten work. By then, she is awake, faced unexpectedly with an entire day to herself. Twenty minutes later, she rides downstairs in the elevator. She nods at the doorman, and wheels herself out onto the sidewalk. In the years since she's tried to navigate these cracks and curbs, it has grown no easier. She arrives at the bus stop, a mere four blocks from her house, half an hour later. The waiting commuters—a black woman in a nurse's uniform, a sweating salesman sucking from his water bottle—avoid looking at her. Ella minds. She minds very much. But it has occurred to her that suffering humiliation may be the same as suffering pain. You wait for it to pass; you believe that it will, and then, in a wash of blue, you are as you were before. When the bus comes, the driver barely masks his annoyance. Ella considers shaking her head, as if she were waiting for another bus. But she meets the man's eyes, and waits the terrible wait while the bus sinks.

They pass through the town. Navajo rugs flap in store fronts; waiters smoke cigarettes outside the restaurants. When they drive by the Coffee Corral, Ella closes her eyes. She thinks of Sheryl as she would a character in a book she's abandoned before finishing.

Ella is unsure what seeing the girl's round, reddened face would do to this comfortable distance, but she prefers not to test it.

As it happens, Sheryl is not in the shop at the moment. Her work for the day, another round of odd couple match-making, is already complete. Lying with her husband in their humid bedroom, Sheryl laughs. "I have a talent for bringing people together."

Buzzy doesn't like the laugh, or this business, not one bit. "You don't mess with people's lives like that, Sher. Trust me. I know a thing or two about messes."

"I didn't make the mess," she tells him primly. "In fact, if you look at it a certain way, I'm cleaning things up. Nice and neat. Everyone gets what he deserves." Yet, some compunction made her absent herself from the coffee shop this afternoon, at the very moment her plot comes to fruition, the very moment Ella's bus passes by.

And so it is that Ella's closed eyes matter, for it is thus she fails to recognize Doug's Nova in the lot. And thus, she does not remark the silhouettes of two men, passing something precious between them.

*

In the afternoon, Mrs. Cartwright was still ill.

"She prefers for you not to see her this way," said Tomás imperiously to the master.

"You should put on your uniform to serve the mistress," said Mr. Cartwright. *For days, Tomás had worn only a ragged blue bathrobe. Now he shrugged, the robe shifting open to reveal the dark hair above his cock.*

"Come on, Belinda," Mr. Cartwright *said. "We'll go for a walk."*

She followed him, his muscular strides leaving deep

prints in the sand, until at last they reached the end of a black jetty. He turned to face her.

"I can't make you tell me," he said. "I can't, and I won't. But if you wish to, I'm ready to listen."

Belinda lacked the guile to pretend she didn't understand. He was talking about what Mrs. Cartwright and Tomás had done in the guest house. What Belinda had witnessed there was no different from what the pair had done in the Great Room, dozens of times. Save that in the guest house, Mr. Cartwright had not been there to watch. Now, he was quivering in front of her, reaching for her.

"Belinda, you are so good. We never should have brought you here."

Belinda saw suddenly that here was her opportunity to have what she'd wanted all along. She could have Mr. Cartwright to herself. And yet, when she finally spoke, it was not her desire that motivated her. She told him what Mrs. Cartwright had done because it was right.

*

The bus reaches the barren outskirts of the town and turns onto the sparsely-developed road between Scottsdale and Tempe. The jostling motion sickens Ella, but she stares out the window, willing her stomach to remain steady. Finally, they reach her destination: a squat stretch of stores with a shoe shop, an insurance agency and a clinic. Until they arrive, she does not know what she will do. But now that she sees it, she knows that she hasn't come here to go inside. She wanted to show the thing inside her, to show it the clinic's curtained windows, its hidden location. She feels that rush again, the one she felt when she took her second test, and senses a response from deep inside her, a kind of knowing. You see? I am capable of it. It is me you will owe your life to, if I decide to give you life. She rides the bus back to her home, barely registering the driver's annoyance as she descends.

Ella does not at first see Doug when she arrives home. Instead she notices the cup from the Coffee Corral, a pink jewelry box lying open on the table. Despite the sunlight, its treasures—the aquamarine necklace, a lost button, missing hairpin—seem dull as tin, like cherished secrets which have been spoken.

*

"Leche," *cried the nurse.* "*The baby, he need* leche." *She placed the infant into* Mrs. Cartwright's *arms and the mother examined her son closely for the first time. He was a murky-colored thing, skin neither dark nor light, eyes neither blue nor green. No father would claim him. But his thin red cry named the one he belonged to; those fists, already bunched into fists, betrayed his lineage. He was his mother's son.*

Belinda was gone. Mr. Cartwright *had left with her. And soon, perhaps even today,* Mrs. Cartwright *would send the nurse away. Finally, she and the baby would be alone. Beneath his wailing,* Mrs. Cartwright *could hear the rumors of their solitude in the dry rustle of the palm leaves, the rasp of the waves hitting the sands. The boy would grow in a universe of his mother, eating from her, sleeping in the curves of her body. He would learn only the language she taught him.* Boy *for* Ocean, Mother *for* Sky.

Like a surfacing swimmer, he mouthed the air in hunger. Mrs. Cartwright *shifted his body closer to her breast and he clamped his gums around her swollen nipple. She was surprised at the intensity of the pain, and the completeness of the quiet.*

The Naked Circus

G. K. *Wuori*

During those first few days Michael kept May in the boathouse. He'd built it of tin and painted it yellow so that it looked like nearly all of the other boathouses there on the south shore of the lake, a cold lake. A chill was nearly always on the water since the lake sat like a long teardrop in the far north country, almost in Canada. Sometimes the water had a reddish hue as though the lake were rusting.

May was a black-haired woman of thirty-seven who'd spent fifty-one days of passage and transfer and sickness and contractors getting to Michael's house, a deal that had been made solely on a computer and, thus, somewhat unique. May's husband knew little of her arrangements, something they'd both agreed upon. May's husband said she would be saving the family and he would not bind her by the old rules.

May had children as well back home, two boys who were both chronically sick. Since both she and her husband knew that he was better with the children than she, there had been no question about her being the one to make the journey. She could be strong for something like that, where she was weak—impatient, she thought, sometimes confused—in responding to her children's needs.

No heroine, though. She would not allow herself to be looked upon in that way. If she had expansive ways, as her husband often said, what somebody had once called, "An eye for the pearl in the honey jar," she had ambitions, too, that something would come of her having been upon the earth.

"My darling, you do not look at things that way," May said to her husband one time, her frankness not unexpected. "If someone gives me a coin I will double it, perhaps triple it. You will admire its beauty. We are like that, but we are not like each other."

Her husband freely confessed as well—delicately—to a certain neglect of her marital needs during this same conversation.

"Necessary," he said, as May sadly agreed with him. The poor man was, indeed, already working twenty hours a day and they had yet to live in a place with locking doors.

"Sometimes," he said, "it is good for one person in a marriage to be incredibly dull, the other less so." May had not understood that at all, though she knew her husband was trying to be kind.

Well, she supposed, he simply did not want her to forget him. She told him she would not. He could see, couldn't he, that how someone lives and how someone loves are often paths that split wide apart. She had monsters screaming at her, living with such force she thought she would go mad. "But I love," she said, "only you. That is my peace. It does not change."

"Yes, yes, yes," he said. "All I ask is that you keep me in mind, that now and again you pull up a memory of me and let me play in your heart and maybe dance playfully in and out of your eyes. I am not being only a general man here, May, like a poet or a negotiator. I am thinking of those times when ardor taps you on the shoulder like some helter-skelter fiend and you have to rent some American boy to fuck the nervousness and all your many dissatisfactions right out of you. All I would ask of you at such a time is that you not think me dead. I would not expect you to tell your lover my name, though you could perhaps say that I was handsome.

"After all," he said, "we have known each other since we were babies. Our muscles are the same, our bones. Perhaps it would be good to tell your lovers your smell is the same as that of your husband. No, no, of course you could never say such a thing; only, don't ever forget it, perhaps make it one of those memories you can never tell anyone, but that you never let slip away completely."

*

Michael bought May for $7500 plus shipping and handling.

At the Port of Leaving Everything (loosely translated), while May was recalling the party her husband had given for her—a One Pot party with a whole barrel of beer—a man approached her with a small device in his hand, a steel machine. Before she could inquire as to his purposes, he'd lifted her shirt and brassiere and May felt the bright light of pain shining in her mind. Looking down, she saw that there was now a wire through her nipple, and a numbered tag attached to the wire—not quite industrial, she thought, yet not all that far from jewelry. She had no time to grimace, however, or to squeeze some tears from her eyes because the man quickly sprayed something from a can onto her nipple and the stinging pain went right away.

May appreciated that thoughtfulness, even as she was being sealed into a ship container with thirty men and two other women. The men were told the women were virginal and that, if they arrived at site in any state less than that, their diminished value would be distributed over all the men, plus a substantial penalty.

Though all the women were beautiful, no one believed any one of them even had a memory of her virginal state. Nevertheless, the journey was all about economics and everyone understood that. The women were not touched beyond a few beatings for laxity or impudence, but that happened to the men, too.

They were given food and water before being sealed into the container, and there were concealed holes in the metal for air. A low barrel soon proved inadequate at holding the waste of thirty-three people.

It was a wretched twenty-two days before they reached port in South America, a dark warehouse in the coastal town of Chrizone. They were stripped of all their belongings and clothing and put on a rickety old bus that had the words *The Naked Circus* painted colorfully on the side. Somebody said their clothes had been taken so that they could be washed and pressed. Derisive laughter greeted the comment, although no one had any other explanation.

Since they'd all felt each other's physical crudenesses during the sea journey, and since each had been struck by someone's sour vomit at least once or heard the unfamiliar eating sounds and sleeping sounds of whomever they'd been next to in the container, their nakedness was only incidental to them—an effective control as they dealt with those who didn't speak a word of their language, a control, too, for those in the group still prone to questioning their overall quality of life: food, transit, these various posings of illicit activities.

As they took their places, naked on the bus, someone said, "Who am I?"

"You're me," came the answer with a great whoop of laughter.

Philosophy, May thought, is never more freely dispensed than it is among those who have been willingly imprisoned. That sounded like something her husband would have said, May decided, except she knew he never had.

They traveled over the mountain places, crossed deserts and farmlands, drove quietly through small villages and cities that thrilled May with their different styles of housing, a love of color that was not her own love, but unique, special. May loved to find soft things before her eyes, not all of this brightness, neutral things—grays, pastels, the silent colors of winter.

Except for traffic, they never stopped in those places, especially since word of their arrival seemed always to precede them. Young people would be in the streets and they would jump up and down trying to look into the windows of the bus. Less energetic people stood on stair stoops or looked down from the roofs of houses to see *The Naked Circus*. May thought their presence seemed expected, as though the bus brought its weary, if occasionally chilly, crew through on a regular basis.

"Is there really such a thing, this naked circus?" one of the women asked the bus driver.

The driver looked around at them and smiled, an exquisitely rolled Cuban cigar in his mouth. He looked at all of them longer than anyone thought was safe given the narrow road they were on. He said something in what someone thought was Portuguese, which no one understood, then finally turned back to his driving.

Their clothes were returned when they finally reached Belize, although, for no reason that was ever given, their small satchels and bags had disappeared.

"Not uncommon even when you travel first class," someone joked. May thought it had been a while since any of them had laughed. A full moon, too, was making magical sparkles over the small chop on the sea, and she hoped some of the others were noticing it. She wished her sick children could see what she was seeing, but it seemed more important just then that the others not forget that the world had some things to offer, that it was good to look at, that it could perform (occasionally) as you needed it to. She said as much during a long silence within the group. The silence remained.

Near dawn, they were put in the cooler of a small fishing boat, about a thousand pounds of pollock, tilapia, and grouper nearby in the early stages of rot. Everyone in the group was hungry, but May thought it unwise to eat even the small bits of flesh some of the men and women were tearing from the slimey fish. Sure enough, there was vomiting within a few hours and it had nothing to do with the roll of the sea—fairly calm at that. There was weakness, even tears. May worried that the poisons leaving with the tears could cause blindness, but that didn't happen. Sometimes she wondered how many of these things she thought she knew were true ever actually were.

*

May's group split up when they got to Biloxi in the Mississippi. Some met entrepreneurs there, others pulled wrinkled papers from within their underwear to see what their next venture required them to do. Of course, none in May's group were friends, none were family, so the bond that was severed was one of discomfort, occasionally fear. They had shared sweat and stink and pain, and nearly all of them knew the secret names for loved ones that had been cried out during a restless or feverish sleep.

Never, May knew, could they exchange true names, and no one had any address at all yet—New York, for most of them; Chicago for two others, and May finally found out that her purchase by the American man was complete, a lucky thing. She was told nothing about the man at the time.

Those remaining, including May, were taken to a huge chicken farm to await their next transport. May loved chicken, but she'd never seen so many in one place at one time. She thought of them as worker chickens, vital in the aggregate, though such details as names, heritage, and place of birth were quickly forgotten. She knew her analogy was as easily attached to people, too.

She'd known people who worked so hard they did nothing else and then they died. It seemed as though their lives were their work and their major accomplishment was their death. May wished she could put it in a more clever way, but the chickens reminded her of her husband. She hoped, once she began sending some money home, he'd buy some cigarettes and heavy beer once in a while.

On her third morning of living with the chickens, a milk truck of shiny metal pulled up and May was put into a small compartment of the big tank that had been walled off from the milk. May thought there was something romantic about traveling with milk. Milk was soft and life-giving; truly, precious stuff. "As am I," she said quietly to herself as she was stripped of her clothing, covered with heavy grease, and pushed through a hole into the compartment.

For a moment, May remembered *The Naked Circus*. It was easy to think of herself as yet one more act. Quite amusing, yes. Quite revealed. Sometimes the traveling shows back home had women well-known for removing their clothing. Only the men were allowed to see that, of course, and they always exited those performances looking slight gray and very sheepish. May didn't think her husband had ever seen one of those shows, but she hoped he had. Being average, as he so regularly thought of himself, did not mean you couldn't climb the hill once in a while to see what lay beyond.

May was in the tank for nineteen hours when she was finally pulled out through the small opening by two men. They were not careful in what they touched of her, although one of them did give her a bottle of water right away. As she was pulled free she could see two other men off to the side exchanging papers. One man looked at the number tag on her nipple, then said something to the man holding all the papers.

She was standing naked in front of four men, and surrounded by hundreds and hundreds of trucks. This must be the end of the journey, she thought, yet nothing was recognizable, no earth signs or things she might think about as being a part of her new home. The air was thick with fumes, too, and the trucks were lit by many, many pink lights on poles high overhead.

It was night, though, and night was familiar. At home, she would meet her husband outside late at night when he came home from work. She walked with him so they could talk before he staggered to their bed for his few hours of sleep. Night had made their marriage, even if it wasn't her husband who had made their children. She was sure her husband knew that, though it wasn't something easily talked about.

"My name is Michael," one of the men said to her. Quite gently, she thought, he placed a blanket over her shoulders.

*

May wrote home:

> He keeps me in a boathouse, my husband. It
> is very safe and it is warm. It is also dark and

> so I bruise my knees constantly. There are so many memories, however, in the slow lap of the water and all the smells—of fish, seaweed, gasoline. When the sun is shining the tin boathouse heats up and I am comfortable. I remember how our own tin houses glow in the sun, and I know that mine must be glowing because at least once, often twice a day, on a sunny day a bird will mistake the glow of my house for freedom and crash into it and die. Sometimes the dead birds float into the boathouse. Do you know that I am writing to you? Can you feel my words on the back of your neck, maybe your knees, as I scratch them out with a fisherman's pencil on an old paper bag?

Michael told her there were snakes in the water so don't even think about bathing in there (Or trying to escape? May wondered—Is that what he thinks?), in the opening where a boat would go. She could relieve herself there. That was all right, of course it was.

"You're not a prisoner," he said, "and this is all temporary."

"This is not your home?" May asked.

"Only a part of my home," Michael said. "The rest is up on the hill. You probably didn't notice it when you first came here."

May wasn't sure what to make of that, if he was ashamed of her or embarrassed, or if she had already displeased him. It could be that he thought her too fat, since it had been two days now and he had yet to feed her. She finally decided it was much too early to try to figure out what any American man might be saying to her. Still, she was very hungry.

On the morning of her fourth day, Michael came down to the boathouse with clothing and food for May.

"Dear Jesus," he said to her, "I simply forgot."

"Things are on your mind," May said.

"I deserve no forgiveness at all," he said, "but thank you."

He brought her puffy baked rolls with butter, grapes, hard-boiled eggs, water, Coca-Cola, and some cheese that smelled like her husband's back—very odd.

The food was in a plastic box, but he also had a paper bag and from the bag he took out a pair of sandals and a white dress. May put the sandals on and then the dress—a cut, she thought, a fashion not at all familiar to her, and she giggled politely.

"Is this something funny?" Michael asked. "Did you think you would stay naked all the time? Do you realize how cold it gets up here?"

May could see that this Michael once again appeared angry with her. She wished she knew how many more failures she would be allowed.

"It is a dress," May said, "an American dress. I have never worn such a thing so it makes me nervous. I'm very sorry. It seems to be a very fine dress."

May took the dress off quickly and gave it back to Michael.

Then Michael said he was sorry—again. Finally, he smiled at May and said, "We're working pretty hard to make all of this as awkward as possible."

"Am I the first person you've ever bought?" May asked.

"Yes. Hence, my bumbling along here."

"Hence?"

"Um—therefore. Anyway, the dress is my wife's and I was hoping it would look on you the way it always looks on her.

"A kind of glow," he continued, "as though no darkness could ever contain her. You both look so much alike, whether hands or hips or lips, a certain way the toes grip the ground, a smell, too –"

Then May interrupted Michael and said, "Do you want to touch me? Do you want to see if I feel the way she feels—or felt? Is your wife still with you? Is she alive?"

"Yes, she is," Michael said. "Would you like to meet her?"

"Of course I would like to meet her," May said. "Will this prove difficult for her?"

"If you could talk to her," Michael began, "if you could listen –"

"Michael?"

"Yes?"

"You say 'if,' but I belong to you. I am owned by you. Perhaps you find that troublesome but I don't. It's why I'm here. If I were firewood you could burn me. I am what you will determine I am."

*

Later that night, May once again wrote to her husband using the fisherman's pencil and a paper bag.

> I am to be another woman, my husband,
> and live in a house where there has
> been much sadness. The woman I will be is
> a dying woman. My name will
> be Carol and you must use that name when-
> ever you think about me. Perhaps
> it would be good to start saying that word in
> front of the children. It is not a
> hard word.

Michael's house had three floors and was sided in cedar. Connected to the house, May noticed, was a small warehouse that held four automobiles, all of them different, and all of them looking very old, like a vehicle her grandfather drove before he disappeared. There were many gables formed by the steep-sloping roof. On the lower floor was a deck that faced the lake and the tin boathouse. May noticed that all of the floors had carpets on them, big and small, and that many of the walls were either marble or inlaid with mirrors. She began to think good fortune was about to strike her like a hammer on a mushroom.

Michael apologized for the clutter and all of the mess. He said his wife had not been able to do her work since taking sick, and for as much as he'd been willing to do it—"she will not allow me to get a girl for the job"—Carol had said no, she would not be given up on that easily.

"It would give me great pleasure, Michael," May began. "I know all about the things that are pleasing to woods, porcelains, ceramics, all of the–"

Michael would not let her finish.

"When it is time," he said.

Together they walked the broad stairway that went upstairs. It was wooden and curved and the hardwood steps sometimes squeaked. May knew Michael was taking her to his wife and she wished she were wearing some clothes. She supposed that was necessary if she was to be the harlot of the house (although Michael had not suggested that—yet), but it was not easy to meet another woman naked, as she remembered from the baths back home. You always wanted to tell the world life was good, but the body was the face of truth. The body told no cheerful lies.

Michael's wife was lying in the biggest bed May had ever seen, a bed Michael said was for kings. It was filled with water that warmed the flesh and gently rocked the spirit. Carol smiled at May and May thought for a moment she was looking in a mirror. Carol was gaunt where May was full, but the sickness had done that. Otherwise, Carol's eyes, her nose, her lips, even the tiniest of clefts in the chin–they were sharing something, as though some kind of genetic flower had put its pollen into the wind many years ago.

"Please get into the bed, May," Michael said as he pulled back the blankets.

Carol said something, but her voice was weak. Still, May said thank you and realized Carol had told her she was beautiful, had said it in words May could not hear. May told herself there are some things a woman–any woman, anywhere–will always hear.

She reached over and took Carol's hand in hers. The hand was very cold. Carol's heartbeat was in May's hand as well, a strong beat but slow, as though the heart was more than willing to go on, but time, that fat house rat, had things to do elsewhere.

*

Michael would not let May leave the bed after that.

He brushed Carol's hair in the morning and brushed her teeth. He put a clean diaper on her, then rubbed her feet and helped her drink some coffee. A sponge bath came later in the morning along with a few delicate touches of makeup.

Michael always entered the room smiling, often reciting some interesting bit of news he'd heard on the radio. He opened the curtains to the bedroom so that the dawn chop on the lake sprinkled the room with sparkling light. Sometimes he sang, quite spirited songs that May, of course, had never heard before. Carol ate little, but Michael fed her whatever she would take down, talking all the while and reading the newspaper aloud.

After doing Carol's dishes, he came back into the bedroom, announced a hearty "Good morning!" and then repeated everything for May.

Carol and May talked all the time. With May right next to her, Carol needed only the force of whispers to break the silence her body had forced on her, the force of weakness and lassitude, the force of a dying that, until May had arrived, had been telling her there were no longer any important things in her life.

Carol began to see that everything was important. She asked May about her homeland, though not about her husband and children.

"Politics," she whispered, "what's that all about? I have heard your country is reaching for democracy. Is that a good idea?"

Before May could answer, though, Carol went elsewhere.

"Plays," she said, "theater—you have countrymen who do that better than anyone else in the world. Do you enjoy that sort of thing?"

May had never seen a theater performance.

"My town," May said, "my village is very small."

"It's all right," Carol said. In only a moment, she was asleep.

*

One morning Carol asked May if she liked martinis.

"What is a martini?" May said. "I have never heard of this martini. Martin, I have heard of. We have something like that name in my country. A martini—is this a small Martin? Now laugh, please. I think I'm terribly wrong."

"It's a drink," Carol whispered, "with a tiny vegetable in it called an olive."

"I know olives!" May said.

"They're very good—the martinis."

Since Michael refused them nothing, they sipped the funny drinks that day from noon until early in the evening, stopping now and then to sleep or doze or simply to stare out the window at the lake.

The drinks made May's toes numb, and they made her think about her husband and her children. She remembered the day he'd walked out of his small shop and she'd been standing there with her dress caught in her bicycle chain. He could have ignored her. He could have ripped the dress out of the chain. He could have laughed at her as some children had already done.

Instead, he'd picked up the rear wheel of the bicycle so that the chain and sprocket would no longer move, and then walked to her house—a long walk—even politely turning his back as her mother came out and helped May out of her dress and into a shirt and a pair of jeans. Carefully, then, he was able to remove her dress from the bike. It was dirty near the hem, but untorn.

They were married one week after that.

*

"Michael?"

"Yes, May."

"It is good for Carol to drink these martinis? They are intoxicating. They are very strong."

Michael said Carol was now at a point in her life where everything was good for her, whether it was strong drink, a rainy day, or the funny calls of the loons on the lake.

"There is no longer waste in Carol's life, dear May, no longer anything inconsequential—especially laughter and, above all, your friendship."

"Sometimes, Michael, when I dream at night, I feel like I float in and out of Carol's body. I can see memories and hear people whispering her name. I can also see children inside her that she never had. They look like my children."

"How sweet you are," Michael said. "I noticed the other day and even more tonight that you're starting to sound like Carol. That pleases both of us. I want you to know that."

"We are very much alike," May said. "Do you know, one night her eyes were dry and hurting her, so I cried my tears into her eyes and she said that made them feel soothed and peaceful. I wasn't sure what soothed meant, but it sounded comforting the way she said it."

Michael quickly left the room after May told him that.

As May weakened from her bed rest and began to lose weight, she and Carol decided to play a trick on Michael, a funny deed to pull some of the misery out of his eyes and send it down to his belly as laughter.

Slowly—May had not been out of bed in weeks—she stepped to the floor. Her legs wobbled and felt like they were made of cooked noodles, but she made it across the bedroom to the dresser. Delicately, she took hold of the hand mirror, surprised at how heavy such a common tool now seemed.

Back in bed, May and Carol were shocked as they shared the mirror, shocked at the streets of sadness lining their faces, shocked at the hills and valleys of woe that marked time's impatient progress. Carefully, though, with May walking slowly around the room gathering the containers and bottles and packets of Carol's makeup, they daubed, they painted, they spotted—they made of each other's face a canvas and pulled from the canvas the most generous and the most raucous of clowns: clowns of beauty and delight. "This passing clown," Carol said at one point, "and her replacement."

"If I am worthy," May said.

"You are more than we had hoped, my darling," Carol said.

"Someday I must tell you about *The Naked Circus*," May said.

The next morning Michael entered the room and looked down at them. He smiled and said, "Carol–," then realized he could not tell which was Carol and which was May.

"A couple of pranksters," he said.

May opened her eyes. "We tricked you because we love you."

"You did a good job. May?"

"It's me. Are you angry?"

"Oh, no," Michael said. "Not at all. You must have had a good time."

"It took so little," May said. "Eventually we decided that Carol was May and May was Carol. We invented new people for ourselves and a new world where everything could be understood. We decided that one of us was dying but that it wasn't important which one. Such joy in that, Michael! For a time, we felt like we were sleeping out under the trees, where you look up at the sky and the stars and you can see anything you want to see. If there are monsters, so also are there heroes. We decided the best kind of hero to be was the clown because you owe the clown nothing but your joy."

"I'm very pleased," Michael said. "I used to make Carol laugh all the time, but lately–well, I mourn her. That's a terrible thing since she isn't even gone yet. She hasn't . . . ."

"Michael?"

"Yes, May?"

"Carol died last night."

Michael left for a few minutes then, leaving May alone and weary next to Carol, alone and saddened, although there had been fright, too, fright during those nameless hours as death came to a body so much like her own she was afraid it might make some mistake. Death could do that, death the only permanent owner of bodies, death who could take possession at will and who was never held accountable.

Michael returned and May thought he would take her down to his room so that she would be out of the way when the emergency people came. He didn't, though. He had some cream he used to clean Carol's face, and then May's. When he was finished, he picked Carol up and left the room with her, returning once again after what seemed like no time at all.

"It's time," he said to May.

He pulled the blankets down to May's waist and, using a small tool, quite silvery and shiny, he clipped the wire and pulled the numbered tag from May's nipple.

It didn't hurt at all, she noticed, and she smiled at him as he smoothed her hair and gave her a sip of water, as the tears rolled down his cheeks, though there were no sobs.

"Go to sleep now," he said. "I know this has been very hard for you."

"There was joy, Michael. Truly, there was joy."

"I know, Carol," Michael said. "I know."

Fifth Annual
Robie Macauley Award Winner

"Through the Water of the Clouds" *by* Sharon May

Judged by Alice McDermott

Sharon May worked in Cambodian refugee camps in the 1980s and later returned to Cambodia to edit the anthology *In the Shadow of Angkor: Contemporary Writing from Cambodia* (U Hawai'i Press). Her stories have appeared in *Tin House, Manoa, Alaska Quarterly Review, Other Voices,* and *Crab Orchard Review*, and cited in *Prize Stories: The O. Henry Awards*, and *Pushcart Prizes.* Two of her stories were included in the 2005 selection of *The Chicago Tribune*'s four Nelson Algren Prize contest winners, an unprecedented double award. Currently she holds a Wallace Stegner Fellowship at Stanford University, where she is finishing a collection of closely linked stories about Cambodia.

"'In 'Through the Water of the Clouds' I wanted to explore love in the midst of trauma. The story haunted me for years and the characters have stayed with me and recur in other stories. I'm interested in ties of homeland and personal relationships, the complex, troubled yet enduring bonds of friendship created in the midst of war. My involvement with Cambodia started twenty years ago, after the collapse of the Khmer Rouge regime, during which nearly two million people died. I arrived as a journalist, come to photograph the camps. I stayed to teach English, learn Khmer, and interview survivors of the Pol Pot regime for the Columbia University Center for the Study of Human Rights.

"People often ask why did I go, but no one asks why I stayed. In Khmer I would say *chap arom*. I've heard this phrase translated as 'interesting,' but literally it means 'to capture one's consciousness.' That's what happened to me. I fell in love with the place and the people. When my press pass ran out, I stayed for two years.

"As an Iranian-American, raised between East and West, I have always felt indebted to both, yet somewhat outside as well. I've been drawn to those caught between cultures, countries, identities. In the transitory life of the border camps, I found something familiar that resonated with my double-edged heritage. I admired the capacity of the people I met, who had suffered unspeakable losses, to retain their humanity. They welcomed me, a stranger, like a sister or an errant daughter, and treated me as a member of the family. This meant the world to me at that time and I still view it as love trumping despair."

Contributors' Notes

KAREN ACKLAND has published short fiction and essays in *Quarterly West*, *Salon* and other journals. She lives in Santa Cruz, CA where she writes marketing materials.

STEVE ALMOND's *Candy Freak: A Journey Through the Underbelly of America* became a cult classic, and he followed with *The Evil BB Chow and Other Stories.* His fiction has been anthologized in *Pushcart Prizes, New Stories from the South* and *Best of Zoetrope.*

ANDREW FOSTER ALTSCHUL's work has appeared in *Fence, One Story, Swink, Pleiades*, and the anthologies *Stumbling and Raging: More Politically Inspired Fiction* and *In Search of the Rainbow Body and Other Works of Buddhist Fiction.* "A New Kind of Gravity" will be included in the anthology *Best New American Voices 2006*. Altschul is a lecturer at Stanford and teaches writing at the U of San Francisco.

JACOB M. APPEL's fiction has appeared in *Agni, Chattahoochie Review, Colorado Review, Gulf Stream, Raritan*, and *Southwest Review.* He teaches bioethics at Brown U. "After years of writing prose, I attended a performance of Sarah Ruhl's *Clean House* last autumn and was bitten by a playwriting bug. I enrolled in a playwriting workshop and discovered how difficult a medium drama can be. 'Measures of Sorrow' began life as a one-act play and, despite all of my efforts, transformed itself into a story. It embodies two milestones: it is my 50th published work of fiction and my 25th submission to *StoryQuarterly*."

DOREEN BAINGANA, a Ugandan writer living in the U.S., has published *Tropical Fish: Stories out of Entebbe,* won the 2003 AWP Award in Short Fiction, the 2004 Washington Independent Writers Fiction Prize, and is a two-time finalist for the Caine Prize for African Writing. Named a "Washingtonian to Watch in 2005" by *Washingtonian Magazine* and a Bread Loaf Scholar, she has had fiction appear in *Glimmer Train, Chelsea,* and *The African American Review.* Ms. Baingana works at Voice of America Radio. "I have always been interested in the question of authenticity and culture, especially African culture. I grew up speaking English as well as my own language and was exposed to western literature, music and other arts, then moved to the US, where I have lived for the last fourteen years. This makes me feel less and yet more African, too, because of the contrast. In early 2003 in Kampala, Uganda, I went to a music festival with an American and was amused and fascinated by our different reactions to the event. I built and twisted that incident into a story to explore some issues of authenticity. Throwing in a hint of love interest was only natural!"

J. T. BARBARESE is a favorite media Harry Potter scholar (*Yes! There is one*) and has a new book of poetry out from Orchises Press, *A Very Small World, Earth.* He has authored two earlier books of poetry and a translation of Euripedes. A 2005 poetry manuscript, *The Black Beach,* was awarded the Vassar Miller Prize, and his fiction has appeared in *StoryQuarterly* and *North American Review.* Over fifty of his poems have appeared in *The Atlantic, The Georgia Review, The Southern Review* and many other literary publications.

RICHARD BAUSCH published his first of nine novels in 1980. *The Last Good Time* (1984) nominated for the PEN/Faulkner Award, followed by five story collections and an anthology, *The Stories of Richard Bausch* (2003, HarperCollins). *Wives & Lovers: Three Short Novels,* appeared in the summer of 2004. Bausch has received a Guggenheim Fellowship, an award from the American Academy and Institute of Arts and Letters, and the PEN/Malamud Award for Excellence in the Short Story. Currently Chancellor of the Fellowship of Southern Writers, he holds the Heritage Chair in Writing at George Mason University.

OLIVER BROUDY is a writer living in New York. His work has previously appeared in *StoryQuarterly, The Believer, Salon.com, The Missouri Review*, and elsewhere.

DANIT BROWN'S stories have appeared in *Glimmer Train, One Story, Massachusetts Review*, and *Denver Quarterly*, among others. She teaches creative writing at Albion College.

MELANIE CONROY-GOLDMAN's fiction has been anthologized by St. Martin and Wm Morrow Presses and her fiction has appeared in *River City, Web Del Sol* and *Tattoo Highway*. She lives in Ithaca, NY where she is working on a historical novel set in the '70s.

ROBERT DAWSON's poems and stories have appeared in *The Atlantic Monthly, Barbaric Yawp, Carolina Quarterly, Ex Post Facto, FICTION, Harvard Advocate, The Harvard Alumni Bulletin, New American Review, St. Andrew's Review, Transatlantic Review, ZYZZYVA* and more. A collection of poems, *Six Mile Corner*, has been published by Houghton Mifflin. He has received grants from California and Oregon Arts Councils, and from the National Endowment for the Humanities. He makes his home in Salamanca, Spain, and San Francisco, CA.

STEPHANIE DICKINSON's fiction has appeared in *Cream City Review, Green Mountain Review, Chelsea, Brooklyn Review, Fourteen Hills, Spoon River Review, Poet Lore, Nimrod, Willow Springs, MacGuffin* and others. She is co-publisher & editor of *Skidrow Penthouse*. Her *Half Girl* won the Hackney Award for best unpublished novel of 2002, to be published in 2005. "'Slave Quarters' is from a group of stories inspired by the time I spent in New Orleans. I was struck by actual slave quarters being rented to students as apartments. How could such places not contain past anguish? In New Orleans, generally, the past seemed to be alive intimately and perversely in the present—the bricks, stones and dwellings their own ghosts."

ELENA GARRO was born in 1920 in Puebla, Mexico, married Octavio Paz in 1937 and moved abroad, living in Madrid during the Spanish Civil War, in Paris after World War II (where they were largely affiliated with the French Surrealist movement), then in Japan. They had one daughter, Helena Paz Garro, before their marriage dissolved in the early 1960s. Garro began publishing in the 1950s, a play *Un hogar sólido*, but her debut novel *Los recuerdos del porvenir* (1963) won international acclaim, winning the Premio Xavier Villarrutia. Other novels included *Testimonios sobre Mariana* (1981, awarded the Premio Juan Grijalbo), *Reencuentro de personajes* (1982), *La casa junto al río* (1982), and *Busca mi esquela & Primer amor* (1996, awarded the Premio Sor Juana Inés de la Cruz). She is also known for vivid and imaginative short story collections, *La semana de colores* (1964), (which includes "El zapaterito de Guanajuato,") and *Andamos huyendo Lola* (1980). After a clash with 1968 student movements in Mexico City, Garro lived in self-imposed exile in Paris and New York for 23 years before returning in 1991 to Mexico. She died of emphysema in Cuernavaca in 1998.

ELENA GARRO nació en 1920 en Puebla, México. Hija de una madre mexicana y de un padre español, se casó en 1937 con Octavio Paz, y poco después, se trasladaron al extranjero. Vivieron en Madrid durante la Guerra Civil Española y en París durante la Segunda Guerra Mundial, donde se relacionaron con el movimiento surrealista francés. También vivieron en Japón. La pareja tuvo una hija, Helena Paz Garro, antes de separarse al principio de los años 60.

Garro empezó a publicar en los años 50, con su obra de teatro *Un hogar sólido*, pero fue con su primera novela, *Los recuerdos del porvenir* (1963) que se ganó el elogio de la crítica nacional y el Premio Xavier Villaurrutia. Otras novelas de Garro incluyen *Testimonios sobre Mariana* (1981, ganadora del Premio Juan Grijalbo), *Reencuentro de personajes* (1982), *La casa junto al río* (1982), y *Busca mi escuela & Primer amor* (1996, ganadora del Premio Sor Juan Inés de la Cruz). Garro es conocida por sus cuentos vivos e imaginativos, reunidos en el volumen *La semana de colores* (1964), donde se encuentra "El zapaterito de Guanajuato," y *Andamos huyendo Lola* (1980). Después del enfrentamiento entre el gobierno de México y los grupos estudiantiles de 1968 en la ciudad de México, Garro se exilió en París y Nueva York por 23 años. Regresó a México en 1991, y murió de un efisema en 1998, en Cuernavaca, México.

REGINALD GIBBONS, poet, fiction writer, translator, literary critic, artist, and Professor of English at Northwestern U, was editor of *TriQuarterly* from 1981 to 1997 and co-founder of TriQuarterly Books. He has published numerous books, including seven poetry collections, most recently *It's Time* (LSU, 2002); a collection of fiction, *Five Pears or Peaches* (Broken Moon Press 1991); a novel *Sweetbitter* (Penguin 1996); and a translation of Sophocles's *Antigone* (Oxford, 2003) with Charles Segal. He has won Guggenheim and NEA fellowships, the Anisfield Wolf Book Award, Carl Sandburg Prize, and other honors, including work in *Best American Poetry* and *Pushcart Prizes.*

PAUL GRIFFITHS lives with his family in Somerville, MA and recently received his second scholarship from the Bread Loaf Writers' Conference. "Postcards from the Flood" is his attempt to synthesize the book of *Genesis*—inspired by *Paradise Lost*. This is his first published work, but there's more at: *www.nationalbestseller.com.*

EDWARD T. GURSKI has been selected as the official translator of Marina Mayoral's stories by the RDC Agencia Literaria of Madrid. He holds a Ph.D. in Spanish from UVirginia and has taught at Virginia, Tulane, and Auburn, publishing articles on Antonio Munoz Molina, Jorge Luis Borges, Juan Carlos Onetti, and other contemporary Spanish writers. In addition to Marina Mayoral, he is currently translator for Rosa Montero and bilingual editor of a series of web-based childrens' books. He has recently completed two screenplays, and a forthcoming memoir, *Swimming Lessons*.

HONORÉE FANONNE JEFFERS has won a Rona Jaffe Foundation award and fellowships from the MacDowell Colony and the Bread Loaf Writers Conference. Her fiction has appeared, or is forthcoming, in *Callaloo*, *The Kenyon Review*, and *New England Review*. A native southerner, Honorée now lives on the prairie where she is working on her first novel while she teaches at the University of Oklahoma.

SARA DANIA KIPPUR, translator of Elena Paz Garro, is a doctoral candidate in Romance Languages and Literatures at Harvard, where she specializes in 20th-century French and Spanish literatures. Her essay on triangular desire in the works of Marguerite Duras won Princeton's R. Percy Alden Memorial Prize in 2002. She first became interested in Elena Garro's works as an undergraduate at Princeton, whose library holds the author's papers. She is researching French-Spanish bilingualism and translation in the works of Jorge Semprun and coediting a special issue on the legacy of Jean-Paul Sartre in *Journal of Romance Studies*, out in 2006.

WILLIAM KITTREDGE grew up on the MC Ranch in Oregon, farmed until he was 35, studied in the Iowa Writers' Workshop and was

Regents Professor of English and Creative Writing at UMontana until he retired. He received numerous prestigious awards including a Stegner Fellowship at Stanford, two Writing Fellowships from the NEA, and two Pacific Northwest Bookseller's Awards for Excellence. He was co-producer of the movie *A River Runs Through It* and became a major cultural voice with *Owning It All*, essays which mapped the emotional terrain of the modern West. His task is introspection, the examined life, a cutting away of rationalizations, a self-dissection. About this story, he says, "This is not part of my novel, but...based on an incident on the Klamath Marsh, in 1944, when I was twelve. My grandfather (not a suicide) brought just such a set of steers from Sonora. They were said to be "like wild dogs with horns," and herding them likened to "herding chickens." The wilder adventure came later, when we tried to ship them off to market. The engineer blew his whistle, and they scattered into the timber. Several showed up hundreds of miles away."

JUSTIN M KRAMON, graduate of the Iowa Writers' Workshop, has fiction coming in *Glimmer Train*. "'The Way People Are...' began with the idea of Clara telling Maureen a story about herself, and she loses the words. I had to tell the story that Clara, the veteran storyteller, couldn't tell."

ARYN KYLE recently won a 2005 National Magazine Award in fiction. Her stories have appeared in *The Atlantic Monthly*, *Alaska Quarterly Review*, *The Georgia Review*, and *Best New American Voices, 2005*. She was a Tennessee Williams Scholar at the 2004 Sewanee Writers' Conference and the winner of a 2005 National Magazine Award in fiction. Aryn lives in Colorado and is at work on a novel.

PAUL MALISZEWSKI's letters to the President have appeared in *Fence*, *J&L Illustrated*, and other magazines. His writing has also been published in *Harper's*, *Granta*, *The Paris Review* and in *Pushcart Prizes Anthologies*.

SHARON MAY, our fifth Robie Macauley Award winner, chosen by Alice McDermott, is profiled on p. 545 of this book. As well as the Macauley Award, this year two of her stories were among four finalists published by the *Chicago Tribune* for their annual Nelson Algren Award. Her stories have appeared in *Tin House, Manoa, Alaska Quarterly Review, Other Voices, Crab Orchard Review,* and cited in *O. Henry Prize Stories* and *Pushcart Prizes*. Iranian-American, May was raised in Central America, on both east and west coasts of the U.S. coasts, and in Southeast Asia. She has edited *In the Shadow of Angkor: Contemporary Writing from Cambodia*, and this year holds a Stegner Fellowship at Stanford.

MARINA MAYORAL was born in Lugo, Galicia, Spain in 1942. Since 1978 she has been a professor at the Universidad Complutense in Madrid where she teaches Spanish Literature. Her works of literary criticism include studies of Rosalía de Castro, Pardo Bazán, Galdós, Machado, and Miguel Hernández. She has published her fiction in Galician and Spanish and been translated into several languages. In Spanish, in addition to the short story collections *Morir en sus brazos*, and *Recuerda, cuerpo*, several novels stand out, including *Contra muerte*; *Recondita armonía*; and *Dar la vida y el alma.*

MARINA MAYORAL nació en Lugo, Galicia, España en 1942. Es Profesora Titular de la Universidad Complutense, Madrid, desde 1978 donde imparte clases de Literatura Española. Entre sus obras de investigación y crítica se encuentran estudios sobre Rosalía de Castro, Emilia Pardo Bazán, Benito Pérez Galdós, Antonio Machado, y Miguel Hernández. Ha publicado varias obras de ficción en gallego. En español, además de los volúmenes de relatos *Morir en sus brazos*, and *Recuerda, cuerpo*, varias novelas destacan incluso *Contra muerte*; *Recondita armonía*; y *Dar la vida y el alma.* Muchas de sus obras han sido traducidas a diversos idiomas.

ALICE MCDERMOTT, this year's judge, is author of three novels: *A Bigamist's Daughter, That Night, At Weddings and Wakes, Charming Billy* and *Child of My Heart. That Night* was nominated for the National Book Award, PEN/Faulkner Award for Fiction and Los Angeles Times Book Prize, with a film version produced by Warner Brothers. She received the National Book Award in 1998 for *Charming Billy*. Her stories have appeared in *Ms., Redbook, Mademoiselle* and *Seventeen*, her reviews and articles in *The New York Times* and *Washington Post*. She has received the Whiting Writers' Award, been two-time finalist for the Pulitzer Prize in Fiction, and currently holds the Richard A. Macksey Professorship of Distinguished Teaching in the Humanities at Johns Hopkins University. She lives in Bethesda, MD.

MORGAN MCDERMOTT'S fiction has won competitions from the Dana Awards, Phoebe, New Mellennium Writings, Random House, *Swink, Meridian,* an AWP Grant for Fiction, as well as a 2004 Illinois Arts Council Award for a story in *SQ39,* plus an IAC Fellowship Award. He has completed a collection of stories that have all been published and is polishing a novel for marketing, all while he and his wife Wendy adjust to the arrival of their first child, 'Chancellor' McDermott, Morgan's new best buddy.

MICHELLE MOUNTS is Assistant Editor at *Harper's Magazine.* She received the Avery and Jule Hopwood Fiction Award while at the University of Michigan, where she was a Colby Fellow. She has a story forthcoming in *Phoebe.*

MICHAEL POORE'S fiction has appeared in *Southern Review, Hayden's Ferry Review, Carolina Quarterly, Black Warrior*, and new work is forthcoming in *Talebones* and *Greensboro Review.* Poore's story in *SQ39* was cited in *Best American Spiritual Writing.* His work will be featured on WBEZ, Chicago Public Radio. He lives in Hobart, Indiana with three dogs and the world's oldest cat.

SHANN RAY's fiction has appeared in *Narrative Magazine, Talking River Review, Aethlon*, and *McSweeney's*. He spent part of his childhood on the Northern Cheyenne Reservation in southeast Montana and has lived in Alaska, Canada, and Germany. His wife wears the garment of praise instead of the spirit of despair. His three daughters shine like the sun. "The story was written after much love and devotion and I hope it holds the same sense of awe, and surprise at life's generosity."

SUSAN JACKSON RODGERS is author of *The Trouble With You Is*, a collection, and her fiction has appeared in *North American Review, Glimmer Train, Beloit Fiction Journal*, and others. She is recipient of a Kansas Arts Commission Fellowship in Fiction and reports, "I wanted to write a short-short that would introduce...a theme of loss ...without being too depressing. My character, a woman maybe a decade older than I am, began listing for me all the things she had lost, and as she recited, the rest of her story began to emerge."

MARK STRAND was born on Prince Edwards Island and educated in the U.S. The many honors for his nine books of poems include a MacArthur Fellowship, and a 1999 Pulitzer Prize for *Blizzard of One*. Poet Laureate of the U.S. in 1990, he is author of a book of stories, *Mr. & Mrs. Baby*, several volumes of translation (Rafael Alberti, Carlos Drummond de Andrade and others), editor of anthologies and two monographs. He is a member of the Committee on Social Thought at the University of Chicago.

MARIA ELENA SUAREZ is a floral deisgner in San Francisco, where she lives with a needy cat, an aimless mathematician, and her husband. "It is in the most physical acts of daily life, whether they be watching television, experiencing violent loss, or wiping up breakfast crumbs, that we exist most fully, and that is where we must scour the walls for something to connect us to each other."

GLADYS SWAN's sixth collection of short fiction, *A Garden Amid Fires*, will be published in spring 2006. Her two novels are *Carnival for the Gods* (Vintage Contemporaries Series) and *Ghost Dance: A Play of Voices*. Two of her books have been nominated for the Pen/Faulkner Award, and her short fiction has appeared in *Kenyon Review, Sewanee Review, Virginia Quarterly Review, Shenandoah, Manoa, Ohio Review* and *The Literary Review. Prairie Schooner* awarded her its Lawrence Foundation Prize, and she has received the Tate Prize for Poetry from *Sewanee Review*. She received fellowships in painting and exhibited at a celebratory Swan poetry reading held at Stephens College in 2004. "A friend, who is in the Coast Guard Auxiliary in Florida . . . told me about an incident when his team searched for a man who jumped from a shrimp boat after being threatened with a knife. Nobody knew what he'd done to provoke such a reaction, and the situation caught me up. What had happened on that shrimp boat? I tried to find out what I could."

LAURA VAN DEN BERG lives in Winter Park, Florida and her short fiction has been published or is forthcoming from *Oasis, Pangolin Papers, The Tulane Review, Wordsmitten Quarterly*, and *Byline.*

MARY MICHAEL WAGNER's fiction has appeared in *Southern Review, Alaska Quarterly Review, Cream City Review, ZYZZYVA* and *Spoon River Quarterly*, among others, and recognized in *O. Henry Prize Stories* and *Pushcart Prizes*. Her plays have been performed by the Drama League of New York, Actors Theater of Louisville and San Francisco's Magic and Eureka Theaters. She has taught creative writing in a residential program for prison parolees and teaches self-defense to women and teens. She hails from Kentucky and lives in San Francisco.

MITCH WIELAND has published one novel, *Willy Slater's Lane*, and completed a collection. Short fiction has appeared in *Southern Review, Kenyon Review, TriQuarterly, Sewanee Review* and others. He is founding editor of *The Idaho Review*. "Some time ago, Cyndi and I decided to sell our entire flock of thirty sheep, after losing money on them for too many years. As if summoned, several Bosnian men stopped by our small ranch one afternoon, wondering if we would sell some lambs. Over the dust and heat of that long summer, the men returned every week or two with an entourage of relatives, eventually butchering every last lamb, ewe and ram in the barn. I found a home for those memories in this story."

G. K. WUORI, is author of *An American Outrage*, a novel, and *Nude in the Tub*, a collection, the novel winning a Book of the Year Award from *Foreward Magazine* and translated for German and Japanese editions. His work has appeared in *Pushcart Prize Stories, The Missouri Review, Shenandoah, Other Voices, New York Stories, Five Points, The Gettysburg Review, Witness, Night Train* and others. He reports, "'The Naked Circus' was inspired by a number of experiences I've had working within the international community. Its core idea, which never appears in the story and is only slightly outrageous, is one of compassionate slavery." Wuori lives in a house with eight gables in Sycamore, IL.

RICHARD LEE ZURAS has recently held fiction scholarships at Bread Loaf and Wesleyan, and his work has garnered a Yemassee Fiction Award. He is currently seeking an agent and/or publisher for his collection entitled *Every Normal Family*. His beloved late father, an ex-CIA agent, is an inspiration for many of his stories.

Past Contributors' News

CHRIS ABANI (*SQ39, SQ40*) has won more awards for his extraordinary novel, *Graceland*, set in Nigeria. Picador announced that he had won the California Book Award's Silver Medal for Fiction and the book was also chosen by Walter Mosley for *The Today Show* Book of the Month.

KERRY NEVILLE BAKKEN (*SQ37*) received the Chandra Prize for Short Fiction, and her short story collection will be published in spring 2006 with the UMissouri-Kansas City/BkMk Press.

RUSSELL BANKS (*SQ19*) was chosen New York State Writer for 2004-2006, following Grace Paley and Kurt Vonnegut with that honor.

J. T. BARBARESE's (*SQ36, 37, 39, 41*) newest book, *A Very Small World, Earth* (Orchises Press) earned raves from Daniel Hoffman: "Every page of this book bears the thumbprint of a poet with an original slant–'*to see the extraordinary/wither into life/and tell its story*'."

T. C. BOYLE (*SQ19 & SQ39*) has a new collection of stories, *Tooth & Claw*, 2005, Viking. Booklist says, "Boyle is also a virtuoso short story writer, and he has never been more enrapturing than in his seventh collection of shrewd and comic tales."

DUFF BRENNA (*SQ38*) reports that his fifth novel, *The Willow Man*, will be launched at the James Joyce Center in Dublin October 7,

2005. Brenna's first novel, *The Book of Mamie*, winner of an AWP Award, will be reissued in a paperback edition March 2006.

JOHN CARTER'S (SQ38) manuscript, *All Night Newsstand,* made finalist for the National Poetry Series and the U of Wisconsin prizes. A second manuscript, *Dinosaurs Again,* has been completed. Recent publication of his poetry includes *ARC* (Canada), *Bombay Gin, The Cream City Review, The Evansville Review, Faultline, LIT, Oxford Magazine* (UK), *Pharos* (France), *Poet Lore, The Republic of Letters, Rosebud* and *Verse* with work forthcoming in *North American Review.*

JOHN CASEY'S (SQ39) story collection *Testimony and Demeanor* will be released in paperback in December, from Vintage Books.

BROCK CLARKE's (SQ38) third book, a collection, *Carrying the Torch,* won the 2004 *Prairie Schooner* Book Prize in Fiction (UNebraska Press). He has stories & essays in *Virginia Quarterly Review, Agni, Land Grant College Review,* and *Writer's Chronicle.* He won an Ohio Arts Council Fellowship for 2005-6, is fiction editor of *The Cincinnati Review,* and was just promoted to Associate Professor at the U of Cincinnati. He visited SQ in Chicago when he read at Northwestern University.

QUINN DALTON (SQ37) arrived in our mail, with fiction in *One Story.*

PHILIP F. DEAVER (SQ33) has a new book of poetry, *How Men Pray,* out from Anhinga Press, a story in *Kenyon Review* and creative nonfiction in *The Louisville Review.* Garrison Keillor on NPR read two poems from his first collection, *How Men Pray* (Anhinga). Thirteenth winner of the Flannery O'Connor Award for Short Fiction for *Silent Retreats,* Deaver has been an NEA and Bread Loaf Fellow, appeared in *O. Henry Prize Stories, Best American Short Stories* and *The Pushcart Prizes.* Many of his stories are set in a fictionalized version of his hometown, Tuscola, IL. He is Assoc. Professor of English at Rollins College, Winter Park, FL.

ANTHONY DOERR (*SQ35*) wrote last year, "I'm traveling right now to promote my new novel . . . I was lucky enough to win a Rome Prize this year, so my wife, I, and our newborn twin boys are moving to Italy in mid-October for ten months. We can't wait . . . First I need to finish this book tour." Rome with twin boys? Hmmm. Sounds classic.

ROCHELLE DISTELHEIM (*SQ36*) expanded her *SQ* story into a novel, *Jerusalem*, which won the Gold Medal for Best Novel-in-Progress from The Faulkner Society Medal.

STUART DYBEK (*SQ36*) is a Lannan Fellow this year. His most recent publication is *Streets in Their Own Ink*, a collection of poems.

XUJUN EBERLEIN (*SQ39*) was a Bread Loaf Scholar and her "Second Encounter" was voted one of Top Ten Online Stories of 2004 by the Million Writers Award.

DAVID EVANIER (*SQ13*) published his fifth book, *Roman Candle: The Life of Bobby Darin*, chosen as a Top Ten Book of the Year by Janet Maslin in *The New York Times*. He received the Aga Khan Fiction Prize, has appeared in *Best American Short Stories, The Paris Review, The Antioch Review, Chelsea, Southwest Review, TriQuarterly* and other journals.

ALICE HOFFMAN (SQ38*)* brings out a new novel this fall *Love, Mercy Hope* (Little Brown), her twenty-first novel.

RICHARD FORD (*SQ39*) has a new collection out, *A Multitude of Sins*, ten pieces he describes as: "About the way people fail each other. Fail themselves, even."

BETH GOLDNER (*SQ38*) had a second book, *The Number We End Up With*, a novel, published last summer to great reviews by *Publisher's Weekly, Entertainment Weekly, Kirkus* and more. "I'll start writing my third book this fall, after nine days at a quiet resort in the Dominican Republic (or Mexico) and getting a dog (via rescue, of course). If it is a girl, she shall be named Mavis. If it is a boy, he shall be named Woof."

KEVIN GRAUKE *(SQ36)* accepted a tenure-track position at La Salle U in Philadelphia, where he teaches fiction writing and American Lit.

ROBERT HELLENGA *(SQ38)* has a new novel, *Philosophy Made Simple,* coming out in March 2006 (Little Brown).

KAUI HART HEMMING *(SQ39)* brought out her first collection, *House of Theives,* (Penguin), doing the book tour with her first baby under one arm. The much praised book, set in Hawaii, deals with "the complications and lonlinesses of life in Paradise."

GREG HERRIGES's (SQ38) article in *South Carolina Review* details filming of *Thomas E. Kennedy: Copenhagen Quartet*, a documentary about Tom Kennedy's (SQ35) work, seen at schools internationally. A new non-fiction book is due out in 2006, *J.D.: A Memoir of a Time and a Journey*, about his meeting with Salinger at his home in NH. Herriges and Duff Brenna (SQ38) have an article coming out in *South Carolina Review.*

DREW JOHNSON (SQ39) writes, "The news on my end is that I'm starting this month in the MFA in Fiction Program at University of Virginia (Charlottesville). A fellow from SQ's past (2001-3 SQ staffer) is incoming with me, Will Boast." Our best to both of them, and lucky UVA.

THOMAS E. KENNEDY, *(SQ35)* now core faculty in Fairleigh Dickinson's low residency MFA, had two books out in 2005: *The Literary Traveler* from Del Sol Press and *Danish Fall*, the last of his "Copenhagen Quartet" (interrelated novels, Wynkin de Worde, Ireland). An essay, "The Bridge Back to Queens," was in *New Letters.*

JHUMPA LAHIRI (SQ30) welcomed a new baby, her second, and is taking some time off to get to know the new addition to the family.

KERRY LANGAN (*SQ35*) is busy at Oberlin College, with stories this year in *Eureka Literary Review, Poemmemoirstory, The Antigonish Review,* and online at *Literary Mama*. Under her pseudonym, Carrie Meehan, she has work in *Working Mother* and *Philosophical Mother.*

JANICE LEVY (SQ40) writes, "In the past year, my eighth children's book, *Alley Oops,* was published—about bullying. I had fiction in *Quarterly West, Green Mountain Review, The Portland Review,* three juvenile pieces accepted by *KidWriter's Magazine*" and I'll have a story printed on a coffee mug—put out by *flashfiction.net*."

NATHAN LONG (SQ40) spent six weeks writing at the Ucross Foundation, is teaching writing at Richard Stockton College in NJ, and has work in *Natural Bridge, The Sun, Tin House, Place*, and *Tusculum Review.*

ANNIE MCGRAVIE, SQ staffer, had three staged readings (Melbourne Australia, Woodstock NY, and Victory Gardens Theatre in Chicago) of *Dandelions*, her latest play (about an improverished community of four elderly nuns, who volunteer for a research project on aging that pays much too well, and turns out to be something quite different from any research they previously had been part of). "I am already at work on my next play, *Anna, The Emperor's Nightingale* (about Anna May Wong, Hollywood actress of the 20s-40s)."

KEITH LEE MORRIS (SQ39) has published two books—*The Greyhound God* (novel) and *The Best Seats in the House* (story collection)—with UNevada Press. *Seats* was first runner-up for *The Southern Review* Annual Short Fiction Award and his stories have appeared recently in *Southern Review, New England Review, Ninth Letter* and *Nightsun.*

ALYCE MILLER, (*SQ38*) now an attorney with part-time solo practice focused on animal law and guardianship for disabled adults, writes, "I have been publishing more nonfiction recently, addressing the complex relationships we have with non-human animals, including a law review article on the plight of wild animals in captivity. I am also working on a novel—that is, for better or for worse, an academic parody set in a fictional Midwestern university—involving lots of deceit and hubris, murder, sex and mayhem. I received a College of Arts and Humanities Initiative grant that allows me leave from teaching this fall so I can work on a series of essays about animals, plus an Indiana U New Perspectives Grant, funding an interdisciplinary conference on animals that I'm directing a year from now, called 'Kindred Spirits.'"

RICHARD NEWMAN'S (SQ39) newest collection of poetry, *Borrowed Towns* (Word Press), appeared this summer. He also has a brand new website: *www.vacuumpacked.net*.

DAN O'BRIEN (*SQ39*) spent last summer in NYC rehearsing the world premiere of *The Dear Boy* at Second Stage—a play previewed at Sewanee Writers' Conference the year before, and read there with Romulus Linney. See Dan at: *www.secondstagetheatre.com/uptown*. He's had more plays published by *Playscripts* (www.playscripts.com) and spent spring 2005 in Sewanee again as a Williams Fellow at the University of the South.

KAREN RUSSELL, *SQ*'s 2002-3 intern *extraordinaire*, has gone on to be extraordinary. Finishing her master's at Columbia University this year, Karen writes: "I wanted to share some unbelievable news: *The New Yorker* is going to publish one of my stories in their Debut Fiction Issue, June 6. *Carumba!*" See more of our beloved Karen on p. 24.

ED SCHWARZSCHILD (*SQ37 & SQ40* and First Robie Macauley Award winner) brought out his first novel, *Responsible Men* (Algonquin), last spring, 2005, and just sold his second book, a collection of stories. *Kirkus Review* printed a glowing account of *Responsible Men* just before publication: "Life gets complicated for a con man with a conscience in a thrilling first novel that's family drama with a strong suspense element . . . From a complicated business deal to a teenager's first kiss, Schwarzschild works with the quiet authority of a master. This is one terrific debut." Ed is on a book tour, taking notes for the next novel. With Kaui Hart Hemmings, Ed will be guest editing *StoryQuarterly41* in 2006 with a group of other Stegner Fellows.

LAUREN SMALL is closing in on the end of "Choke Creek," the novel that grew out of the short story "Livia" in *SQ37*.

GEORGE (G.H.) SMITH *(SQ38)* gave up law practice to write and has moved to an island off of Washington state, a 100-yr-old farm with two ponds, an orchard, and a huge barn—"Paradise in many respects." Three poems have been accepted by *Cafe Review* in Portland, ME.

SARAH STONE *(SQ36)* co-wrote a textbook with her husband, Ron Nyren: *Deepening Fiction: A Practical Guide for Intermediate and Advanced Writers* (Longman). "We've tried to make it useful for individual writers as well as workshops. We own great books of essays about writing, some terrific beginning texts, but we couldn't find books that specifically used examples and exercises to address intermediate/advanced questions—like revision—for writers who are no longer beginners; or anything on the artistic implications of different craft choices. We spent a few years writing this book. (It contains a section on the writing process and life, and a mini-anthology of stories: North American and international, classic and contemporary.) It's available primarily online, either at the Longman site or Amazon."

Edward Schwarzschild
"Marvelous. . . .Impressive." —Ha Jin
Coke
Responsible Men
A Novel

HOUSE OF THIEVES
Stories
KAUI HART HEMMINGS

My Sister's Continent
gina frangello
isbn:0-9703212-9-5
price: $12.00
distributor: spd
forthcoming December 2005
FRANK
r.m. berry
isbn: 0-9703212-7-9
price: $12.00
distributor: spd
forthcoming October 2005
FRANK
R. M. BERRY
My Sister's Continent
Gina Frangello
these fictions do not follow the rules. risk is worth it.
10:01
lance olsen
available now
10:01
lance olsen
isbn:970-3212-6-0
price: $12.00
distributor: spd
available now
many ways to get it,
many ways to say it
cris mazza
isbn:970-3212-5-2
price: $12.00
distributor: spd
many ways to get it
many ways to say it
cris mazza
chiasmus press www.chiasmusmedia.net

Taste the difference!
BLACK
WARRIOR
Fresh
REVIEW